CW00641779

A BATTLE LOST

Dave Shaw

FuelledbyAnger Publishing

A Battle Lost

By Dave Shaw
FuelledbyAnger Publishing

Copyright @ 2022 Dave Shaw
Cover design by Beyond Book Covers

All Rights Reserved
No part of this publication may be reproduced, stored in a retrieval system, distributed, or transmitted in any form or by any means, including photocopying, recording, or other electronic or mechanical methods without the prior written permission of the author.

All the characters in this book are fictitious, and any resemblance to actual persons, living or dead, is purely coincidental.

First printing May 2022

ISBN Print Book 978-1-7396756-0-8

Dave Shaw
Cheshire UK
www.dave_shaw1@sky.com

It is hard to thank everyone who has supported or at least tolerated me through this journey without forgetting anyone, so if I do, please accept my apologies and feel free to remind me.

So, thanks to my early readers who gave me advice and constructive criticism and helped me create something that I hope is readable. Rich C, Anne T, Malice B, Edona G and Michael S. Thank you all.

Thanks also to Yvonne at WireRose for the editing, and Beyond Book Covers for the fantastic artwork.

A Battle Lost

The following pages were found by workmen repairing the infamous Peremoss Bridge. The pages were found wedged beneath a concrete railway sleeper, pushed into an artillery shell casing and sealed with a greased cloth. The shell casing was handed over to the team of archaeologists excavating the old Human Advancement Party bio-research labs where so many died during the civil war of 2160–2164 AL (After Landing).

This astounding discovery comprises the memoirs and thoughts (confession?) of Daniel Shaddick, the renowned guerrilla leader who disappeared after leading an attack on the bio lab facility, shortly before the cessation of hostilities.

Shaddick was a constant thorn in the side of the much-feared Bio Legion, and is credited with severely disrupting Bio Legion supply lines, thus allowing great advances to be made against them by the armies of the Free State Coalition. Shaddick's disappearance has been the subject of much discussion, not to mention myth and legend. This amazing find of revealing papers at last answers the question of what happened to him, and also goes some way to explaining the origin of his almost legendary fanaticism.

Maria Phibbs PhD 2215 AL

All Aboard

Some may call it luck or a lack thereof, some may call it an accident of circumstance; myself, I believe it to be a question of geography. When war broke out between the Human Advancement Party (H.A.P.) and the Free State Coalition, I just happened to be on the wrong side of the lines. There I was, twenty-four years old, living in a small town called Westridge in the foothills of the Jeral Mountains, a town I confess I was utterly bored with. It was late spring, the last of the winter tourists had left, and the summer tourists had not yet arrived. I had already charmed my way to intimacy with all the local girls who could be so charmed, my funds were low and my credit with the three local bars that stayed open off season was frankly exhausted. The motor bike on which I loved to race recklessly through town was broken, and in my naivety I was convinced that there was nothing more for a devil-may-care young man to occupy himself with. To make matters worse, my parents were abroad on holiday and due back in a couple of weeks, and my sister was married and living up north (facts that became something of a relief), and as a consequence I had been left caring for my six-year-old brother, Mathew. At that time of my life I saw such a task as something of a burden and I confess that I was not the most attentive of older brothers; in fact, I could scarcely find time for him at all.

I had paid attention to neither politics nor the worries of my elders, and so the outbreak of hostilities and my harsh introduction into current affairs came as something of a shock. On this particular day it was almost noon, and I was still lying in my bed, fully clothed from the previous night's drinking and petty gambling, listening to Mathew playing outside.

Content that the little tyke had once again managed to get himself up, dressed and fed, I allowed myself to close my eyes once more, just for a few minutes you understand.

I think it was the silence that finally woke me; All the normal sounds of the town were absent, it was as if an enormous collective breath was being held, and then from the distance I could hear a regular crunching, rattling sound that grew louder and louder. I got out of bed and splashed cold water onto my face. I could hear panicked shouts and wails of fear, yet these were somehow muted in comparison to the shouted orders and the shrill of whistles. Panic gripped me and an understanding of sorts dawned. I grabbed my leather bike jacket from the back of the chair, and as I shrugged it on I heard the unmistakeable sound of boots on the stairs. The door crashed open and standing before me was a soldier clad in black and grey with the electric-blue emblem of the H.A.P. on his sleeve. He carried an ugly squat black weapon that reduced me to terror as he pointed it at me. 'You. Out.'

He stood to one side and gestured with his gun. My hands raised in fearful supplication, I walked past him. At the top of the stairs, he helped me on the way with his boot and I tumbled terrified and sore to the bottom step where I was grabbed by two more soldiers and dragged outside.

It seemed that the whole population of the town had been collected and herded together in the central square. The look of sick fear on the faces of people I knew being held within a cordon of heavily armed soldiers awoke something in me, and for the first time in an age I became concerned for the welfare of my brother. As I joined the other captives, I began to thread my way through the crowd, stopping to exchange words with those I knew, asking for news of Mathew. It was only as people began to sit down that I caught sight of him. He was standing with our neighbour, Hilda Bancroft, a matronly woman of fifty or so. Mathew was wearing his favourite white T-shirt, red shorts and brown sandals, and his bright blond hair shone out like a halo. One arm held onto Mrs Bancroft and the other clutched his constant companion, his tatty blue teddy bear. His face was red from crying but when he caught sight of me he choked back his sobs and smiled, showing his small, even teeth. He ran over, relief evident on his little face.

'Danny!'

I ruffled his hair in the distracted way that older brothers have, 'Hey, kiddo. You all right?'

He looked up at me and nodded, 'What's happening? I'm frightened.'

'I'm not sure,' I told him, 'but don't worry. I'm sure things will be all right.'

That was the first and possibly greatest lie that I told him. I took his hand and led him back over to Mrs Bancroft. He sat down beside her and asked her the usual inane questions such as, 'What's happening?' and 'What do you think will happen?' There were of course at that time no reasonable answers, and perhaps due to some innate optimism of the human race, none of the guesses or suppositions from those townsfolk nearest to us even touched upon the horrible truth of our fate. The most we could reasonably ascertain was that the H.A.P. had made a pre-emptive strike and that it looked as though civil war was now inevitable.

We sat there through the heat of the day. I was, I suppose upon reflection entirely bored, I tried to answer Mathew's questions, but for the most part I bade him to sit still and play with his teddy bear. It never occurred to me to be frightened as I reasoned that if we didn't upset the men with guns by trying to leave the square, or even by asking any of them questions, then they would have no reason to display any kind of violence or hostility towards us. Although in truth I did feel that I had been somewhat roughly manhandled from my house to the square, they were in effect doing their job. I didn't like the way I had been treated, after all they could have asked, but I was certainly not going to raise the issue with anyone. I decided to treat the whole experience as an extended fire drill. At least it wasn't raining. I did wander around a little, chatting to others of my age that I considered to be friends, but strangely, even though on a night out we could talk for hours about almost nothing, the conversations drifted into awkward silence after a few minutes. Talk of shared excess the previous evening seemed somehow out of place and no one knew what was happening. We therefore found ourselves with nothing to say. I did, however, happen upon Mr Campbell, my old Social History teacher from school. He was wandering around in the same familiar playground-supervisor pose that I remembered from school, hands clasped behind his back, pipe clamped between his teeth and a distant look in his eye. I decided to chance my hand and see if he not only recognised me, but if he could also shed some light upon our current situation.

I stood before him and caught his eye, and nodded at him in greeting. He took the pipe out of his mouth and ran his fingers through his thinning grey hair. 'Mr Shaddick, as I live and breathe.'

I grinned, glad that he remembered me. 'Hello, Mr Campbell. I didn't think you would recognise me.'

He gave a sort of half laugh, half snort. 'Not recognise you? Mr Shaddick, if I may be frank, as you are no longer a student of mine, you were the very bane of my existence for two long years: wilful, stubborn, lazy and disruptive.' He gestured at me with his pipe, 'and those were your good points.' He ran his hand through his hair again. 'The worst of your crimes, however, was that you were a clever young man who refused to learn. That was what always disappointed me the most.'

I looked him in the eye. I think he could tell I was annoyed, but instead of a pithy retort about how his lessons were dull, I swallowed both my pride and anger, twin bitter tastes I was unused to, and asked him if he knew what was going on. I received a disappointed shake of the head.

'Really, Daniel. For such a bright boy, it amazes me how little you actually know of anything. Where would you like me to start?'

I thought for a moment, 'You know, who these soldiers are, and what they want.'

He tapped out his pipe on his heel and placed it in his pocket. 'I spent two years trying to teach you almost exactly that, and now you want a brief summary of two years' worth of lessons and hundreds of years of history?'

I grinned at him, 'Please.'

He sighed, 'All right, Daniel. I should at least be pleased you finally want to learn something.' He drew a deep breath. 'Right, several thousand years ago, a colony ship was launched from Old Earth and aimed at this Earth-type planet, New Albion, in the hope that we could land, settle and grow in an environment that was not so overcrowded and destroyed. Are you with me so far?'

I nodded and made a rolling hand gesture for him to continue.

'After countless generations, the ship arrived and promptly crashed whilst trying to land somewhere down near the equator. There are a couple of nations who claim that their country was the actual site of the landing, and there are a number of theories and a corresponding number of probable sites… however, I digress. The crash killed thousands of those on board, not to mention causing a slight change in the atmosphere that destroyed many of the indigenous humanoids; a task that it appears, was eagerly completed by our ancestors in the next few decades. But that is another story. Anyway, the survivors found that many of those who had travelled in sleep could not be woken. However, the long-dead scientists and astronomers on Earth had been correct, and they had indeed landed on a planet very similar to the one the ship had left all those years ago. They were thus able to survive. They farmed the animals they had brought with them, planted the crops, thrived and increased in number. People formed groups and moved away to other continents, forming the countries and populations we have today.' He paused and drew breath. 'Still with me, young man?'

I nodded, amused that even now he still treated

me like I was stupid.

'Now, Daniel, this is the important part, or at least from our current perspective. The survivors and their descendants attributed the loss of so many of their friends and families on the colony ship to the failure of technology; high technology and flying in particular became something of a taboo. Indeed, two thousand years after the landing when attitudes have relaxed and the benefits of technology have been observed, flying is still seen as both dangerous and a religious offence. Which brings us to today. Some people advocate the use of technology and the advancement of science, and the debate has coloured and directed political debate for the last decade. The south of the country is run by those who support the growth of technology and the application of science, whereas the north remains far more conservative. The opinion of those in the north is that the combustion engine, transport and conventional medicine are fine, but flying and the higher sorts of science like genetic manipulation are not. Regardless of our opinion, Daniel, it seems that those in the south have chosen to force their opinions upon us.' He took his pipe from his pocket, put it in his mouth and spoke around the stem. 'So there you have it, young man, a brief history of why we are standing in this square.' He smiled, 'I wish you well, young man.'

I nodded my thanks but he had already turned and vanished into the crowd.

The acquisition of a little understanding did nothing to make the situation more enjoyable, and the restless dull day stretched into the long evening when cramp and full bladders brought further misery to us all. Darkness allowed the shy to relieve themselves, and hungry and cold with an encroaching sense of fear, we slept where we were. In the cold grey light just before dawn, we were roused by boots, whistles and orders, then formed into lines regardless of age and gender, and made to shuffle past a series of tables where an officer and a pair of soldiers were sitting. Name, age, address and occupation were given at the first table; a stamp of indelible red ink on the back of the hand at the second; and most welcome, a hunk of bread and a cup of water at the third, before each line was carefully but brutally shepherded down to the station with kicks and prods from the wire stocks of machine pistols.

Throughout all of this I held tightly onto Mathew's hand as I and the formidable Mrs Bancroft, defiant in her floral print dress, tried to protect him from the worst of the abuse. At the station, still in our lines, we were thoroughly searched and all our valuables such as money and jewellery were taken from us, as were any tools such as pocket knives and cigarette lighters. We were, however, allowed to keep one inoffensive item each: Mrs Bancroft kept her comb; I kept the pack of cards I had in my pocket; and Mathew kept a tight hold of his old blue teddy bear.

After being searched, we were herded (how appropriate a term) onto a long line of box cars, the previous occupants of which had clearly been animals. The train wagons stank, and packed with slightly too much frightened humanity in the rising heat of the day, they only got worse. The jolt of the train moving off was accompanied by a rising murmur of fearful exclamation. There was no food, no water and it soon became apparent that there was not enough room for all of us to sit down at once. By some unspoken consensus, those of us still hale and strong remained standing, allowing the old and the very young to sit. Mrs Bancroft, bless her, stood for as long as she could in the thickening air of the sweltering box car, before I suggested that she sit with Mathew on her lap, thus taking up less space. This she did and she sat holding him close and rocking him gently as he slept with his head on her shoulder, sucking his thumb, with his teddy held in the crook of his elbow. I was hot, tired, scared and could you believe it, bored. It was then that I remembered the pack of cards in my pocket, and so took them out and began shuffling them as something to do. It was not something I was used to doing standing up but it passed the time and helped me ignore the constant murmur of conversation and complaints that surrounded me with its soft waves of despair. How long I stood, constantly playing with my cards, I don't know.

The murmured conversation within the train had become a low-level, almost unheard hum, broken only by the occasional update on our increasingly southwards geographical location shouted out by Lewis, the local train enthusiast, a fairly dull sort I had known at school. As time passed, and station name after station name was called out, my back hurt, my legs were cramping and my thirst had grown from a slight annoyance to a problem I couldn't continue to ignore.

I think it was as the train changed direction at a set of points that the jolt made me drop a couple of my cards; that was the first bit of luck I had that day. Cursing under my breath, I bent my aching back and began rummaging through the filthy straw at my feet, trying to pick up the cards, hindered by the sway of the wagon. As I reached for the last card, my fingers brushed against something buried within the straw and animal filth on the floor. I plucked it out with my fingertips and was surprised to find that within my grasp I held a small leather purse. Its size and contents led me to believe it had been dropped by a drover and not someone of wealth, but within it was, in my current situation, a king's ransom. One large copper and two small silver coins – such luck! I pondered a while about how best to use my new wealth and in the end, just as night began to fall, decided to exchange a coin with one of my fellow captives for a spot against the wall of the wagon so that I could at least lean against something and take the weight off my back for a while. Although it didn't seem fortunate at the time, Holt the butcher drove a hard bargain and it cost me a silver coin to exchange places with him. My second stroke of luck came about as I moved towards my space on the wall. The change of temperature as night arrived was condensing the humid atmosphere of the box car and moisture was beginning to form on the walls. My thirst was great and trying not to think too hard about the origin of this bounty, I was, I confess, the first to start licking the rough wooden walls of the box car.

My thirst somewhat abated by the admittedly foul providence, I decided I could use another coin in exchange for a position at the small metal grate in the wall where I could finally get a breath of some fresh air and a restricted view of our passage through the countryside. It cost me another silver coin but as I put my mouth to the grate and took in my first breath of something other than a foetid soup for the first time that day it seemed worth it. The moon was bright and I managed to work out that we were heading south and possibly east, a region I knew only vaguely, but it helped somewhat to at least find our direction. Since Lewis had fallen silent a few hours ago, I passed the word around that we were heading southeast and it was decided that we must be travelling deep into H.A.P.-controlled territory. Dark stories came back to me on the ebb and flow of conversation concerning the practices of the H.A.P. in the south and I began to worry. The worry became fear as time passed and the train continued its relentless passage through the night. I was close to panic as I fumbled around in my pocket for my last remaining coin, the large copper one, wondering how I might buy myself some new advantage. It was at this point that we passed through a town, and in the reflected lights coming from the station I could see that one side of the coin was damaged-it was flattened along one edge and narrowed as if it had been crushed. A thought occurred to me and I nervously measured the flattened edge of the coin against the slotted head of one of the screws holding the grate securely in place. It fitted the slot like a screwdriver, and in excited anticipation I applied pressure. The screw turned! I realised now that with time and patience I may be able to escape!

I loosened the screws one after the other, until after about an hour, such as I could measure time, they were almost out and the grate held in by only a thread. With some quick bargaining for a brief swap at the grate with another of my coerced travellers, I made my way back over to Mathew and Mrs Bancroft. I shook Mrs Bancroft awake and told her that there was a chance I could escape and maybe find help. To be truthful, getting help was not really a concern to me at that time, not compared to the chance of escaping from that awful train. Mrs Bancroft looked at me as though I was something she had found on the bottom of her shoe, and to be fair I deserved it, but at the time I was filled with a righteous indignation. I was going for help, damn it!

'What about your little brother, Daniel? You can't leave him here. Lord alone knows what will happen to him.'

I shrugged, 'I will try to take him with me of course.'

The stray wisps of her grey hair moved slowly as she shook her head. 'Daniel, he is only six, how on earth do you expect to jump from a moving train with him?'

‘I will wait for a river or something,’ I said with a touch of exasperation, ‘Anyway, I will ask him.’ I gently woke Mathew and he smiled up at me from his place on Mrs Bancroft’s lap.

‘Hello,’ he said and held up his teddy, ‘Harvey says hello too.’

I smiled back and once more ruffled his hair. ‘Hey, Matty. I might be able to get off the train; would you like to come with me?’

He looked confused, ‘How?’

I held out my arms to pick him up, ‘Come with me, little fella.’

I picked him up and wormed my way back to my place at the grate, displacing the man holding my spot. I put Mathew down and winked at him. ‘Watch this.’ With a heave I pulled off the grate, turned it on its edge and threw it out of the hole. Cool air flooded in and I could hear the sighs of relief from the other captives in the box car. Like a dog, I stuck my head out of the hole and let the wind rush past me, blowing my hair about and filling my cheeks. I pulled my head in and looked at Mathew, wide-eyed with surprise, ‘We just wait for the right time, kiddo, and then we jump.’

His face coloured and I thought he was going to

cry again. 'But, Danny, I'm too small to jump off a train.'

Ignoring the wisdom of six-year-old boys, I told him not to worry, that we would wait for the right time.

'Just don't leave me, Danny. I don't want to be left on my own,' he said a look of panic on his face.

I made some reassuring noises and turned my attention back to the hole in the side of the box car. Even though I am fairly tall, at a hair under six feet, I have a fairly narrow frame and reckoned I could, with a little effort, squeeze my way out of the hole without much difficulty. Although the night was well into the small hours, from my vantage point I was afforded a reasonable view of the countryside in monochrome, silhouetted against the light of the still bright moon. After a while I perceived that we were travelling through a wide, flat valley and I could see into the distance that the rail tracks curved as they went over a bridge. Unlike most of our long night journey, which, apart from the occasional station, was travelled without the benefit of lighting, the bridge was illuminated at regular if fairly spaced intervals. I presumed that this was to warn high-masted ships but in truth I had no idea. Beneath this bridge flowed a wide river and, assuming it was also deep, I thought that this would be my chance of escape. I knelt down to speak to Mathew and outlined the plan to him.

'We can jump out here, Mathew. I can hold you and when we hit the water I will keep you safe and take you to the shore.'

He clutched his teddy tightly to him with both arms, and shook his head. 'I can't, I'm too little, it's too far and I can't swim.'

Exasperated by his objections, sensing the onset of his tears and truthfully not really caring if he came with me or not, so desperate was I to make my escape that I swore under my breath, 'Don't be such a baby. We need to get off this train and get help or something.'

His voice was a whisper as he choked back a sob, 'I can't.'

'For God's sake, Matty, this could be our only chance to get off this bloody train! We don't know where it is going or what is going to happen to us when we get there. We are coming to the bridge and we are running out of time!'

There was a disturbance in the dark and Mrs Bancroft moved into the pool of moonlight coming in through the hole in the wall. 'What's going on, Daniel?' she asked with her hands on her hips.

Quickly I outlined the situation to her, how I was going for help and how Mathew was refusing to come with me. Her face was caught in a wash of illumination as we passed the first of the lights leading up to the bridge, showing the anger and irritation on her normally placid face.

'Are you out of your mind?' was her response. 'I really don't care if you knock your own brains out or drown, you have always been trouble, but to put this little angel in danger is something you are just not going to do.'

The set of her body told me her mind was made up, so I muttered something about getting help again and turned once more to Mathew.

'What do you think, Matty? Are you coming with me?'

The little shake of his head again and the whispered 'I can't.'

Hot with rage, and desperate to move as I felt a change in the vibration of the train as it started crossing the bridge, I gestured wildly with my hands. 'Well I'm going.' I thrust the copper coin at Mrs Bancroft, 'There. Mrs Bancroft will look after you for now.' I knelt and gave him a brief hug.

Two things happened as I stood: Mrs Bancroft

slapped me hard around the face and hissed at me, the weight of venom and disgust hurting more than the slap.

'You filthy, filthy coward you.' She paused, obviously searching for the right word. 'Lowlife!' And with that she turned her back, her shoulders shaking with rage.

I smirked at her back and shrugged my shoulders. *Water off a duck's back, old girl* I thought to myself. Mathew threw his arm around my leg and gripped fiercely, trying to tug me deeper into the confines of the carriage. 'Don't leave me, please, Danny. Don't leave me, I'm scared.'

I peeled his fingers from my leg and backed towards my exit. 'Look, little man, I have to go. It's important. I need to get out, you know, find help and stuff. It's no good staying here, is it?' I shrugged helplessly. 'I mean. Look, I just have to go. Okay?'

I pulled myself away, and the man I was then began to worm his awkward way out of that hole. I remember I leaned out of the hole backwards and managed to sit on the lip, reached up with my hands and found a ledge I could grip and pull myself up with. The train was about a third of the way across the bridge at this point in my escape. I looked ahead and saw the approach of another light, and fearful of being noticed by the guards, I pulled my head back in again. Mathew was on his knees in the filth of the carriage, tears streaming down his face as he clung to his teddy and cried. Mrs Bancroft knelt next to him, rubbing his back and making sounds of comfort. His distraught wails were so loud I could hear them over the rest of the noise in the carriage. Pulled once more by the strings of guilt, I looked out at the bridge and decided that I would just have time for one last attempt to placate Mathew before it was too late to jump. I quickly slid back into the confines of our prison and knelt on the floor in front of my little brother.

'Hey, Matty, don't cry. Look, it will be fine. I jump out of the train, get help and come and rescue you, okay?' His howling stopped and he looked up at me and wiped the snot and tears from his face with the back of his hand. 'I will come back for you, Mathew, don't worry. I wouldn't leave my little brother for long, would I?'

His words came with difficulty, his throat constricted from crying. 'How do I know you will come back?'

Running short of time and getting more than a little desperate to make my escape, I did the only thing I could think of doing. I reached over and pulled his beloved teddy bear out of his hands.

'Look,' I said, 'this is your teddy, isn't it?' with the stress heavy on the word 'your'.

'He's called Harvey, Danny.'

'Okay, little man. Harvey is your bear, not mine, so if I take him with me, I have to come back to give him back to you. Grown-ups call it a guarantee, okay?'

He nodded with that grave understanding singular to children. 'But I don't want to lose Harvey. He's my friend.'

I sighed, 'I know, Matty, but he is the only thing you have to guarantee that I will come back. So no more tears, let me take the bear and I will see you soon. Yes?'

He stood up and nodded. I held out the bear to let him give it a goodbye kiss on the top of its head, tucked it inside my jacket, winked at him and smiled. 'Stay with Mrs Bancroft.' Now in a feverish haste, I began to wriggle my way out of the window. The train was too close to the end of the bridge for me to worry about being seen as I thrashed and pulled myself up, got my legs out by kicking and twisting and found a slight lip around the bottom edge of the box car I could rest most of my weight on. I gripped the bottom edge of my exit hole and prepared to jump. As I gathered my courage, I looked one last time into the carriage. At that moment we passed another of the bridge lights and for a brief instant it flooded the scene before me with a brightness akin to daylight. The car was packed with people, some lying down, some standing; one or two watched me with interest. But in the middle stood Mathew, in his little boy's brown sandals, his favourite red shorts and white shirt, his soft halo of blond hair, his little face red from crying, and his bright blue eyes.

Oh, his eyes. Mute anguish in a little boy's eyes.

I jumped.

IN OVER MY HEAD

I didn't know until later how far I had dropped. All I can say is that at the time it seemed like eternity. An eternity in which I was chased all the way down by the demon of my conduct lashing me with whips of guilt. The air rushed past me as I fell with my arms outstretched towards the train as though I could somehow defy gravity and my decision, haul myself back into the train and beg forgiveness from my brother.

It was I suppose, with hindsight, an odd moment to experience something of an epiphany, but I believe that when throwing myself from a moving train some forty feet above an estuarine river of indeterminate depth was as good a time as any. So, weighed down with guilt and heavy with self-loathing, I hit the water.

The shock was immense: a full body blow to my back that wracked my body with pain and knocked the air from my lungs as my fall pushed me deep into the cold, cold tidal surge. I have only fragments of memory of my time in the water, more like half-remembered echoes of a dream than a true recollection. Images of weight, cold and panic and the desperate painful need to draw breath. My memories begin again at the point I was rescued, for rescued I was.

Once more, fortune had cast her benign gaze my way: the tide was moving in and had swept me up river, where the growing dawn light had revealed my limp body bobbing in an eddy to my trio of rescuers. I fleetingly recall being dragged from the water, the mumble of voices as my chest was pumped to empty my lungs and the warmth of a blanket being thrown around my shoulders. As the growing heat of the morning sun slowly brought me to something that resembled life, one of my rescuers brought me something hot to drink. I shall never forget how she looked the first time I saw her. She was beautiful, odd but beautiful. She was tall and slender, and moved with a grace that suggested she owned the world. Long black boots, tight black jeans, black leather jacket (almost the same as mine), and long black hair that fell to the middle of her back. Her face was pale and flawless with full red lips and a ring in one side of her perfect nose. Her slightly elfin ears were pierced twice on each side, and the delicate arches of her brows were quizzically raised above her eyes. Her beauty, however striking, would for me never catch as much attention as her emerald green eyes flecked with hints of gold. Eyes that weighed me up and seemed to look straight at my soul.

'Drink this, Fish.' Her voice was strong, her accent southern.

I managed a nod.

'Join us when you feel like it.'

I nodded again and watched as she stood and walked over to the others who were sitting by a smokeless fire within a copse of trees beneath the sheltering lee of the cliff-like riverbank. As I revived, I began to take more interest in my surroundings. The trees and vegetation were brown tinged and sickly at a time when they should have been lush and verdant. A sooty pall hung in the air, and apart from the restive sounds of the river coming from my right, it was very quiet. There was an absence of both birdsong and the furtive noises made by small animals as they forage and move through the undergrowth. The part of the valley we were in felt more like autumn than spring, and the questions created by this seeming oddity of nature pushed me to my feet more than any state of recovery. As I made my way the short distance to the small group of my rescuers, I unzipped my jacket, and as I did so, a little blue bear fell out and landed at my feet. My eyes blurred with tears as I bent to pick it up. I held it to my chest for a moment, and then wrung out as much water as I could. Unable to confront or deal with the wave of emotion caused by the sight of Harvey, I stuffed him back in my jacket and stumbled over to the fire.

The three looked up as one as I approached. There were two men and the girl. The men were sitting on a log on one side of the fire and the girl on her own opposite them. The older man, a guy around his mid-sixties or so, gestured towards the space next to the girl.

'Welcome to our disparate circle of outcasts and vagabonds, young man. Take a seat.' He waited until I was seated and then introduced himself and his companions to me. Sometimes he controlled the narrative, and at other times one or the other of his companions would fill in some detail. His name was Godfrey and he had until recently been a fisherman with a small house on the Peremoss Point. The slender blond man with the spectacles was Alex; he was a geologist who had been spending time researching rock formations in the area. The girl introduced herself as Venice and she happened to be in the area to visit Godfrey, who was her grandfather. The facts as they were unveiled were basically thus: just over a month previously, Godfrey had been out on a fishing trip on his small boat with Venice, who had taken a break from work to visit her grandfather, and, as she put it 'Clear my head and get some perspective'. Whilst out at sea, an armoured column had rolled onto the Point, followed by a large number of troops who started to construct defensive positions. Godfrey had sailed his boat further out to sea in an attempt to be less visible, waited until nightfall and the change of the tide, and then sailed up the river under the cover of darkness and made camp upon this spot. It was a site he knew well from his years living in the area; a site that was difficult to get to and protected from overhead observation by the large overhang of rock.

For the next couple of weeks they had survived on the equipment they had in the boat (it seemed that Godfrey always planned ahead) and they had lived mostly off fish they caught in the river. During this time they would venture out from their campsite and spy upon the activity taking place on the Point whilst avoiding armed patrols. It was during one of these trips that they had seen the glow of a campfire and decided to investigate. At the camp fire they had discovered Alex, who seemed blissfully unaware of the activity going on in his environment and who luckily thus far had not been spotted by any of the patrols. His camp was well stocked with provisions, as he was intending to stay in the area for a month or so to investigate what he called 'various interesting strata'. Concerned by their warnings, he had packed up his camp and Venice had led him to their shelter as Godfrey 'sanitised the camp site'. Until my arrival three weeks later nothing much had occurred to unsettle their routine; the same was not to be said for the activity on the Point.

The building work had taken place at a fantastic rate. The whole of the Point had been cordoned off by a large fortified wall some half mile off the end of the Peremoss Bridge where the promontory was at its narrowest point. A large tower had been built at the end of the Point, seemingly the focal point of an industrial unit that soon began to belch out black smoke. Indeed it seemed that the smoke and effluent that poured from these sinister buildings were the most likely cause of the pollution in the air and in the water. It had tinged the river valley with the touch of autumn, replacing the usual verdant blush of spring. This industrial quarter was itself surrounded by a wall. Barrack blocks had been built between the two walls, as had a number of razor-wire fences arranged in squares surrounding a number of regular pre-fabricated huts. All this had happened within two weeks, and Godfrey's supposition that the razor-wire compounds were for prisoners proved to be true as the first train loads of wretched humanity began to arrive over the bridge, to be marched into the compounds and from there to work in the dark factories.

As the silence grew after the telling, Venice turned her head to look at me, 'So what's your story, Fish?'

I stared into the fire for long moments unable to bring myself to speak, embarrassment and shame temporarily robbing me of my voice. Venice made a sound of irritation but her grandfather calmed her with a gesture of peace, 'Give him time, lass.'

At last I reached into my jacket and retrieved Harvey. Unable to meet their eyes, I addressed my story to the little blue bear in a voice cracked with emotion. When I had finished, silence greeted my words and I looked up to face their condemnation. Alex wore a look of horror, Godfrey remained impassive, and Venice, well her look was the most odd. It seemed to be a look of speculation and appraisal. She tilted her head and looked at me with those amazing eyes.

'Not just a fish, a cold fish!' She got up and knelt before me, one hand resting on my knee.

'Welcome to our group', she said. 'What is done is done, what happens next is what matters. Finish your tea and get some sleep, we will talk later.'

With that, she rose and kissed me briefly on the forehead before returning to her seat. I found a bedding roll set out for me beneath the shelter of the rock, and with the burning tingle of her kiss still hot against my cool skin, I slept.

It was dark when I awoke. The fire had been smothered and the others sat talking in a group, their own blankets draped across their shoulders to ward off the chill. I rose stiff and sore with the gait of an old man and shambled over to join them.

Alex stood and offered me his hand. 'God, hope I never have to make a decision like yours' he said, 'Alex Avery, geologist and now a fugitive of sorts. Pleased to meet you.'

I shook his hand, relieved at the warmth of his smile, and took my place with the others, my presence transforming the triumvirate into a quartet. As I sat down, Godfrey began to speak, his voice calm, reassuring, and seemingly imbued with confidence. 'Alex and Daniel,' he nodded at us, 'not many people apart from my family know this, but I was not always a fisherman; that is the occupation I chose in my retirement.' He smiled at his granddaughter. 'Before I retired I was an officer in the army, special forces to be precise.' He paused to let that information sink in.

Well, I thought, that explains a lot.

He continued. 'Ultimately our position here is untenable: low on food and supplies, deep in enemy territory, not to mention subjected daily to this unknown pollution. I can help us move cross country with a fair chance of avoiding detection if, and only if, you do as I say.' He paused to look at us again, making eye contact with each of us in turn before resuming his briefing. 'Now, being able to move is one thing; knowing where to move to is very much another, so if any of you have any ideas or information about the current political and military climate, or know of a safe place for us to head to, now is the time to share. Daniel,' he said, 'you are the most recent to arrive amongst us and to my knowledge the only one to escape internment in the camp. Have you any ideas?'

I looked about for a moment, as if searching for inspiration, before confessing my lack of political savvy and my ignorance of current affairs up to the point of my capture. As I spoke, however, a thought entered my head. Initially it seemed like a meagre offering, but the thought grew more insistent until at last it coalesced into words and poured from my mouth. 'I can't tell you much about troop placements and military stuff,' I explained, 'but I do know that all the stations I saw on the way here seemed to be under the control of the H.A.P. and I know for certain that my home town of Westridge is in their hands.' I thought for a moment. 'Actually it is probably a staging or marshalling area for them. I mean they have removed the entire population as far as I know, so that would seem likely.'

Godfrey nodded at this. 'You are probably correct in that,' he said. 'I imagine the Jeral Mountains represent the front line at present. That would fit with the political map of party voting in recent years and the mountains do form the geographical north-south divide.' He gestured for me to continue.

'As I say, I don't know much about the military stuff, but what I do know is the area around Westridge. I know the hills, I know the paths into and through the mountains and most of all I know the caves and gullies. I could hide a thousand men in that area,' I boasted. 'After all, they seem to have put everyone else who knows the hidden places of Westridge and the lower slopes of the Jerals into the camp behind us, and from there we could, with a bit of luck, cross the front line into friendly territory.'

Alex raised his hand as if to speak, but Venice

got in before him. 'Fish, you're sure that trying to hide on the front line is a good idea, and next to one of their bases?' She gave me that look again. 'Seems a little crazy to me, or at least a bit suicidal.'

I shrugged, it was a valid point and one I had not taken time to think about. I was about to apologise when Godfrey interrupted.

'Ven,' he said, casting a warning look her way, 'it's not that crazy at all. It's a good two hundred miles to the Jeral Mountains from here. On foot, even with my skills, it would take us more than a fortnight to get there. Rest assured,' he said, marking the ground with a stick, obviously thinking hard, 'by the time we get there the front line will be well north of the mountains. This lot are well prepared, already mobilised and well drilled. Whoever it is the north find to try and stop them, they are going to get seven shades beaten out of them until they can organise properly.' He grinned, 'Anyway I like the idea of hiding under their noses.' He dusted his hands together. 'Anyone got any objections? Good. Daniel, put the brew on. There is a little stove in the camp box over there,' he said, pointing to the box Alex was sitting on. 'Tomorrow we break camp and head north.'

I made the brew and handed out the hot mugs of tea. It was good to have a plan but emotions warred inside me. I needed these people to help me survive, but could my already shattered senses and my newly awakened conscience allow me to once more turn my back on Mathew and save my own wretched skin? I plucked up courage and spoke to Godfrey about the turmoil that nipped and frayed at my already ragged sense of worth.

He sat me down and spoke. 'Safety, planning, then action. Don't worry, we will do our best to help him.'

Hardly reassured by his words and still consumed with self-loathing, I nodded and managed a weak smile by way of thanks. Later that night he led me out of the camp site and, after crawling over rock and thorn for what seemed like hours and hiding from a patrol doing a sweep of the surrounding area, he brought me to a spot overlooking the fortified factory camp that Peremoss had become. I watched the brightly lit scene as vehicles and machines moved about under the glaring arc lights, men shouted and the factories belched black smoke and glowing cinders into the air. Worst of all were the lines of prisoners that were herded into the factories to replace exhausted ones that stumbled back to their huts, too tired to even notice the whips and casual violence offered by their guards. I watched for about an hour, and for about an hour hot tears rolled down my cheeks until all that I saw was refracted a thousand times in the diamond gems of my worthless tears.

After a while Godfrey motioned that we had to leave. I silently bade my little brother a last farewell and followed Godfrey into the darkness. After we returned to camp, I huddled in my blankets and stared at the little blue bear I held in my hand. Such a small thing to be the object of so much tenderness, faded blue and threadbare in parts, worn shiny from constant childish affection, one ear ragged from where Mathew used to teethe on it. After a moment I began to whisper, telling Harvey what a shit I was, how I was a worthless brother and a waste of space. I told him of my anguish and shame, and promised I would try to do better. I do not know what possessed me to do that, to open up to a little blue teddy bear and admit my failures, maybe it was the lack of judgement in his black button eyes, or perhaps I felt on some level I was talking to Mathew. All I know is that it helped me in some way to ease my conscience and from that point on, when I couldn't sleep or stress threatened to tear me apart, I would turn again to my little blue confessor.

Somewhat shriven I slept, but sleep was no restful affair, watched as I was by the mute anguish in a little boy's eyes.

One Step at a Time

Some ungodly time before dawn Godfrey woke me. He and the others had already packed away most of the camp. He asked me to pack up my own kit and then join him at the riverside. I made my way towards the others collected at the water's edge, somewhat unsure of my footing and still a little groggy from sleep.

In a low voice, Godfrey told me that we had to get his small boat out of the water and hide it under the rock overhang. It had been well camouflaged, but the risk of discovery was too great. We couldn't use the boat, however, as it was both a little small and had no engine, relying on its sails or oars.

'Damned if I am leaving them this little beauty,' grumbled Godfrey, running his hands with affection over the smooth boards of her hull. 'Come on' he urged, 'Let's get her dry.'

After a short struggle against the flow of the river and the slope of the bank, we hauled her up, stowed her beneath the rock and covered her with branches. That done, Godfrey handed us each a rucksack. The weight was immense and only a glimpse of a mocking grin from Venice caught in the growing light prevented me from complaining. Burdened like mules we stood before Godfrey. The sky was light to the east, an orange glow tipped the high hills there, and to the west stars still shone, not yet ready to relinquish their dominance of the night sky. It was all in all a magical moment. Yes I was scared, yes I felt like I was turning away from my little brother, and yes my back felt as if it would break beneath this weight I carried, but the idea of movement, of action, seemed right. I trusted this old man with the gleam in his eyes; this was what he had spent most of his life doing, and he seemed eager to embrace all that he had been. I looked across at Venice at that moment and felt that I could follow her for ever.

Godfrey spoke, 'Right, follow me. Keep low, stay quiet and do what I do. If I drop, you drop, if I run, you run, Okay?'

We nodded each in turn and with a wave of his hand he led us north, through the tangle of rocks and scrub. A vain hope, a foolish path and a crazy idea, our journey may have been all these things as it began; where it would end was at that time a blissful mystery. Those who grasp at Fate will ever have her twist and turn, trying to sink her teeth into the ones behind.

That day for me was murder. Pure. Bloody. Murder. Yes, I was an accomplished guide and walker, but the packs I was used to carrying held little more than a first aid kit and my lunch, I was used to making the tourists carry the rest! Coupled with the back-breaking strain of my pack and the rubbing of my still damp boots was the constant gnawing fear of discovery. At first, as we wound our way north through the wooded hillsides, following the course of the river north, I tried to keep my ears tuned for the drone of propellers, and my eyes on the sky for the tell-tale black dot of an enemy bi-plane. I saw no planes but tripped constantly over roots and rocks, and as the heat of the day increased and my fatigue and aches became overwhelming, I ceased looking or caring. My feet were on fire, my shoulders were rubbed raw and my lower back protested with every step I took. During one brief rest, as I leant against a tree, too unsure of my strength and will to risk sitting down, I stopped Alex as he walked past me. 'Al,' I beckoned him over with a nod of my head. 'I am struggling a bit,' I admitted with an apologetic shrug. 'Not sure I can go much farther. Any ideas?'

He handed me the staff he had cut for himself, 'Here, have this. I will make another one.' He patted me on the shoulder, 'It helps if you can focus or think about something to take your mind off it.'

He passed me his water bottle. I took a grateful swallow, having already emptied mine. He clapped me again on the shoulder. 'Don't think we will be going on for much longer; be dark soon and we need to make a camp. Remember, Dan, focus on something and after that it's just one step at a time.'

I smiled my thanks and handed back his water bottle. I was about to take my place at the end of the line when Alex gestured me ahead.

'I will go last,' he said. 'Make sure you don't drop behind.'

I smiled tiredly at him, 'Thanks, Al.' I stepped onto the trail behind Venice.

She turned her head and fixed me with her cool gaze. 'Keep up, Fish.'

Then she turned her back to me and strode off after Godfrey. I stared at her back for a moment, and then a little lower, at the confident stride of her perfect legs and the flex of her perfect behind as she stalked along the trail. I grinned to myself: focus on something to take your mind off it, Danny, and then it's one step at a time. Like a bear after honey I set off through the trees, musing to myself that she had as fine a figure as a fellow could follow.

When we stopped for the night and set about making camp, I was dog tired, sore and reeked of sweat. This, however, did not prevent Godfrey from giving me tasks. I collected dry sticks for a smokeless fire and dug a shallow fire pit with a circle of stones around the top to prevent the fire spreading. Then I was sent for water from a small tributary that fed the estuary river, a water source Godfrey assured me would be safe to drink from. After I had filled the water bottles and cans, I took the opportunity at the water's edge to strip off and wash, the cold stream water soothing the raw skin on my shoulders and numbing the blisters on my feet. I don't think I had been sitting in the stream for more than a couple of minutes before a voice made me jump.

'I hope you filled the bottles before you polluted that stream.'

It was Venice. I jumped up startled, forgetting I was naked. 'Er, what? Erm, yes.' I managed to reply.

She just looked me up and down with that mocking smile upon her face. 'Not bad.' If anything her smirk grew bigger as I flushed red.

She turned back to the trees, 'Hurry up with that water, Fish.'

I scrambled out of the stream, dried myself on my shirt, dressed and hurried back to the camp. Alex had laid out the bed rolls and made simple bivouac shelters above them. Venice had lit the fire, and with the arrival of the water, Godfrey began to cook.

When we at last began to eat, Godfrey began to talk. With words and hands he entertained us with some of his war stories. How he had blown up such and such bridge on some river here, and how he had infiltrated an enemy camp there and even the way he used to clean his guns. If I'm honest, only a few days previously I would have paid no attention at all, but tonight, sore as I was, tired as I was, between mouthfuls of some sort of stew, I paid at least some attention. Anything to take my mind off the pain in my feet and the ache in my shoulders, and to mute the voice of my conscience clamouring to make itself heard in the depths of my skull.

Godfrey talked at length, stories about his time as a partisan, examples of misdirection and hit and runs, and his favourite methods of using explosives and so on — a whole host of terms I had never encountered before. I distinctly remember wondering how on earth he had survived a life packed with such terrifying adventure.

I was fairly relieved when after a while he stopped speaking and looked up, something of a smile on his face. 'That's enough for tonight. Danny, take first watch; Ven will relieve you in three hours.' With that he kicked soil over the fire and climbed into his sleeping bag and closed his eyes. It had not even occurred to me that we would need to mount a watch, but with a moment's reflection I saw the logic in it. Although I was desperate to lie down and sleep, I forced my aching body to stand, and entirely unsure of what I was doing, moved slightly away from the camp circle into the trees, and for want of a better direction, faced back the way we had come. Three hours later, inordinately proud that I had not fallen asleep, I felt Venice tap me on the shoulder, and I reeled drunkenly to my bed roll, checked that Harvey was safe and fell asleep. Godfrey woke me with a toe in the ribs early next morning. Stiff as a board and feeling like glass, I helped pack up and clean the camp, wincing as I moved. I touched my toes a couple of times to stretch the knots out of my back and my legs, helped Alex set his pack upon his back and staggered as he returned the favour.

I nodded my thanks at Venice when she threw me some bread and a piece of fruit, nodded again to

Godfrey that I was ready and, chewing hard on the slightly stale bread, I followed after the others.

That day passed in much the same way as the previous one had, with the notable exception that Godfrey would fall back to walk alongside me every so often and tell me another of his seemingly endless supply of war stories. Distracted as I was with my own thoughts and the view before me, I wished that the old man would just shut up and go away and I groaned inwardly each time he returned with a spry step, a smile and another damn story.

Any residual energy I had soon fled as the spring sunshine warmed the air beneath the trees. My attempts to keep an eye out for danger dwindled to the occasional glance about me as my pains returned with a vengeance and I focused once more upon putting one foot in front of the other behind the girl I would have followed anywhere.

The only other notable occurrence of the day happened when we stopped briefly for a break around noon. We had come to another of the many small streams that flowed from the Salus Hill range to our east to join the Tarma River and Peremoss Estuary on our west, the river that we had followed now for a day and a half. This time I had decided to remove my pack, to allow blood to flow back into my arms and to enjoy the almost weightless feeling one can experience when removing a heavy weight from one's back. I was walking up and down, swinging my arms and generally tentatively stretching my various protesting muscles. Venice was sitting beneath a tree leaning back on her pack, sipping from her water bottle and smoking a cigarette. Godfrey was sitting on his pack, busy with map and compass whilst Alex, ever the scholar, was looking at rocks in the stream bed. He kept bending down and fishing out an example that caught his eye. He would hold it up in the sunlight and examine it for a moment before tossing it back into the water and selecting another. He had done this some half a dozen times when he made what I can only describe as an excited squeak. His hand darted into the water, he pulled up another rock and floundered and splashed to the bank waving his new rock above his head. 'Look!' he cried, 'Look.' He thrust an elongated rectangular-shaped rock at me.

I took it from him without conscious thought and turned it over in my hands. It was perfectly smooth and a pretty dark green colour. But apart from that and its obvious rather regular shape, flat and oblong with the slightly fatter end bevelled to something resembling an edge, I failed utterly to see what had got him so excited. 'That's nice,' I offered.

He looked at me for a moment, baffled, and then realised that I was entirely ignorant of what I held. He grinned at me and shook his head. 'What you have there, Danny, is a polished hand axe from the late Stone Age.'

I looked at it again with fresh eyes. It was definitely axe shaped but it still failed to kindle any excitement within me. 'That means what exactly?' I asked.

He took it back from me as though ignorance could defile his treasure. 'I am a geologist, not an archaeologist,' he explained, 'although the two fields do on occasion meet, especially when it comes to artefacts made from rock.' He turned the axe head over in his hands. 'This is over four thousand years old, it shows that the indigenous people lived here for millennia.' He paused, sensing my lack of interest. 'It is also worth a fortune.' Now he was speaking my language!

He hurried off to show the other two his find. I spent the last few moments of my break filling my water bottle, and I have to confess, keeping an open eye for more stone axes.

Later that afternoon, Godfrey signalled for us to stop and gather round. 'There's a small village on the other side of this hill,' he said. 'We don't know what to expect there; it could be friendly or it could be crawling with enemy troops. At any rate, we are not going through it.' He looked around and fixed us all with his gaze. 'We are not even going to be seen, you understand me?' We nodded in understanding and he continued, 'We will steer slightly away from the village, but there is still a road we have to cross. When we get to that road, I will cross first and then when I am sure the coast is clear I will beckon you over one at a time. Ven first, Al last. Okay?'

We agreed, and with exaggerated care that must have been slightly comical to the former soldier, we began to move through the trees with as much stealth as we could manage. It was absolutely nerve wracking, but strangely I was enjoying myself. I stopped noticing my aches and pains and somehow tuned myself into my surroundings in a way I had never done before. Indeed, I was inordinately proud of the fact that I was the first to hear the two men walking towards us through the trees. I tapped Venice on her boot, and she looked back at me, a fierce expression on her face. I gestured at her to warn Godfrey. Almost as soon as she touched his foot, he heard them for himself. He made one of the hand signs and gestures he had been teaching us to stay down and fade into the bracken and undergrowth.

Tense with fear and excitement, I lay there as the two men, probably on their way to cut wood judging by the tools they carried, passed within only a few feet from our hiding place. After that encounter, for which I received a welcome pat on the shoulder from Godfrey and an even more welcome half-smile from Venice, crossing the road was easy. One at a time we scampered over the hard surface and disappeared into the trees on the other side.

We walked on much later than usual that night, probably by another few miles. We were all truly tired when we stopped and made a quick camp, a practice we were becoming quite adept at. After we had eaten and listened to another story from Godfrey that had me wanting to bang my head against a tree, he made us all a cup of tea and congratulated us on how well we had done that day.

'In case you are wondering why we walked further today, lady and gentlemen, it's because tomorrow we have to cross the river. We can't continue north for much longer. We have to go west at some point and it is likely there will be more troops the further north we go, thus making the crossing more difficult.' He looked around and smiled at us over the rim of his mug as he took a swig, 'The only sticking point is that there is a town in the way, one we will have to go through. There is too much activity there to try and swim the river, and we are not going to look suspicious and try to sneak across the bridge at night. What I propose is that Alex and I saunter into town in the morning, make a recce and then come back and formulate a strategy for crossing.' He shrugged, 'Who knows, there may not even be any troops there an' we can just waltz in and out again.' He grinned again, 'Sleep well, kids; tomorrow it gets interesting!'

Next morning, I awoke tense and nervous, aware that today would bring new trials and tribulations. Alex was quiet and subdued; only Godfrey seemed unaffected. He smiled as he took his time over breakfast, putting the kettle back over the fire to make another brew.

'Might as well make a leisurely breakfast', he grinned. 'No point going in too early, that would be suspicious!' He ruffled Alex's hair as he walked past him. 'I'm not unknown here in Oldbridge, I have picked up supplies from here before so it should be a piece of cake. Walk in, see what sort of enemy presence there is, if any, and then come and get you both.' He rummaged in his backpack for a moment and pulled out his map case. 'Right, you two.'

Indicating Venice and myself with a nod of his

head, he traced a path on the worn map with a blunt finger. 'This is the proposed route we will be taking to the Jeral Mountains. Study these maps well, I am leaving them with you for now. Getting caught with maps by suspicious people is not a good thing.' He looked up at the sun and turned to Alex. 'Right, young man, it's about ten; let's be off.' He picked up his stick, threw the dregs of his brew onto the ground, slung his pack over his shoulder and grinned at me. 'Right, Danny, you are in charge. Keep quiet, stay alert and I will see you in a while.' He kissed Venice on the forehead, 'See you later, love,' and with a wave disappeared into the trees.

After they had gone, I thought about asking Ven to clear the camp up, thought better of that idea, and did it myself. After our presence had been disguised and everything packed up and ready to move, I joined Venice under the shade of a large beech where she sat smoking a cigarette and studying the maps. I sat down beside her, cadged a smoke and watched her in silence for some minutes as she frowned over the map. Emboldened by our solitude or perhaps no longer able to contain myself, I asked her a question. 'You always been close to your grandfather?'

She turned her head and fixed me with that gaze. 'Since I was about fifteen, yes.' She looked back at her map.

'So what happened when you were fifteen?'

'My parents died.'

'Oh.' I was silent for a while. I finished my cigarette and buried the butt in the earth between the tree roots. 'How?'

She looked up from her map, sighed deliberately, and then carefully folded it up and placed it back within the case before exaggeratedly turning her full and wonderful attention towards me. 'Nosey Fish, why would you want to know?'

I shrugged helpless and embarrassed, 'I just want to know you better I reckon.'

She arched her eyebrows at me. 'Ok, you get to hear this once and no questions or mentions later, understood?'

Fascinated by her, what could I do but nod?

She lit another cigarette, lay back against the tree and closed her eyes. 'I was born in the town of Seline in the southwest. My mother was Godfrey's daughter and like so many she sought a completely different way of life to that of her parents. My grandparents' life was the military, and as a consequence my mother spent most of her childhood on various military bases in the area, and occasionally overseas, depending on whereabouts grandfather was posted. Anyway, when she came of age, she left that world behind her and discovered religion.' She paused, gave a slight shake of her head and continued. 'Through religion she discovered my father, a very devout man, who attempted to take the scriptures literally and thus live his life. My mother followed his every lead; soon they were married and then I was born. Life was ok, if you disregard the harsh discipline of the religious school to which I was sent, or the strict observance of prayer, not to mention the avoidance of sin, which as you might imagine was everywhere in my parents' eyes. When I was about ten, my parents began to get heavily involved in the Saviours Way militant religious group.' She opened one eye and looked at me. 'Have you heard of the Pilgrims Path Movement and the Sky for Angels campaign?'

I shook my head.

'So you won't know about the Aylcton Tor martyrs, then?'

'I think I heard of them. Something to do with aeroplanes I think.'

Venice closed her eyes again and drew on her cigarette, 'Something to do with aeroplanes he thinks. Yes something to do with aeroplanes. Fish, your lack of knowledge about anything astounds me. In concise form, Fish, although the human race has made great engineering and scientific progress over the years, for instance a multitude of lethal land-based war machines and the current cloning situation to mention but a few, in the field of flight, until recently, religion has held sway. Sky is for the birds and if the creator had intended us to fly he would have given us wings.' She paused again, considering. 'I am going to assume that you are aware of that particular tenet of our society.' She waved her hand to forestall my answer. 'I suspect that this was as much a practical consideration as a theological one, as the couple of attempts that have been made at powered flight in the past have ended in disaster, thus to some degree reinforcing the religious argument. Anyway, a few years ago, when I was about thirteen or fourteen, people began to experiment with powered flight again. I think the military were impressed with its tactical potential, but it caused an enormous amount of friction within the religious community. The Pilgrims Path, of which my parents were prominent members, started the Sky for Angels campaign and protested and picketed any military base they suspected of working on aeroplanes. To cut a long story short, a couple of short stays in prison later and me handed to the care of my grandparents, now retired, my parents along with about two hundred other religious fanatics actually witnessed the first successful short powered flight by a military-built bi-plane at the Ayleton Tor base. In some sort of religious fervour the base was stormed, the aircraft and the pilot ripped to pieces, and subsequently nearly all the protestors, my parents included, were mown down with heavy machine gun fire.'

She sat up, reached down and picked up her water bottle. Lost in thought she slowly unscrewed the top, took a sip, replaced the cap and continued. 'So, my parents died and now mankind can fly.' Another shrug. 'Fair swap I call it. So I continued to live with my grandparents. My grandmother died when I was sixteen and I moved back to the house in Seline that my parents had owned. Grandfather moved to Peremoss for a bit of solitude I think, although I have visited him every couple of months for the last three years.'

She opened her eyes and saw my raised eyebrows and the unasked question. 'Me? Well you know what I said earlier about children not following the paths of their parents? When I was seventeen and the money had run out, I got a job dancing in a club. When I was eighteen I got my tattoos done, and let me tell you, Fish, the most interesting thing that I have discovered is that in the small minds of some people, sin is just a different word for fun.'

As I silently (for once) digested this information, my thoughts were interrupted by the sound of something stumbling and crashing through the undergrowth of the forest. I leapt to my feet, my staff in hand ready to run at the first sight of danger. The undergrowth parted and a bruised and scratched Alex fell at my feet.

'They took Godfrey,' he gasped.

I helped him to his feet, relieved that for the moment at least, I was still safe. I gave him a drink of water from my canteen, and sat him down by the tree. Venice, for the first time since our misadventure had begun, lost her composure. She was white and fear had filled her eyes. She grabbed at Alex as I sat him down, harpies' talons clutching at his jacket.

'Where is my grandfather? What the fuck happened?' She shook him and I pulled her away, giving her the canteen. 'Venice, drink. Let him talk.'

'We got to Oldbridge without any problems', he recalled. 'Saw a couple of people on this side of the river, collecting wood and things. Godfrey waved to them and they waved back. We got onto the bridge itself; there were no guards on this side … I don't know why, but there was a guard post on the other end of the bridge with two guards in it.'

Alex paused and took another sip of water 'Godfrey told me to relax, act naturally and let him do the talking. The guard post was a sort of small square box behind a low wall of sandbags, and a pole barrier across the road that could be raised to let traffic through. They stopped us and searched our packs. Godfrey told them that we had been on a fishing trip up on one of the lakes in the Salus Hills for the last ten days. The gear we had supported this story and Godfrey claimed that we lived on the far side of town and were just on our way home. The guards told us that we would need papers and to get them from the police station, and they let us through.' Alex paused, rubbed at his face and looked up again.

'Then it went wrong: we were only a few feet away from the checkpoint when someone Godfrey knew saw him. The stupid fool waved to him and shouted out, 'Hey, Godfrey, what news from Peremoss?' That was it, the guards told us to halt, we turned and in the moment it took them to ready their weapons, Godfrey was on them. As he fell with both the guards in a tangle he roared at me to run. I did and here I am.'

Venice sat with her head in her hands. Maybe she was weeping, but knowing that she would hate me seeing any weakness I ignored it. I don't really know what prompted me to say what I said next; it may be that I knew that without Godfrey we stood little chance of surviving the near future. Maybe it was because I wanted to impress Venice (and by all and any gods I did) or it may have been my guilty conscience, tweaked as ever by the image of mute anguish in a little boy's eyes.

My mouth opened, and I heard myself say, 'So let's go and get him back.'

The look on Ven's face was worth my rash pronouncement. It was a quizzical look of hope and disbelief, which transformed into a look of determination. She nodded.

Alex was less convinced, 'But how? Danny, there are armed men in the town.'

Still somewhat shocked by the audacity of my own mouth, without too much conscious thought I explained. 'We always knew this was going to be dangerous. We are to all intents and purposes fugitives and we are in a region that is now controlled by an armed force, a force we are in hiding from, a force we are trying to escape from and, need I add, a force from whom I have recently escaped and who still hold my little brother captive.' Rather glibly I shrugged. 'It is hard to imagine that we could escape this area without having to resort to some sort of violence. Now our best hope of escape has been captured, we have to rescue Godfrey if we are to have any hope of fleeing to the north. Remember what Godfrey has taught us: evaluate, plan and execute.'

I drew breath, and held up my hand to forestall questions from the other two. 'Alex, tidy up a bit and go into the woods, collect firewood or something and see if you can engage one of the townsfolk in conversation. I don't care what you have to tell them, maybe you could tell them the same fishing story that Godfrey used and find out the situation in the town, find out how many soldiers there are, where they are and where their operating base is. Venice will stay at the camp and see if there is anything we can use as a weapon in our kit, and I will go and have a look at the bridge and plan a way of getting across.' I looked at my wrist, forgetting for a moment that my watch had been taken from me. 'You both have watches?' Alex nodded and Venice showed me hers upon her wrist. 'Right, Ven, can I borrow yours?' She nodded, undid the strap and threw it towards me. I caught it and as I strapped it on nodded at Alex, 'See you back here in two hours.'

Alex paused at the edge of the trees and turned to look at me.

'It will be fine, Alex,' I said. 'Just find the information we need, and don't try and think about the next part.' I gave him the best smile I could manage, hoping that it looked more sincere than it felt upon my face. I knelt by Venice as she opened Godfrey's rucksack. I touched her lightly on the shoulder. It was all I dared. 'We will get him back.'

She nodded at me, her lower lip held in her teeth. I stood and left for the bridge.

My trip to the bridge was uneventful, or at least free from drama. I had to lie still in the undergrowth twice to keep my presence hidden from anyone, but soon worked my way to the edge of the trees that ran down almost to the river. I stayed still and observed the comings and goings of people in the town. Not many at all crossed the bridge or used the small road that ran between the trees, a road I recalled from the maps as heading to the village we had bypassed the day before. One or two people made their way back across the bridge into the town burdened with firewood. All these people collecting wood was an indicator that something had interrupted the usual coal supply, although whether the wood was being stockpiled against winter or was for more immediate use, I could only guess. Each person was stopped by the guards on the bridge, who were no doubt a little more vigilant than they had been before they captured Godfrey. There were, as Alex had recounted, two men at the far end of the bridge in a small guard box behind a low sandbag wall. I could see a way across the river but could not in my time observing detect a pattern in their behaviour that would allow us to cross undetected.

I slithered back into the undergrowth and made my way back to camp. Alex had already returned and he and Venice were conversing in low voices as I stepped out of the concealing undergrowth and into the small clearing. Both greeted me: Alex with a smile and Venice, her face still tight with worry, with a small nod. I grinned back in return.

'So, Alex, what did you learn?'

His smile widened into a grin to match my own. 'It was easy, Danny. I helped some woman collect sticks. I pretended that I was from the next village and had wandered a bit far. I told her it was difficult there at the moment, she agreed and then told me about the occupation and how much life had changed.'

'So?' I gestured, 'Numbers? Disposition?'

'There are fifteen troops left in the town, the rest moved out once the place had been pacified she said. There are now two on watch on each side where the main road enters the town, and the other ten soldiers and their officer are based in the old police station. Apparently that is where they are holding a number of prisoners, you know the type, vocal or aggressive locals, as well as one or two people not from the town who are being detained.' He looked at Venice, 'That is probably where they are holding Godfrey.'

I patted him on the shoulder, 'Nice work, Alex. Just what we needed.'

I looked closely at them both. Venice was quiet and deep in thought, while Alex looked like a young boy on the first day of school, torn somewhere between excitement and terror, and unable to decide which camp to land in. For myself I was in a strange state of calm, not backing away, and probably for the first time I could recall, determined to try or die, both for the admiration of the most enigmatic person I had ever met and in an attempt to silence the demons that nagged at me from the dark spaces within my brain.

'This won't be easy,' I continued. 'I do have a general plan, although there is one big part that is missing. I can get us both across the river, but I need a distraction so that we can climb the banks and get behind the guards.'

Venice looked up at that point and smiled, the

first true smile I had seen from her since Godfrey had been captured. Her smile turned into a small laugh. 'Don't worry, boys. I think I can provide the distraction.'

I cocked my head to one side. 'How?'

She smiled again. 'You will know it when you see it.'

I shrugged, 'Well if you are sure. Don't do anything too dangerous.'

She shook her head and laughed. 'What? Like three unarmed civilians attacking a unit of heavily armed and trained soldiers?' She gave me a brief but delicious hug. 'Silly Fish.'

I smiled my bashful smile, 'Good point, Ven.' Her mention of weapons triggered a thought, 'Did you manage to find any weapons, Ven?'

She shrugged. 'There is a big hunting knife, a hatchet and a couple of other largish kitchen knives but that's it, I'm afraid.'

Alex spoke. 'I'm going to use the hand axe I found. All I have to do is make a handle for it.' He saw me look pointedly at my watch. 'Oh, don't worry Dan, it will only take a short while.'

I paused, unwilling to say anything that might

undermine his confidence. 'Well if you think it will work, Al, it's up to you.' I selected the hatchet, drawn by the lethal-looking small-edged chopping blade, balanced by a sharp curved spike on the back, and handed the hunting knife to Venice. Alex selected a branch to use as a shaft for his axe, and I ran a stone over the edge of the hatchet, trying to get it as sharp as I could manage. Venice rummaged around in a rucksack finding us something to eat.

'The plan is,' I stated between strokes of the stone, 'we cross the river as soon as it gets dark, Venice provides the distraction, we run up the bank behind the two sentries, kill them as quickly as possible, and strip the bodies of weapons and uniforms. We then hide the bodies, and you two put on their uniforms and head through the town to the other sentry post. You kill the two sentries there as silently as you can, cut the communication lines and then fire a gunshot to let me know that you have succeeded and then I will storm the police station. Any questions?'

Alex sat open-mouthed; Venice frowned at me.

'It sounds okay, Fish, right up to the point where you take on eleven heavily armed men by yourself, then it seems to get a little,' she searched for the right word, 'fantastic.'

Maybe bravado had been wreaking havoc with my brain chemistry, maybe I was feeling reckless, but it sounded like a reasonable plan to me. I winked at her. 'I will have the element of surprise, but if there are any left you can help me finish them off when you get there.' I saw the question in her eyes and held up my hand to forestall her. 'The prisoners should be safe in their cells. I don't believe that the soldiers will want to waste time harming them whilst they are under loud and vigorous attack by persons unknown.' I took a couple of practice swings through the air with the hatchet. 'Eat, rest, and try to relax because when it gets dark our world changes.' With that I sat back against the tree and closed my eyes. I was far from sleep and utterly terrified but now was no time to show it.

All Change

As the daylight began to fail, we gathered our belongings together and slowly made our way towards the river. We put our gear in a heap and covered it with branches. I paused for a moment to take Harvey from his place in my pack and I propped him in the fork of a tree from where there would be a view of the bridge. I am unable to say for certain why I did this other than that I felt somehow that in some way Mathew, wherever he was and whatever hell I had left him to, might understand that at last I was in the act of keeping my promise. I kissed the little bear's head before I set him on his perch and whispered 'I am on my way,' in his fluffy ear.

The moon that night was quite bright in a cloudless sky, but this presented no problem as it cast one side of the bridge into shadow. I took a deep breath and nodded to the other two, 'Right, let's go.' I smiled at Venice, as close to tears from fear as I had ever been and half joked, 'See you on the other side.'

She whispered, 'Good luck.'

I turned then and slid into the water, chased onwards by the mute anguish in a little boy's eyes that made a mockery of my fear. Gods, it was cold in the shadow of the bridge. Wordlessly we eased forwards, communicating with nods and hand signals. Once we had travelled over half the distance I knew it would be almost impossible to spot us from the sentry box, which was sited a few yards back from the end of the bridge. This knowledge eased the fear of discovery, but the fear of the next action grew until I was a vibrating bundle of near-panic. I kept nodding to Alex. I could see that he was at least as afraid as myself; his eyes rolled and his hands shook. In the arch at the far side of the bridge I held his shoulder and motioned for him to breathe. He visibly relaxed and I spoke almost without noise into his ear, 'When I go, you go. Okay?'

He nodded and I slid away from him to the other side of the bridge and waited for Venice to distract the guards. Caught in a strange sense of detachment, I no longer felt the cold, and the noises of the night seemed louder as I waited; I could hear the sounds of small animals and the whispering of trees. As I tuned in to the sounds around me, I realised that I could also hear the murmur of the sentries on duty, the low quiet sound of two men talking in hushed tones, airing, most likely, grievances against officers, fellow soldiers and this dull little town to which they had been stationed. Presently, the murmur of their voices stopped. There was silence for a few brief seconds then a very audible 'What?' followed by an amazed 'Saints, look at that.'

There followed the sound of them moving, and when their quick footsteps passed overhead on the bridge I moved, praying that Alex was moving with me. I surged up the low but fairly steep bank, clutching at small bushes and handfuls of reeds to assist my progress. I reached the top and swung onto the bridge. The soldiers were standing together, their eyes on something before them – what it was that held their attention I could not see as they themselves obscured my view. They stood with their weapons held before them, yet in a posture that somehow did not imply threat. They were, it seemed, totally oblivious to my presence behind them. A glance to my left showed Alex coming onto the bridge; his face, probably a mirror of my own, was grey and fearful. I nodded briefly to him and he readied his stone axe. I ran the short space between me and the sentry and swung my hatchet into the back of his neck just below the rim of his helmet. It was a good and solid blow and I believe he was dead in an instant. I was aware of Alex striking the other soldier as I caught the body of the man I had killed in an attempt to deaden the sound of his fall. I pulled the corpse over backwards on top of myself to cushion the falling body with my own; it was in that instant that I saw what had so enthralled them.

Venice was naked. That is except for her boots. She was walking slowly forward, moving with a feline grace and her body, it was… no. I shall not attempt to describe for you the perfection I beheld. Some small memories a man must cherish for himself, memories to treasure and remember in the hard times in life, small talismans of warmth that ease the icy holds of fear and hunger, a currency of survival if you will. There have not been many men, I think, who first beheld the naked body of the woman who was to become their greatest love as they cradled the body of the first man they had killed. My soul sang with joy at the same instant as it was plunged irredeemably into perdition.

I tore my gaze away and looked to my left where there was a struggle occurring. Alex had failed to kill his man, his damned axe had broken, the shaft he had made had snapped on impact and now he lay on the floor grappling with the soldier.

To his credit, however, he had jammed his forearm into the soldier's mouth to prevent him sounding an alarm and the gun lay on the ground where it had presumably been dropped when Alex struck him. As I wrestled myself clear of the body to go and assist him, the glorious naked Venice sprinted up, pulled the knife from her boot and slid it into the soldier's rib cage. The body kicked and then relaxed and for the moment, at least, we were safe.

I nodded at Venice, and she turned and flitted back through the shadows of the bridge. I helped Alex to sit up and I bound the bites on his arm with a sleeve ripped from my shirt. He was shaking and crying. I held him close for a while and whispered words of encouragement into his ear until his shaking stopped and he regained some of his composure. I was glad to do this and thought nothing less of him for his display of emotion. Indeed, the act of calming and reassuring him helped me to control my own frayed nerves, the platitudes I had whispered being for myself as much as for Alex.

If you have never killed a man in anything less noble than self-defence, or the defence of your loved ones, then I implore you, for the love of all the saints and martyrs, don't. You will never be fully human again.

A fully clothed Venice returned and helped us

to drag the bodies back to the sentry box. She hugged us both and I whispered my thanks into her ear for her help. She told me not to mention it, and so in all the time we were together, right until the end, I never did.

We stripped the bodies and Alex and Venice donned the light grey uniforms and black webbing. The weaponry we claimed was fairly impressive. Each man carried an assault weapon with a folded bayonet, two spare clips of ammunition and two grenades. I took the grenades for the coming lunacy of my attack on the police station, leaving the guns and ammunition for the other two. It was as I was casting my gaze around the interior of the sentry box, just to make sure we had not missed anything, that I saw in the corner the weapon that was to become the one I have been most associated with – the riot shotgun. On inspection it carried a full twelve rounds, and after familiarising myself with the mechanisms and the safety switch, I tied it to my back using the other sleeve from my shirt to hide it from frontal view.

I stuffed the grenades into my pockets and the hatchet handle into my boot, and turned to inspect the others. I really had no idea at the time about the correct appearance of a H.A.P. soldier, so I made sure they looked the same and that no blood stains showed. I extended the bayonets on the weapons and nodded. 'That's as good as it's going to get, I think. Remember, go the back way past the square so no one on duty outside the police station will see you, kill the other sentries, cut communications and alert me with a shot.' I grinned with what in truth was probably a very sickly grin. 'Easy really. Good luck and I will see you in a bit.'

Venice smiled at me and visibly composed herself, 'We will be fine.' She took Alex by the arm and led him out onto the street. 'Come on, Alex, we can do this.' She looked at me, her eyes hidden by the shadow of the helmet, 'Be careful, Fish.' Before I could answer she had turned, and with a confident stride, Alex in tow, she set out to do unspeakable things in the attempt to rescue her grandfather.

Before I followed them into the town, I had a thought and sprinted back across the bridge. I retrieved Harvey from his place in the tree, tucked him back into my shirt and jogged warily into the town.

There were a few parked cars at the side of the main road and I used these for cover as I approached the junction where the road entered the square. I stopped before I came into the square, lay down in the shadow of the building on the corner and wriggled forwards so I could look around the corner into the square at floor level. The police station was the second biggest building on the square after the town hall and the only one that was brightly lit. The bright lights were, however, casting deep shadows at the side of the steps up into the building. There was obviously some form of curfew in operation as there was no one at all on the streets and all curtains were drawn with only faint slivers of light showing from occasional gaps.

I realised that I should be able to take the alleyway that ran behind the houses, circle the square and use the alley at the side of the police station to get behind the sentry to hide in the shadows and wait for my signal.

I took Harvey from within my shirt, kissed the top of his head and whispered, 'I'm coming, little brother,' before setting him down on the floor on the corner to watch.

Knowing that time was short, I backed away, stood up and began to jog down the dark alley. As I ran I could not help but wonder to myself how on earth I, a lazy self-obsessed individual, had organised and begun a daring raid to free an old man. Yes I would count him as a friend and yes the opportunity to ingratiate myself with his granddaughter was important to me, and yes I owed an enormous emotional, psychological and fraternal debt to

Mathew… but this? This was madness, this was almost certainly suicide. As I reached the corner and turned to move past the back of the town hall, three points occurred to me: firstly, where in the name of the Eternal had I gained this ability to plan; secondly, where in the name of the Saints had I begun to lead; and thirdly, by the Martyrs I was enjoying this!

I rounded the last corner and began to move back towards the police station. Luck was with me: no dogs had barked, nothing had tripped me up in the darkness and there had still been no gunshot. I was only slightly concerned for the others; I believed that surprise was completely on their side and that despite my misgivings about Alex, the wonderfully competent and resolved Venice would see him through.

I took my hatchet out of my boot and eased slowly down the side of the building. Crouching down I peered around the corner. Luck was still with me. The guard was facing away from me in the act of lighting a cigarette. As his flint failed to strike, it took only a moment to cross the well-lit corner of the building and crouch down in the shadow by the steps. His last smoke underway, the guard stood at ease with his back to me, one hand on the strap of his slung rifle. He was completely relaxed and looked neither left nor right as he blew smoke rings into the night sky. I, on the other hand, waited coiled and tense, like a runner on a starting block. I had not long to wait at all. The soldier in front of me had smoked about half his cigarette when I heard the crack of a gunshot break the silence of the night. The guard turned, startled, but I was on him in an instant. I pulled back on the barrel of his rifle, staggering him off balance and I swung my hatchet into his throat. I swung again, left my weapon where it stuck and turned my attention to the building behind me. I knew it would only be moments before someone came to enquire about the shot, so moving in feverish haste, I took the shotgun off my back and laid it on the top of the steps.

There was a window on either side of the door and a grenade is more than heavy enough to break glass. I pitched two in quick succession through each window and as the muffled crump of detonations sounded, I crouched and picked up the shotgun. Smoke and screams billowed from the windows and the double doors flung open. A soldier, his shirt smouldering and cuts cross-hatching his chest and shoulders, burst into the square; almost on reflex I shot him, throwing him back into the building. I followed him in.

I do not in truth remember much of what happened after that. I know I must have been screaming as afterwards my throat was raw and my voice strained. I remember a red jittery panic as I pointed the gun at anything that moved and pulled the trigger. I have a vague impression of a number of bullets whining past my head, fired by a soldier behind a big desk, and I remember as a bad dream the sound of a click as my gun emptied. I don't remember leaping the desk and clubbing down the soldier with the heavy wooden stock of my gun. This I must have done, however, as I was still repeatedly doing it as I sobbed, shook and vomited over the gruesome corpse of my antagonist when my breathless companions rushed to my help.

Venice, helmet off and in her stolen uniform, was as welcome a sight as I have ever seen. She handed me a bottle of water, her concern writ large upon her lovely face. She looked around the room at the torn and broken bodies; words I think failed her and she nodded but once. It took me several attempts to open the bottle and drink, but my shaking began to subside.

You have to love those with a scientific mind: Alex focused my attention wonderfully with a quietly spoken, 'There's one missing.'

I looked at him in horror, 'What?'

‘Look,’ he said, ‘nine bodies here, four outside, there’s one missing.’

Almost as one we turned our heads and looked at the door that led to the cells.

‘There must be one on guard in there,’ he suggested.

Cursing myself for the oversight, I picked up my gun from the floor and loaded it from a box of ammunition on the desk. I controlled my adrenaline shakes and firmed my resolve. ‘There is only one thing for it. Alex, you yank open the door, I will dive through and try to get him before he gets me. Ven, you stand to one side and shoot him if he gets past me.’

Venice gave me the look that all women give idiotic males from time to time, as she rolled her eyes and shook her head. She walked up to the door and knocked on it.

‘Any soldiers in there, I suggest you surrender immediately,’ she called through the door in a loud clear voice. ‘You are on your own and there will be no help coming.’

Astounded as I was at her brilliance, I was yet more astounded when a voice shouted back.

‘Ven, is that you?’

'Grandfather?'

'Yes, love. Come in, it's okay.'

With the only girly shriek I was ever to hear Venice make, she wrenched open the door to the cells. Alex and I followed close behind her.

A very bruised and battered Godfrey was in a cell at the far end of the corridor, his arms through the bars, choking the life out of the missing soldier, who was released and dropped to the floor as we entered. All the other cells were occupied: there were five cells in all and three or four people in each cell. They were starting to make the beginnings of a racket with shouted enquires and pleas for release, until Godfrey's military bellow for silence momentarily ended their clamour.

Venice had found the cell keys on the desk at the end of the corridor, and after finding the one for the cage Godfrey was in, was enjoying something of a tearful reunion with him. Unwilling to watch this scene, I stationed Alex at the door and told him not to let any of the occupants of the cells past until I had questioned them about their alleged crimes and allegiances.

It was in the end easy to recognise those who were to be deported: it was all of them – seventeen unaware souls who were to be consigned to the same fate as my little brother. They all wore the red stamp on the back of their hands and had been arrested for such minor offences as complaining to their new authorities, being members of the town council and, in the case of one, for insolently returning the stare of the officer in charge of the town. I let them all out and this time stood at the double doors myself to prevent anyone leaving. The sight of all the bodies in the main room subdued them somewhat, as Godfrey, professional as ever, collected weapons off the fallen. I held up my hand for silence. I never intended to make a speech, raw as my throat was. I was just going to explain what had happened and warn them of likely reprisals and to not direct their anger against us in the event of this happening. But speech it became and yet another twist of fate in the life of me, Daniel Shaddick, layabout and wastrel.

'Gentlemen,' for they were all men, 'my name is Daniel Shaddick. The red stamp on the back of your hands tells me that you were going to be deported.' I held up my hand and let them see the ghost of a red stamp on the back of my own. 'A few days ago, in sight of the very camp I was being taken to, I escaped. Fortune was on my side and I met these people who are here with me. We were trying to head north into Coalition territory but unfortunately one of our number,' I indicated Godfrey, 'was captured yesterday. We were unwilling to leave him in the hands of these military thugs, unwilling, through our inaction, to allow him to be herded into a camp and forced to work on behalf of the H.A.P. war effort. I would ask all of you gentlemen to forgive us this slaughter and forgive us too any injustice our action may bring to you and yours, but the capture of our friend we could not let lie. I would ask you to return to your families or flee and hide as you see fit. When the wagon comes to collect you, if I were you I would not be here. We had intended to reach safety. This now will be more difficult, but a small price to pay for freeing a handful of the unjustly incarcerated, and one I may have to pay again as I have little idea of what the future has in store for us all. I do know, however, that it will be difficult. It would seem that the previous uncertain political situation has now become a military one and that forces have been unexpectedly and ruthlessly mobilised. If the pattern we have observed thus far is any indication, there is much territory already under the control of the H.A.P. Undesirables and trouble makers have been removed and indeed at least one whole town has been emptied to create a military staging post for the army. I for one have no intention of surrendering my liberty.' I patted the shotgun slung across my chest and grinned at the small group of shocked and nervous men. 'This is my get out of gaol free card, and the dream remains, freedom or bust!'

Silence greeted my speech for a few brief moments, followed by some whispered words from a few of the men until the biggest of the group stepped forward, his hand extended.

'I'm Harry Glover. Run a couple of trucks I call a haulage firm, or did 'til these bastards took them. I will have a word with my missus, and if I know her at all, she won't mind if I come with you; fact I reckon she will insist.'

Another man came forward. He was small and fairly portly, and he introduced himself as Oswald Walton, until recently the mayor of the town. He had no family other than the townsfolk and he too would be grateful to tag along. The third man to come forward was a slender rangy sort, not unlike myself in build. About eight years my senior, he was wild-eyed and filthy with longish hair and a beard, a gold tooth and an impressive collection of tattoos. He called himself Jimmy Parker. He was not from this town, he explained, but was a mechanic by trade and his wife had thrown him out a few days before. He had missed the occupation of his town by sleeping off a three-day drinking binge in a ditch. After that he had been too afraid to go home and explain to the new authorities where he had been, and ended up wandering here, where he got caught anyway.

That was how I gained my other lieutenants, or captains, call them what you will. They were the first to volunteer themselves and for the most part men with nothing much to lose and a deep belief in justice. Harry was hugely strong, very steady and reliable. Oz was an officious little man, passionate about whatever task he had been set and very good at planning. As for Jimmy, he was reckless and daring, drank too much, enjoyed making others laugh and was all in all the most charismatic man I had ever met. They were all to become close and trusted friends of mine.

In all, twelve of the men for one reason or another decided to chance their hand and join with us. At this point, Godfrey took over. He looted a watch from a dead soldier and checked the time before issuing orders.

'We leave in four hours; longer than that will not be safe. Communication has been cut but if other units fail to get through they will realise that something is amiss. Get some food and some sleep, gather things you will need, say your goodbyes and be back here in time to leave.' He stopped one of the men who wanted to come with us. 'You, help me burn all the records they have in this place and see if we can find any maps or useful military documents, anything that could give us an insight into what we face.' He looked up, 'Go on, the rest of you. Get out of here and I will see you in four hours.'

A Brief Respite

I wandered outside into the fresh night air, and still in something of a daze I went back to the corner of the square and picked up Harvey. I kissed the top of his head and tucked him back into my shirt. I began walking along the road, heading back to pick up our belongings. The night air was warm, and after a moment the sounds of the night began to wash over me, chasing from my head the remains of the awful terror that had gripped me and smoothing the sharpest edges on the jagged recollection of taking life, leaving me in a state of almost calm. I heard footsteps on the road behind me. There was no need to turn, I knew only one person who walked like that. I held out my hand and as she caught up with me, Venice took it in her own, interlocking her fingers with mine.

Sometimes there are no words to convey emotions. She, unable to express her gratitude and regret or her horror and remorse, said nothing. I, unable to tell her that risking my life and condemning myself to a fugitive existence were an insignificant example of what I could do should she but ask, said nothing. We walked in silence – her hand in mine said it all. As I retrieved the kit we had hidden, the moonlight must have caught my face. I hadn't even realised that I was crying, but I was; a product of joy or remorse I know not, but I suppose with all that emotion kept tight inside something had to give. A tear had rolled down each cheek and Venice saw them in the lunar glow. She reached up with both hands and used her thumbs to wipe them away. Then she kissed me. I have never felt such passion and emotion in a kiss. The moon and the stars could have ceased to be and the world could have burnt around me, and I would have been unaware of anything but her lips on mine and the shape of her body in my arms. I recall sharing a long kiss, an age wherein each understood completely the other, but even so, all too soon she broke away. Almost overwhelmed, and unwilling to break the spell with an ill-placed word, I sought solace in silence and action and passed her some of the kit to carry. I shouldered my own burden and hand in hand and wordless we walked back into the small town.

When we arrived back in the square, there was something approaching chaos beginning to ensue as townsfolk exiting their houses to investigate what all the shooting had been about thronged around the released prisoners. It appeared that some were jubilant and others were terrified. The large, calm presence of Harry who was standing with his arm around his wife, was for the moment preventing either panic or celebration, depending upon the inclination of the individual. There were at a guess around three hundred people standing around shouting questions, praise or damnation.

Dropping the packs I carried, and giving a last reassuring squeeze, I reluctantly released my hand from hers and clambered onto the top of one of the cars parked at the side of the square. I passed unnoticed for a moment until I stuck my fingers into my mouth and released a shrill, piercing whistle. Heads turned towards me and I heard Harry bellow, 'That's the man you should speak to, that's Daniel Shaddick.'

People began to gather around the front of the car where I was standing. More questions were shouted, insults too. I waited in silence as they gathered before looking over my shoulder to catch a reassuring smile from Venice. I held up my hand for silence.

'Ladies and gentlemen, please go back to your houses, homes and families. This event tonight should not concern you. We have no intention of causing trouble for you, we are not here to liberate the town or bring the wrath of the H.A.P. down upon you.' A thought occurred to me, 'In fact, I would suggest that as soon as we leave, one or two of you should drive to the nearest large town and inform the new authorities of what occurred here tonight. This I believe will somewhat allay suspicions of collusion and perhaps cause the H.A.P. to show you a little leniency.' I raised my arm to fend off another barrage of shouts. 'In a few short hours we will be gone; the less you know the better, don't you think?' I paused. 'In fact, for the sake of your families and your loved ones, it would be better for you if you claimed you had seen nothing tonight and stayed inside. I am sure there will be questions; tell them what you like, tell them armed men killed their soldiers and freed some prisoners, but if you tell them you spoke to us, what are they then going to believe? So go home, go to bed and forget you saw us.'

Somewhat muted, the obviously worried crowd began to disperse. One or two groups lingered so I jumped off the car and beckoned to Oz, who looked up and came trotting over, struggling a little with the rifle he had claimed. 'Oz, these are your people,' I gestured at the fifty or so who lingered. 'Tell them that you would have been in a camp tomorrow if not for this, remind them of the work you have done on their behalf and plead with them to go home and allow you this chance of freedom.'

I shrugged and nodded my head towards the steps of the police station where my ragtag but heavily armed group of volunteers waited. 'And if that doesn't work get that motley bunch to persuade them gently inside.' Oz tried to salute, but I stopped him, 'Don't salute me, Oz. I'm not a soldier I'm just a bewildered man caught up in events beyond my control.' I grinned at him and winked, 'I make most of this up as I go along.'

He smiled back a little nervously, 'Okay, Mr Shaddick,' he said, 'I will get it done.' He turned to walk away, took a half step and paused. 'And thank you, Mr Shaddick.'

I shook my head at his bizarre formality and sat on the front of the car. Venice joined me and leant against my shoulder. 'Thanks, Fish,' she murmured. I put my arm around her shoulder and gave her a hug. We sat like that for a moment until Harry arrived in front of me, his small wife in tow.

'That was nicely done, Daniel, thank you.' I nodded in response and he continued, 'Daniel, I would like you to meet Sara, my wife.'

I stood and shook her hand. She smiled warmly at me and grasped my hand in both of hers.

'Thank you so much,' she said, her eyes sparkling with unshed tears. 'Harry has told me what you have saved him from… I couldn't bear the thought of my Harry in a place like that. Now I know he could maybe stop with me but he is too big to hide.' She smiled up her husband, 'I know that he will still be in danger with you, but if he can get over the border I could stop worrying about him, knowing that he is safe.' She let go of my hand to put both her arms around the big man's waist, 'You will keep him safe for me, young man, won't you?'

'Mrs Glover, I will do my very best to keep him fit and whole until he can return to you,' I solemnly declared, meeting her heartfelt plea with as honest an answer as I could summon.

Harry kissed his wife on the top of her head, gave her a squeeze and told her that he would follow in a few minutes.

'I don't know much about military matters,' he claimed. 'Done a fair bit of hunting though, so I'm not a bad shot. What do you want us to do?'

I thought for a moment, 'Post a couple of men on sentry duty at the guard posts on the road, have a couple more small patrols in the square and around the town and report to Godfrey in the police station. Get Jimmy to keep the rest of the lads together in the town hall. Anyone who feels the need to ask more questions or air more worries, get them to speak to Oz.' I yawned, the events of the night finally catching up with me. 'I would be grateful if you could make sure everyone was together in time to leave. As for me, I need to find somewhere to get some sleep, I think tomorrow is going to be a hard day.'

Harry smiled at me. 'Thought of that,' he said. 'Already asked Sara to run you a hot bath and make you some food. You can both stay at mine until we leave.'

I slapped him on the shoulder. 'Harry, you are a godsend, thank you.' I looked over at Venice, 'You coming, Ven?' She smiled her beautiful smile at Harry. 'You had me at hot bath.' She jumped to her feet, 'Let's go.'

Harry's house was quite a large town house, brick built and well-crafted with lead-panelled windows complete with shutters. He led us inside. 'Welcome to my humble home. Sara likes to keep it nice,' he said, pointedly taking off his boots. We did the same and followed him up the tastefully decorated hall past rows of ornaments into the kitchen.

Sara had a large pot of stew on the stove and

gave us a big bowlful, along with a large chunk of fresh bread. It was easily the best meal I had eaten since before my parents had left for their holiday. Venice and I were silent as we ate. Harry watched us as he ate his own meal, obviously full of questions but too kind-hearted to interrupt us as we ate.

As we neared the end of the meal, Harry gestured towards the back stairs with his crust, 'Soon as you are done, the bathroom is straight up those stairs. Help yourself to towels and whatever you need.'

Sara rapped him over the head with a wooden spoon. 'Don't speak with your mouth full,' she admonished. She turned to address Venice, 'Ladies before gentlemen. You first, love.'

Venice finished the last of her bowl, stood, thanked Sara warmly and disappeared up the stairs.

Sara pressed a hot mug of tea into my hands and sat down. She looked at her husband who nodded and asked, 'So what happens now, Daniel?'

This was a question I had been asking myself as I ate. Something resembling an idea, or at least an idea of an idea, had been forming as I enjoyed the warmth and the food. I find that being asked a direct question helps focus various threads of imagination and supposition until they coalesce into a solid thought, particularly when you suddenly understand that despite your misgivings and your own lack of belief in yourself, you have, for better or worse, a responsibility for other people's lives; and almost worse than that, you have a responsibility towards their loved ones. I took a deep breath and began, the plan finally taking shape as I spoke.

'When we leave just before first light, most of the group are going to head north. We will do this in two groups, one group with Godfrey and Venice, and another with you and Oz in charge.'

Despite his obvious need to ask questions, Harry was astute enough to let me finish.

'You will travel at night and rest up in the day – choose woods and ditches to hide in; there is too much risk of discovery if you hide in buildings and barns. If all goes well, you should be able to cover the distance in a little over one week. I will show you on the map later where we will meet up; I have a safe place in mind. From there we will journey into the mountains and try to find a way across the front lines into friendly territory. I will lead a third group, mostly volunteers with Jimmy as my second.' I paused, took a sip of my tea and continued. 'We will head south to that village down river and cause some commotion there, and after that we will head southwest and attack a couple more random

H.A.P. targets. Hopefully this misdirection will concentrate the search away from the two groups heading north and make your trip easier. After a couple of days we will disappear and head north ourselves and join you at the meeting point. I will have a look at some maps later and work out where an attack would cause the most confusion.' I looked up and smiled, 'That is as much as I have so far.'

Sara reached over the table and placed her hand upon mine, 'Young man, this is the second time you are going to risk your life for Harry. Oh, I know the first time was just coincidence, but you are doing it again and willingly. You are incredibly brave, but why would you risk your life for people you hardly know?'

I managed a strained smile, 'I have a debt to pay, Sara, and this is the only way I know how.'

She scrutinised me carefully, her warm brown eyes studying every twitch and frown made by my face. She patted my hand. 'Don't let those demons drive you too hard,' she said.

Embarrassed, I concentrated on my tea, swirling the dregs around in the bottom of the mug until a towel-wrapped Venice appeared at the bottom of the stairs.

I offered my thanks for the food and headed

upstairs for a bath. I stripped off my dirty clothes, set Harvey to one side and slid into the hot water. I closed my eyes and relaxed, floating on that moment on the edge of sleep where thoughts are hard to grasp and emotions become ill-defined. I sensed a presence with me in the bathroom and the bath shivered slightly as someone sat upon the side. I opened my eyes and focused on the towel-wrapped Venice, who sat there regarding me with her quizzical gaze.

Somehow unperturbed by my nudity, I offered her a shy smile. She returned it and then knelt at the side of the bath, picking up the soap and slowly beginning to wash my back. It was blissful and natural, and at that moment it seemed as if I had known her forever. I closed my eyes again and revelled in the sensation. After a while, I sluiced the soap off and stood. I took the towel she handed me and dried myself off. I wrapped it around my waist, took Venice's proffered hand and followed her into a bedroom. We climbed between the sheets and lay nose to nose for a moment staring into each other's eyes.

'You are doing well, Fish,' she murmured. She moved her head slightly and kissed my mouth. 'Thank you for giving me my grandfather back.' Then she draped her arm over me, rested her head on my chest and closed her eyes. Without rancour or regret I held her gently and closed my own and drifted into sleep. As usual, as I drifted off I recalled the mute anguish in a little boy's eyes, but for once I could look back with something other than shame. 'I'm on my way, Mathew,' was my last thought before I was claimed by sleep.

Two and a half hours is not much rest but it was the best sleep I had had in an age. I was woken, feeling surprisingly rested, by Harry with a discreet tap on the door. Venice was already up and gone. 'Sara has washed and dried your clothes. It's almost time to move. Got a brew waiting for you down here.'

I hauled myself out of bed, retrieved my clothes and dressed, then headed down the stairs. On the table next to my cup of tea was a package of food and a freshly cleaned Harvey.

'I put some food together for you for your journey, love,' said Sara. 'I hope you don't mind but I cleaned your little bear as well.'

I heard the unasked question and smiled, 'Thank you, Sara, you have been wonderful. Thanks for cleaning Harvey; my little brother will be grateful when I get to give him back.'

Somehow, probably due to the fabled intuition

that women have, Sara understood the meaning of my statement, if not the details. She put her hand to her mouth, and her eyes misted as she came forward to give me a hug. 'You just make sure he gets it, then, Danny.' She paused, thought for a moment and said, 'I have an idea. Tell me if it's daft, but how about if you happen to come back this way and need somewhere to stay, if it's safe I can leave a bear or doll or something in the top window of the house.'

'Mrs Glover, that is a great idea.'

Venice was at the bottom of the stairs, and she pondered the idea for a moment. 'How about you leave a bear or a blue doll in the top right-hand window if it is safe and in the top left-hand window as a warning?'

Sara smiled at Venice. 'Hello, love. I will do that, and I will spread the word to a few I can trust to do the same.'

Venice thanked her, and nodded her head at the door. 'Come on, Fish, things to do.'

Getting her hint I nodded back, 'See you outside in a short while, Harry. Thanks again, Sara, and I hope I will see you soon.' In the hallway I packed my food parcel into my backpack and shrugged it on. I pulled on my boots, slung my gun over my shoulder and stepped outside.

It was raining slightly, the indecisive sort of rain that could be over in a brief sharp shower but instead lingers, bleeding moisture into the air and making everything damp over a protracted length of time. I shuddered slightly, already missing the warmth. Determined but almost consumed by my nerves I trudged back towards the police station with Venice lost in her own thoughts at my side.

Godfrey had cleared the bodies from the station and laid them in a sheet-covered row in front of the building. It was a good idea to treat these H.A.P. dead with respect; it could certainly do no harm to the prospects of the town's inhabitants when the soldiers arrived. All the volunteers, or to be rather more accurate, the rabble of desperate or frightened fugitives who had decided to throw their lot in with us, were standing at one side of the main room. Godfrey was sitting on the edge of the large desk at the other end of the room. He looked tired but quite happy. His face lit up as Venice entered behind me and a smile creased his face as she sat down next to him. I, too, walked over to the desk and bent a little to whisper in Godfrey's ear.

'Godfrey, I have no fucking idea what I am doing. Oh, I have a kind of plan, but to have these people's lives depend on it … on me … seems, well terrifying and possibly fatal.'

Against all my expectations, Godfrey winked at me. 'You have done all right so far, lad. Ven trusts you and you freed me. These people have decided to follow you.' He smiled slightly, 'Welcome to the horrible business of leading. Although to be fair, if I think you are making a right-balls up, make no mistake I will take you to one side and tell you. So what's the plan?'

Briefly I outlined it, and he nodded. 'Good enough. Show me where this meeting point is, then.'

I studied the map of the area, showing the foothills to the south of the Jeral Mountains. It took me a moment to familiarise myself with the map until at last I was able to stab a finger down on the place we would hopefully meet up.

'This is it. There is a village called Sheps Clough; I used to visit it quite often. In this small wood here to the southwest there is an ideal meeting place. I know a man, name of Kennet, runs an illegal distillery from his farm. The entrance to the cellar where he stores the liquor is in this wood. It was an old manor house or something, got abandoned and fell down. Only the cellars are left and Kennet covered them over and built his hidden door. Look for a big tree stump about my height. It's hollow, so climb to the top and lower yourself down, and there is a trapdoor in the bottom that opens into his cellar. It is quite large, will easily accommodate all of us and I doubt very much that it has been discovered by the H.A.P. When we have all met up we can scout the area, move to one of the caves I know about, and from there plan how to get across the frontline. We should have a good view of the plain on the north of the Jerals so it will be a matter of observation and timing.'

'Very good, lad. That sounds ideal. I will leave you to organise the groups and I will speak to you later.' I nodded to Godfrey and turned to the waiting men.

'Gentlemen, we are going to split into three groups. I need three men to travel with Godfrey, Alex and Venice. No don't move yet, let me finish. I need three men to travel with Harry and Oz and I need three to come with me and Jimmy. Now the first two groups are going to travel north, moving at night and hiding during the day. Oz, if you and Harry, when he gets here, could speak to Godfrey, he will show you where you are going, give you some maps and suggest a route for you. The three that come with me and Jimmy need to be volunteers and they need to be fairly fit because we have the dangerous part. We, gentlemen, are going to stage a number of attacks to the south to draw away the H.A.P., to help the other two parties get away. We will then make our own way north and meet up with the other two groups. If you have any questions talk to your group leaders. Now, you have five minutes to talk amongst yourselves and then I want my volunteers to step forward. Thank you.' I beckoned Jimmy over and his smile said it all.

'Thanks, Danny. Didn't think you would pick me.'

I patted him on the shoulder. 'Jimmy, you are the craziest guy we have and what we are going to do is crazy so I thought that you would be just the man for the job.'

His grin got wider. 'No way am I the craziest,' he said. 'That title definitely belongs to you.'

I laughed, 'You might be right at that. Come on, let's look at some of these maps whilst they try to decide which amongst them wants to be a hero.'

I left Jimmy looking at the maps with Godfrey, Venice and Oz and went outside to sit on the steps to have a smoke and contemplate the enormity of the situation. My contemplation only told me one thing and that was that the situation did not bear thinking about. As I was sitting there I saw Harry approach. He had two men with him. I raised an eyebrow at him and looked pointedly at the two newcomers.

'All right, Danny?'

'Not bad, Harry. Could you speak to Oz when you go inside, he will bring you up to speed.'

'Okay, boss. Will do.' He gestured at the two men, 'These are the boys who are going to drive to Woodhouse to tell them about the attack.'

'Okay, Harry. Thanks. Go on in, I will follow in a minute.' I studied the two men for a moment. 'Thanks for doing this ... no don't tell me your names, it's safer that way. Head to Woodhouse about an hour after we leave, that will buy us time but still make it look like you have been prompt in reporting a terrible attack.' I stood and shook their hands, 'Drive safe and be careful, be as honest as you can without mentioning you spoke to me. Also, if they ask tell them I went south.' I grinned, 'I really am, and in a couple of hours they will really believe you!' I nodded at them. 'Thanks again. I and the whole town will remember you for this.'

They made their goodbyes and wished me luck. I watched them walk away, turned, and went back inside. I had five volunteers waiting for me, all eager lads. All of them had used guns before although none had any military service. In the end I picked the middle three, assigned the eldest to Oz and

Harry and the youngest to Godfrey's group. Before he went to join Godfrey I spoke to him, partly to mollify his feelings and partly to alleviate one of my concerns.

'What's your name, fella?'

'William, sir.'

'Well, William, the reason I didn't select you for my mission is that I have a more important one for you. You will be travelling with Godfrey, Alex and Venice. I am sure you have noticed, but Venice is the only girl in our group … your job is to be her bodyguard. Keep close to her, look after her and keep her safe for me. Would you do that for me, William?'

He fiddled with the strap of his rifle and looked at the floor before trying to come to attention. He saluted, 'Yes, sir. I will do my best, sir.'

Despite my distaste, I let the sir and the salute pass without comment; they were obviously important to him. 'Thank you, William, I will see you at the rendezvous.' Pleased with my recollection of the military term, I nodded his dismissal and raised my hands for silence.

'Gentlemen, if you could split into your groups, please. Those with me wait outside. Make sure you have food and water as well as ammunition for your weapons. I hope you also have bed rolls and clothing. All ready? Good. I will be with you shortly.' I waited for my men to head out of the door. 'Right, for the rest of you, Godfrey will tell you all the details. I would appreciate it if you would listen closely to him as well as Venice and Alex, as your liberty as well as your lives may depend on their advice. Well, gentlemen, that is about all I have to tell you. Travel safely and I will see you in about eight days. Be careful and good luck.'

Godfrey stood and began addressing the assembled group. Alex approached me. He looked uneasy; in fact, he looked positively ill.

'Danny, there is something I have to say. Can I have a word please?'

'Of course you can, Alex, what would you like to say?'

He indicated the cell room, 'Not where others can hear.'

I nodded, 'Okay, Al. Lead on.'

He shut the door behind us, and spoke in a rush of words that indicated he had kept them bottled up for some time. 'Danny, I … it's just that … well I can't, won't, kill anyone. I couldn't on the bridge.

Venice had to kill both the other sentries as well. I can't do it, Danny, even the thought makes me ill. I came close before on the bridge. Saints know I tried, but I can't do it. I just, please don't ask me to do it again, I can't.'

I held out my hand and as he accepted it I pulled him into an embrace. 'Al, I understand completely. You are a good friend, you have helped me a lot, and in a short space of time we have both been through an awful lot. I can honestly tell you that I hate the idea of having to kill people, but as you know, they have my little brother, so sooner or later I am going to have to get through them to get him back. Honestly, Alex, it is only the chance of some form of redemption that lets me do it.' I gave him a wry smile. 'If it helps, I was horribly sick afterwards.'

I let him go and held him at arm's length. 'Just let us make it to the border and I will try my best to get you across. I promise that I will never ask you to take a life for my sake, okay?'

The relief on his face was obvious, 'Thank you, Danny.'

I winked, 'See you in about a week, Al.'

Venice was sitting on the big desk next to my kit. Her smile made me forget my fears. She helped me shoulder my backpack and handed me my shotgun. 'I found these for you, Fish,' she said and handed me three grenades she had found. She indicated the damaged police station and grinned her wicked grin, 'Seems like you are pretty good at using them.'

I smiled back, once again struggling to find words to express myself to her. 'Thanks, Ven.'

'Have you got Harvey, Fish?'

I patted the front of my jacket, 'Always.'

She put her hands behind my neck and pulled me towards her. She kissed me fiercely, almost painfully. 'Keep that little bear safe, Fish. See you in a few days.' With that she stalked across the room, her head held high. I raised a hand to wave my goodbyes to the others in the room, and on a whim picked up off the desk the big note pad that was to become my journal, and stepped outside.

Snowball

Jimmy had the men lined up waiting for me. He walked along the short line of men introducing them. 'Paul, Caleb, Duncan, we are all ready. Danny, just say the word and we will follow.'

I grinned sheepishly, 'Actually I was hoping you would lead the way. We are going to that village just south of here and I don't know the area like you do.'

He laughed, 'All right, Dan. It's called Welby. We can be there in an hour on foot.'

'All right, Jimmy. After you, fella.' I turned to the other volunteers. 'Keep quiet, eyes open and make sure your safety catches are on. I don't want to accidentally wake anyone. You hear or see anything suspicious, tap the man next to you on the shoulder and get off the road. This walk will be the most time you have to relax for the next few days, so enjoy it, and thanks again for your help.' I gave the thumbs-up to Jimmy, who gave me a half-mocking salute and led us out of the town on the road towards Welby.

We were quite silent as we walked. Apart from the odd rattle of equipment (something I would have to address in the near future) and the occasional crunch of a stone underfoot, nothing really broke the stillness of the night. Animals rustled in the undergrowth at either side of the road and insects buzzed and clicked in staccato conversation. With my senses alert for danger, I still somehow found my thoughts wandering. I remembered a dry dusty classroom, a history lesson at school, how a general or someone had crossed a river he was not supposed to, and how it had started a war.

Well I, too, had crossed a river and my life had changed dramatically. I recalled how in some ancient language the general had made one of those pithy comments that history is littered with, sort of literary points of reference that hold the past together. I could remember neither the words nor the translation, but could only imagine that if his frame of mind was anything like my own, then what he had said was probably 'What the bloody hell am I doing?' It had been, I mused, the most eventful, the most frightening and yet the most joyous day of my life. I had freed an old man and killed nearly a dozen people. I had been kissed by a Goddess and then spectacularly fallen asleep with her. I seemed to have recruited some sort of militia and now I was on my way to probably kill again. Why? It could be that I was doing this for Venice and Godfrey, so they could escape to the north, or maybe it was because it helped silence the nagging of my conscience and made me feel that I was at last helping Mathew. Maybe it was that the other freed prisoners were looking to me for salvation. It was in all fairness a combustible cocktail of need, want, circumstance and event. My feet, it appeared, were on a path that now must be walked. The only destination lay at the end, and to stop meant failure and death, maybe for me, certainly for those who had put their trust in me. Some great politician had once said 'Cometh the hour, cometh the man.' I just wished he would bloody hurry up and get here.

I almost ran into the back of Jimmy as he stopped. To ask the reason for stopping was unnecessary as I could see a faint glow of light through the trees ahead. I motioned to the men and we moved off the side of the road into the trees. We wormed our way slowly forward. We had by my reckoning about an hour to go until dawn, and I wanted us all to be in position by then. There was an area of cultivated land between the trees and the village, but this was split by drainage ditches and provided plenty of cover. I could see two bored-looking sentries on the north side of the village. Bored was good; it meant that our attack on the town had thus far gone unreported. In the shelter of the remains of a stack of hay in the corner of one of the fields I bade the men take a drink of water as I tried to think of a plan.

'Jimmy, take Duncan with you and scout around the edge of the village. Find us some transport, there must be a truck in one of these barns. We have nearly an hour until dawn. When the guard changes we will be able to hit four of them at the same time. As soon as you hear gunfire, I want you to arrive as fast as you can in the truck and get us away as quickly as possible. If you can't find a vehicle or you don't think you can get it to start, get back here in…,' I looked at my watch, 'forty minutes, then we can come up with another plan. If you don't come back I will assume all is well and proceed with the attack.' I grinned at him in the dark, 'and for God's sake don't get caught without making a lot of noise and alerting us.'

'Gottcha. See you later, fella. Good luck.' With that, he and Duncan crept towards the east side of the village until they were out of the line of sight of the sentries, whereupon they rose to a crouch and headed off in search of transport. I knew the plan was risky and depended upon a number of uncertain elements, but we were here to cause a commotion. It was not my intent to kill all the soldiers as we had done at Oldbridge, which was just as well really as I was unwilling to undergo a similar experience twice in one day. The sky was beginning to glow with a hint of orange as I spoke to Caleb and Paul.

'Right, lads, it is nearly time; the sentry change will be here soon. I am going to move closer.' I pointed to the barn at the edge of the village, just a short distance to one side of the two sentries. 'This ditch runs almost all the way there. Once I get to the end of the barn I will wait out of sight of the guard post. That is where you come in. When the other soldiers arrive for change over, wait until all four are together then open fire. I will move around the back of the barn and make sure that none escape. Okay?'

They nodded and began nervously checking their weapons.

'Just remember, breathe steady, relax and squeeze the trigger. As soon as you see me wave to you, come running and wait for Jimmy. Safeties off and don't shoot too soon. Keep your heads and I will see you soon.'

Getting to the end of the barn undetected was easy if a little wet. I crouched down, muscles tense, and willed myself to relax. I had only been in position for a couple of minutes before I heard the sharp retort of rifle fire from behind the hay stack. Like a sprinter at the sound of the gun I was up and off. I ran along the length of the back of the barn, my legs pumping, shotgun in my arms. I slid to a halt at the corner and stepped into the open.

Three of the four were down, the last had found cover and was trying to return fire. With much more calm than I felt, I shot him in the back and waved to the two men. I heard the roar of an engine as they came running across the field chatting excitedly to one another. I turned to see a H.A.P. army truck tearing through the village at great speed. I had a moment's panic when I feared all was lost, but as I raised my gun, the truck slewed to a halt and Jimmy stuck his grinning face out of the open window. 'Taxi, anyone?'

Weak with relief, I barked a command at the men, interrupting them looting the bodies of the men they had killed.

'On the truck. Now.'

We scrambled on board; I jumped into the front with Jimmy. 'Duncan?'

'In the back.'

'Good. Head southwest if you can, let's carry on with our diversion. What the hell is making you grin like that, Jimmy?'

He laughed loudly, bounced the truck over a pothole and banged his foot hard down on the accelerator. 'This must be a supply truck or something. There is a heap of guns and explosives and stuff in the back.' He went silent for a moment as he slid the truck around a tight bend in the road. 'There were two men unloading it. Young Dunc locked one in the shed they were putting stuff into and the other kinda got stabbed and I threw him in the back.'

I sat back in my seat, patted my jacket to check that Harvey was still secure, lit two cigarettes and handed one to Jimmy. I put my feet up on the dashboard and tried to portray as much nonchalance as possible. 'So let me get this straight, Jim. We have just killed some soldiers, one of whom we have taken with us, and now we are making our escape in a massive rolling bomb, which incidentally you seem to be trying to make explode by the way you drive.'

Jimmy grinned and nodded, 'Aye, boss. That's about it.' He rooted around in his jacket and pulled out a hip flask, took a swig and passed it over. I savoured the sting of the whiskey as it slid down my throat, took another sip and handed it back. 'Just slow down a bit, Jimmy. If we get there too quickly I won't have come up with a plan,' I winked. 'Anyway, don't forget about those poor boys in the back.'

I took a map from my pack, and studied it for a few minutes as we bumped and rattled along the road. The roads in the backwoods of the country had always been fairly poor. It was something of a joke that people living in the east knew if they were travelling west because the roads got bigger and better. I suppose it had something to do with the wealth of the area and the number of people living there, but as everyone elsewhere seemed to know, the hill country had always been backward. As I looked at the map, we slowed and bounced over a level crossing. I realised with some emotion that it was the Peremoss line. I touched Harvey on the head for luck and continued trying to work out our next step into the unknown. So far our luck had held. How long could it last?

'Jimmy, head for Market Grafton.'

'Okay, boss. You got a plan yet?'

Duncan stuck his head through the small hatch in the back of the cab. 'Erm, sir, we were wondering… can we throw this body off the truck? It's taking up too much room. It's not nice to look at either.'

I looked at Jimmy and grinned, and my smile got wider as a thought came to me. 'Leave it where it is for now, Duncan, It may come in handy. Oh, and tell the others they did a great job.'

'Thank you, sir. I will.' His head disappeared back into the confines of the truck.

'All right, boss, I can see those wheels turning. What have you come up with now?'

'About ten miles outside of Market Grafton, there is a wood that we pass through,' I said, pointing at the map. 'Stop there and I will explain the rest then.' I stuck my head through the hatch to talk to the others. 'We will be stopping in about half an hour. Sleep if you can, eat if you can't. One of you keep an eye out for pursuit, and remember to watch for planes!'

I held my hand out to Jimmy and wordlessly he passed me his flask. I took another swallow and passed it back. I tucked my hand inside my jacket and with my hand resting on Harvey's head I leant back and closed my eyes. I didn't think I would sleep, but I must have done, because in what seemed like moments, the truck had stopped and Jimmy was shaking me awake. We were on a wide part of the road that bisected a fairly large and well-established woodland. I shook my head to clear my thoughts. 'Good spot, Jim. Just roll her forwards about fifty metres from the crest of that next rise, and park with the back end angled towards the south.'

Once he had killed the engine, I threw my kit out onto the road, picked up my gun and walked round to the back. 'All right, lads, down you come; this is as far as we go on this ride. Duncan, can you and Caleb please bring the body out, thank you. Right, if the rest of you can just wait over there I will have a look at the new toys we have been given.'

I climbed into the back. There were crates of ammunition, grenades, weapons and a couple of crates of explosives. Jimmy hopped up onto the tailgate.

'What do you reckon, Danny?'

'It's a good haul, fella. It's enough to start a bloody war.'

Jimmy laughed, 'You already did that, boss, and this will just make it bigger.'

'Maybe, but we can't take it all, so we are going to leave it for the H.A.P. to find!'

I jumped back down. 'Right, listen up, here's

the plan. There are some nice new assault rifles here; everyone gets one. Caleb will hand them out, Duncan will find the right ammunition, but don't take too much, it's heavy. Paul, you get out a box of grenades and some packs of explosive. When you have done that, drag some boxes into the woods behind the truck and make an obvious trail, we will refine it in a bit.'

I put my hands under the arms of the dead soldier. 'Jimmy, grab hold of the legs.'

Between us we managed to manhandle the corpse into the driver's seat and I shut the door. Jimmy looked at me with a 'what the hell are you up to?' look upon his face. As I climbed in from the passenger side with a grenade, pulled out the pin and wedged the grenade with the lever still in place between the door and the seat, he laughed.

'You sneaky sod. Nice one, boss.'

His smile got wider as I tied a length of cord to the dead soldier's webbing, passed it through the hatch and tied the other end onto the pin of another grenade, which I placed into one of the boxes of explosives. I put the lid back on the box with a slight gap at the end, small enough that the grenade would be unable to pull out, and placed a box of ammunition on the top and others to either side of the explosives.

I climbed carefully back out of the truck and shut the door, and went to see how the men were getting on. They had all found themselves nice new weapons, and were loaded down with ammunition and grenades. I chose not to say anything: they could start discarding some superfluous items when they realised how hard it would be to carry all that for any length of time. There was a pile of discarded weapons at the back of the truck, which included a couple of heavy belt-fed machine guns with bipods. Whilst the men (they were boys really, but it seemed unkind to call them such) made the false trail into the woods to the south, I spent a few minutes figuring out how these weapons worked. I confess I was a little perplexed and ended up calling Jimmy over to see if we could work it out between us. It was fairly simple in the end. I had been trying to fit the ammunition belt from the wrong side! I showed Jimmy where I wanted the machine guns putting, mid-way between the top of the rise and the abandoned truck on the north side of the road. I inspected the trail the others had made and deemed it satisfactory. It looked to all intents and purposes as if a number of men had moved a large number of heavy boxes out into the trees. I ushered them back onto the path, and with a couple more grenades and a length of twine left another surprise for anyone foolish enough to investigate our trail.

'Right, lads, here is the plan. I think a large town is too much for five men to attack, even if it is us.' I waited for their enthusiasm and bravado to fade. 'So they are going to come to us. By now every occupation force in every town will know there is a stolen truck heading southwest. They will also suspect that the people who stole it were responsible for the attack on Oldbridge and they know we attacked Welby because we stole their truck and left survivors. We will have been seen on the road and I expect blocking forces will be moving towards us as we speak.' I looked at the sky. 'In fact, I am expecting an aeroplane to come over us soon, as I imagine they will have them flying over the area as spotters.'

I prudently moved us all under the tree canopy and continued. 'I don't know how many men they will send but they will assume that a single truck, already loaded, will hold about ten men at most. So I don't think they will send more than three truckloads to find us; in fact, I am hoping it will only be two. This is what will happen: I believe that they will stop their vehicles on top of the rise, and as soon as they see the truck, the soldiers will get out, form up and investigate the vehicle. There will be a bang followed by a really big bang. Keep yourselves hidden behind a big tree until the bang stops. Jimmy and Caleb, you will then start shooting with those big machine guns, rake anything that moves. Duncan, you will have a box of grenades, so throw as many as you can as fast as you can. Paul, you and I will wait in the trees at the top of the rise and kill the drivers and anyone left with the vehicles. That is if everything goes how I think it will. However, and this is important, there are two conditions: firstly, if more than thirty troops arrive, we fade into the woods and meet up three hundred metres north of here. Second, Jimmy is to fire first, the others follow his lead, because if more than twenty are left standing after the big bang we retreat into the woods and fade away. We will have made our point and I don't want anyone to die just for a higher score card, understood? Any questions? Right now it's just a question of waiting. Jimmy, show Caleb around that big gun and then cover yourselves with leaves and stuff. Good luck, fellas.'

With that I nodded my head at Paul, 'Let's go,' and we headed to the top of the rise. Once there we camouflaged ourselves and I settled down to wait.

It was a lovely spring morning, the birds flitted from tree to tree, flies buzzed and the warm spring sun seemed to be making the plants grow up around me. I swear I could almost hear the bracken growing. Left alone with my thoughts, I worried about the others. I worried about Venice. Were they making good their escape? Was this all worth it or was it a pointless endeavour? Maybe they had already been recaptured? I shook my head; it did not do to dwell upon such thoughts. I convinced myself that they would be fine and were now hidden for the day. Once I had persuaded myself of their safety, my thoughts once again turned to Mathew. I hoped to all and any gods that he was safe and unharmed for both his sake and mine, for how could I save myself without first saving Mathew? I closed my eyes and again slid my hand inside my jacket to touch that little blue bear. I whispered my mantra, 'I am on my way, little brother. Just hang on for me.'

My reverie was interrupted by a droning noise and I whispered across to Paul, 'Keep still. Aeroplane.' A shadow flitted across the ground in front of me and I could hear the engine note change as the pilot started to turn and then circle the area, once, twice, a third time and then he flew off to the west.

It was about half an hour later, as my bladder was beginning to cause me some discomfort and I was trying to decide whether or not I should slip deeper into the woods and relieve myself, that I caught the sound of machinery, carried towards me on the gentle breeze. My bladder forgotten, I strained to hear more, to try and ascertain what sort of vehicle had been sent against us. It was certainly not a truck I could hear, and with growing foreboding I realised that the sound I could hear was the sound of tracks clanking as they turned. *Not tanks. Please don't let it be tanks*, I thought, motioning to Paul to stay down. Closer and closer the sound came, until a large dark shape crested the top of the rise, closely followed by another. I sighed with relief in my hidden position in the wood. Not tanks, but some sort of tracked and armoured troop carrier. I relaxed slightly as they came to a halt side by side just down from the top of the rise, a little further down than I had anticipated, but now I was behind them.

The machines were large and grey with the blue emblem of the H.A.P. above another of crossed rifles, with the legend 1st C.L. written below that. I had no idea what this meant, nor could I spare time to think about it as I looked at the soldier on the roof of the machine, alert and focused, tracking the abandoned truck with the huge twin-barrelled machine gun he was operating. A whistle blew and the doors at the back of the armoured vehicles flew open and men spilled out to take up defensive positions at the rear of the machines.

Slowly and cautiously, two groups, one covering the other, moved towards the truck, covered all the while by the big machine guns whilst the drivers waited in their seats. I took time to do a quick count of them as they went. Including the two in each vehicle and the officer, there were around thirty of them. I smiled to myself. Game on.

The officer sent four of the men to run past the truck and see if anything was waiting for them on the other side. After a quick look, one of the men signalled to the officer the all clear, and the officer approached the truck with a number of the other soldiers. He walked around it for a couple of long minutes. He looked into the back, saw the trail we had made, and sent two men to follow it. He spoke into a field radio, straightened the cap on his head and walked to the driver's door. *Open it*, I willed. *Just bloody open it.*

I have to say, in retrospect, that it was probably the best and luckiest plan I had ever conceived. The timing was perfect. He wrenched open the door, and as he did, the two soldiers who had been following the trail found the surprise we had left them. The officer turned his head at that bang and completely failed to see the grenade land at his feet.. One of the other soldiers saw it and dived to the floor as the officer was lifted off his feet in a bloody ruin of well-tailored authority. As his body sailed backwards through the air, I remembered my own warning to the men and ducked my head back behind the large tree. The explosion was enormous and a great wash of heat rolled over me. There were agonised screams and cries and the constant popping of ammunition as some of the rounds that had not been flung through the air like shrapnel exploded with the heat.

I took a deep breath, signalled vigorously to Paul and sprinted towards the back of the troop carrier. Jimmy, bless him, opened up with the machine gun as we broke cover and sprinted for the first vehicle. I threw a grenade on top, caught Paul's eye, pointed towards the front and drew my finger across my throat.

Leaving Paul to finish the driver, I ran on towards the second machine. The sound of gunfire and exploding grenades was deafening and got louder as the soldier on top of the other machine opened up, firing into the trees. There was a little ladder at the back of the carrier and I climbed it as fast as I could, my heart pounding in my chest and my bladder beginning to clamour for attention. I got to the top of the machine. The soldier was standing in a hatchway, only his upper body visible as he concentrated on blazing away at trees. He sensed me as my shadow fell across him, and as he turned in shock I pulled the trigger twice and he slumped down into the interior of the vehicle. I scrambled over the gun and looked down just as the driver tilted his head back to look at me. His face shattered in a mist of red as I instinctively pulled the trigger.

The truck had all but disappeared, just a smouldering wreck of twisted chassis remained in a large blackened crater. The blast had vaporised some of the soldiers, and those who had escaped the bomb lay in scattered untidy piles of blue, grey and red. The occasional muscle twitched and a body jerked in agony, but none remained able to fight. Just for the record, I did not piss on the dead, nor did I express my contempt by urinating maliciously in their direction; I simply could not hold on any longer and had to relieve myself over the side of the troop carrier. Jimmy has made much of this and always uses the tale to let new recruits know what a hard man their boss is. But I suppose that tale is better than the alternative one where I tried to hide an embarrassing wet patch from my fellows.

I jumped down in the suddenly silent aftermath; although, silence is a relative term, as the occasional scream or moan replaced the harsh noise of gunfire and explosions. Jimmy was wandering in a dazed sort of way amid the piles of the fallen. He had found a pistol and was calmly despatching any horribly wounded soldiers he encountered. Paul for some reason had failed to kill the driver of the other troop carrier and was now holding him at gunpoint, sitting against the side of his vehicle with his hands on his head. I admit I rolled my eyes in disgust at this added complication but gave him a reassuring nod as I walked past to join the others. It was then that I realised one of our number was missing.

'Jimmy, where is Duncan?'

He looked around, 'Shit, I don't know.'

'I will go find him. Ask Caleb to help Paul guard that driver; we can ask him some questions later.' I gestured at the bloody ruin of bodies around us. 'You all right with this -', I paused, searching for the right word, 'task?'

He shrugged, 'I reckon it's a kindness.'

'Thanks, Jim.'

'No worries, boss.'

I left him to his work and walked into the trees.

The force of the blast had ripped many of the leaves off the trees and piled up loose branches into tangled drifts against the bases of some of them, as if a giant hand had cleared a space. Duncan was not hard to find for he was still in position lying prone over a half-full box of grenades. I ran over to his side. He was a mess: a bullet from the big machine gun had caught him in his side under his arm. Presumably, as he rose up to throw a grenade the bullet had passed right through his upper torso, leaving a large wet wound on the far side. The sight of his lung rising and falling as he tried to breathe brought bile into my mouth. Mercifully he was unconscious. I slung my gun over my back and knelt, and as tenderly as I could I picked him up. I stumbled back out onto the road and half ran with my burden into the shade at the side of the first troop carrier.

I confess I was in something of a panic, as I washed his face with water from my bottle and tried to get him to drink a little of it. I looked up at Paul, who was staring in horror at his wounded friend.

'Get that soldier to find a first aid pack.' I did what I could, which is to say almost nothing. I had never encountered anything more serious than a cut or a sprain, but I knew that when something leaks you have to plug the holes; so I cut his shirt off, sprinkled some antiseptic powder into the wounds, pressed some dressings against them and wrapped his upper chest in bandages to hold them tight. I also injected him with some morphine from the first aid supplies found in the vehicle. His body seemed to relax as the morphine took hold.

'Jimmy, grab his legs and we will put him into the back of the other carrier. I think we will take that one.' I paused, 'You can drive that, can't you?'

A slightly subdued Jimmy nodded, 'Sure, boss. Give me a few minutes in the driver's seat and I will get the hang of it.'

I struggled for a moment to open the double back doors and support Duncan at the same time, but I found the catch and they swung open. I laid him on the floor and put an abandoned greatcoat under his head in an attempt to provide him with some comfort. Realistically, with the amount of morphine I had given him, he would not have felt it even if I had laid him down on broken glass, but there are some things that should be done and I felt keenly the duty of care I had to this boy. I stood with my head bowed by the low roof and absentmindedly wiped the blood off my hands with a cloth Jimmy passed to me.

My internal dialogue had called him a boy. I pondered a moment upon the changes that the last week had rendered upon me. I was certainly no more than a year or two older than Duncan, yet he and the others looked to me for direction and I perceived them as young. Jimmy was older than me, called me boss and seemed to thrive on creating murder and mayhem at my request. I sat down on one of the small hard benches lining the side of the machine. I stared at Duncan lying there, his skin pale, his breathing shallow and his blood slowly seeping in scarlet surges through the results of my inadequate medical intervention.

What next? I put my head in my hands, and rubbed my face. There were a dozen others following my instructions, trying to find safety. How had we got this far? They needed me to survive, yet if we carried on like this it seemed unlikely that any of us would. Saints, I was tired and hungry, I missed Venice, and I missed my old life. But who else was there? I owed it to Mathew. I would rescue him and carry whatever burdens that I incurred in the process. If it was my fate to be reduced to bloody ruin before I achieved that, then so be it. It was some small consolation to me that those with me were volunteers, but still, I had no doubt that Duncan would die.

I once again pulled Harvey from his place in my jacket and sat and turned him over and over in my hands. It was a cold truth that in the heat of violence I would be responsible for the deaths of more young men. I vowed I would try to be frugal with their lives. My thoughts were interrupted by Jimmy knocking into me as he unceremoniously threw the two bodies out of the vehicle. I looked around, slightly confused, tucked Harvey back into my jacket and stepped outside into the sunlight. I sensed the others watching me. Indecision was replaced by decision as a thought occurred to me. 'Jimmy, check the gun on the roof of that other carrier. I threw a grenade up there but we need it working. Caleb, you and Paul tie the hands and feet of that prisoner and chuck him in the back of this vehicle. Caleb, get in with him and keep an eye on him. Jimmy and Paul, get on those big machine guns. That aeroplane will be back and I want it knocked out of the sky before we move. We don't want it informing anyone which direction we are travelling in. Remember, fellas, it's a moving target so aim in front of it. If you want me I am going to check these vehicles for documents and maps … oh, and put one of those helmets on; it might confuse the pilot into coming in straight and low.'

There were only a few documents in the first vehicle. I found them in a box at the front after I had pushed the remains of the gunner out of the way. They were underneath a neatly folded greatcoat that looked as though it had belonged to the officer, judging by the decoration upon it.

In another storage area beneath the bench I found some packs of rations and sat with the papers on my knee, eating some sort of bean surprise with a hard biscuit as a spoon as I tried to make sense of the documents. There was a rolled tube that when I slipped the rubber band off and opened it turned out to be a fairly detailed map of the area. It was similar to the one I already had but there were notations on the page that I believed to be the names of units in other towns. The other bundle of papers contained some sort of movement orders that showed that this group of the 1st C.L. were an emergency detachment sent to investigate reports of insurgency and attacks upon H.A.P. soldiers. I smiled to myself: at least part of the plan was working. The rest of the column were heading north and the orders detailed that this group were to rejoin the main column once the threat had been dealt with. I turned over the page, and the beginning of an idea came into my mind when I saw that the officer had written down his call signs.

I heard the low sound of the aeroplane approaching. I took the officer's coat, grabbed a helmet off a rack and jumped outside. I yelled up at Jimmy and Paul. 'Fellas, don't shoot that bloody plane; in fact, give it a cheery wave when it flies over. Don't track it with your guns, and try and look fairly relaxed.' They both waved to show they had heard me. I pulled on the greatcoat, sat the helmet on my head and waited for the aeroplane to appear. It came in low along the path of the road, flying just higher than the tallest trees. I copied the stance the officer had used when he had got out of the vehicle and stood with my legs apart with my thumbs hooked into my belt loops. As the other two waved, I threw what I hoped was a smart salute, waved and jumped back into the vehicle. I flicked the on switch on the radio; it flickered with green light and I caught the end of a transmission from the pilot.

'Do you receive? Over.'

I picked up the handset and pressed the button.

I had no idea about radio protocols, or the way in which one was supposed to speak. All I had was a few vague ideas from war stories and films, along with the call signs I had found and the name tag on the coat I had borrowed.

'Randle, officer commanding, repeat, over.'

'Eagle One to Charlie Lima One, what's your status? Over.'

'Heavy casualties, Eagle One. Situation under control, hostiles eliminated, bringing one in for questioning. Will give full report on our return to column. Over.'

'Roger, Charlie Lima One. Suggest you contact column with ETA. Out.'

I heard the plane circle and the engine labour as it climbed for altitude before heading back the way it had come. I stuck my head out of the doors and shouted to the other two.

'Gather up some uniforms, fellas. Hats, coats, boots, the lot. We are joining the H.A.P.!'

I checked that the prisoner was secure and that Duncan was, as far as I could tell, no worse, and told Caleb to get some of the rations together and make a meal. He nodded and saluted. It must have been the officer's coat, but I let it pass as throwing the odd salute around was going to come in useful in the next day or two. I sat at the radio for a while, experimenting with switches and dials until I found how to change the range and the channel. I then flipped slowly through the channels until I found one that mentioned Charlie Lima. I listened in for a few minutes until I was sure, took a deep breath, pressed the transmit button and spoke.

'This is Charlie Lima One. Do you receive? Over.'

'This is Charlie Lima Six, receiving. What's your status, One?' I repeated what I had told the pilot but added that we had been ambushed by a large force, all but one of which had been eliminated. I told the voice on the other end of the radio that I had lost some fifty per cent of my force, that one of the vehicles was damaged and that I would have to drop it off with an engineer group in Market Grafton, after which I would rendezvous with the column on the Forton road somewhere south of Junction, the town where all the rail tracks met, in forty-eight hours.

'Roger, One. Charlie Lima Actual wants a full report at his command post upon arrival. Confirm.'
'Roger, Six. Out.'

I switched off the radio and headed back outside. I sat down with my back against the troop carrier, and Caleb handed me a cup of tea. 'Thanks, mate. That's wonderful.'

'Anytime, boss.'

He went back to the stove he had found. I lit a cigarette and closed my eyes for a moment. I heard someone sit down beside me. I knew it was Jimmy as I didn't think the other two were confident enough to be that familiar. Without opening my eyes I took a sip of tea. 'All right, Jimmy?'

'Not bad, Danny. You want something stronger in that brew?'

I opened my eyes and held out the tin mug. He splashed some whiskey into it and I raised it in a silent toast.

'What next, Danny?'

I looked at him and shook my head. ''What next?' he says. Next… I'm going to finish my brew and my smoke, eat some food and have half an hour with my eyes closed.'

He looked thoughtful for a moment, 'You sure we got time to linger?'

I nodded. 'I think so. I spoke to …' I waved my hand in a vague circular motion in the direction of the dead soldiers '… their, well, our commanding officer for the moment I suppose. We should be undisturbed for a bit.'

Jimmy helped himself to a cigarette from my packet, lit it and shook his head. 'You know what? You have got some big balls on you, you really have.'

I grinned at his compliment, 'Don't forget my lucky streak.'

He smoked in silence for a while. 'Seriously, what next?'

'Well, you are going to find a way to fuck with

the engine on that other vehicle. I want to find a way to make it run but rough. Then we are going to take them both to Market Grafton. Just before we get there we will sabotage the engine and leave the damaged one at the depot for repairs. Then hopefully we might get a couple of days unhindered driving north. But before we drop the machine off for repair, I'm going to booby trap it.'

He clapped his hands in delight. 'Brilliant! Blow up the workshop — nice idea.' He frowned slightly, 'But how are you going to do that? They will surely notice a bomb when they repair it, and if it explodes before we have gone far… well, I don't see that it will take them long to put two and two together, if you see what I mean?'

'You do it like this,' I said. I took a grenade off my webbing and put a rubber band from the map over it so that it held the lever onto the body, and then pulled the pin off. 'You take this here grenade and you drop it into the fuel tank. It takes a while, anything up to a month, but the fuel eats through the rubber band, the band snaps and the lever flies off. Bang!'

Jimmy nodded in admiration, 'Where in all the hells did you learn that?'

I grinned at him, 'Apparently it's a technique

utilised by partisans. Just something I picked up off Godfrey.' I drained my tea, 'Right, Jimmy, get some food, select the best of the weapons and ammunition and load them into our transport. Don't forget those explosives. Get Paul to keep an eye on our prisoner and to use more morphine on Duncan when needed, then wake me in half an hour.' Jimmy saluted me by tapping his borrowed helmet with his hip flask, 'Okay, boss.'

My eyes were shut before he had scrambled to his feet.

I was woken with a gentle shake and another mug of tea after what seemed like a very brief half hour. I shook my head to clear my lingering fatigue and climbed stiffly to my feet. I thanked Caleb for the tea and asked him how Duncan was doing.

He shook his head, 'Not well, boss.'

I knew that at the very least these young men were acquaintances, and in all likelihood friends, and so I felt some sympathy for him. I patted him on the shoulder, 'Right, let's move. You okay to ride on top in the gunner's chair, soldier?' He nodded again, and I could see my careful choice of words visibly stiffen his resolve. He snapped off his attempt at a salute and climbed onto the roof of the troop carrier. I went over to the driver's side and asked Jimmy to show me the controls. They were fairly simple and after a few moments I nodded at him, 'All right, Jimmy, turn this thing around. I will drive the other one and let's go and cause some more trouble.'

Jimmy smiled again and took a sip from his flask. 'Always a pleasure, boss.'

The journey towards Market Grafton was perhaps the calmest couple of hours I had experienced (whilst being awake) in a number of days. I felt secure in the knowledge that we would not encounter any more problems at least for a short while. Yes, Mathew was still a captive; yes, the fate of Venice and Godfrey was as yet undetermined; and yes, there was a young man in the back of the other vehicle who was dying because of my own personal crusade. But, aside from those considerations, for the moment at least, no one was trying to kill me or ask me questions I was unable to answer. The only thing I really had to do was follow the vehicle in front. We rolled through the occasional village and small town, but where there were barriers they were lifted for us as we approached, and we continued unopposed.

I stopped behind Jimmy when he pulled up at the side of the road at a sign stating that we were two miles from our destination. Jimmy hopped out of his vehicle, took some tools out of the back and sauntered over to the front of the vehicle I was in. I joined him at the front and helped him lift the engine hatch. He set to work with a long bar, a big wrench and a hammer, and after a couple of minutes of loud precision destruction, he stood back with a satisfied smile upon his face 'That should do, Danny. I reckon she will run for about half an hour before she stops. She ain't gonna run well and she will be a pig to drive, but she will get a few miles at least.'

He slung his tools back in the lead carrier. I stuck my head in the back, and after asking after Duncan, asked Paul to take position on the gun on my carrier for sake of appearances. I started the engine again. I have no idea what Jimmy had done to it, but he had done a bloody good job. It sounded terrible: it rattled and banged and poured smoke from one of the exhaust stacks. I had to try and keep the engine revs up and changing gear became a matter of delicate timing. Moving somewhat slower than before, we followed the signs and drove into town.

Market Grafton was a fair-sized town with a heavy troop presence, but once again the barriers were raised for us and we were waved on our way. I smiled slightly to myself, musing upon the fact that this sloppy approach to security would no doubt change after the details of our current escapade were fully realised, and never again would we be able to drive unhindered into the heart of an enemy-held town.

I was slightly concerned that we would not be able to find the depot. After all, I was dressed as a high- ranking officer, who unusually was driving his own vehicle. My hair was way too long for a military haircut and to be honest I don't really think my bearing and poise would have held up to scrutiny for very long. As such, I didn't think that asking for directions was a very good idea, and if I looked something less than soldierly, then Jimmy was even worse. The very thought of the piratical Jimmy with his gold tooth and tattoos asking a young trooper for directions made me smile. We stuck to the main road through the town, looking down every side road and junction in the hope of spotting the depot. Our luck held, and as we neared the outskirts of Market Grafton we saw a large complex surrounded by barbed wire with numerous vehicles parked in rows. I stopped my vehicle by the open gate just short of the guard post. The engine shuddered to a stop as I switched off the ignition and slid out of the driving seat on the blind side of the guard house. I beckoned Paul down off the roof gun.

'Paul, I need you to run over to the guard post.' I straightened his helmet and collar. 'Tell them that you are dropping off one troop carrier, damaged, by order of Major Randle. Oh, and get a receipt; this looks like the type of army that runs on paperwork.'

Paul looked horrified, 'But they will know I'm not a soldier. I will get us all caught.'

I smiled at him, 'Paul, you look smart and young. They will just think you are a green recruit. Look how easy it was to drive through the town; they are not expecting any sort of espionage, spies or saboteurs here today. Walk briskly and smartly and nobody will suspect a thing. Oh, and if they ask, tell them we don't have time to drive it in because we are due to join the colonel at Junction ASAP.' He still looked sick and so I gave him my biggest grin and cursed myself inwardly as I said, 'Have I been wrong yet?'

I waited until Paul approached the guards and, whilst they were distracted, climbed into the back of the other carrier. A couple of minutes later, a beaming Paul jumped in waving a piece of paper. 'It was easy, boss. They never even questioned me.'

I gave him a smile, 'See? Good job, fella.' I signalled Jimmy, and with a lurch the vehicle set off heading north on the road to Junction.

The prisoner was still bound, and sitting on one of the benches, a blank look in his grey eyes as he just mutely watched us. There was no sign of hostility or anger on his face and he just seemed to calmly accept the situation. Caleb was still tending to Duncan. He had changed the dressing I had applied and was holding a damp cloth to Duncan's pallid sweaty forehead.

'How is he doing, Caleb?'

Caleb shrugged, the strain of the last few hours showing on his face, 'I don't think he is in pain, Daniel sir, but his breathing is bad and he has lost a lot of blood.'

'You are doing a good job, Caleb. Let's just see if we can keep him alive long enough to get to some help.'

He gave me a nervous smile and returned to his patient.

I took off my officer's cap and hung it on a hook riveted to the bulkhead. I kept the coat on though; it was warm and fitted well. I took my shotgun off the rack, and after emptying it began to clean it, teaching myself how to take it apart and reassemble it. The soft click of metallic parts and the smell of gun oil seemed somehow therapeutic and my mind began to relax, occupied as it was with the simple task at hand. As is often the case when the mind relaxes, I began to question my actions: was this the right course to be following, was there any way to stop this wild rollercoaster ride, and perhaps seek another way to free Matty? Once I had met up with the others, would I be able to say that at least I had tried enough to regain some of my lost honour? After a moment I reached into my jacket, pulled out Harvey and sat him on the bench in front of me, where his black button eyes stared into mine to remind me of the awful thing I had done and the enormity of the task in front of me. It was going to be, I reflected, resolved once more: a long road to redemption, one that was going to be hard and possibly fatal, certainly if not for me then for those who aided or followed. Is there a balance, perhaps, like a set of judgemental scales wherein the lives of volunteers are weighed against the life of a small innocent six year old? And if so, how many lives of decent hard-working people who fought to make a difference equated to one small boy? I closed my eyes for a moment and saw again the vision of Mathew that plagued me and ever pricked my conscience; one brief glimpse of the mute anguish in that little boy's eyes was enough to convince me. The answer was simple. All of them.

That is not to say that I was a monster who held scant regard for other people's lives. Yes, I had always been callous and selfish but never malicious. However, my redemption and the life of my brother were to become my all-consuming goal and as such, lives would be lost but never needlessly and never in vain.

Paul had managed to make tea despite the motion of the vehicle. I drank and ate some more of the nasty ration pack food from the foot locker. I untied the gag from around the prisoner's mouth and released his hands so he could eat and drink. As he did I sat across from him, holding a pistol pointing at his head. I didn't take my eyes off him for a moment as he ate. He kept his eyes down, ate quickly, finished his drink and meekly held out his hands to be retied. As I pulled the gag back over his mouth, he nodded and in a plain monotone voice said, 'Thank you, sir.' I nodded but refused to reply, and once he was bound and gagged again, he sat as before, observing meekly but not reacting.

It was beginning to get a little stuffy in the back, with the aroma of cooking and sweat mingled with the smell of blood and antiseptic, so I opened the long hatch in the side of the vehicle and let fresh air flood in. It was a lovely day outside, warm and sunny, and as we rolled along, the tracks clanking and creaking as they bit into the road, it was hard to believe that there was a war on and that we were audaciously driving a stolen enemy vehicle north through occupied territory. There were men working in the fields, none of whom raised their heads as we went by, hoping I suppose that we would pass as swiftly as possible and leave them to their toils.

Strangely, it was the cows grazing the fresh grass that lifted their heads to watch us pass. It amused me that the only attention we had had thus far on the journey came from herds of bovine spectators. I was sure that there was symbolism of some description there but at the same time its significance eluded me.

The hours passed as we rattled north. I sat with my arms folded, staring at my feet, forming and discarding plans as they came to mind. The core of the plan was as ever to get to the hidden cellar, but what was I to do with our added complications? I had a dying boy by my feet and a prisoner to contend with. I was fairly certain that Duncan would die; I presumed it was just a matter of time, and that we would somehow have to inter his body before we continued. The prisoner would be more of a problem: he would hinder our escape, and at some point presumably attempt to escape or alert his fellow soldiers to our presence. I could of course march him outside and shoot him, but for the moment I was wearied of killing and there was a chance that he could hold useful information, if I could find a way of getting him to talk. He would also be an asset once we managed to cross the front lines and hand him over to friendly forces. Thus far I had mostly made up my plans as I went along, and thus far I had been lucky, but luck could not last forever and I was trying to do my best to formulate a plan that would see us out of this mess.

I was still having ideas, ones that were becoming increasingly fantastic, and disregarding them as ridiculous, as the light began to fade from the sky and night arrived.

Duncan's Hour

Just before full dark, an exhausted Jimmy pulled up and stopped. I put Harvey back into my coat and got out to speak to Jimmy as he stretched his legs and eased the cramp from his back. I lit him a cigarette, he took it gratefully, leaned back against the side of the machine for a moment and closed his eyes.

'Get us a brew, Dan. My bloody flask is empty and I'm parched.'

'Sorry, fella. Of course.' I spoke to Caleb through the open side of the carrier and asked him to make Jimmy a cup of tea.

Jimmy looked at me for a moment, 'Okay, boss. What's your plan?'

'To be honest, Jim, I have spent the last eight hours trying to come up with one. We have to get past Junction and keep heading north – that part is easy. The rest of the unit we liberated this vehicle from are expecting us soon, and so we will have to ditch it and head out on foot, but we have Duncan and the prisoner complicating things at the moment. How far are we away from Junction?'

'About a mile I reckon; that's why we are running dark.'

'Right, so we drive a little further, abandon the carrier and head out, but how we are going to carry Duncan and escort the prisoner I have no idea yet.'

'You could, you know,' he mimed firing two shots.

'I thought of that, Jimmy, but I don't want to. Besides they would hear the shots. Anyway, neither of us is going to shoot Duncan because the other two would have a fit.'

'Aye, Dan, you're right. Best we just let you wing it as always, eh?'

In the end it was poor brave Duncan who provided the solution.

Caleb came up carrying a mug of tea for Jimmy. 'Dunc's awake, sir. Wants to speak to you.'

Jimmy grinned at me and raised his brew in mock salute, 'Wing it, boss.'

In the back of the vehicle, Duncan weakly held out his hand. I held it in both of mine and put my ear near his mouth so I could hear him speak. 'I'm dying, aren't I, sir?'

The solemnity of the moment struck me and I knew this was no time for platitudes or glib lies; he was owed more than that and only raw honesty would do. 'Yes.'

'How long?'

I studied his cold skin and his laboured breathing, and weighed the strength of his whispered words. 'A couple of hours, Dunc. I'm sorry.'

He acknowledged his fate with an almost imperceptible nod of his head. His lips moved and I leaned closer to catch every fading word. He told me his plan.

It was simple, brave and daring. It would save us a lot of time and once again throw any pursuers off our tracks. I was astounded that a dying man could have conceived of this idea and was willing to sacrifice himself in an attempt to make good our escape. His plan involved getting him onto a southbound train, packing him with explosives and putting a primed grenade in his hand, which he would hold tight until the last of his strength failed him. Releasing the lever would set off the grenade and cause a chain reaction that ignited the bomb, causing a large blast as far to the south as he could manage, while we hid on a northbound train from which we would jump as close to our destination as possible. He was obviously resolved upon this course of action and I thanked him and told him that his sacrifice would not be in vain.

'Just tell my mum I was brave.'

I wiped a tear from his cold cheek, 'I will tell her you saved all our lives, and helped us escape.'

He nodded once. 'Good enough. Thank you.'

I stroked his head for a moment and said nothing, overwhelmed with the selflessness of his decision, before going back out to tell the others of the plan.

And so it transpired, we crawled the vehicle as close to Junction as we dared, finally pulling up in a copse of trees overlooking a railway siding serving a branch line with a number of trains on it. Luck was with us once more as the night was dark, with the forming clouds of coming rain obscuring the moon. After we had removed our personal weapons, I let a gleeful Jimmy booby trap our abandoned vehicle. I crept as close to the sidings as I dared and watched the comings and goings of the soldiers in and around the trains. There were two patrols with slung weapons walking in pairs around the perimeter, and on each of the trains was a flat wagon carrying some sort of large artillery gun. I realised we could get close to the trains by sneaking up behind the signal hut and hiding under the stairs until the guards had passed on their circuit. The troops manning the guns were inattentive and at that angle would be unlikely to see us. All that remained was to select each train and find a place to hide both us and the valiant Duncan. Ascertaining which train was heading in which direction proved to be easy, as the northbound trains were filled with equipment, crates of ammunition and lines of armoured vehicles and fuel tankers. These trains were on the nearside tracks; those that I could only hope were going south, which were mostly empty and presumably heading back for re-supply, were on the far tracks. There was one train that had a hospital carriage, reminding me that somewhere others were also putting up a fight and confirming that we did at least still have a safe destination.

I crept back to the others and while Jimmy rigged up a bomb on Duncan's harness, I told Caleb and Paul to stay with the prisoner and wait for our return. I let them say their strained goodbyes to their friend, and between Jimmy and myself we carried him as gently as we could into the shadows of the signal box. I watched three revolutions of the guards' circuit, and when I was sure of the timing sent Jimmy off ahead and followed, struggling under the weight of Duncan. We had to hide beneath one of the nearside trains to avoid another patrol, and when it had passed we scrambled out from our shadowy refuge and ran across the small gap to the empty trains. Hidden once again beneath one of the flat bed wagons, Jimmy and I had a hurried conversation about where best to hide Duncan, and quickly decided to lay him on top of the broad front axle of the wagon and tie him in place with some straps off our webbing. In this position he would be too high up to be seen by anyone not on their hands and knees and also placed where the explosion might rip off the axle and derail the train. Working quickly, we secured him in place. I primed the grenade in his webbing and placed his hand where he could hold the lever in. Satisfied that Duncan's plan might just work, I leant across to whisper in his ear. 'Gods bless you, Dunc. Hold on for as long as possible. I swear I will tell stories about you that no one will ever forget.'

He smiled weakly. I could see him trembling with fear and resolve and he was clearly crying as he struggled to draw in enough breath to speak, the finality of his situation lending him a confidence he had not previously shown.

'Danny, will you just piss off.'

I squeezed his arm, ducked under the side of the

wagon and crept back towards the signal box. I left Jimmy keeping a watch and hastened back to collect the others.

They were sitting in the darkness, guns trained upon the captive and they started slightly as I slithered down the bank to join them. I cut the rope binding the prisoner's feet and tied it around his neck so it would become a choke hold if he tried to run or lagged too far behind. I rechecked his gag, making sure it was secure, and led him towards the waiting Jimmy, with the other two following on behind.

When the patrol passed again, Jimmy darted to the back of the nearest loaded train. I watched tensely as he ran up the steps at the back of the wooden carriage and opened the door. He stuck his head in for a look, beckoned faintly in the dark and disappeared inside. He shut the door behind himself as another patrol approached, and once they had passed we ran as quickly and quietly as we could, the prisoner trailing meekly behind us. One at a time we mounted the steps and Jimmy helped us up into the carriage. I pushed the prisoner up before me and let Jimmy take charge of him, as I hauled myself in and shut the door. There was a bar on the door and I dropped it into place before taking stock of my surroundings.

We were in a carriage filled with crates, so as

silently as I could I motioned to the others to begin quietly moving some of them to make a space to hide within. It was a nervous wait as we crouched in our hidey hole waiting for the train to move off. I know I can speak for all of us (prisoner excepted) when I say that our thoughts were with Duncan. We heard a train move off about half an hour before ours did, and I could only hope that it was the train carrying Duncan to his final fiery end. I am not a religious man; indeed, I think the entire concept of religious devotion to be quite ridiculous, but in that dark cramped space waiting for the train to move and fearful of discovery, I confess I beseeched any spirits who might be listening to give Duncan the strength to hold on to life and his grenade for a little longer and to bless him and receive him with open arms when his strength finally failed.

I cannot know what agonies that poor young man endured, his life slipping away, his body jolted by the rhythm of the tracks as the ground passed swiftly a couple of feet below him. I can only imagine his struggle to hold onto his life, his hand gripping the grenade with desperate strength until his vitality finally faded and the jolting of the train shook his grip loose to leave his hand dangling briefly to knock against the blurring sleepers.

Presently we heard a whistle and the carriage

jolted as the train began to move forward. It was, I admit, a huge relief to be moving without either having been discovered or any alarm having been raised by an explosion. I organised a guard rota for the prisoner and we took turns to catch some sleep.

I awoke when the air pressure changed. Jimmy had opened the door to peer outside. The dawn light was beginning to bathe the sky, the train was alone on the tracks as it headed northwards, and with a shrug Jimmy stepped outside onto the small platform on the back of the carriage and lit a smoke. I took a drink from my water canteen and went out to join him.

'Anything happen whilst I was asleep?'

'I saw a flash to the south about an hour ago. Hell, am I going to drink to that boy's memory.'

I nodded, 'I don't think I will ever raise a drink again without mentioning his name, I reckon he had more courage than I will ever find.' I finished my cigarette and flicked the still-glowing butt into the turbulent slipstream of the train, and went back inside to explore.

The carriage was mostly filled with crates of food. I forbade Paul from opening any packets whilst we were on the train because the mess created would give an instant warning that someone had been aboard, and it would not take long to associate the abandoned troop carrier with evidence of fugitives upon the train. I did, however, get him to select a couple of crates of tinned goods that we would take with us when we went. I for one didn't want to have a long, hungry wait at the rendezvous point.

We were remarkably secure in this carriage. It was on the end of the train and could only be accessed from the side or rear, so I had no fears of a security patrol check unless we stopped at a station. This in itself was unlikely as the train was already loaded and therefore it was only a remote possibility that it would stop before its destination. I continued exploring the cargo stowed aboard. It was, as I have said, mostly food, but at the front end of the carriage, there were three big olive drab chests. Inside the first was a small selection of what I can only describe as precision instruments. They seemed to be range finders or something, with angles and numbers and parts that slid with little tuning dials. They certainly invoked within me the latent schoolboy horror of the maths class. In the second chest were radios not unlike the ones we had used on the troop carrier, although these were smaller and a little more portable.

The third held only three black cases, something

like a suitcase although a little longer and not as wide. I flicked the catch on one and within were three finely made sections of a long grey sinister-looking sniper rifle. I stood looking at it for a couple of moments before turning my head to catch Jimmy's eye and beckoning him over. 'You think we can risk taking one of these?'

He stood, like me, still and silent for a moment, running over the pros and cons of helping ourselves to some of the items in the crates. 'I reckon we could take a couple of the radios; it might take a while for their absence to be noted in the stores. By the time they have matched up the loading manifests we will be long gone.' He rubbed his face in thought, 'I suppose there is always a chance the discrepancy will be put down to clerical error. I don't know about the other instruments and those natty-looking rifles though.'

'I was thinking much the same, Jim. A couple of radios would be very useful, not only to communicate, but also to listen in on what they are up to. Right, decided, we take a couple of the radios. I'm inclined to take one of the guns too.'

'Be careful, Danny. One crate that doesn't match the inventory can be explained as error, but two?'

'Yes I know, Jimmy, but I'm thinking about Venice.'

He laughed, 'She sure is a good-looking girl, but do you really think this is the time?'

I punched him on the arm. 'Shut up a minute, Jimmy, and listen. If this thing we have started escalates, and I think it is going to, then Ven is going to want to help. I would rather she was as far from the bullets and bombs as possible.' I indicated the rifle, 'With this she could be half a mile away and still have an active part in any scrap.'

'Point taken, and I agree with you. Hell, if it was my missus though, I would want her right on the front line, preferably with a target painted on her head. It's a good idea though, and I suppose a sharpshooter looking out for us would be a fine thing to have. Still, can we risk taking one?'

My decision was already made, but I pretended to think for a moment or two. 'Yes, I think we can. Let's just hope they don't open the boxes for a while.' I paused, 'Any chance you could find a way to damage those range finder devices? Not visibly of course, just a tweak here and there, a slightly bent pin or something?'

Jimmy grinned again, 'That's why I like you, Danny, it's an evil bloody mind you have. I will have a look and see what I can do.'

Throughout the long, slow day we rattled our way steadily north. I gave the prisoner a drink and passed the time in quiet conversation with Paul and Caleb, both of whom were more than a little subdued at the death of their friend. I tried to lift their spirits and let them know how well they were doing and not to be sad at Duncan's passing but to be both proud and grateful as his actions had bought the breathing space we needed to get away.

Jimmy finished tinkering with the geometric devices, and I got him to help Caleb and Paul put the crates back where they had been when we boarded the train. Apart from the radios, rifle and two crates of tinned goods, we were leaving everything as it had been.

'Sir, when do we get off?'

I smiled at Paul, 'In a bit. We wait until dark and when the train slows to climb a slope as we get into the foothills, then out the back we go.'

He nodded, 'What then?'

I took out my map and tried to work out roughly where we were. 'I reckon that if we time it right, we should only be around eight miles from where we are meeting the others, so a brisk walk across a bit of rough country and then a long wait for the others. I hadn't planned on overtaking them, but it will be nice to arrive first. We will probably have just over a week of waiting until they arrive.' I smiled at him, 'Plenty of time to relax, and if I know my friend Kennet, there will be some quality booze available too.'

Jimmy shook his empty hip flask forlornly, 'I will drink to that.'

As darkness fell, I checked over our equipment and looked over the floor to make certain that we had left nothing behind. I lined the group up against the wall of the carriage. 'Right, first off go those crates of food, and then Jimmy, Paul, the prisoner and Caleb. I will shut the door and jump last. Land loose and roll, and don't forget to unload your guns before you jump; I don't want one going off by mistake. Jimmy, make for the crates and get them off the track in case of a following train. Caleb and Paul, collect the prisoner and join Jimmy. One of you help with the crates if you need to, the other guard the prisoner. I will join you there and then we head for the rendezvous. Anybody got any questions?' Heads were shaken in the negative and I opened the door and waited for an opportune time to make our exit.

Refuge

Eventually, after what seemed a long wait, when the train began to grind up the first slopes of the foothills of the Jeral Mountains, I became reasonably confident of our position. We hit two slopes and at the start of each Jimmy looked at me quizzically; each time I shook my head and motioned him to wait. As the train began to climb the third slope I picked up a crate and manhandled it over the platform and dropped it as gently as I could onto the track. We were still doing around fifteen miles an hour, and the crate soon disappeared into the darkness. Jimmy was waiting with the other crate, dropped it over the back and with a nod at me, followed it over the rail. I gave it a space of a couple of seconds and sent Paul off the back, followed by a clearly terrified prisoner, whom I tried to lower as gently as you can lower a struggling, terrified man. Then Caleb followed with a brief salute. I admired his spirit, gathered my kit and the rifle case, and checked that Harvey was secure under my jacket.

That fact that I was once again jumping from a moving H.A.P. train in the darkness clutching Harvey was not lost upon me, and as my shoulder hit the dirt and I rolled to a slightly bruised halt, I saw again the same image of my brother kneeling in the dirt of that other carriage. Although I was further from Mathew than I had ever been, and his rescue seemed as improbable as ever, I somehow felt a shade less shame as once again I was beset by the memory of mute anguish in a little boy's eyes.

I scrambled to my feet, shook myself free of memory and debris, collected my kit, checked Harvey was ok and jogged down the track to meet the others. Paul was limping a little, having hurt his ankle when he jumped, but after a few moments walking around cursing, he seemed to be ok. The prisoner was standing at the side of the track, and I was struck by his lack of hostility or defiance. Jimmy had already collected the crates, and with me leading the way guarding the prisoner and the others carrying the crates between them, we made our way into the night.

It was a still, dark night; the temperature was low and we were graced with the odd shower that did nothing to improve the collective mood. I led us west along small country lanes, keeping the Jeral mountain range on my right. Reference to the map was unnecessary as the countryside was familiar to me, and I knew that as long as we travelled west it would not be long until I could pinpoint our location. I kept alert for any signs of enemy soldiers and strained my senses for the distant sound of motors or footfalls in the dark. The night remained quiet, and apart from the odd farmstead we had to move around, occasionally provoking the barked enquiry of farm dogs, our journey was uneventful.

After nearly three hours of careful walking, burdened as we were under our packs and purloined equipment, I was glad when I at last recognised to the south the dark outline of the wood I sought. I stopped briefly to let the group bunch up and inform them that we were nearly at our destination, and then led them into the fringes of the woodland.

After a couple of moments' consideration, I decided to blindfold the prisoner just in case he ever escaped, shortened his leash and led the group to the small clearing with the tree stump. I whispered the secret of the entrance in the hollow stump into Jimmy's ear and he led the other two off to open the trap door into the cellar, stash whatever they were carrying and return to help me manhandle the prisoner up to the top of the stump and down into the cellar.

Once inside, I shut the trapdoor over my head

and breathed a sigh of relief before fumbling in the dark to find the storm lantern that Kennet kept in an alcove at the foot of the stairs. Warm yellow light filled the room with its welcome glow, causing us all to blink our eyes as they adjusted to the glare. The cellar smelt of earth, wood and alcohol, and as Jimmy's eyes adjusted I could see him staring open-mouthed at the big copper still and the racks of earthenware jars full of Kennet's finest hooch.

'God damn, Danny! You brought me to paradise.'

I laughed, 'Help yourself but be careful; it's got one hell of a kick.'

'Won't your friend mind?'

'Don't worry about it, Jim. I will square it with him tomorrow; he should be here in the morning when he has finished feeding his livestock.' I paused, and added, 'That is if he hasn't been taken.' I turned to the others and pointed to the stove, 'I'm cooking hot food tonight, lads. Take the weight off your feet, eat and have a drink. You deserve a night off; we have had a hell of a journey and you have done really well. We will be here for the next few days until the others catch up with us, but starting tomorrow, a sentry in the woods at all times and the stove only gets lit at night. But for tonight, you have a fallen friend to remember, so let your hair down and enjoy yourselves.' I raised a finger in the air and pointed at each of them individually. 'But quietly.'

I made something that was forever after called camp casserole: a couple of tins of some sort of meat, with a couple of tins of vegetables thrown in, heated, stirred and served. I never was much of a cook, but it sufficed for the night.

I finished eating, put my plate in a bucket on the floor, lined up a row of tin mugs on the rickety table in the centre of the room and splashed a liberal dose of Kennet's best into each of them. I gathered the others around me and handed out the mugs.

'This drink goes to the first of our fallen: a brave volunteer, a young man in his prime who paid the ultimate price in his desire for freedom. His dedication and self-sacrifice have humbled me, I am proud to have known him and ashamed that my actions led to his death. I will always carry that shame and I will always remember him and hope you, too, will spread word of his deeds and keep his memory alive.' I raised my mug, 'To the noble Duncan. May songs be sung about him.'

The others echoed my toast and I finished my drink with a few swift swallows and bade them relax and get some rest.

Caleb and Paul ate and quietly drank together, speaking softly of more simple times and toasting the memory of their friend, until a combination of strong alcohol, food, warmth and general fatigue overcame them. Within a few minutes of each other they fell asleep either side of the stove. Jimmy had been sampling various jars, and finding one that he proclaimed superior, came and sat by me, where I was relaxing with my back against the wall of the cellar, my legs stretched out in front of me. He passed me the jug and I held it up in salute, 'Duncan.' It was the same eye-watering fire that I was used to, and after imbibing enough to numb my throat I passed the jug back, lit us both a smoke and closed my eyes. I enjoyed his silent company as I let my body relax properly and slowly began to feel all the aches and pains of our journey as my body protested about the unaccustomed abuse. Jimmy broke the silence.

'Danny?'

I opened one eye, 'What?'

Jimmy pointed a dirty finger at the prisoner, 'What about him?'

At somewhat of a loss for a coherent and logical answer at that time, and prompted by the devil in me, I hit upon a solution to that particular problem.

I shrugged, 'Whilst we are here, you are in charge of him. Right now, I haven't a fucking clue what to do with him.'

Jimmy grimaced, 'Thanks a fucking bunch.' He paused and then brightened noticeably, 'Can I question him?'

I opened both eyes and turned my head to regard him, 'You can ask him questions by all means, but only questions; I don't want you trying to promote him to loquaciousness with sharp things.'

He laughed and gently shook the bottle in front of me, 'I got a better idea.'

I snorted, 'Jimmy, the things you will do to find a drinking buddy. Fair enough, I have no problems with that. Now sod off and let me sleep.'

'Righto, boss.'

My eyes closed, and with my hand resting on Harvey's head I muttered, 'I'm doing my best, Mathew,' then fell asleep.

I awoke a little groggy and stiff. I rose to my feet and stretched. The dim light of the dying storm lantern was just strong enough to allow me to read my watch: it was a little after eight am. Paul and Caleb still slept, as did the prisoner, his head resting on a rolled up coat, a small pool of vomit by his open mouth. I wrinkled my nose in disgust, determined that I was not going to be the one to clean it up. Jimmy was absent, so I presumed he had gone outside. I picked up my gun and went looking for him.

He was sitting against the stump with his eyes closed and the morning sun upon his face, his arm still wrapped around the spirit jar. I jumped down beside him and he opened his bloodshot eyes and nodded a greeting. I replied in a similar manner, and took a quick walk to the edge of the clearing. Everything seemed quiet so I sat down beside him. 'Mornin', Jimmy. You okay?'

He just nodded once in reply.

'You get anything out of the prisoner?'

He nodded again.

'And?' He regarded me for a moment, took a swig from the jar, rinsed it around his mouth and spat it on the floor. He rubbed his face and stared into the distance for a while. 'I got him to talk.'

'So what did he say? Did you get his name?'

'It's the strangest thing, Danny. If I didn't know better I would have just woken up and thought it was some crazy drunken memory.' He saw my look, 'Hey, I wasn't that pissed.' He drank from the bottle again, and this time swallowed it. I declined the proffered vessel with a wave of my hand and waited for him to talk.

'I didn't find out his name, Danny, because he hasn't got one. Hell, I ain't even sure if he qualifies as human.' He made a zipping motion as I opened my mouth to speak, so I sat back and listened. 'He is called Unit 0231 batch 0014 private first class of the first Clone Legion. That's the group we blew up the other day. Most of them it seems, apart from officers, non-commissioned officers and a few regular troops, were clones. Hell, I've heard stories that some scientists in the south were fucking about with that sort of shit, but it seems they have done it, perfected cloning, apparently to such an extent they are growing their own fucking troops.' He shook his head and stared at the floor, 'It makes me feel really strange, like the world has changed and I never even noticed. It's like the world just got a bit scarier.

It's so fucked up, 0231 knows all sorts of combat and weapons shit. When I was plying him with booze, you know, just a little sip at a time, I gave him one of those pistols to play with. I took out the clip and handed it to him and just asked him random questions, and all the time I spoke he was pulling that pistol apart and fitting it back together like he has been doing it for years. So then I asked him a few questions about grenades and tactics; he told me all about the latest grenades and what their payloads and capabilities are and then he told me how to assault a bunker at a unit level. To be honest I have no idea if what he was going on about was right or not, but he says he was.' He paused and made quotation mark gestures with his fingers, '"Brought on line knowing all this stuff." The thing that really fucks me up though, Danny, the thing that has most screwed with my head this morning, is the fact that he was only brought online six months ago.'

He took another drink and went silent. I put my hand on his shoulder and stood. I left him staring into the distance and went into the trees, both for security reasons and to clear my head and think. It was fairly monumental news, at least to me. I imagine there were plenty of people on both sides of the border who were fully aware of the advancements in science, but I, freshly cast from my little bubble of ignorance, had no idea. Even Jimmy had heard rumours about it, but the very idea was news to me. I couldn't see what difference it made to me: Mathew was still held captive, and throwing an indeterminate number of fully trained troops that could be formed for replacements at an undetermined speed into this particular equation really had only a slight impact on my already almost impossible task. Still, I thought that the Coalition armies might be even more eager to get their hands on him.

I crossed back over to Jimmy and nudged him with the toe of my boot. 'Did he say how long he took to…' I searched for the right word, 'form?'

Jimmy squinted up at me, 'I thought that, Danny, but he has no idea. I suppose it's like asking a newborn how long they were in the womb,' he laughed. 'Well, at least a newborn that was fully aware.'

'Fair enough. Thanks for that though, Jim. I appreciate the effort.'

He got to his feet and prepared to head back into the cellar. 'Well, I'd better go and take care of my charge,' he smiled at me before he disappeared down the stairs. 'I'm going to call him Adam.'

Caleb and Paul awoke and I gave them half an hour to freshen up and collect themselves before taking them on a tour of the wood and showing them where I wanted them to stand sentry.

'There will be a skinny, balding man in his fifties coming through here in a short while. Let him pass without challenge and see if you can avoid being seen by him,' I grinned. 'Consider it a test. Jimmy and I will take over from you around lunch time. Keep a sharp eye out for anything unusual: troop activity, aeroplanes, that sort of thing. If you do see any troops, keep hidden and come and tell me. At some point the others will arrive, so keep an eye out for them as well, although I don't think they will be here for a few days yet.' Just out of devilry, I threw them a salute, to which they responded in kind, and smiling to myself I headed back to the stump to wait for Kennet.

I didn't have to wait long. Simon Kennet sauntered into the clearing and stopped dead when he saw me, his mouth agape. 'Danny?'

'Hello, Si. How's things?'

He spat, 'Well, apart from most of my customers from Westridge getting carted away to fuck knows where and most of my other customers too scared to come out of their houses, not to mention all those gun-carrying goons wandering about the area, everything's just bloody peachy. What the hell you doing here anyway? I thought you'd been taken?'

I nodded, 'I was. I jumped off the damn train, thought I would come back to somewhere I knew and hide for a while.'

'You heading for the caves?'

'Just so. I reckon it will be as safe as anywhere at the moment. Oh, by the way, I got a few people with me and I owe you for a couple of jars of booze.' I took a pistol out of my pack, checked it was loaded and handed it to him, 'That should pay for the drink and the inconvenience.'

He inspected it for a moment, 'I reckon it will at that. You got me curious now, young Danny. A few others? I think I want to hear this story.'

So I sat him down and told him the tale so far. I had known Si Kennet since I was a small boy when I used to make deliveries for him on my bicycle for pocket money, so I spared him no detail other than the part where I left Mathew behind. It must have been obvious to Si that I failed to mention my brother, but to his credit he didn't ask. He sat silent for the telling, and when my tale drew to a halt, shook his head.

'The thing that gets me most, Danny, is how a bone-idle scoundrel like you would become the leader of a group of armed fugitives.'

I could only raise my hands in agreement, 'Aye, it's funny how the world works.'

He snorted in agreement, 'You got that right. You say there are more coming?'

'Yeah, another dozen or so. They should all arrive in about a week.'

'Fair enough, Dan. I ask just this: don't do anything to get me and mine into trouble. I don't mind you staying here until you all meet up, but for the love of God don't go starting any fights on my land. You cause trouble, then I don't know you. Okay?'

'I hear you, Si. We will just lie low for a while. No trouble I promise, and as soon as all the others get here we are gone.'

'That will do. I ain't too happy about it but as long as you keep your word and leave as soon as you can then I don't mind hiding you from those bastards in the H.A.P. Hell, they took most of my cows, requisitioned for the war effort or something.' He spat again, 'Is there anything you need?'

I rubbed my growing beard, 'Well, we could use some soap and a razor, and maybe a bit of advance warning if the H.A.P. come sniffing around.'

'Soap and razor I can do. I ain't going to risk myself warning you but I will keep an eye open for them.'

'Thanks, Si. I owe you big time. Just keep up the same routine and you won't attract suspicion.'

'All right, Danny.' He shook a finger at me, 'Don't drink all my booze.'

I agreed and watched him walk off back towards his farm. His readiness to help was a bit of a relief; he could be a thorny old swine at the best of times. Obviously he felt that hiding us evened the score for his lost livestock. I could sympathise with the need to lash out at the loss of something precious; I for one was nowhere near done with the lashing. I just hoped that I could make my anger felt by those who had wronged me and stolen my brother and my idle, easy life. I already knew something of what I had to do to rescue Mathew, and had some idea how difficult it would be. Once again I just hoped I would survive long enough to do it.

I turned my thoughts to our hideout, and over the next few days I organised the cellar, cleaned and oiled the weapons, counted ammunition and supplies and arranged cleaning and sentry duty. There were two of us on guard at all times in eight-hour shifts, with the other two looking after the cellar and keeping an eye on the prisoner, Adam. Jimmy's supposition that the clone would be amenable to direct commands was correct, and for the most part we left him unbound as he readily carried out commands to wash dishes, fetch more water and clean up. All these tasks he did with good grace and returned meekly to be bound at night time if he was so ordered. We spent time engaging him in conversation, and after some initial false starts he began to develop some conversational and social skills. It was, as Jimmy said, quite interesting to watch his military conditioning break down simply by including him in the group. When I got a chance I would question him about H.A.P. tactics, weapons and command structures, but he was often reluctant to talk about these issues. I still believe that there was some sort of embedded mental block that prevented him from discussing military subjects with his captors, but whenever his talking stopped and he appeared to freeze, his mouth moving but unable to form words, Jimmy would pass him a mug of hooch and within a short time he would begin to talk again. We learnt a lot from him in this way. Although I failed to understand much of what he talked about, I made notes and determined to share my findings with Godfrey upon his arrival. I did learn, however, that he had been brought online at a military base near Forton, a large port city on the south coast, and that they were brought online in batches of a thousand. I noted this information down alongside the rest and hoped that it would come in useful at some point in the future.

The radios we had taken from the train were left

unused for the moment, both to save battery power whilst we were in hiding and not on active operations, and to prevent any H.A.P. commands being overheard by Adam, potentially activating some conditioning trigger that could cause him to become difficult in any number of ways, and also undoing all the progress we were making with him. But for the most part the routine of those few days was relaxing and easy. We saw some troop activity in the distance to the north, but the small wood we were hidden in remained blissfully untroubled. I had arranged the sentry duty so that I would be on the lookout to the south from midnight onwards as I believed that this would be the most likely time for the arrival of the others. My assumption proved to be correct.

Reunion

I was standing in the thick undergrowth, my stolen coat wrapped around me against the cold night, looking and listening into the darkness for anything at odds with the normal sounds of the night around me, when I heard a noise. I have learnt since that there is a particular sound a group makes when trying to move silently; this with hindsight was that sound. There was the odd sound of a footfall on uneven ground, the type of step one might make when the level of the ground being stepped onto is slightly at odds with the ground one's foot has just left, causing a slight overbalance or heavier step. There was also the sound of equipment knocking gently and rhythmically together. Any party, no matter how well they have padded and wrapped equipment to silence it, will make noise if they are as heavily burdened as these clearly were.

I knew it was one of the parties from Oldbridge, and not a patrol of soldiers, simply from the way they moved and the sounds they made. I debated whistling to guide them to where I was standing, but remembered that they would be certain that they were the first to arrive. To avoid causing alarm, I held my peace and waited for the first of them to draw level with me on the small path into the wood. I could tell from his stance and shape in the darkness that the man at the front of this group was Godfrey. My heart, I confess, leapt: Venice was at least likely to be safe.

I called out his name quietly. He motioned with his hand and the small file of people stopped as he crouched on the path, his gun pointing at the patches of densest shadows.

I stepped slowly onto the path and repeated his name, 'Godfrey.'

He relaxed and straightened, before stepping forward and giving me a brief, fierce hug.

'I don't know how you got here so quickly, Danny, but you are a welcome sight.'

'You all get through?'

'Aye, no problems, young man. A few uncomfortable stays in ditches, but by and large no problems.'

I squeezed his arm in thanks. 'Just head along

this path, the stump is in the middle of the clearing. Kick one of the boys awake and get him to make some food and a hot drink. I can't come with you,' I grinned, 'I'm on guard.'

Godfrey cuffed me gently across the back of my head, 'The boy is learning. Thanks, Danny. See you when your shift ends.'

I shook hands with Alex, William and the other man whose name I could not recall as they walked past me. My eyes straining, I searched for the fabulous silhouette that would herald my encounter with Venice. She came walking out of the darkness last in the line. I could see that she was tired beyond exhaustion but I couldn't help myself; I stepped forward to greet her. She opened her arms and I held her tight for a moment; even hot, tired and unwashed she still smelt great. She kissed me on my cheek, murmured, 'Thank you, Fish' into my ear and disappeared up the track. I do believe that the next few hours were some of the longest I have ever known. Venice was only a couple of hundred metres away, and here I was, stuck, ostensibly keeping a lookout for enemy troops, but in reality doing more to set an example than to keep us safe. But the time passed as time always eventually does and when Caleb came to relieve me I gave him a quick report and hurried over to the hidden cellar.

Godfrey's group were mostly asleep, Godfrey included, lying stretched out on the available floor space, much of their abandoned kit piled on the rickety table up against the far wall. To my delight, Venice was sitting by my pack, drinking a mug of tea. She smiled at me when I descended the stairs and held out another mug she had made for me.

'Thanks, Ven. You okay?'

'Hey, Fish.'

I sat down beside her and enjoyed the feeling of my shoulder resting against hers. 'You get here okay, Ven?'

She looked at me like I was an idiot, 'Apart from seven days of bad sleep in trees and ditches and eight nights of hard walking, yes we got here okay.'

I was kind of glad to hear the acid in her voice; she had obviously managed the trek mostly unscathed. 'Was it your idea to ask William to watch over me, Fish?'

I studied her face in the dim light. 'It was, Ven. The boy needed a purpose and I felt I had left him out by not taking him with me to cause the diversions. Why?'

'He takes the job just a little seriously, that's all;

it's like having a bodyguard and waiter combined. It takes some getting used to, but thanks for thinking about me. What puzzles me though, Fish, is how you got here so quickly. We made good time and seriously thought we would be the first to arrive, whereas you were supposed to be last and yet here you are.' She flashed me a smile, 'I can't say I mind that either.'

I smiled back, 'We jumped onto a train heading north and then jumped off again a few miles from here.'

She tapped me on the nose with her finger, 'Clever Fish. Tell me, where is the other boy you took with you?'

So I told her.

She sat for a while, smoked a cigarette, and stared at the roof of the cellar, clearly lost in thought. 'You know how to inspire loyalty in others, Fish, I will give you that,' she said at last.

My own reply was slow in coming as I pondered that statement. 'I wouldn't say I know how to, Ven, it just sort of happens. Oh, I have always been able to talk to people, but it is only since all this began that I have found out that people actually want to come with me once I decide to do something crazy. It's as if they are blind to the consequences and that a little bit of hope or a chance of excitement makes them oblivious to the possible fatal end to this venture. All I do is say I am going to do this thing, or go to this place, and they all decide it's a good idea and want to come along, when really it's a terrible, dangerous and foolhardy idea.'

'Ah, but you do at least think and you do at least put yourself in as much danger as anyone else. And even though I know you have an agenda,' she leant across and patted the bulge beneath my coat she knew was Harvey, 'you do your best for those helping you.'

'That reminds me.' I stood and went to the rack of shelves and brought back the gun case I had taken from the train. 'I got you a present.'

She swivelled the case on her knee, flipped the catches and opened the lid, and stared for a moment at the dull grey lethal weapon in the case. 'Wow, Fish, this is what I mean: you do the right thing at the right time. This is beautiful.'

'Isn't it? It reminded me of you.'

She raised a perfect eyebrow at me.

I smirked, 'Well-engineered, graceful and bloody dangerous.'

She elbowed me in the ribs, and was eagerly

removing sections of the rifle and working out how they fitted together, as, warm and comfortable, I fell asleep.

I awoke a few short hours later, ate some cold food and went over to Godfrey, who seemed to have everything under control.

'Hello, Danny. Glad you got here. Ven told me the story—nice work. Shame about the lad.' He rubbed his hands together, 'Right, I have reorganised the watch; we have enough people here now to make it much easier. I have had Jimmy and the others show us new people around so that we are familiar with the area and what to expect. I'm impressed, Danny; this is an excellent hiding place.' He paused, 'Oh, I have banned excessive drinking. Too much alcohol with too much rest time is dangerous. Okay?'

I nodded.

'Good. Right, Jim has introduced me to the prisoner. I am surprised you stopped to take prisoners, but now he is here we will have to decide what to do with him.

'I know, Godfrey. I didn't intend taking prisoners, but one of the boys refused to shoot him and took him captive instead.' I handed him my notebook, 'I took notes when we could get him to talk, and I suggest that you read them before we reach a decision. It's my belief that we should try to get him across the lines; I think he may prove a useful asset to the Coalition.'

Godfrey brandished the notebook at me. 'Right you are, Dan. I will read this before we talk. I suggest you start planning what we do when the others get here. Oh, and Danny, thanks for that gift you gave Ven; she has really taken to it. Even though she would never say this, and I never told you, we all know what a (he stressed the word) "long" range weapon means. It makes the idea of my Venice having to fight a little easier to bear.' He smiled warmly at me, 'So, once again, thanks. Right, I am going to read this. I suggest you talk to a few of us new arrivals; don't let them think your group is exclusive.'

I waved my goodbye and taking heed of his advice began to circulate amongst the new group. I got a warm hug off Alex; he seemed even thinner than usual, but just as nervous as always. I chatted for a few minutes with him. I told him that I had not forgotten my promise but he would have to stand guard until we got to safety.

'That's okay, Danny. Godfrey has had us all on watch duty, or pulling stag as he calls it, so a few more nights won't kill me. Ven told me of your eventful trip. Glad I didn't come with you; sounded a little too exciting for me.'

'I think, Al, the word exciting almost covers it, but does seem to gloss over the terrifying aspect a little. I'm glad you got here safe, fella.' I gave his arm a slap and went to welcome William and the other man, who introduced himself as Andy.

It occurred to me that only a short while ago I hadn't cared in the slightest what people's names were, as long as they did as they were asked and helped me towards a particular goal. Names had seemed a trivial matter. Surprisingly, it seems the death of Duncan had awoken a streak of humanitarian sympathy within me that I was unaware I possessed. I thanked them both for their efforts and told William he had done a wonderful job of looking after Venice. I showed them around our cosy little den, listening to the story of their journey, listening to their hopes and fears and trying to make them smile and forget that the hard times had only just begun.

The group soon got organised into a routine. It was two days before Harry and Oz turned up with their group, and in that time I put Venice in charge of the sentries, with orders that anything unusual must be reported to her. I put Adam the clone into the care of Alex, and each night Godfrey, Jimmy and I went on roving patrols of the area, trying to map enemy positions and plan the route through to the hills near Westridge. The area was almost free of troops, according to Kennet who made his daily journey to visit us. Sheps Clough had no permanent troop presence, although a patrol came through every other day. We encountered only one patrol in the time we were out on our circuit and that was ten miles to the north, the furthest distance we dared travel if we were to return to the cellar before daybreak. Although I truly wanted to ambush the small squad of H.A.P., my common sense prevailed this time, so we hid in a ditch instead and let them pass, oblivious to the malice with which I beheld them a few scant steps away.

The main north-south road was busy with military traffic and at quiet times when the wind was right we could hear the sound of bursting artillery shells, a sound I had thought to be distant thunder until Godfrey kindly educated me with a laugh and a shake of his head. By the time Harry and Oz arrived, tired and hungry but in one piece, I had a fairly reasonable plan put together for our journey into the cave system of the Jeral Mountains. It would be a twenty-odd-mile hike at night almost back to Westridge. A mere half a mile from the outskirts of the town there is a stream that flows through a deeply cut ravine, rushing out of the hills before flowing into the river that meanders across the plain. We were to make for this and go on to Bright Scar Falls.

The plan was to do the hike in short bursts with me scouting ahead where necessary, even though the stream ran perilously close to Westridge and the occupying garrison stationed there. Once we were into the cut, the stream angled off to the west again, leading us about three miles further away from Westridge, where we would be safe from anything but direct overhead observation. If we followed the stream northwest towards its source we would come to a waterfall. There was a small cave behind the waterfall that a number of people knew about, but I could only think of five or maybe six people who knew the cave's secret. After all, I had found it, and due to my covetous nature had only told my closest companions about it – and they were all interred at Peremoss camp.

I gave Harry and his group a day to rest, eat and relax before we set out. Besides, his arrival coincided with the patrol through Sheps Clough so I used this time to get Oz to inventory our remaining food and split it into individual rations so that each would carry their own food. He also divided the ammunition equally and tried to make all the packs a similar weight. He positively thrived on this task and it was his enjoyment at organising that first made me decide that if we ever needed a quartermaster, then Oz was definitely the man for the job.

On the day of our departure, I had asked Kennet to light a bonfire in his yard if the H.A.P. were in the area. I had Venice watching the yard through the scope on her new rifle whilst I organised the rest of the group into an order of march, discussed the route with Godfrey and Jimmy, and basically tidied up the area to remove evidence of our presence. Dusk arrived with no sign of a warning fire from Kennet, so I marshalled the group on the edge of the wood and waited for the sun to set behind the horizon. I had marked different points on the map that the group should make for in a sequence. I would move about half a mile ahead with Jimmy and scout each location in turn and wait for the others to catch up before running on ahead again to secure the next rendezvous point. My orders were simple: if they heard a gunshot they were to retreat back to the cellar and rethink and plan without me; otherwise, they were to keep moving as fast as they dared, and if dawn arrived before we had made the mouth of the stream then we would hide for the day in the woods around Spinsters Mere, the last piece of thick cover about four miles from the entry to the ravine.

I had Godfrey make one final check for loose

equipment or badly secured items that would rattle and bang as the owner jogged through the night. With a significant look towards Godfrey, who confirmed that the time had come, I flashed a smile at Venice, tapped Jimmy on the shoulder and we jogged off into the night heading through the fields onto the back country lanes that offered the quickest, quietest and most direct route between our destinations.

The only sounds in the night were our footfalls on the road as we headed for the first destination on the map. This was my area and my country. I had grown up (at least physically) in this area so I needed no map. I was a little concerned that the group would fall behind, but I trusted the well-trained and practised skills of Godfrey to navigate without hesitation. The curfew that was in place worked to our advantage: we saw no one and any who saw us were not about legitimate business themselves and therefore kept their own presence quiet. It would prove to be difficult for them to tell anyone that they had seen us without admitting that they had broken curfew themselves, thus leaving me fairly relaxed about the issue.

We made Gorse Bank, our first rendezvous, with no difficulty and waited in the dark with only a passing fox to register our arrival. Some five minutes later the rest of the column caught up, and with a brief stop for some to catch their breath and take on water, Jimmy and I headed off into the dark again. It was easy jogging along the quiet roads and the next two stops were free of incident. One or two of our recruits were showing the strain, particularly Oz who was a good deal older than most of us and carrying a little extra weight. Godfrey seemed to be fine: decades of hard soldiering had set him up well and even though he was in his later years he still possessed plenty of energy and drive. Venice I was more concerned about, but the scowl I received at my quiet enquiry told me that I had nothing to worry about. I checked the time with Godfrey and we conferred quietly. We were slightly ahead of schedule and gaining the safety of the caves seemed a definite possibility before we ran out of night. I blew Venice a kiss just to annoy her and set off for the next point.

The rest of the trip was across country, although apart from the dry stone walls and the odd hedge, the only obstacle slowing us down was the uneven ground. If you are used to walking over rough ground it doesn't present too many problems – you step a little higher and put your feet down a little lighter, but it is an acquired skill and I could only hope that those in the party unused to cross-country walking acquired the skill quickly before anyone turned an ankle and slowed our progress.

Fortune, however, favoured us and the group proceeded well, apart from the odd tumble on the tussock-strewn turf. I was, however, far more alert and on edge as we neared the final part of our journey. The closer we got to our destination the more likely it was that we would encounter a patrol. If, as I surmised, Westridge was being used as a forward base, then it was likely to be both heavily guarded and patrolled. About one mile out from Spinsters Mere, I heard sounds in the night, the clink and rattle made by careless marching men. In the lee of a stone wall I motioned Jimmy to halt and whispered into his ear. 'Patrol coming. Move back and find Godfrey and get them all to find cover, then wait fifteen minutes and move forward. I will wait for you here.'

He tapped his understanding on my leg and headed back to warn the others. The patrol passed off to my left, unaware that they were under scrutiny, and after a tense wait Jimmy appeared once more at my shoulder, a wary group behind him.

Godfrey came to the front. 'Everything okay, Danny?'

I nodded. 'So far. They have moved on, but this is probably their patrol route, so keep low and quiet.

Me and Jim will make it the rest of the way to the mere. Give us five minutes' head start, move them fast and stick to cover. I will see you at the mere.'

Godfrey grinned at me in the gloom and I realised my advice was pointless: he was after all so much more experienced than me.

'I got this, Dan. Don't get too far ahead.'

Moving swiftly across the patrol route, heading from cover to cover, we soon covered the ground to our last meeting point. Once we reached the wood surrounding the small lake, I sent Jimmy to perform a circuit of the trees to check that they was clear to move through. When the rest of the group caught up, I had them wait with me in the shadows until Jimmy completed his reconnaissance and gave us the all clear. I gave him the thumbs-up and he led us on the quickest path through the wood where I drew the group together and quietly outlined the next part of our journey.

'If we head due north from here, we come to the stream we need to follow. The ground starts to get steeper from hereon in. Keep off the tops of the rises and follow the low ground; it does mean you have to walk slightly further, but it's so much safer. When you come to the brook, it is fairly easy to follow. It floods every few years, so the banks are quite an easy route through the hills for a couple of miles, at least until you reach the edge of the mountains. That, my friends, is where it gets more difficult. The stream comes out of the mountains in a bit of a gorge, which is when you have to get your feet wet. Cross the stream and stick to the left-hand side; it makes for easier walking because there are fewer deep holes and eddies on that side. Although in some places you will be waist deep, keep going as that is as deep as it gets. If for some reason I am not waiting by the mouth of the cut, make your way upstream until you reach the waterfall. There is a cave behind it that will offer shelter. If all goes to plan, all you need to do is follow me. You are all doing well, and we have a little over two hours until light. As long as we can get into the gorge before light we will be fine, so take a drink of water, and in five minutes Godfrey will lead you out. I will meet you at the mouth of the gorge.'

It was, for me, the easiest part of the trip, deep into familiar territory, moving over ground I had travelled many times before. I led us through the low hills and hummocks ever upwards into land that became progressively steeper. I could sense the safety of the ravine getting closer, and although I kept alert for more patrols, the chances that we would run into one were slight. It was difficult ground to traverse and so they probably stuck to the flatter ground to the south. So slight was the chance, in fact, that at one point I almost started whistling as we jogged along, but fortunately caught myself in time and shook my head in silent self-remonstration. I might pretend confidence and authority in front of the rest of the group, but by the Saints, I was so green and amateurish and of course, thus far, really bloody lucky.

Once we reached the mouth of the ravine, I breathed a large sigh of relief and relaxed. No matter what happened now, even if the rest of the group got killed or captured, I knew that I at least would be safe. I was confident that there was not a man at liberty who knew these mountains and its caves like I did, and that if I had to I could head upstream and disappear. That is not to say that I wished that to occur. After all, I owed a considerable debt to my three original rescuers and felt some responsibility towards those others who had fled north with me in the belief that to follow me meant heading to safety. Then of course there was Venice. The beautiful, obscure, enigmatic Venice. She confused my loyalties. I had vowed to rescue my little brother and I would do everything I could to arrange matters towards that end. But Venice … well although I had not known her for long, I had willingly given her a piece of my meagre soul and I would do anything for her, anything that is, just so long as it didn't clash with my other great resolve.

There was a lot of light coming from Westridge perched above us to the east, and so as I was waiting I crawled up the bank between myself and the town to see what had become of the place where I grew up. There was clearly a large base in what had previously been my home town. I could see that there was a chain link fence around the perimeter, presumably topped with wire, although the distance and light made it impossible to tell. There were guard towers at each corner with two on the gates and another set by the train station. Although it was still very early in the morning, the town was well lit and there were some troops forming up in the town square. Vehicles were moving on the streets and the train station seemed busy. I would at some point have to circle around the town to see what other changes had occurred in the areas hidden from my view, but for now I had seen enough.

It unnerved me slightly that the place where I had so recently been at ease was now so dangerous and forbidding; it is an odd sensation to realise that one has lost one's home. Anxious to avoid being seen or noticed by the large dogs held on leashes by the perimeter guards, I slid back down to Jimmy and, I admit, gnawed upon my finger nails as I waited for the others to appear.

The false light of dawn was beginning to glow in the east when the harried members of the following group caught up with us. I nodded, both relieved and pleased to see their tired faces, and led them into the stream. The water was cold and a little deeper than usual due to the last of the spring thaw coming off the mountains, and it took a moment to adjust to the lap of cold water around my groin. The way forward was slow and steady. I took my time and pointed out the deeper spots and submerged rocks to Jimmy behind me, who in turn passed this information down the line. My feet were numb and I was thoroughly soaked after wading through some waist-deep holes before I heard the sound of the waterfall pounding into the stream bed after its long drop down the mountain side. We rounded the last bend in the rushing stream bed in the first true light of the morning, and there before us was Bright Scar Falls. In the summertime this place is beautiful, with the thin bright ribbon of water falling around a hundred feet from the wooded side of Scar Fall Peak. There is wet green moss on the rocks at each side of the falls and the spray from the long slender waterfall catches the sun and shines with all the colours of the rainbow. Despite the noise I had always found this to be a wonderful place of peace, and as such I had often brought tourists by the overland route to stare at this wonder of nature, but

I had never shown them the cave behind the blue-and-white curtain of falling water. After all, few happy hiking tourists want to get cold and wet an hour's walk from dry clothes and comfort. Today, however, the falls seemed slightly forbidding and stark, almost monochrome in appearance as the rising sun lit up the cascade of water, whilst we in the ravine were still walking in shadow along the cold bed of the rocky stream towards the incessant rumble of the falls.

I led us around the left-hand side of the deep plunge pool that over time the falls had etched out of the rock and up onto a ledge that was the remains of a previous wider plunge pool before the constant flow of water had delved a little deeper with its persistent erosion. The rock ledge was wet and slippery and I signed for caution before heading tentatively for the spattering edge of the cascade where the flow was at its lightest. I was, as ever, stunned by the freezing shock of gallons of water breaking over my head as I forced my way into the vertical flow. Once behind the curtain and away from the worst of the downward pressure, I thrust my arm back out past the falls and when I felt the grasp of a hand I pulled. Once each person was through, I pushed them to the back of the small cave and reached my arm back once again. In this manner, I helped everyone through but by the time we congregated at the back wall I was white with cold and shivering badly. Jimmy, bless him, handed me his flask and I took a good swig and handed it to the next in line. Jimmy didn't seem too pleased to be sharing, but I gave him a wink and he shook his head in mock disgust. I spent a few moments windmilling my arms and jumping up and down to get my circulation going again. After enduring the hot needles of pain in my fingers, I prepared to relinquish my long-held secret in the twin names of safety and security.

'Right, Danny, show us this secret of yours.'

'Watch and learn, Godfrey. Harry, pass me that rope you are carrying.'

Harry slowly unwound himself out of his rope, and with a smile at my bemused companions I confidently strode the four paces to the back of the small cave and disappeared. There is a flat rock at the back of the cave with a narrow gap behind it. The gap is impossible to spot from anywhere but directly alongside it. It is only a shallow gap of about five feet, but if you follow it upwards into the shadows, there is an opening at the point where the back wall meets the roof. This opening is an entrance into the cave systems of the Jerals and when I say that it is impossible to spot, I do not exaggerate. I had found it from the other side when I had been exploring the unmapped areas of the system. I had been amazed at the discovery and absolutely startled when I realised where I had emerged. I climbed slowly and painfully, my limbs numb and exhausted. I knew, however, that I had a stash of equipment a few metres inside where it became much wider and higher. This was gear that I had accumulated on a number of exploration trips over the last year, both as spares and as a resource for further exploration. I struggled over the lip of the hole – it was the size of a large pipe and even the biggest of us would be able to crawl up it without difficulty. I tied the rope to one of my previous anchors, groped around for my torch and signalled for the others to start the short climb.

The bore that I was in widened shortly after the opening and became a large enough space to stand, and it was here that I lit a lamp, bright and welcoming in the otherwise utter blackness of the underground. There was not really enough room to pass one another in the narrow choke point, burdened as we were, so after the first climber, Alex, who seemed to be paying more attention to the rocks than he was to climbing, made his way into the pipe, I told him to help the next one up and then to head for the light. They began dropping their packs off as they arrived into the circle of light, and they slumped wearily to the floor. Like me they were drenched and cold. I took a moment to head back and pull up the rope after Harry at the back had arrived, before returning and instructing them to strip off to their underwear and find dry clothes in their packs. I busied myself at the same task, and was kind of glad when Venice stepped out of the circle of light to change. I laid out my damp bed roll on the sandy floor, checked that everyone was dry and if not warm, at least more comfortable, before asking that the last person to lay their bed out turn off the lamp. I put Harvey under the bundled clothing I was using as a pillow, stroked his damp little head and closed my eyes. I was just drifting off to sleep when the light went out and a cold slender figure climbed in beside me. I kept my eyes shut and smiled contentedly as she wriggled herself comfortable. She threw her arm over me and placed her head on my chest, and I fell asleep stroking her damp hair.

I opened my eyes to total darkness several hours later. The number of bodies in this small cavern had done much to raise the temperature, and I was if anything a little too warm, although that may have had something to do with the delectable form still lying half on top of me. Unwilling to move, but aware that I had much to do, I lay still for a while enjoying this selfish moment before guilt kicked in and I slowly slid from under her. I pulled the blanket over her and in the darkness kissed her cheek before questing my way through the slumbering group on my hands and knees and heading once more for the cave at the back of the falls. I lowered myself down the rope, took off my clothes and stepped through the glimmering curtain into the full light of day. Even standing as I was in the shadow of the mountain, it took a while before my eyes adjusted to the brightness. Once they had, I scanned the limited amount of sky that I could see from the bottom of the ravine for aircraft, and the tops of the ravine for movement. Satisfied that there were no evident threats, I took a deep breath and dived into the freezing waters of the pool. The shock woke me fully and knocked the rest of the cobwebs from my head. I scrubbed myself as well as I could with handfuls of gritty sand from the bed of the stream, and content that I had done something to clean off my reeking body, I began looking for firewood. There was plenty to be found at the edge of eddies, trapped in tangled lumps on outcrops of rock and beached on water-cut ledges on the sides of the ravine. It was only after I struggled through the waterfall with my first armful that I hit upon the idea of taking down the rope and using it to tie large bundles together, which I could then tow upstream and through the blanket of water. I thus occupied myself for a couple of hours until I had a large pile of wood stacked in the cave. I dried myself off with my shirt, dressed and then shinned back up the hidden fissure and reattached the rope. I could tell from the glow that the lamp had been relit, and although we were for the moment safe from discovery, I did inform them that the light could be seen from the cave behind the falls. I assured them that for the moment it wasn't a problem, as it couldn't be seen outside the curtain of water, and we would be moving deeper into the caves as soon as everyone was ready.

I sat down beside Venice who gave me a small smile and playfully pushed me away calling me wet fish. I pinched one of the biscuits she was holding and jumped up before she could retaliate. Taking Harry with me I went to haul up some of the wood I had collected.

Once a reasonable amount had been brought up, I split it into piles, told people to leave their packs where they were and grab an armful of timber. I organised them into a line with a light in the middle of the group, another at the end, and me with my miner's hat and lamp at the front. It wasn't a short route I took them along, but the walking, although made complicated by innumerable bends in the old water course, was easy as the floor was flat and sandy and the rock walls smooth and rounded. I ignored any of the occasional side branches to our route and pressed along the largest cut through the rock. After twenty minutes' walking, in which time only Harry had encountered the need to duck, I drew the group up suddenly when I felt cooler air against my skin. I turned to face them and stood with my arms out to prevent any who tried to stumble past me.

With the air of the showman I am occasionally known to display, I asked them to stand completely still and turn off their lights. I pulled a flare from my caving utility belt, and reached up and switched off my own lamp. I turned, lit the flare and hurled it into the vast open space before me.

'Lady and gentlemen, I give you what I call Shaddick's Cavern.' I was expecting the gasps, and rightly so; the red-lit view before us was amazing. We were standing high on a ledge, the same ledge I had once climbed to upon a whim that led to my discovery of the route to the back of the waterfall. The roof stretched up into the blackness above us and the floor lay forty feet below. The falling flare lit up beautiful forms of rock, stalactites, stalagmites and pillars where the two had joined. It illuminated an area several hundred feet across and was reflected briefly in the deep, dark underground lake that occupied the far end of the cavern before finally landing on the sandy floor where it spluttered and sparked for a few moments before going out and plunging us once more into absolute darkness.

I clicked my light back on and saw the amazement on the faces of the party.

Godfrey shook his head in wonder, 'Hells, Danny, we could hide a thousand people in this space.'

I flashed him a grin he could not see. 'I know. Might be a bit hard to feed them though.' I set a lamp near the edge of the rock ledge and unrolled a long lightweight rope ladder that I had fastened there what seemed like an age ago. 'Right, everyone, just throw your firewood over the edge, and make your way down one at a time.' I handed Godfrey my lamp, 'You go first, Godfrey. I will help them onto the ladder.' I helped him balance as he mounted the swaying ladder, and when he had descended he flashed the lamp twice and the next in line went down.

Venice was the last to climb down before me. With her dancer's grace she smoothly mastered the ladder and descended rapidly. I joined them at the bottom. After checking that everyone was okay, and helping Godfrey select a dry sandy spot for the fire, I realised I would need some assistance and so took four of the others back up onto the ledge with most of the lights and spent the next couple of hours transporting all the packs, kit, weapons and food back to the main cavern. The equipment was lowered on ropes as were the weapons, although I made sure they were all empty before I sent them over the edge. We joined the others at the small but brightly burning fire. As Oz organised the ingredients of a meal, I took Godfrey and Jimmy over to look at the lake.

Standing at the black water's edge, the dark water lapping at the toes of my boots, I showed them a trick I had discovered whilst exploring the pool. 'Watch.' I held my helmet lamp close to the water and after only a few seconds a good-sized pale fish rose lazily towards the light. 'This pool is full of fish, and they respond to the light. I have not tried catching any but I reckon we could.'

'Are they blind, do you think?'

'Some might be. They seem to sense the light somehow although I think you still get fish coming here from further downstream.' I shone my light around, indicating various features. 'There is a chute of water comes in over there on our left. It flows fast because the hole it comes out of is narrow, but I don't think it produces enough water to create this lake.' I paused and threw in a small stick I had brought with me. 'See, it flows to the right but there is a strong current. I think the water wells up from below and flows out to the east. It probably joins the Tarma River when it finally makes it out of the mountains, or some other stream between here and there. I don't really know, I'm just guessing, but fish seem able to get in and out.'

Jimmy was on his knees sipping water out of his cupped hand. 'This water,' he exclaimed, 'it's really pure and cold.'

Godfrey laughed, 'Probably because it has been filtered through all this rock. No dead sheep or human waste in this I should think. Back in a minute.' He headed back to the fire.

Jimmy borrowed my torch and went off to investigate the spout of water pouring into the western side of the underground lake, leaving me sitting in darkness, accompanied only by my thoughts and the splash of water. It was strangely peaceful and I spent a short but productive time pondering what I should do next. The bobbing of the light signalled Jimmy's return. 'You all right, Jim?'

'Aye.' He scratched his bearded chin. 'That spout gives me an idea.' His waved hand negated a response. 'Let me think about it for a bit; will let you know when I have sorted it out.'

'Fair enough.'

Godfrey returned with a long stick, and after lashing his knife to one end, borrowed my lamp. 'Let's see if we can catch some of these fish.'

Jimmy and I left him to it and went back to the fire and chatted with the others. Caleb had filled a pot from the lake and was heating it in the embers at the edge of the fire. I liked Caleb – anyone who put the kettle on was all right in my book. I cadged a smoke off Ven who blew me a smoke ring kiss, and deciding I had missed out something important, I went to speak to Alex. 'Hey, Al, everything all right?' 'This place is amazing! I could get my PhD studying this place.'

I laughed, 'Just as soon as the war ends, eh?'

He smiled, 'I suppose so.'

'How are you coping with Adam? Was he any trouble on the way here?'

'You know, Danny, that's the thing, not a moment's trouble out of him. He seems to thrive on orders; tell him what to do and he does it. We did gag him on the journey just in case he called out, and I had Paul and Andy keeping an eye on him, but no trouble at all.' He pointed to Adam sitting on a rock to one side of the fire. 'I don't think he knows what to make of it all; it is so far out of his limited experience and battlefield training. He just seems to have sort of shut down and only responds to orders. I even had to order him to go to sleep last night.'

'Thanks, Al. I appreciate it,' I patted his arm and he nodded his thanks.

I picked up one of the lamps and showed Oz a raised area at the back of the cavern where the bed rolls could be placed, and led him behind a row of stalagmites and showed him a deep crack in the floor. It was a metre wide at most and when I dropped a stone into it, it fell so far we didn't hear it land. 'This will be where the latrines are, Oz. It's not entirely pleasant and we will need to get some planks or something to make a bench, but it's better than having to soil our living area.'

Oz nodded thoughtfully, 'And it will take forever to fill up … maybe if we shovel some sand over it every couple of days it would keep the smell down.'

'Good idea. Oz, would you mind if I put you in charge of the camp and our supplies?'

'Daniel, I would be honoured. It will be good to have something productive to do.'

When we walked back to the fire, Godfrey had speared a number of fish and he was spitting their cleaned bodies over the fire. It looked as though tonight we would eat well. With everyone gathered around the fire I decided to make an announcement. 'Lady, gents, welcome to my little cavern. I know you will be safe here in this cavity at the root of the mountain, and as of now Oz is in charge of the camp, our supplies and organising work details. Yes, that's right, we have a lot to do if we are going to stay here for a while, but I will discuss that with you tomorrow. Tonight we are going to eat our fill, relax and get the best night's sleep we have had since this all began. To that end, Jimmy, break out that flask you stole from Kennet and hid in your kit, … no, don't give me that innocent look, I heard it sloshing all the way here.'

With a wry snort of amusement he took out the flask and began pouring generous measures into proffered mugs.

I raised mine in a toast, 'To safety and friends and friends who are safe. To the missing and the loved and the loved who are missing.' I drained my mug in one swallow amid the quiet murmurs of agreement and closed my eyes against the vision of mute anguish in a little boy's eyes that I saw in the bottom of the empty vessel. I held it out for a refill.

I sat down, my feet stretched out towards the fire, feeling the warm glow of Kennet's moonshine spreading through my body. I was lost in quiet contemplation when I realised Godfrey had stood and raised his mug in the air above him. 'Venice, gentlemen, tonight we are all safe. Most of us here owe our freedom, freedom from the gods know what fate, to the bravery, passion and ideas of Danny. Ever since I got captured he has led from the front, always had a plan, inspired others and brought us all here to this wonderful shelter. Now I admit when I first met him I didn't think he had what it takes, but despite his own considerable personal burden, he has taken the time to help us all. Venice, gentlemen, a toast if you will, to the man with the plan and the will to carry it out: Daniel Shaddick.'

I was surprised and embarrassed by the noise of my name being shouted in salute. I waved with a sheepish grin on my face and took another sip from my mug to hide my embarrassment. I lowered it to see Venice kneeling before me, her head tilted to one side as she scrutinised my face. I regarded her back silently, unwilling to disturb the closeness of the vision before me. She leaned in and suddenly those beautiful full lips were pressed against mine. I responded avidly and after a long moment when I had begun to run short of air she pulled away, 'Thank you, Fish.'

Andy slapped me on the back, 'Yeh, nice one, Fish.'

Venice stood up, the light from the fire giving

her an angry demonic look. She thrust her face towards Andy and he recoiled from the violence he saw displayed there. 'No one calls him Fish,' she hissed at him, 'No one but me. You don't have the right, you don't have the reason and you don't have permission. You fucking understand me?'

Andy held up his hands in surrender. 'I got it.'

'Not finished. You call him Daniel or Mr Shaddick or you can even call him sir.' She pointed at me. 'That man rescued you from the work camps, led you here and gave you another chance. Have some fucking respect, and if you or any other man calls him Fish or anything that implies disrespect, I will personally cut their fucking balls off when they're asleep. Do I make myself perfectly clear?'

A pale Andy apologised to Venice and then, as a short afterthought, to me. I raised my mug to him by way of response and he returned to the camp fire, no doubt to spread the word that Venice was not to be messed with. I was certainly never called Fish by anyone other than Venice in all the time she was alive.

I remember talking to Venice, our bond seemed to be strengthening and I enjoyed every second of her presence. The raw whiskey, the heat from the fire and my general exhaustion soon had me nodding off, despite the noisy revelry. With my head leaning back on the cool rock wall, I slowly drifted off.

I think there was singing.

Plans and Action

I awoke in the dark. I knew I had been asleep for a long time as the fire had died down to a red glow and I could hear the snoring of slumbering bodies. Someone had draped a blanket over me and I shrugged it off to go and stoke the fire. My mouth was dry and my head ached a little but I managed to throw some wood on the fire, collect a pan of water and start making tea. I remember thinking it would be nice if we could find a source of milk so I wouldn't have to drink it black all the time, but hey, black tea was better than no tea. That reminded me, I also needed to find a regular supply of tea. I made another mental note and added it to Oz's suggestion that we needed a shovel. As I slowly stirred the tea bags in the water, waiting for it to boil, I suddenly had an idea of where I could find much of the equipment we needed.

Sometime later when the tea had been drunk, a sparse meal had been eaten and the banging in my head had muted to a murmur, I gathered the principal members of the party together in a circle. Using the light from one of our oil lamps, with a stick I drew a map in the sand that showed the cave system as I knew it, dictating key elements as I drew them. 'This is the main cavern where we are. There are two entrances: the one we came in through that leads to the falls, and another that can be accessed from the old tin mine above us. The mine has been abandoned for a good while now. Some of the old men from Westridge worked it when they were young but the seam ran out and they started mining elsewhere. Not long before the mine closed, they broke into a much smaller cavern a couple of hundred metres higher up and a little to the west of this one. It wasn't that impressive and after a quick exploration no further ore seams were found in it. The floor was mostly full of water but the dry areas were used as a miners' mess, workshop and a store depot for props and things. It has been empty for years, but about twenty years ago some hopeful prospectors used explosives to do some blasting to see if they could find any more ore. One of the charges cracked the floor, drained the pool and exposed a natural pipe at the back of the small cavern that leads to this one, coming out at the back of the west wall over there.'

I indicated it with a wave of my hand. 'It wasn't investigated much at the time because there was a long sump full of water that no one dared to find the edge of.' I looked up. 'When you investigate a sump you don't go any further than half the distance you can make holding your breath. There is no telling whether there are any air pockets or an end to the sump ahead of you, so you travel for about thirty seconds and then turn back; otherwise, you may never come back. Anyway, five years ago the sump dried up; now it's just a very wet muddy hole three feet in diameter and about sixty metres long. Two other caving enthusiasts from the town and I were the ones who found that it had dried up enough to be passable.' I grinned, 'To be honest we were looting scrap from the old mine and one of the others noticed that the water in the sump had mostly gone. So, anyway, one thing led to another and we came back with better gear, ropes, helmets, etcetera, and had a look.'

I pointed with the stick. 'You come out of the old sump here, and there is a dry stretch of thirty metres before the main channel enters another sump. After thirty seconds of crawling through that cold water you are still completely immersed, with no sign of air, so where it goes I don't know, although I would think that it comes out of the north side of the mountain somewhere. But on the dry stretch before the unexplored sump, there is a fissure. It's a little over three feet wide, can be walked at a stoop, and it winds its way down to this cavern. I was the first to go down it, that's why I claim this cavern as my own.' I shrugged and smiled, 'Well, finders keepers, eh? I have brought a few people here and the cavern is known about; however, the entrance we used is not. That's my secret.'

Harry spoke up, 'You said there were two entrances from the mine?'

'Sorry, Harry. Yes I did. There is the main mine entrance and then the gallery that runs off it comes straight past the edge of the small cavern. The gallery bypassed the cavern, but sort of just clipped the edge. They even put a door in and shored up the breakthrough.' I quickly sketched in the sand. 'The mine has two levels with numerous side tunnels off each main gallery. The upper gallery is accessed down a short side tunnel and up a ladder, and that tunnel breaks through on the north side. It is not an entrance as such as it would be a horrible climb to it from the bottom of the valley. It comes out on an almost vertical cliff with a nasty scree slope at the bottom. I think they followed the ore until they broke through the side of the mountain, but they used the hole they made to tip waste rock off the edge so there is a wide ledge there with an incredible view. There is also a perilous little track that winds up the side of the mountain all the way to the peak, but it's not for the faint-hearted. I like to think the miners used to sit on top of the world to eat their lunch.'

Godfrey coughed and borrowed my stick to indicate the area he was concerned about. 'What about the main mine entrance? Is that easily accessible?'

I nodded. 'It is. There is a drivable track that becomes impassable to vehicles half a mile from the mine entrance. There is a quarried-out area there where they built the ore crushing plant with a small railway track that leads to the mine entrance. The carts were pulled by pit ponies then, and the metal tracks and any remaining carts were sold for scrap about five years ago.'

Jimmy burst out laughing, slapped me on the shoulders and offered me a swig from his flask. I grinned at him, took a swig and resumed. 'The track carries on past the mine entrance and on up the side of Beacon Peak, the mountain to the east of this one. There is a ski lodge there that gets fairly busy in winter but tends to close for the rest of the year. One of the men from the town was caretaker there and he used to come up a couple of times a week just to keep it clean and sort out any problems.' Godfrey pointed at the main mine entrance again.

'So, anyone can just walk into the mine and find our front door?'

I shook my head, 'The people who still own the mine seem to have got very annoyed about their old equipment going missing and they have put heavy steel doors on the mine entrance, padlocked with a heavy chain.' I winked at Jimmy, making him laugh again. 'I know they are heavy because I couldn't move them even when I tried to lift them off the hinges with a bar.'

Venice smiled and cuffed me across my head. 'What about the path, thieving Fish? Can we block it?' 'Well, it is narrow and has a sheer drop on one side. I think if we have our own padlock we can use the main entrance for bringing stuff in and it will look untouched. Alex, can you have a look at the path to see how difficult it would be to collapse? We have got a small amount of explosive left. If we take away the path, this mountain almost becomes an island, but if there are people here we can rig up a rope and pulley system for bringing goods in via the main entrance at night.'

'Okay, Danny, I will take a look for you. Anything to be useful.'

'Thanks, Al. Once I have shown you all the way out, I will send a couple with you to keep watch whilst you do your work. Right, that's it for now. Oz, I will leave you in charge of this rabble, the rest of you grab what you need and I will show you around the mines. Prepare to get muddy in the sump.'

After a few hours exploring the routes in and out of the cavern, we washed off in the lake as close to the outflow as we dared to avoid polluting the water. We dried off and dressed and I gathered the others to go and find some much-needed equipment. I left Oz and Andy to watch the camp and to keep an eye on Adam, armed the rest and led them up to the big double door of the mine entrance. I produced an old worn hacksaw from the remains of the tool store in the small cavern, and with Harry, Jimmy and I taking it in turns we slowly sawed through the chain that held the doors closed. It was just starting to get dark outside when the chain finally parted and I took time to outline the plan before we opened the doors and headed outside. Alex, with Paul and Caleb to keep watch for troops or aircraft, would examine the side of the track to see if it could be collapsed. Harry with two others would sneak down the path to the old ore crushing plant to see if they could find any useful pulleys, chains or tools, whilst the rest of us headed up the path to the ski lodge to see what we could loot. I shook hands with the others and wished them luck. 'Oh, and Harry, see if you can find a 'D' shackle to refasten that chain from the inside.'

He waved his understanding and headed off down the track. It was really quite a pleasant climb up to the ski lodge and the night was warm and overcast for once as we filed up the fairly well-maintained track. I hoped that the H.A.P. had not yet occupied the building. I didn't think they would have as it was difficult to access and the big machine they had there to maintain the ski runs had been brought in during the depths of a cold winter when the ice and snow smoothed out the rocks and slopes it needed to traverse. I remembered that it had still taken two days for the delivery team to get it to its new home. It might, I thought, have made a good vantage point, but although the view was awe-inspiring, it was really only a view of the valley and the slopes of the mountain in front of it. So, alert but mostly unconcerned, we trekked the four or five miles in silence.

The lodge was as I remembered it: a large flat building with a steeply sloping roof, two visible floors and a basement beneath. There were no lights on and the place seemed somehow forlorn without the presence of holidaymakers.

With a smile I stopped Jimmy from breaking the lock on the door, and rooted around under the big rubber welcome mat. I held the key up for him to see.

'Local knowledge, my friend.' He grinned appreciatively and we filed inside. 'Right, go through top to bottom, and bring anything useful back here to reception. If we can't take it all tonight, we will have to risk coming back tomorrow. Ven, could you take a couple with you and search the top floor, please? Godfrey, the same in the basement; Jimmy, the garage; and I will take this floor. Torchlight only please, people. Happy hunting.' Shortly, a pile of pilfered items began to build up in the centre of the reception hall. Tools from the garage, bedding from the wardrobes upstairs, food from the cupboards and freezers in the kitchens, climbing gear, shovels and sleds from the basement, and the alcohol I liberated from the bar area.

Jimmy reappeared from the garage with parts he had removed from the slope tractor. At a glance these included the fan, some belts, the alternator and a big battery.

'What you want with those, Jimmy?'

He grinned at me, struggling with the weight of the battery, 'It is just a little something I have in mind.' He paused, 'Reckon we could do with some lights,' he said, pointing at the ceiling.

I was about to order the stripping out of some of the light fittings when Godfrey stopped me with his hand on my arm. 'Danny, when they find that this place has been looted and all the lights are missing, the first place they will look is somewhere dark.'

I felt myself go red, and felt the fool for not having realised that. I did my best to recover my composure and flashed him a smile. 'Good point. Thanks.'

He smiled back and nodded and so I issued the order to find some lights that would not be missed. Venice discovered some boxes of festive lights in the attic. They were multi-coloured but still, they were lights. Jimmy came back from the garage with a couple of inspection lamps, and I detailed two of the team to start loading items into backpacks and onto the sleds. Godfrey, with help from one of the others, reappeared from the cellar lugging a small portable generator. I gave him the thumbs-up and gestured to the large pile of pilfered property in the centre of the room.

When the first of the sleds were loaded, I sent most of the group with Jimmy to return to the mine, with instructions to pile the stuff up in the entrance and return as quickly as possible. It was something of a risk, but I judged that there would be enough time before daybreak to make a second journey, and with the amount of supplies we had found, it would be a stretch to transport it all in two journeys even with the use of the sleds. With the first group gone, I returned to the kitchens and with the Venice's help pulled hobs off the cookers, collected various utensils and added them to the pile. Once I had done this, I went outside, uncoupled the gas bottles, dragged them out of the small lean-to at the back of the kitchens and loaded them onto a sled.

Godfrey raised an eyebrow. 'I understand the need for those hobs and the gas, Dan, but that will be one heavy load.'

I shrugged, pretending a nonchalance I didn't feel, knowing that it would be heavy, but I could not afford to be seen taking it easy. 'It's all downhill; I'm more likely to need a brake man than any assistance pulling it.'

'Well, if you are sure?'

I nodded, 'I am. Anyway that generator is going to take some moving. Will you be all right with it?'

He grinned, 'Don't worry, Danny. I have already designated a couple of the younger lads to pull it.'

I waved the rest of the group on their way with their burdens of supplies and waited in the cold, dark lodge for the first group to return. Alone with the silence, sitting in the dark, I held Harvey in my hands. My mind whirled with a nervous cocktail of problems and solutions, half-formed ideas and plans, fears and worries, responsibilities and duties and above all, promises that I had made. I could at the present moment see no rational way of achieving anything resembling the keeping of my word to rescue my brother. It seemed to be only something a character out of a fantasy could ever hope to achieve. There were, as far as I could see, only two ways of entering the factory complex at Peremoss: either I could sneak in and rescue Mathew, or march up to the gates with an army at my back, kick them open and as in the previous scenario, rescue him. The thoughts were too big and immense. It felt like I was trying to juggle with live grenades and I confess to a few minutes' panic there in that deserted ski lodge. That was until I remembered the warm spring day when I had walked behind Venice. I smiled in the dark and put Harvey away with a pat. One step at a time, Danny. One step at time.

I had pretty much regained my composure by the time the first group returned, and I directed the loading of the rest of the supplies onto the sleds. I locked the door as I left, put the key back under the mat and as a bemused Jimmy looked on, prised open one of the windows with a crowbar from the garage. I caught the look Jimmy gave me. 'Don't want them to think it was anyone local.' He nodded his understanding. I took hold of the rope at the front of my sled and spent the best part of the next two hours sweating, slipping and struggling as I cursed and growled my way down the track back to our retreat.

On my arrival, I dropped the rope and blew on my blistered hands. It felt good to straighten my back for what seemed like the first time in an eternity. I leant back against a tree, took a long drink of water from a proffered bottle and caught my breath. I stretched my back with a satisfying crack, asked Venice to organise the storing of supplies, and told Jimmy to go and see if Harry needed any help and to check on the progress Alex was making. I checked that my weapons were in place and turned to face the trek back up the mountain.

'Where you off to now, Fish?'

'Going back to hide our tracks.'

I blew her a kiss and headed back into the night. I used my hatchet to lop a couple of leafy branches off a tree a little upslope, tied them to my belt so that they dragged behind me and began the exhausting process of walking up to the lodge and back again, smoothing out the worst signs of our passing as the branches dragged over the ruts and footprints we had left. It was easier coming back down, but I was at the limits of my endurance. Sweat ran down my face and my eyesight was blurring as I fought to beat the sunrise back to the cavern. In this I failed: the new day was about twenty minutes old as I started down the last section of slope before the mine entrance. I dimly remember Harry and Venice hurrying from the shadows of the mine entrance to support my arms and half drag, half carry me into the waiting darkness, before Harry shut the doors behind us. With the weight of the branches lifted from me I reeled like a drunk towards the main cavern with Ven leading me and Harry propelling me from behind. I remember sitting down in darkness that was faintly illuminated by a small fire and the bobbing light of the odd torch. I drank a mug of tepid tea, someone threw a blanket over me, and I was gone.

When I awoke stiff and sore several hours later, it took my mind a few moments to work out what was different. It slowly dawned on me that I could see! Not well I grant you, but there was definitely a light source in the cavern. I got up, clutching my blanket around me, and stared amazed at the transformation that had taken place as I slept off my labours. There were paths along the floor from area to area, illuminated by the multi-coloured glow of festive lights. One of the inspection lamps hung over the cooking area and another over the main bench where I had piled my maps and things. Somewhat in awe I followed the glowing path down to the water's edge where I could see plenty of activity around some sort of device. I heard footsteps behind me and a warm hand grasped mine, warm lips kissed my cheek and a hot mug was pressed into my other hand.

'Come and look at this, Fish. It's brilliant. Jimmy might be half crazy but it seems he might be half clever too.'

Down at the water's edge, Jimmy had built a contraption consisting of his scavenged parts and some other bits that I could only assume Harry had brought back from the factory.

'All right, Danny?'

I nodded, 'What's this then, Jimmy?'

He beamed at me and gestured with a wrench, 'The fan off the truck. Bent the blades around so they catch the water from the spout better, held under the flow by this gantry, linked by the fan belt to the alternator which is wired to the battery, and that powers all these lovely lights. As long as the water flows, we have light. Just a shame we have no converters so lights is about all this will power.

Anyway, we've got the generator if we want to power anything that needs more juice.'

I took in the sight of his contraption, and looked at the lights that cast their soft glow in the vastness of the cavern. 'I'm impressed, Jimmy. Good work.'

He mock saluted me with the wrench and carried on making some adjustments. Venice led me along the water's edge to the other end of the lake to where Godfrey was organising a team digging out two rectangular holes.

'Hey, Danny. We did some good work last night. Good to see you back on your feet.'

I gestured with my chin, 'What's with the holes?'

He smiled in the dim light, 'Baths. When they are two feet deep, we will open them up to the water, then we have somewhere safe and level to wash. They will of course be very cold but the water will always be clean, and they are next to the outflow so our drinking and cooking water won't be affected.'

'Good idea. Thanks, Godfrey.' I paused and added, 'Can I have a chat with you later, please?'

'Of course you can. You go and get something to eat; Oz has organised the canteen so just ask him. I will come and see you as soon as I'm done here.'

'Thanks, Godfrey.'

I turned and let Venice lead me to the canteen where Oz was busy organising and counting the food we had taken from the lodge.

'Everything okay, Oz?'

The little man beamed at me, absolutely in his element. 'Fine. Just fine thank you, Daniel. All weapons and ammunition in that alcove over there,' he said, gesturing to the back of the cavern, 'all domestic items over there,' pointing to the higher area we had previously slept on, 'and all foodstuffs here,' gesturing at some rough shelves behind him. He patted the tool chest that Jimmy had brought from the lodge, 'And all the booze locked in here. Godfrey says that it stays locked until you say otherwise.' He turned back to one of the boys stirring a pot on the gas hob and handed me a bowl of some indeterminate meat in gravy and another large mug of tea.

'Great job. Thanks, Oz.'

He smiled his happy smile and returned to his organising. I sat on the sandy floor, and leant my back against the rock. Venice knelt beside me, 'I'm going to check the sentries. See you later, Fish.' Momentarily surprised that we had sentries, I nodded back. 'Okay, Ven. See you later.'

She smiled and headed towards the exit and I turned my attention to my food.

I finished eating and drank my tea, ruefully bemoaning the current tobacco shortage. Then I took my bowl back to one of the lads manning the stove and was sitting cleaning my shotgun when Godfrey arrived.

'You wanted to talk?'

I finished drawing out the barrel, 'I did.' I put the gun down beside me and gestured at Godfrey to sit. 'What the hell do we do next?'

Recruit, Train, Consolidate and Attack

'What do you want to achieve, Danny?'

I gestured at Godfrey, waving my half-full mug of tea. 'Well, I suppose ultimately, the plan is to rescue Mathew, only now I have got even more dependants. I've stirred up some terrible trouble and I feel further away from helping him than ever.'

'You do realise, Danny, that the only way you were ever going to get him back was by force? It seems improbable that you were ever going to effect his release with a strongly worded letter or by walking in and asking nicely. You have to stop being naïve, young fellow. You have already started your war against these people, and you have made some great progress already, if only through accident or coincidence.' He paused and looked at me steadily for a moment. 'You, Danny, have the makings of a great leader of men. You have charisma, people will follow you and they will listen to what you say, but you have to keep winning. All your ideas so far, from the moment you freed me from the cells up to our retreat to this great hideout, have been inspired. Keep it up and you could actually achieve the rescue of your brother.'

I snorted and took a swig of my tea.

'Seriously Danny, you are good at coming up with a plan and you can think on your feet. You do need to take more of an interest in the people around you though, not just the key members of the group. If you want to win this thing you have to inspire more loyalty. The odd pat on the back and shared meal or smoke goes a long way with the average man, particularly as you will be asking them to put their lives at risk for you time and again, but it may be an idea to remind them that they will be fighting to free their own friends and family too.'

I looked at the small group of refugees I had brought with me. 'I don't know if this lot have had any of their friends and family taken.'

Godfrey smiled at me, 'Not this lot as far as I am aware, no, but the next lot may have.'

My mouth dropped in surprise, 'What next lot?'

His smile turned into a big grin, 'If you want to free your brother, we need a lot more people. We need to recruit, train, consolidate and attack. First job is to train the ones you have here with the aptitude, as your ersatz officers and non-commissioned officers in the partisan force you will be leading. I will do the training and also the weapons training initially, until others can take over that part. Your job is to come up with the plans and the overall strategy. These will be discussed with your right-hand men and then we will plan how to accomplish them. Then you carry out that plan, and when I say 'carry out that plan', I mean that you will lead from the front and be seen to be doing so. You got that, Danny?'

I sat mouth open, mug dangling forgotten in my hand, 'Erm, I think so. Feeling a bit out of my depth to be honest with you, Godfrey. Where do you want me to start?'

He stood and brushed the sand off his trousers, 'I am going to gather your key people together and start teaching them some useful things. You are going to work out where to find some new recruits. Come and tell me when you have a plan.' With that, he stalked over to the bench and sent Alex looking for Harry, Jimmy, Oz and Venice.

I sat in the gloom, one hand resting on the little

bear's head, slightly aghast and a little worried at both this side of Godfrey and the seeming inevitability of the future course of events. I sat in the gloom and worried. I sat in the gloom and desperately tried to conceive of a recruitment drive for those with suicidal leanings. *Come and join our little war. You may lose your life or perhaps a limb but hey, it might be a laugh.*

I spent perhaps a week watching Godfrey train our little group in everything from map reading to weapons use and maintenance. He took them up the mountainside to teach them how to snare animals and forage for things that could be eaten. Out of sight of the others he taught me the same things until I could strip down any of our weapons in the dark and find food on a hillside, and knew how to make the best use of explosives. We generally did this as I took my turn standing sentry duty. When I asked him why I didn't just join the others, he told me that they needed to assume I could already do these things.

'A leader must appear competent, he must seem to be worthy of respect. You cannot be seen to make the same mistakes as your troops, you have to inspire confidence and infallibility to get them to follow you.' He threw a question at me, 'Have you worked out where to find any recruits?'

I shook my head and finished assembling the pistol with my eyes shut.

We had sentries stationed at the exit of the cavern, at both entrances to the mine and at an observation post at the top of the mountain, up the narrow track from the upper gallery exit. Once the men had become used to the monotony of sentry duty, and a little more skilled in the art of fieldcraft, Godfrey and I began taking them on short night patrols in the surrounding area to watch troop movements in and around Westridge. It was on one of these patrols as I lay in the bracken watching the lights of my home town that an idea began to form in my head. I knew how we would find our recruits.

After we had returned, I approached Godfrey. 'I know where we are going to find our recruits.' He made a rolling motion with his hand and I continued, 'We need to stop one of the prison trains and ask for volunteers.'

Godfrey gave a sigh of relief, 'That's my boy. I wondered how long it would take you to work it out. I was going to have to give you a clue if it took much longer.'

'What? You already knew where to find them?'

He grinned at me, 'Of course. Where else are you going to find a substantial number of people willing to fight a well-trained army? You need desperate people whose lives are already forfeit. I'm glad you worked it out for yourself. Now you need to come up with a plan.'

The plan, in the end, was fairly easy. I spent a few hours examining the maps we had, and reconciling them with my local knowledge. The plan formed and when I was decided upon a course of action, I discussed it with Godfrey.

'Good plan, Danny. Now get your officers together and give them their tasks.'

I sent out word and my small group of leaders assembled around me to listen to the plan and their part in it.

'Right, Oz, I want you to stay here with Al and five of the others. Your job is to prepare this place for anything up to three hundred more people.' I held up my hand as he started to protest, 'I know, our food will only last a very short time with that many more mouths, but I will sort that problem out later, ok?' He nodded and I continued, 'Venice, you and William will provide cover from a distance, should it be needed. Harry and Jimmy, you come with me and the rest of the group.' I grinned, 'We are going to rob a train.'

I took them to the map table and pointed out the

terrain around Westridge.

'It seems that the enemy are fortifying the town, and to do this they have ironically started bringing people back into the town to do the work. Here is the plan. This section of track starts a fairly steep climb here at Binghams Cut, and then curves up and around Plover Hill. The basic idea is to release the last carriage of the train just as it starts the ascent, drop a tree behind the carriage so that it doesn't roll back too far, open the door, and there you go: new recruits.' I looked up beaming to face some rather bemused faces. 'I gather there will be questions?'

I looked at Jimmy.

'Not from me, boss. Just let me know what you want me to do.'

'How are we going to get everyone back here, Fish?'

'Once we stop the carriage and we have our recruits, assuming any want to come with us, you and William will leave your position here on the flank of the hill and act as forward scouts. Jimmy and I, with Caleb and Paul making sure nobody lags behind, will lead the new volunteers around the mountain and enter the complex up the rope from the top gallery entrance. Al will drop that for us, and Harry with the rest will act as a blocking force in case of any pursuit. Harry, follow behind us to here. Wait for an hour at this point on the trail, and if no one follows come in through the waterfall entrance.'

Harry nodded, 'Fair enough, Danny. Just one question though: how are you going to unhitch the end carriage from the train?'

I smiled at him, 'That's the tasty part of the plan. Ven, how good is the silencer on that rifle of yours?' She tilted her head and gave me a half grin back, 'You didn't hear me practising the other day, then?'

I conceded the point, and indicated the H.A.P. greatcoat I wore. 'We can scrounge together a bit more uniform. When the train comes through this point here,' I pointed to another spot on the map, 'there is a set of points and a signal hut. I take Paul and Caleb with me, overpower the signalman, tie him up, and signal for the train to stop. After I jump on the back we let it continue. I stay on the back until it comes out of this wood here. If there are guards on the roof, Ven can remove the last one as the train clears the wood. I get up onto the roof and as the train makes the climb I jump down between the carriages. As the train slows, I wait for the inertia to take the weight off the coupling, and release the carriage. I'm hoping the guards will be in the front carriage as normal but they might be on the roof. If so, Ven, you may have to remove them.'

She nodded in agreement.

'When the carriage rolls back a little way to where we have blocked the track, we release the prisoners, let the carriage roll all the way back and make our escape. Easy!'

In the end the plan worked fairly well, if not for the oversight that it would be two days before another prison train came through. This caused us a couple of uncomfortable nights but it gave us plenty of time to rehearse, cut down an appropriate tree and observe the comings and goings of the signalman. In the end, that worked slightly to our advantage as we were able to waylay the poor man on his way to work. We gagged him and tied him up but made no secret of the fact we were members of a vast and growing resistance. I even managed to let slip that we would be heading back to our base at Little Junction after the raid. I love the tactic of misinformation; it is a great game. Luckily, both for my endeavours and to save Venice an unpleasant task, there were no guards on top of the carriages (although this would change in the very near future!) and I was able to get into position easily. When the carriages bunched up as the train started the climb, I was able to release the end carriage and cling to it as it ended its forward momentum and rolled slowly backwards to a halt against the fallen tree.

There was much commotion and shouted questions from inside the packed carriage, as I positioned my men in a broad well-armed semi-circle around the side door, smashed the lock off with my hatchet, threw the door open and announced dramatically, 'Welcome to the resistance.'

Obviously this caused some consternation and, I admit, confusion. Some were surprised that there was a resistance, and I did somehow neglect to tell them that there were only about twenty of us all told. Some were annoyed to be confronted by more armed men, and all were concerned about their immediate future. I helped them down one at a time and asked them to form up alongside the carriage. They were all men between the ages of about sixteen and fifty, and to judge from their accents they were from all parts of the country. I held up my hands for peace, patted the little blue bear under my coat for luck and gave them my best recruitment speech.

'Gentlemen, my name is Daniel Shaddick, leader of the resistance, or at least until I win or fall. I know you have all been taken from your homes and your loved ones, dragged unwillingly from all over the country to serve as little more than slaves for the armed might of the H.A.P. I know for a fact that this train was taking you to the town of Westridge, where you would have been forced to pour concrete and dig trenches until you can dig and pour no more. Now it may be that once exhaustion claims you, a drink of cool lemonade and a sit in the shade would perhaps be offered. It is also likely that whips and boots will get you back on your feet until you drop once more. Then when the job is complete you might get a cheery handshake and a pay packet, or you could be put back on a train to continue your work elsewhere. Or,' I paused, 'you could be shot once the work is done.'

I waited a moment for my words to have effect and as the men began to talk amongst themselves again, I once more raised my hands. 'We of the resistance offer you three choices; three more than you will ever be offered by the H.A.P. The first choice we offer is that you can stay on the train, claim that you wanted nothing to do with us and submit yourselves to the embracing lash of your overseers. The second choice is that you disappear into the countryside and try and make your way home to friends and family, and trust that they will be able to hide you and feed you until this chapter of unpleasantness has been consigned to history. The third choice we offer you is to join with us, be fed, trained and equipped and allowed to strike back at your oppressors, gain vengeance for your losses, live the lives of men, become a thorn in the side of the enemy, make a difference and give hope to all those that suffer. The choice, gentlemen, is yours.' I looked at my watch. 'You have five minutes to decide.'

I let them argue amongst themselves for the five minutes and then bellowed, 'Time is up, gentlemen. Those who want to, get back in the carriage; those who want to try and make it back to their homes off you go and good luck; those with fire in their bellies enough to fight, form up on my left and start practising trail discipline. That is traps shut, eyes open and do what you are told. Your lives will depend on doing what you are told as soon as you are told, if we are to get you safely back to our base near Junction.'

It was a fairly reassuring sight to see that only a half dozen of the weaker souls climbed back into the train carriage, and around forty made their brief farewells and disappeared into the trees at the top of the embankment, leaving some one hundred and eighty hardy men who had for whatever reason decided to throw in their lot with ours. It took longer than I had planned to get us all back to the mountain. In the end, I decided to lie up in some woodland and wait for dark before moving across the open ground. I sent one of Harry's boys ahead to explain our delay and spent the time moving amongst our new recruits, talking to them and getting their stories. Some were men who had refused to join the ranks of the H.A.P. Some were those who held political sympathies at odds with the government; some were of foreign nationality, northerners working in the south; and the odd honest, small-time crook who had been sentenced to work in the labour gangs.

Presently I deemed it dark enough for our journey and led the men on a circuitous path through ravines and cuts, over spurs of rock and through small streams to the scree slope at the base of the mountain. Alex was waiting and threw down knotted ropes. At my urging, the new men followed Jimmy and Caleb up into the waiting shelter of the old mine. We kept them hidden there, fed and rested if damp and uncomfortable, for two days before leading them to the cavern. Two days to assess their resolve, two days to hear their stories and grievances and to try and filter out any men who would be likely to run. In truth I trusted them all; each was hungry and each bore the marks of heavy-handed treatment and not one had any praise for their former captors.

More than one cried when I led them into the large, dry cavern lit by the low festive glow of looted lights. I handed them over to Oz, who gave them soap and towels and showed them where to bathe. When they were dry and fed, I had Godfrey and Oz line them up, and ask them about their trades and skills, after which they were given a number and organised into ten squads under the command of one of the originals. Jimmy, Harry and I took direct command of three groups each, whilst the last group was assigned to Oz to help him with his tasks.

That night we threw another party for the newcomers. I myself spent most of the night sitting shoulder to shoulder with Ven, drinking sparingly and thinking furiously about how best to train, equip and utilise my new force. At one point I was coerced into standing and giving a welcome speech, where I thanked the men for joining the cause and told them that their training would start tomorrow. I don't really remember the talk I gave, pre-occupied with bigger issues as I was at the time. The main issues that presented themselves were how to feed and arm this many men. I sent a couple of the originals out with a small group of recruits to see Kennet and purchase some supplies off him: relatively small amounts of corn and vegetables, nothing above an amount that could logically be explained to the new authorities should they question his productivity. I questioned men about their previous locations and asked them for any relevant information they might have overheard. I stationed Alex on the top of the mountain, in the hide we built up there, to monitor radio traffic with one of our captured radios; and I stared long and hard at the maps, measuring distances and trying to estimate carrying capacity and quantities of supplies needed.

'Godfrey, the only way I can see us getting these supplies is from another raid. We could raid the warehouses at Westridge, but that would give the enemy a large hint about the area we are operating from. Little Junction is out of the question: it is likely to be swarming with troops after I let it be known that is where we were from. I am thinking somewhere on the west coast but that is a big distance to travel on foot. Any ideas?'

'I think what you need to do, Danny, is hit a supply convoy heading to the front. It will contain weapons and ammunition as well as food and medicine. Not only that, it is already heading this way. The idea of a target on the west coast is a good one though. I suggest that you take out the guard, drive the trucks as close to here as you can, unload them somewhere safe and bring the supplies in a few at a time by hand.'

I drummed my fingers on the desk, thinking hard. 'So, what do we do with all those empty trucks?'

Godfrey just laughed, 'That I will leave up to your imagination, Danny.'

It was later that night when I came up with the solution. I had done my leader-of-men bit as suggested by Godfrey. I had walked among the men, talking to them, asking how they were settling in and other such banalities. Their gratitude was quite remarkable as was their renewed sense of purpose, not to mention their respect. I strolled over to where Ven sat cleaning her rifle and chatting to William. I passed her a cigarette and told her that I was having difficulties tying together all the loose ends in the latest escapade.

She smiled warmly at me, her beauty as ever catching my breath in my throat. 'Talk it through with me, Fish.'

I finished recounting the idea to her, and she nodded in thought. 'I like it. They are expecting trucks full of supplies to be heading north. As long as we don't do anything too stupid, I doubt very much that any alarm will be raised.' She looked at me again after a moment. 'They are also expecting empty trucks to be moving south along the main road.'

I grinned my understanding and leant forward to kiss her. 'Put them back where we found them.'

She kissed me back, 'Exactly, Fish.'

I laughed out loud, not something I did often at that time, 'That should confuse them.'

I gathered my captains about me. 'Jimmy, you and I will bring a squad each. Venice and Will, you are coming. Oz, see to the running of the base. Harry, you are in charge of area defence whilst I am away. Keep your head down and tread carefully – I promised Sara I would keep you safe.'

Harry nodded his great head, 'I will be having a word with you about that when you get back.'

I noted the serious look on his face and nodded, 'Okay, Harry, granted. But for now keep the base secure. Alex, keep on the radio. I will send a message when we have the wagons.' I turned to Harry. 'Harry, you will meet us here,' I pointed at the map. 'It is a picnic area just off the main road to Westridge. You can help us unload before we take the trucks back, okay?'

He nodded his understanding. Alex nervously put up his hand.

'Yes, Al?'

'What is the message going to be? Make it short, otherwise they can track your location.'

I smiled, 'You will appreciate this one, my friend. It will be 'stone axe'. Just reply 'understood' and then I will turn off the radio.'

He nodded and smiled, 'Good enough. Thanks, Danny.'

'Now, I don't know how long this will take; it could be three days, it could be ten. Just stay calm, keep up the good work and prepare for our return. Any questions?'

There were none so I instructed everyone to prepare to leave as soon as full dark arrived. The trouble with summer was that the nights were so short; therefore, you had to move quickly and plan all the places to wait out the day in advance. Who would have thought that rescuing Mathew would involve so much mathematics? I smiled grimly at the brief vision of mute anguish in a little boy's eyes. I'm getting there, little brother. I'm getting there.

It was a hard march. We moved as ever at night, heading at a jog from point to point, trying to cover at least twenty miles a day, until four days later we reached the coast road. We settled down in some thick woodland and I let the group enjoy the short spell of inactivity and the smell of the sea as, in pairs, we watched the road and I tried in vain to come up with a plan to halt a convoy.

Providence smiled upon me again when one of the men watching the road came hurrying back to tell me a motorcycle despatch rider had stopped his machine a few yards from their position, and was coming into the trees. Inspiration gripped me and suddenly I knew what I was going to do. The reason for the stop became obvious when I saw his splay-legged stance before the tree, and in accordance with the laws of decency, I allowed him to put himself away and button his fly before I slammed my hatchet into the back of his head.

We dragged the body back into the trees and stripped it. I ordered that it be buried, and I put on the dead man's uniform before going to examine the bike. In the maintenance of honesty I was actually really excited about going for a ride – it had been a while. Big engine, big wheels and half a tank of fuel. This looked like a promising day. I opened the bike panniers and extracted some of the messages that were being carried, mostly for some town or other I had vague recollections of to the north of the Jerals. There would be time to examine them and see if they contained anything useful when I got back.

I threw my leg over the bike, kicked it into life and pulled down my borrowed goggles. I showboated with the throttle, grinned at the tree line where I knew the men would be watching, steered back onto the road and accelerated away, heading north up the coast road. I have to admit that the war was not a time of joy for me. However, that day, riding a powerful motorcycle on a clear, warm morning, weaving in and out of the mostly military machinery that was using the road, thundering past convoys of transporter trucks carrying tanks and armour, heavy fuel bowsers and trucks full of soldiers, I had a wonderful time. Indeed, for a whole half hour I completely forgot my woes and my goals and luxuriated in the feel of the wind upon my face and the roar of the engine in my ears.

I swerved past laden supply trucks, exchanged nods with southbound despatch riders and, joy of joys, even engaged another northbound rider in a race for a short while, until with a long beep of his horn he pulled off the main coast road onto a side road. As I flashed past, still gripped with adrenaline and the joy of the race, I realised that the side road actually led to a large lorry park and refuelling stop with a number of buildings I reasoned to be a mess hall and barracks block. There was another side road that rejoined the main road a short distance ahead, as would be expected with this type of facility.

The sight of this facility reminded me of my

mission, and, as ever, loose thoughts swirled around my head until they coalesced into an idea about ten miles further up the road. I drew to a halt at the side of the highway, and when a gap in the traffic presented itself, I performed a swift U-turn and headed back the way I had come. I proceeded at a more sedate speed as I had no wish to be recognised as the reckless rider who had been heading north only a short time earlier. After a long fairly pleasant ride I discovered that there was another refuelling stop almost exactly one hundred miles south of the first one I had seen. By this time I was really low on fuel and had decided to chance my luck and pull in at the military convoy stop to get some more. Unsure how to proceed, I stopped short of the pumps and pretended to tinker with my bike engine to wait for another despatch rider to enter the fuel station so that I could mimic his actions. I did have a tense moment when I was approached by an inquisitive sergeant who wanted to know if everything was okay. I stood at my best impression of attention, grateful for my dust mask and goggles. 'No problem, sergeant. Just a loose spark plug lead; have it fixed in no time.'

'Very good, trooper.' He paused and looked towards the fuel pumps, 'Remember to hand in the right fuel chit when you top up.'

'Yes, sergeant.'

Well that simplified matters for me. When he turned and walked back to the shade of his office, I did a quick inventory of the pockets in my borrowed uniform and found a handful of tickets, some stamped north and some stamped south. Freed of my need to wait for another rider, and in truth feeling a little lucky after my encounter with the nosy NCO, I rode up to the fuel station and handed the ticket to the soldier manning the pumps. There was a brief conversation about the road and traffic, I scrawled a signature on the proffered clipboard that matched the name on the front of my uniform shirt, nodded my thanks and set off heading south.

As before, I waited for a break in the traffic, changed direction and headed back northwards to rejoin Venice, my men and the next dirty chapter in my desperate little war. We hid the bike in the trees and lay up to wait for nightfall. I explained to Ven, Jimmy and the squad leaders that we were just waiting and watching the traffic on the road. I was assuming that there were truck rest depots all up and down the road at regular intervals, and that the convoys would stop at night, but only observation would confirm if this was a fact. We were about thirty miles south of the nearest stop, and, as I had hoped, the last convoy of trucks came past us just before midnight. I know that later in the war the trucks ran all day and all night with a change of drivers, but that was after the Coalition counter-attack and the H.A.P. began to use supplies in greater quantities. At this time, however, the war was progressing well for the H.A.P., and as long as they had enough men and supplies to roll up the inadequate forces set against them, the supply train was quite a leisurely affair, very much to the advantage of a small band of desperados.

The next morning, I detailed a couple of the troops to find a stream and fill our water bottles. We ate a little dry food and I explained the plan to capture the trucks without a shot being fired, before lying down on the floor with my feet propped up on a log and enjoying the lovely weather as we waited for night to arrive again. It's funny, really, how much waiting there was to do. In all the time I was fighting to free Mathew, there were great swathes of slow monotony, endless hours of ceaseless sunshine, downpour, ice or snow to endure before brief lightning-fast bursts of horrific stomach-churning action. No matter their duration, they seemed to be over in seconds and they left you shaking and reeling, and uncertain that you had actually survived. I never did get used to the nervous tedium of waiting, but I did learn to fool others that I was calm. Initially, before the infrastructure of our resistance was put into place, I was often busy planning and organising merely for survival. Later, however, I was allowed to concentrate more on offence, which led to more waiting: either waiting to signal the attack myself or waiting for reports from those I had sent out to attack a target. I always felt that after a fight the waiting around was good, something I had deserved perhaps, but I was never comfortable waiting to attack – I was always keen to get to business. I think that perhaps this was due as much to my need to perform a live fire testing of the veracity of my plan, as to wanting it to be over; although, ironically, if by testing the plan it was found wanting, we were in all likelihood screwed.

After dark, I checked the troops, their kit and their understanding of the plan. I sent three of my squad a mile south down the road, as I planned to hit any convoy coming past between half eleven and twelve. These three were to fire warning shots if another convoy approached after this time. I tried to straighten my despatch rider's uniform as best as I could, and around eleven I pushed the bike back onto the edge of the road and sat astride it, waiting. I waved to one convoy and then another whenever the glare from their headlights caught me, until just before midnight as the lights of what I hoped was the last convoy of the day got closer. I gave the signal to Jimmy to light a small fire at the side of the highway, before I parked my bike in the centre of the road and stood before it waving my torch in circles at the approaching line of trucks.

Dutifully, and happily for me, the lead truck ground to a halt before me, and the others in line stopped in turn. A head leant out of the window.

'What the hell have you stopped us for, rider?'

I shouted back that there had been an accident a mile ahead, that there was fuel oil spilt across the road and that they were to wait there until further notice, on orders of the colonel. The last bit was pure inspiration as I felt that perhaps the word of a scruffy despatch rider needed a little more weight behind it.

There was some cursing and slamming of doors as drivers got out to investigate the cause of the halt. Most were unhappy that they had been forced to stop such a short distance from warm food and a decent bed. I held up my hands in supplication and addressed the lead officer, a lieutenant.

'I am sorry too, sir, as it happens. I am not too happy about missing my supper, either.'

'Are you being insolent, trooper?'

'No, sir, not at all.' I pointed to the unattended fire at the edge of the trees, 'In fact, I have put a kettle on the fire so that you can all have a brew whilst you wait. Wash some of this road dust away.'

The officer straightened his belt, 'Thank you, private. Most thoughtful of you.'

I saluted, 'With your permission, sir?'

He nodded.

I turned to the drivers, 'Grab your cups, lads, and follow me if you want a brew.'

In all there were ten men in eight trucks: one driver in each with an officer accompanying in the front truck and a sergeant in the one at the back. They all fell to and followed me over to the fire. The water had nowhere near boiled, but I wasn't going to waste tea on them anyway. I lifted the kettle, made to pour for the officer, then pretended to slip and drop the kettle in the fire. At the shower of sparks my men came surging up out of the darkness, cutting and stabbing with knives and bayonets. I thrust mine into the stomach of the officer just as Venice stabbed him from behind, and our eyes met as he crumpled to the floor between us. Outnumbered more than two to one, and the officer's side arm the only weapon not left in a truck by these complacent amateurs, I was overjoyed at our success.

We stripped the bodies and threw them into the backs of the trucks where we covered them up, cleaned the blood-soaked soil and the ashes from the side of the road, and sprinkled fresh soil over the aftermath before inspecting the trucks.

We didn't set off at once as there was yet more waiting to be done. We had to time it so that we could arrive and refuel as if we were the first convoy on the road that day. So I sat and fretted and made sure that everyone had their fuel requisition slips, that the drivers had their uniforms straight and as clean as we could get them, and that the men and the decidedly female Venice, who we could not fit onto the trucks or afford to be seen, respectively, had enough supplies to make it back to base. I left Venice in charge. I had no need to ask the others to follow her orders and nor would she have thanked me for it. I merely stated that Venice was in command of the overland party and left it at that. I believe my reputation at the time was already sufficient (largely thanks to Jimmy) for them to fear not following my orders. I kissed Venice firmly and passionately in front of the troops to a subdued cheer, and waved her off as she led the majority of the ambush group back home.

I had Paul wear the officer's uniform, for two reasons really: firstly it fitted him quite well, and secondly there was no place on earth where Jimmy would ever look like an officer. Still, Jimmy was our best driver and so he was happy to don a trooper's uniform and climb behind the wheel. I decided that I was not going to travel on a truck; I kept my motorbike and rode ahead to keep an eye out for trouble and to act as a surprise element if trouble found our little convoy of bandits.

The men on duty at the fuel pumps took no real notice of us. The fuel requisition slips were handed over, the newly promoted Paul scrawled a signature on the clipboard and we set off northwards. The journey was uneventful for the most part, but I knew that we had to hurry to make the turn-off that would take us to the rendezvous with Harry, before the first southbound convoy came through. So I hurried and harried them, riding ahead and falling back and trying to press them to greater speed. I pulled up at the junction and waved them into the turn. About a mile off the main road heading towards the hills, I drew alongside the lead vehicle and shouted through to Paul.

'Channel three five two, code word 'Stone axe'. Break contact. Okay?'

He nodded and reached for the radio. I saw him speak the call sign, he acknowledged the reply, then turned the radio off and gave me the thumbs-up.

We got to our rendezvous in the late afternoon, and as quickly as we could we unloaded the supplies and buried the bodies. To my great relief there was a large amount of food and plenty of weapons and ammunition, as well as several boxes of medical supplies. Harry with his section, the men not on guard and the men that Oz could spare, began the long job of carrying it all into our hidden cavern. I left them to it, and with the other drivers we returned the trucks to the coast road, waiting for a gap in the convoy traffic. We slipped past the northern depot in the dark with our lights out, coasting slowly down the slight incline of the road with our engines off. When we got to the ambush point we turned the trucks north again and parked them at the side of the road. I detailed Jimmy to lead the other men home and, taking a couple of the explosive charges and detonators I had removed from the supply trucks, I headed south into the night. I pulled up shortly before the southern depot and parked my bike in the trees.

Their security was lax and it was a very casy task to sneak past the single sentry and place the charge on one of the fuel storage tanks. I set the fuse for about an hour and wormed my way out of the depot on my stomach, crawling from cover to cover until I made it back to the trees. I was a good sixty miles up the road when an enormous fireball erupted behind me. Smiling and well pleased with myself, I rode through the early hours of the morning to make it back to the base. I hid the motorcycle in the thick undergrowth of a small copse a few miles from the cavern. I camouflaged it well and removed all the identification plates as well as the panniers, and made my way back to await the returning groups.

I spent the next couple of days helping Oz sort out the looted kit and outfitting our new volunteers. I was overjoyed when Ven returned and nearly as happy to see Jimmy when he arrived a day later.

Godfrey and Alex looked through the despatch messages that the rider had been carrying. I asked them to inform me if they contained anything useful and went to spend some time with Venice. She was, as ever, a delight to spend time with. There was never any need to be anything but myself with her. To her I was just Fish, the man she had pulled out of the river. She knew my faults and foibles and for a short time in her company I could forget my role as Commander Shaddick and relax.

But as ever, when I got too comfortable, guilt drove me on. The more inactive I was, the more I was haunted by the vision of mute anguish in a little boy's eyes, so after a couple of days of idleness I began to plan again. I gathered my commanders around me.

'Gentlemen, what is it that we need most?'

I gave Jimmy the finger when he cried out, 'Booze!'

'Seriously, we have some two hundred men, all organised, and trained as well as we could manage in a few short weeks. We have supplies and weapons, but what else do we need?'

I knew what we needed. I knew because Godfrey had told me the day before, and the question was rhetorical. Godfrey had once more decided that I should look the part of leader; so, when no suggestions were forthcoming, with only a slight smile from Godfrey, I spoke again.

'What we need is something for these men to do. They are eager to get stuck in but how do we move two hundred across the country? Too many to hide and too few to really accomplish anything. Yes, we could take out some targets, but how long before we encounter a force large enough to destroy us all, or they capture someone who can tell them roughly where our base is? What we need is both more men and the paperwork that will allow them to move around the country. They need new identities so that they can move back to the areas they know and await missions whilst we gather and train more people here.'

'What we need, Fish, is more women too.' I cocked my head at that, 'Go on.'

'There are plenty of women and children being taken too. If we recruit some of them it will be easier to move people around as happy families rather than a big bunch of suspicious-looking men. Anyway, Fish, I dare you to tell me that women can't fight.'

She had a point, she always did. So, I sat my captains down and we discussed long into the night what could be done. The upshot of our discussion was that we would have to raid another train or holding camp as well as a major supply depot and make off with all the paperwork we needed, as well as the photographic and printing equipment to forge our own documents. It might sound like a far-fetched idea, but it was the only real way any of us would be able to move around freely without arousing suspicion. We could, it was argued, stay hidden, but then the targets we attacked would have to be close to the base and that would soon show up as a pattern on the map, leading to the discovery of our location. However, even though the need to free those undesirables the H.A.P. had put into camps was something of a personal crusade of mine, I understood that the need to find identification papers was a priority. If we could gain legitimacy of travel for the men we had stationed here, we could form them into cells in different parts of the country and train the next group whilst the cells under my instruction hit targets up and down the length of the nation.

To this end I went amongst the new recruits, asking if any of them had been forced to work at a supply depot or one of the administration centres that were being built up and down the country. The results of this questioning led me to the conclusion that we had to enter the administration facility at Junction as it was the main administrative centre away from the capital in the south, and, as it happens, one of the men, a small thin man called Ferret by his friends, had been a sewer worker in Junction and swore he could get us under the base.

I selected Jimmy, as ever, for my right-hand man and hand-picked ten of our best. I explained to Ven that although I wished she could be at my side, there would be no opportunities for a sniper on this mission. I was expecting an argument but for once there was none. She just nodded and smiled and wished me luck. I suppose with hindsight it was probably the thought of wading around in sewers that helped to convince her that staying at the base was the more appealing option.

After I had selected the men, Harry came over to have the conversation I had promised. He was obviously ill at ease and I took him up to the top of the mountain to our eagle's nest in the bright fresh air. 'So, what's troubling you, Harry?'

He scratched his head and stared out into the middle distance, 'Not sure how to begin, Danny. It's about Sara.' he sighed and I nodded for him to continue. 'Well, I promised her to stay safe, and you promised her that you would keep me from harm's way … it's just that I can't do it, Danny. I can't stay safe and out of the way whilst others are putting their lives on the line. I don't know what to do. I'm torn between doing my fair share and fighting these horrible people, and keeping my word to my wife.'

That I think summed up the noble Harry in one. When offered a chance to sit out conflict in relative safety and comfort, most would jump at the chance. No doubt I could have found him something to do that kept him out of harm's way, but it just wasn't in his nature.

I thought about his predicament for a while, his need to help and his concerns for the feelings of his wife. 'How is this for an idea, Harry? Once we get some papers sorted, I can organise some of the younger lads into a sort of courier service, then you can write regular letters to Sara, letting her know that you are safe and well, and away from the trouble.' I paused and considered my statement for a moment. 'If the worst should happen, Harry, we can let her know it was just an unfortunate accident, a car crash or something. You get to fight and Sara thinks you are safe – that way you can both sleep easy.'

He smiled in relief, 'That would work. Thank you, Danny.'

I shook his hand, 'Who knows, maybe soon you will be able to go and see her.'

He nodded vigorously, 'I could, couldn't I? That would be great.'

'In the meantime, Harry, you are in charge of the defence of the base. Go to Godfrey if you need advice. Keep the patrols close and avoid any contact. Look after Ven for me and I will see you soon.'

I left him enjoying the view and returned to the mine to prepare my team. After some deliberation I decided to travel on foot again. I had thought about stealing onto a train or a truck and getting a ride southeast to Junction, but decided it was too much of a risk. If there had been only a couple of us then I probably would have, but as it was we packed our kit, picked up our travel rations and set out when it became dark. For the majority of the journey, once we were away from any towns and large villages, we stuck to the roads, turning aside and hiding in the ditches or trees at the side if any vehicles approached. So, it was in this manner that we made good speed towards the city, arriving on the outskirts at the end of our fifth night's travel. I had the team lie up in an old deserted barn well away from the main road on the open farmland that surrounded the suburbs at the edges of the city.

The city itself was much like any other, with suburban houses surrounding the older city centre proper with its crowded housing, markets and shopping areas. Junction had a large railway station where most of the tracks from the south converged, as well as industrial and administrative quarters. I assumed that the administrative buildings near the centre of the city would be where we would find the equipment we needed, but assumption wasn't really good enough so Jimmy and I decided to risk sneaking into the city to have a good look around.

It was quite an adventure, really, and for the most part made me feel like I was twelve again. I gave orders for the rest of the men to stay put, remain quiet and wait for our return. If anything happened they were to keep Ferret safe as he was our ticket into the sewer system. Jimmy and I, armed only with our hidden pistols, crept through the early dawn, moving from house to house, keeping to the shadows and back alleys and moving always towards the busier heart of the city. We were clearly in a fairly affluent area. The houses were large and well built with spacious gardens and cars on the driveways. We hid from postmen doing their rounds and scurried quickly past houses with attentive, noisy dogs until the sun began to climb higher in the sky and the roads began to get more crowded as people came out of their houses to go to work or school. We took refuge in some thick bushes at the bottom of a garden and waited for the morning rush to subside.

Adrenaline can only get you so far: I was exhausted and confess to falling asleep for a short time. Jimmy woke me around ten o'clock, his crazy smile plastered all over his face. I looked at him, my eyes narrow, knowing only too well that smile meant he had been up to mischief of some description. 'What have you done this time, Jimmy?'

It was then that I noticed he was wearing clean jeans and a shirt.

He pushed a leather briefcase towards me, 'Open it.'

I did so to find that it contained a shirt, a smart

pair of trousers and a jacket. I liked the idea. In these clothes we should be able to make an unobtrusive entry into the city, and as long as we could avoid patrols and checkpoints we should be able to have a decent look around before returning to the squad. 'Where did you get these, Jim?'

He shrugged, 'They were hanging up on a rack in a garage a few houses down. Took the briefcase thing as well. It's gonna come in handy.'

'How so, fella?' I started to take off my old clothes as he spoke.

'It's a scam I used to pull when I was a bit younger. One smart-looking fella knocks on the front door when the husband has gone to work, pretending to sell something nobody would really want, or something that the woman of the house would leave to her husband. You know, try to sell them a swimming pool or life insurance, something like that. When she comes to the door, the other fella goes in through the back door and looks for a purse or something valuable to steal. But nothing too obvious, something that won't be missed until they look for it. If the woman's shoulder bag is there, lift the purse out and she won't know it has gone until she needs it again, then she will probably think it has been mislaid. Anyway, you will have plenty of time to get clear.'

'Jimmy, I am not sure that stealing from people is going to help our war effort.'

'We need money, Dan. We catch the bus into town, buy a sandwich and some smokes, you know, look normal. We only need a bit of cash but without it we will go nowhere.'

I had to concede his point, so for a brief moment of my life I became a petty criminal and a fake door-to-door salesman. But first, Jimmy had to shave me with that wicked razor he kept in his boot. If you have never been shaved by a grinning maniac whilst hiding in some bushes at the end of a garden, using water from an ornamental pond and a razor you know has been used to kill, then to be honest I am not sure whether to feel sorry for your lack of excitement, or abjectly envy your quiet existence. May you live in interesting times indeed.

When he pronounced himself satisfied, I dressed. The trousers were a little long but they helped to cover my dirty boots. I wiped the dust off my old briefcase and prepared to rob a house. We chose the one next door; apparently it had a richer feel, and I suppose the open back door helped too. 'Remember, Danny, confidence. Stride down the drive like you own it and knock loudly, and then sell them something shit. When you have done, just keep walking slowly towards town. If I get nothing we will try again a few streets over. When I walk past you, if I stop at the bus stop all is well; otherwise, follow me until we find another house.'

I bundled our old clothes into the briefcase and sauntered down the driveway as if I had just made a call. I walked up the driveway of the house next door and knocked smartly on the door.

'Yes?'

I gave my best smile to the pretty blonde woman who answered the door. 'Are you the lady of the house, madam?'

She looked me up and down and straightened her apron, 'Yes.'

I gave a small bow. 'Madam, I represent Barnet and Boon.'

She held up her hand, 'Are you selling something, sir?'

'Yes, madam. We sell the finest bespoke children's tree houses, in a range of styles, sizes and colours.' 'No, thank you. I'm not interested.'

I proffered my briefcase, 'Could I at least leave a brochure with you?'

She looked at me as though I was crazy, which to be fair was not too far off the mark. 'You are aware there is a war on?'

I nodded, 'Yes, madam, but we still have to make a living.'

'Why don't you sign up with our other brave boys?'

Suddenly I didn't feel so bad about robbing the silly cow. I bade her good day and walked back down the path and slowly towards the town. Jimmy overtook me and I caught him up at the bus stop, so presumably all had gone well. We were the only two waiting there.

He smirked at me. 'Bespoke fucking tree houses? In war time? Bloody brilliant! She was loaded; got her purse.' He handed me half the cash. 'You don't know me from now on. You take the lead for now and I will follow. If we swap every few hundred yards or so it won't look so suspicious. On the way back, don't stop here; let the bus take us further on. We don't want you being seen by that woman again.'

I pocketed the cash and nodded my agreement. I climbed aboard the bus when it arrived and ordered a return to the city centre. Jimmy behind me ordered a single and we sat away from each other.

When I disembarked at the city centre, the military presence was, I am grateful to say, somewhat less than I had imagined it to be. However, there were plenty of off-duty soldiers wandering about in the cafés and shops, interspersed with the normal civilian population one would expect in a city centre. Listening to conversation between some soldiers in a shop where I bought some cigarettes and a paper, I learnt that there was a big base in the industrial part of town and a heavy guard presence at the station. I bought a coffee at a small café in a plaza and sat down to read the news. Apparently the war was going well. The unenlightened soldiers of the north were being pushed rapidly back, several large towns had been captured with minimal losses, the pre-programmed soldiers (I could only imagine they meant the clones) were performing well and the H.A.P. expected to have captured the capital within a month. Obviously I didn't believe all of this. I realised that the Coalition were being pushed back but Alex had intercepted radio traffic that suggested resistance was fierce and the outnumbered Coalition were only very slowly giving ground. I noted with some grief that some suspects had been executed in reprisal for some stolen supplies. Sickened and feeling guilty I folded the paper and left it on the table.

I finished my coffee and nodded to Jimmy, who

appeared to be buying a hat at a nearby shop. We exited the plaza and wandered towards the council district. Access to the central square where the government administration buildings were located proved to be impossible for us. There were soldiers stationed at all the entrances and a checkpoint on the road in and out. People entering the square were clearly having their papers checked before they were allowed in.

I gestured discreetly for Jimmy to stay put and made a circuit of the buildings around the square until I found one that suited my purpose. It was a large department store with a number of floors. I smiled at the lift attendant and asked to be taken to the fourth floor, the men's clothing department. I gave him a small tip and wandered amongst the latest range of menswear, looking for a window that overlooked the square. As it transpired, I had to try on a suit so that I could get into the changing room and stand on the bench to look out of the window at the square beneath me. A significant number of troops were on guard in front of various buildings, but the building that interested me most was directly across the way from my window. It was The Department of Civilian Processing, a fact I was informed of by the H.A.P. banner above the large double doors. Satisfied I knew which building I was looking for, and familiar with the layout of the square, I exited the changing room and handed the suit back to the helpful young assistant. I did buy the tie.

Jimmy and I spent a couple of hours wandering around the city centre, turning down side streets or entering shops if we saw a patrol coming our way. There were also a number of men who appeared to be civilians, but who clearly worked for some branch of the H.A.P. They were obvious by their uniform lack of uniform, so to speak – the same long coats and hats and a peculiar authoritarian manner in their speech and demeanour. It was clear that the ordinary folk were giving them a wide berth and I thought it prudent to do the same.

I bought some strong-smelling mint salve from a pharmacy, and at a baker's treated myself to a fresh greasy pasty. It was the best thing I had eaten for a while, so with a touch of compassion, I bought another dozen and went to catch the bus back to the suburbs. From there, with as much inconspicuousness as I could manage, I meandered back out into the countryside. I changed back into my old clothes and returned to the barn.

The men had been keeping watch and opened the door at my arrival. A short time later Jimmy returned, and as the men gratefully devoured the lukewarm food, he and I compared notes. I consulted our map with Ferret, and as dusk arrived we headed southwest through the fringes of fields and trees that backed onto suburbia. As you can imagine, the large sewage works stood alone down a long, narrow access road screened with trees. We could smell the place from a fair distance before we arrived, and I could tell from the glances that the others shared, that none of us were looking forward to actually having to wade through shit.

For that is what we had to do. The sewage processing plant sat in a quarried depression in the open fields, presumably to hide it from view and gain the required fall for the liquid to travel. There were men on duty but no guards that we could see. The small office building at the far end of the compound was well lit and it was clear that the technicians on duty were monitoring their dials from the comfort of the office.

Ferret crawled over to me. 'Wait here a minute, sir. I got to go get something.'

I patted his arm in agreement and watched him slither off into the compound, heading towards a small concrete building situated between two great settling tanks. He came back a few moments later holding a helmet with an attached lamp, the type that miners use.

'You ready, sir?'

'Just a moment, soldier.' I smeared the menthol salve over my top lip and handed it down the line where the others did the same. Only Ferret refused, laughing quietly to himself. I tapped him on the shoulder, 'Lead on.' We wormed under the chain link fence, following the aptly named little man, dropped down some ladders, and hurried across the open floor of the plant to the foot of another set of ladders that led up to the looming mouth of a large sewage outfall pipe. One at a time we climbed the ladder to the concrete lip at the side of the pipe and disappeared into the foetid darkness.

Ferret was waiting, and as each man entered the pipe he threaded a rope through their belts. Demanding silence in a whisper, he headed to the front of the file just ahead of me, and calmly led the way into the pitch black. Thankfully, there was not much liquid under our feet and the smell was not too bad. After what seemed like miles, but was in all probability a trek of only a few hundred yards, Ferret turned on his helmet lamp, an act that left us blinded and blinking and cursing his lack of warning until our eyes had accustomed to the light.

'It's okay to talk a little here and switch your torches on, sir.'

‘Thanks, Ferret. Where are we?’

‘This is an overflow and bypass pipe for heavy rains. Usually doesn’t run ‘til autumn. We follow this south until we reach the great gallery and then take a pipe that leads us under the central plaza. Easy enough for now but I promise you it will get nastier as we move on.’

I gave the signal to move forward and followed the little man as he worked his way along the brick-lined tunnel. The air got thicker and the smell worsened as we progressed. Being used to caves and similar myself, the tunnels held no fear for me. Even the occasional rat we saw fled when the light from our torches touched it, but the smell was another thing altogether. I have no idea how one gets used to that loathsome reek. The menthol on my lip helped, but the thought that it was only going to get worse failed to cheer me up at all.

The large gallery was something else. It was a huge, dark space under the city with numerous pipes that poured ordure into the central sump where it gurgled and festered and flowed into unseen exits.

Our lights failed to illuminate the far side and rats scurried and chattered everywhere in the darkness beyond the glow of our lamps.

'Keep to the walkway and follow me, sir. Watch your footing and walk careful. You fall down there and you're a gonner even if we can haul you out.'

I passed the message down the line, and placing my feet carefully on the slick green surface, edged around the walkway, following Ferret as he made his way into the gloom. Presently he stopped at a pipe a little less than six feet in diameter that issued large volumes of brown watery foulness. He rubbed at the filth on the wall by the mouth of the pipe, exposing a large letter A and the Roman numeral for three.

'This is the one. Careful now.' He stepped into the flow of filth, and I, three short feet of rope behind him, could do little other than follow.

It was foul. A stinking torrent of human waste, knee deep on the submerged ledge that ran along the side of the pipe. I had to lean forward to clear the roof with my head, bringing my face closer to the swirling tide of shit that ran past me.

'Stick to the side now, sir. Too deep and fast in the middle; it will have you away in no time.'

I followed Ferret as he waded happily up the tunnel, his short stature and wiry body allowing him to walk unhindered in the confined and odious passageway. The journey for me was a nightmare. Stooped and confined, my back ached miserably and the smell made me retch. I tried not to picture the shape of the items that bumped into my legs as I sloshed and stumbled up what could only ever be laughingly labelled shit creek.

Four hours the journey took from when we entered pipe A III. Four hours in which we jumped across converging pipes, ducked under foetid flows joining the pipe at head height, and scrambled over slick filthy nests of pipework that blocked our path. Four hours in which I puked my guts up, got covered from head to foot in the flushed waste of a city and yearned with every fibre of my being to be able to straighten my back.

After I had lost all sense of time and could think of nothing but the pain in my back, Ferret finally came to a halt.

'We are under the central plaza now, sir. There are four access points on the square. Where do you want to come out?'

I used my finger to draw a map of the square in the filth on the pipe wall. 'This is the building we want to get into. Where is the closest sewer access?'

He thought for a moment. 'This building here on the corner next to the one you want, there is an access comes up in the rear courtyard.'

Desperate to be out of this hell I gave a firm nod, 'Okay, that's the one.'

'I'll just go and find it. Wait here, I will be right back.'

With that, he untied the rope that joined us together and disappeared. He came back a few minutes later and led us to the foot of a ladder. 'Here we are, sir – Access 113b.'

It was just past one-thirty in the morning by my watch. I gave orders to turn off all lights and wait for the command before following me up. Lady Luck was smiling on me again, for when I forced the cast iron cover up enough to suck in a welcome lungful of fresh air and take stock of my surroundings, I realised that the sewer access was located between the back wall of the courtyard and the waste bins for the hotel. I whispered back down the shaft and within a couple of minutes ten stinking foul and nervous men were crouching in the darkness behind the bins.

There were lights on in various windows of the hotel and it seemed that the bar and restaurant were still doing a roaring trade despite the hour. The building next door that we needed to enter was silent and dark and I could only hope that all the staff from the Civilian Processing building were making merry in the hotel. Still, here I was, crouching behind the bins, filthy and reeking and short of nothing but a plan.

It was one of the new boys who came up with the idea. He tapped me on the shoulder and pointed upwards to the iron fire escape that clung to the side of the building. I gave him a grin, and keeping an eye on the doors from the kitchen, he and I ran across the courtyard to the fire escape. I put my hands together and boosted him up, from where he dropped a rope so that one at a time the men could dart from the shadows and join us on the creaking iron. As slowly and carefully as we could manage, we crept up the ladder, ducking down as we passed the yellow glow of occupied rooms until we reached the upper floor. With my knife I popped the catch on the window of an empty-looking room and slid inside. A quick check revealed that the bed was unoccupied and the cupboards and wardrobe held nothing but bare hangers.

Deciding to push my luck even further, I went into the bathroom and stood fully clothed under the shower until the worst of my journey had washed off. I returned to the room dripping but cleaner and insisted that the others did the same. Water would dry but the filth we carried would herald our presence like a marching band. We dried ourselves off as well as we could with the hotel's towels. I thought with a grin that I should complain to the management that the number of towels provided was insufficient for ten men from the sewers, and that if they wished for my return custom they had better rectify the situation.

My grin remained as I looked up and saw the ceiling hatch that led to the attic. I had two of the men lift me up and I clambered into the surprisingly large space. I shone my torch around briefly, and stepping carefully on the wooden beams made my way to the end window. At right angles to this building, the gable end window of our target building was only a few short feet away. I returned to the hatch and helped the rest of the men up. There was no need to stress the need for care and silence, for we all knew our lives depended on our stealth.

I beckoned Jimmy over to the window to look at our target. He nodded, worked his way slowly back and began carefully rooting through all the various pieces of hotel junk that had been stored up there. He returned presently with the side plank from an old bed frame, and between us we slid it out of the window to rest it upon the window ledge on the building opposite. I almost burst out laughing at the silent argument we had in the dark with gestures and head shakes, until I managed to demonstrate quite eloquently I believe, using mime, that it was his damn fool idea so he was going first.

He grinned at me and motioned that I should hold the plank still. He shuffled across on his hands and knees. It was the work of moments for him to open the window and so, many feet above the ground and the patrolling troops below, we each crawled along a discarded length of bed frame until we all congregated in the office of Civilian Processing. The building was deserted: five floors of empty offices filled with books, labels and paperwork. Half of the floor below was given over to the machinery we sought: hand cranked presses, sheets and sheets of blank identity papers and photographic equipment. But it was in the main office on the top floor where we made the important find. Along with the clean uniform of a major, Jimmy found a whole bank of rubber stamps. To be truthful, they were of no concern to him as he had discovered them whilst searching the office desks for something to drink, coming up trumps when he found a crystal decanter of fine brandy in the major's office.

I began directing the men to steal what we needed when I was gripped again by devilment, inspired I believe by both recklessness and the fear of braving the sewers again, something I think would have taken more resilience and courage than I possessed. I picked up a camera, made sure that the heavy curtains on the photo booth were shut, and sat a bemused Jimmy down, smoothing back his hair before taking his picture.

‘What the hell did you do that for, Danny?’

I gestured to all the equipment in the room, ‘Why go down the sewers when we can just walk out of here?’

He took a swig from his crystal decanter; I took one too and passed it over to the rest of the squad. ‘You know, that’s not a bad idea.’ He clapped his hands together, ‘You sure we got time?’

I gave him my nastiest grin, ‘Of course. I got a plan.’

We cleaned up as well as we could in the wash rooms. I had everyone strip off and use the soap to get as clean as possible. A few brave souls accepted a shave from barber Jimmy, and as soon as I could I began taking photographs of the men. Once I had done, Jimmy and a couple of others went back into the hotel to steal clothes, money and bags from sleeping guests and staff quarters.

Just before he crossed back into the hotel, he turned to me and said, ‘You sure we will get away with this?’

I just grinned at him again.

'Oh fuck, Danny, I'm looking forward to this.'

I looked at my watch; time really was going to be short. I got Andy to familiarise himself with the press and learn how to feed blank sheets over it. I had another of the men practise laminating photographs onto the papers on another machine, and whilst the rest of the men were stockpiling as many blank sets of identification papers as they could carry, as well as the stamps, ink and chemicals used in the process, I disappeared into the developing room to process the photographs. It was something I had done at school and, to be fair, I didn't do a bad job at all.

If we wanted to be out of there by four, which was my plan, I really had to hurry. I gave the completed photographs to one of the men and had him cut them to size. Using a couple of finished sets of papers that were waiting to be issued as a template, I invented names, dates of birth, home towns and occupations for all of my men. I forged the signature of the major, stamped them all with the correct stamps and handed the documents to Ferret so that he and the others could put them through the machines and complete our fake documents.

Once this was done, I sent the men back over to the hotel with all the portable items we could carry that we could use to create more sets of papers. I then had a couple of the lads strip out the mechanical parts of the machines, the rollers, printers and binders. I reasoned that Jimmy would be able to fashion something similar to the original machines back at the cavern as long as he had all the complicated internal parts. I sent the last of the men back to the hotel and spent a few moments scattering paperwork around the room and soaking it in the highly flammable developing chemicals that we had left behind.

As the chemicals soaked into the wooden flooring, I changed into the uniform of the major, complete with a new pair of boots, then splashed more chemical thinners around the upper floor. I poured what was left down the stairs and flicked a glowing cigarette butt down the stairwell from where a light blue flame raced out in a widening circle. As quickly as I could, I hurried back over the bed bridge to the hotel and dropped into the room where the men were waiting.

'It appears that the building next door is on fire.' I grinned at the men garbed in a collection of clothes, from waiter and chef to smart businessman and tourist. 'Wait for the alarm, boys, and then rush out of the hotel in panic. You all got the right papers? You all have some cash?'

There was a chorus of quiet 'Yes, sirs' and I nodded. 'Be ready, don't run too fast, mingle in the crowd that forms to watch and when the shops open, go and buy an outfit more befitting the occupation on your papers.'

I heard Jimmy snort and I grinned, expecting his outburst. 'I ain't even sure what the fuck a bloody ornithologist is.'

'They wear a lot of tweed, Jimmy.'

'Tweed? You are a sick man, boss.'

I told the men to wrap their filthy old clothes into sheets or pillowcases and to put them into the bags they all carried, along with the various items we had looted from the office of Civilian Processing. They were instructed to dispose of the clothes somewhere on their journey back. I suggested that over the next day they should take trains and buses north, travel as far as was sensible and make the last stretch of the journey on foot at night time. I checked everything was safely packed, gave their papers a quick inspection, made sure they knew the names and occupations they were to travel under and waited for the alarm to be raised.

As soon as we heard the clatter of the alarm bell, we exited down the fire escape in pairs, joining the bewildered and panicked residents of the hotel in their exodus. Flames billowed from the windows and the roof next door, and tongues of flame licked and lapped at the red-tiled roof of the hotel. We joined the throng of panicked guests outside in the square as the fire brigade arrived. As the men merged with the crowd, I had a great time bellowing conflicting orders and creating more confusion, whilst giving the impression of trying to organise the crowd and the work of the fire fighters. Once the roof of the offices had collapsed and the firemen turned their full attention to preventing the blaze from spreading to the hotel, I perceived that my work there was done. I faded from prominence, sought an early opening café and settled down to a large breakfast with a big pot of tea. Somewhat fortified, I walked to the station, where I presented my papers, exchanged salutes with the guards and boarded a northbound train.

As the train pulled away, I caught a glimpse between station buildings and made a note of some sort of camp, well guarded, surrounded by barbed wire and populated with an assortment of ragged civilians.

The train was packed with troops. I, of course,

sat in first class, where I bluffed my way through some conversation with other officers by explaining that I was heading north to assume command of a company in the 1st C.L., which led to a conversation about the abilities and faults of the clone troops or, as the officers dismissively called them, Tubes.

It was interesting to note that they were happy to use them as disposable troops or cannon fodder, sending them to attack positions that would have galled regular troops; but, while they held great respect for the discipline and skills that their in-utero programming had instilled in them, they definitely saw them as second-class soldiers. They viewed them as highly trained and disciplined but utterly unable to think for themselves or adapt to any given situation without orders. It seems that the officers and NCOs were vital to the cohesive operation of the clone units. I mentally compared this information with what I knew about Adam, and concluded that perhaps in the future more sharpshooters might be required.

I refrained from asking questions about the progress of the war, information I would probably be expected to be aware of, and decided to be discreet, pretending to sleep for much of the remainder of the journey. About twelve miles south of Westridge, where the flat plains of the south began to blend with the steeper ground of the Midlands, lay the small village of Mallowdale. It was here that I decided I would make my exit.

'Well, gentlemen, it has been a pleasure. Thank you all for your company, but this I believe is my stop.'

One of the other officers looked at me, a quizzical look upon his face. 'Surely, major, you mean to travel to Westridge?'

I brandished my papers at him. 'I am not due to report until tomorrow and I happen to know a delightful young lady who resides in this burgh … I hope to report in tomorrow with a slight smile and a scratched back.'

They laughed at this and I endured the slapped back and the vigorous handshake, bade them good hunting, picked up my bag containing the embossing plates, tipped my cap and sauntered to the station gate.

As for the rest of the journey, I followed the usual routine of waiting unseen for dark. In a gentle yet persistent rain I made the journey to the wet entrance, where I took off my uniform jacket and cap and waded into the water.

Just before I ducked past the falls I was

surprised to be challenged. With hindsight I am pleased that I was, but at the time I merely felt annoyed.

'Halt, what's the password?'

'How the fuck do I know what the bloody password is? I've been away for nearly a week. Tell Oz to let me know what the password is before I actually go on a sodding mission.'

'Oh, it's you, sir. Sorry, sir.'

I passed through the curtain and nodded to the two men guarding the entrance. 'Good work, fellas. Keep it up.'

I was the last to arrive, having had to wait for dark unlike the less conspicuous members of the team, and my arrival prompted a great cheer in the base of the mountain.

Venice was pleased to see me and showed it with in her usual welcome style. The rest of my captains shook my hand and Godfrey for once was effusive with his praise.

'Excellent work, Daniel. Excellent. Jimmy told us how you burnt the building down and got everyone away in the panic.' He clapped his hands, 'Now we can really start to make a difference. You stole exactly what we needed and we have enough blanks to make a couple of thousand sets of paperwork. I will get Alex to start working on the new identities first thing tomorrow.'

I was glad to be back and pleased at how successful the mission had been, so I unlocked the tool chest and handed out bottles; not enough for everyone to get drunk, just relaxed, but I made sure that those who had been on the mission with me got very relaxed. In one of those moments of inspiration, such as I often have during periods when I have attempted to alter my blood chemistry, I pulled one of the medals off my stolen tunic, stood on top of a rock formation and demanded silence. I made a speech about how great all the men under my command were and how proud I was to lead them. I thanked all of the men from the mission by name but saved Ferret until the last. Him I called up to the rock and presented him with the medal, calling him our very own brave and dependable sewer rat. Poor fellow, he actually broke down and cried at the applause, and I believe he was still following me around telling me what an honour it was and how grateful he was when I finally fell asleep.

We put those identity papers to good use over the next few months. Men were given new identities, organised into local groups and sent back to areas they knew to form resistance cells. They were told to stay inconspicuous, keep their weapons and equipment hidden in safe places and await the arrival of one of the captains before attacking any targets. They were to gather information on troop and weapon movements and organise a safe house for others to visit. I explained to them the code of the toy in the upstairs window of the house, wished them well, told them to wait for me to arrive and saw them off. To be honest, I did not have much at all to do with organising the cells. That was all Godfrey's work. He gave them extra training and taught them all they needed to know to survive as partisans in a hostile urban environment. I just planned on visiting them from time to time to use them and the knowledge they had collected to attack the H.A.P. and cause as much damage and mayhem as possible.

Obviously, not all of the men could or would leave. Some had nowhere else to go and others like Ferret and my captains preferred to stay at the base. The ones who chose to remain numbered around sixty and became the core of the resistance. I used them for local work and training new recruits, and I took some of them with me as extra manpower when I visited the groups we had set up around the country. They also worked as couriers for what had become the intelligence section under Godfrey and Alex, coordinating the groups and running messages from cell to cell.

Possibly the most worthwhile result of all our new paperwork was that I was finally able to take Harry back to Oldbridge to visit Sara. We had set one of the older men up as a taxi driver based in Mallowdale. It was a properly registered company with legitimate plates and licences. We had put ten years on his age when we gave him his identity papers, making him too old to be called up. As a result, he was often called upon to run us around the country when other means of transport were inadequate or too risky. In fact, this scheme worked so well we ended up with small taxi companies around the country, which proved invaluable for moving weapons, ammunition and men from place to place.

Posing as father, daughter and son, Harry, Ven and I drove through various checkpoints, where our excellent genuine forged papers aroused not the slightest suspicion, and into the town of Oldbridge, past the scene of my first small massacre. We drew up a few doors down from Sara's house. I asked Harry to go around to the back door, as the fewer people who saw him the better, given that there would be no mistaking that great frame of his. Noticing with a smile the blue doll in the right-hand upper window, I knocked on the door.

Sara was as neat and tidy as always. She recognised us instantly, but unsure of the reason for our visit and probably and rightly apprehensive of the news we carried, she merely offered a tight, nervous smile and invited us in. I took off my boots, remembering her fastidious nature, and we followed her into the kitchen.

I winked at Ven and she let me lead as Sara began fussing with the teapot. I could tell she was desperate to hear about Harry but couldn't quite bring herself to ask.

'Sit down, sit down. It's lovely to see you both, I must say. How have you been? Is everything okay?'

I adopted my favourite poker face. 'We are fine,' I stressed. 'It's about Harry.'

She leant back against the worktop, her hand flying to her mouth. The sharp intake of breath was clearly audible. 'What about Harry?'

Venice cracked first. 'He's at the back door; you might want to let him in.'

I swear that I had no idea that plump women of a certain age could move so fast. One moment she was leaning back against the kitchen worktop and the next instant she was wrenching open the back door to be enfolded in the embrace of the giant Harry, sobbing into his shirt. Ven looked pointedly at me and then the kettle and we got to our feet and finished making the tea, all the time looking out of the window whilst Harry gently held his wife and assured her over and over that he was fine.

We had a lovely evening and Sara's joy affected us all. We stayed the night and got the taxi back the next morning after a fine breakfast, Sara's protracted thanks, and further admonishments to keep Harry safe.

Gerry, the taxi driver, dropped us off in some woodland close to the base and we returned through the mine to the cavern and the war.

MY WAY

With our ease of movement around the country assured, it was time once again for more recruits. This time, as Venice had insisted, we decided to try to rescue women and children as well as men. In a way I was looking forward to receiving this latest batch of refugees as it would allow me to go back into the field and continue to cause mayhem and disruption to the supply lines of the enemy.

This next mission was more complicated than most. Oh, I had no doubt that we could waylay a train and make off with the passengers, but how would I get them to the base? I could not risk leaving another empty train near to Westridge, which meant that either I would have to release the prisoners at a point further away and risk an overland trek with women and children in tow, or once again some sort of misdirection would have to be used, coupled with a short journey across country.

In the end, the planning proved extensive and

problematic. As the pieces of the plan finally came together, I made a couple of journeys south to blow up railway lines and attack supply convoys in different areas, both to keep up the momentum of our resistance and to keep the various resistance groups around the country active, give them victories and purpose, and keep up their morale.

One of the men was infiltrated into a truck company running stone from a quarry in the east Jerals to various places in the south. This provided ballast for roads and railways as well as delivering to the large concrete works at Dunsop some fifty miles southeast of Little Junction on the main road to the capital at the naval city of Port Redmire. In addition to the truck, which would be used to move the released prisoners northwards, men had to be sent out to scout the various rail points that would need to be changed to send the train in the direction we required. A diversionary attack on the coast road also had to be timed to coincide with our escape. But perhaps the most difficult task was finding a place where we could hide and feed all these people whilst they were waiting to be moved. This place of relative, if temporary, safety had to be close to the rail lines and on the return route of the stone wagon, so that the driver could maintain his routine whilst running fugitives northwards to safety at the hidden base.

In the end, after scouting out the terrain, I decided on a small area of woodland where the road passed through one side and the railway through the other. It was a fairly desperate plan, and it relied on the various cells carrying out timed assaults at different points both to lure away the H.A.P. and to prevent them from being able to organise a thorough search of the area in which we would be hidden with an unknown number of men, women and children.

The other main consideration was the weather. We were well into autumn: the nights were cold and the days were not much better. I put out the call and congregated some fifty men in the woodland to organise bivouacs, and to have blankets, warm clothing and food ready to welcome the new arrivals. These men would arrive a couple of days before the prisoners, and after the last one had left, clean up the temporary camp and disappear back to their homes.

After all the convoluted and difficult planning, it was a relief to actually begin the mission. I sent out the men whose task it was to move the points on the track, reminding them to disconnect the cable so that the signalman would not notice that the points were moving, and to reconnect it once the train had gone past. Venice and Will went to take up their position near a bridge halfway between Junction and Little Junction. I sent Jimmy off to organise the various diversions and I chose fifteen men, including Caleb and Ferret, to come with me on the main mission.

We used assorted identities and occupations to get into Junction, where we booked into various rooms around the town. We met in a bar near to the station and as night fell, gathered our equipment. We crawled in ones and twos past the gauntlet of searchlights that lit up the holding pens of the transit camp and the sentries who marched in pairs around the yard. The prison train that would be taking the undesirable group of humanity to some fresh hell was easy to identify. It stood at a platform across from the camp, bars on the windows and the sliding doors of the wagons open, ready to engulf and transport more unfortunates away to an uncertain and sorry future.

There were six wagons in all and a guard carriage at the front. I had a hunch, prompted by the locked doors on the last three wagons, that only half the train would be filled from this transit camp and that it would stop to collect more prisoners somewhere on the journey. This prompted a brief conversation and a fairly major change of plan; the original plan being to hide our larger weapons, break into the camp and be herded aboard with the other prisoners. The new plan, however, gave us the opportunity to keep our long weapons and avoid the risk of being caught breaking into the camp, illuminated by spotlights as it was, and guarded by sentries and dogs. I talked to Ferret and asked him if he would be okay with the task I had for him. He, as ever, grinned and nodded. I don't know if he relished adventure or was a man truly without fear. I asked him if he could break into the holding camp on his own with no weapons and circulate amongst the inmates, asking them not to be alarmed if there were men waiting in the wagon they were assigned to.

'Ferret, find the ones who seem to be in charge and let them know that there is going to be a rescue attempt. Get them on your side, and ask them to help spread the word to ignore our presence. However, and this is really important, they must not display any difference in their behaviour. Don't let them show their hope or there will not be any. You understand?'

He nodded again. I patted him on the back and we slithered forwards under one of the raised station buildings. I stayed there and watched him, remarking to myself once again upon the aptness of his moniker as he wormed his way past the guards, moved into the shadow of the lights, made a small hole in the fence and merged into the camp.

I rejoined the rest of the men and, resolute, we all slid aboard, climbing silently onto the roof of one of the locked wagons, prying up the ventilation hatch and sliding down inside. I stopped Caleb before he entered the dark wooden box, and whispered to him through the open hatch.

'Caleb, change of plan. Shut the hatch on us and try to make it fit properly, then consider your part done. Make your way home.'

He was a good lad and understood the need for my decision. My view of the night sky disappeared as he closed the hatch and slid slowly back into the darkness.

It was tense in the dark of that wagon; our silence had to be absolute. I allowed none to sleep for fear of loud snores and I admit that whilst I remained hidden from view I chewed away at my nails, hoping desperately that I had made the right decision and that we would pass unnoticed by the guards. I had to content myself with the idea that even if they did decide to use this wagon, it was unlikely that they would check it first. As long as we kept in the shadows and managed to stop the first to board from speaking, then we could well get away without being discovered.

It was just starting to come light when I heard the whistles. Momentarily I panicked, thinking we had been discovered, when I realised that the prisoners were being roused. I watched intently through a small gap between the boards, ready to give an order that might result in a short, desperate and deadly fight to escape. I was horrified by both the number of guards and the condition of the small tide of humanity that was being herded towards the wagons. I was fairly sure that once the prisoners were loaded, a small section of the soldiers would join the train for its journey, with the rest staying to keep order at the camp and the station. Our job would be too difficult otherwise, and the mission would have to be abandoned. However, looking at the distraught adults and the crying children sickened me and provoked within me horrific memories that made me clutch at the little blue bear under my coat, grind my teeth in anger and bow my head in shame at the vision of mute anguish in a little boy's eyes.

I vowed that I would release these poor souls no matter how many guards they assigned to the train. Someone once told me that you should be able to look in a mirror and be proud of the man you see looking back at you. I, for one, would ever be ashamed by my reflection, and even if I accomplished the impossible and rescued Mathew and could bear to look into my own eyes, I would still be haunted by the shadow of the cowardly man who abandoned his brother to save his own wretched skin.

You should be proud to look at the man in the mirror. These guards had sealed their own fate and I was not going to allow them even the slightest chance of redemption. I saw one of them move towards the door of our wagon and gestured frantically to the men to hide in the shadows in the lee of the door. I held my breath, gun cocked, safety off, my back pressed hard against the wooden wall of the wagon as the door opened and light flooded in. The guards started shouting orders at the prisoners, and with kicks and shoves forced them onto the wagon. The first prisoner to enter was a young harried woman with large dark eyes, clutching the hand of a weeping gaunt child. She hesitated slightly when her head turned towards me. I smiled at her, brought my finger to my lips to indicate silence and winked. She proved herself to be a woman of some strength and will as she gave me the slightest smile back and turned to help others onto the wagon. I still think it was her lack of reaction and her calm presence of mind in helping others onto that wagon that prevented the alarm from being raised, and my respect for her was immense. That was how I met Hannah, the woman who would go on to make Jimmy's smile even broader and become a member of Ven's sniper team.

The door slammed shut, the train moved off and we stood silently amidst a group of expectant staring faces. I kept my finger to my lips to prevent questions but after a time I smiled at the throng and bade them talk amongst themselves.

'No questions and no shouting, please, people,' I whispered as loudly as I dared. 'Let us get on with our job and we will see what we can do about getting you out of this box car.'

Footfalls on the roof above attested to the presence of a guard, and I had the men ready themselves in silence. I asked the prisoners to make some space for us at both ends of the car, and put one of the men to work loosening the boards there with a pry bar, but with strict orders to leave them in place. We waited for the killing to begin. I kept an eye on our route using trees and bridges as markers to try and estimate our speed. My reckoning was not too far out and only moments after I whispered at the men to make ready did I hear the guard above our heads exclaim loudly before he landed with a dull thump on the roof and slid off the side.

I grinned at the sound: Ven was doing her part

of the job. I slashed my fist downward, cried 'Now!' and the men exploded into action. We ripped the loosened boards off and I led the men up onto the roof. Two went to the rear to deal with any guards on the back of the train and I led the rest forward. There was only one guard still standing as we raced forward, jumping the gap between box cars and sprinting towards the front. Speed, surprise and violence of action were our best weapons here. The remaining guard turned upon hearing us and raised his weapon. My beautiful sniper didn't let me down and he failed to get a shot off before an invisible force hit him in the back and he fell onto the track below. I raced straight over the guards' carriage, leaving the others to hurl grenades through the roof hatches and open up with their weapons before entering to make sure that none of the soldiers lived.

I jumped over the last gap to land in the back of the locomotive, seeking to pacify the driver and get him to continue on his present route, though I hadn't allowed for the driver's mate, who nearly finished my campaign with a well-swung shovel. I ducked the blow and caught him behind the head as he overswung, and beat his face against the iron side of the locomotive until the fight went out of him. The driver just stood at the controls, shock written all over his face. I gestured with my pistol,

'Just keep driving, sunshine. Face forwards and keep it moving.'

'Yes, sir. Anything you say, sir.'

Barrett, one of my team, jumped onto the engine. 'Train captured, Commander Shaddick. No hostiles left aboard.'

I thanked him and told him to take the men back to the car we had so recently exited and get some sleep.

'You be all right here with this one, sir?'

'It's all under control, thanks, corporal. Just send someone forward in a couple of hours.'

'I will come myself, sir. Count on it.'

I dismissed him, 'Go and get some sleep … Oh, and find Ferret and tell him he did a great job.'

He scrambled back onto the carriage and I turned my attention back to the driver. He was obviously terrified and I could see him plucking up the courage to speak. 'Go on, driver. What did you want to say?'

'Begging your pardon, sir, but did he just call you Shaddick?'

'He did.'

'*The* Shaddick? Daniel Shaddick?'

I laughed at him, 'How many Danny Shaddicks do you think there are that attack trains and kill soldiers?'

He thought for a moment, 'Just the one I suppose.' He shook his head and held out his hand, 'My name is Thompson.'

I shook it, 'Nice to meet you, Thompson. Just you keep driving and we will get on fine.'

'My missus will go batty when she hears that I shook your hand. She thinks that you are some kind of hero.'

'Well that's good of her, Thompson. I know there are many who see me as some sort of traitor.'

He shrugged, 'It all depends on which way you voted before the war I reckon. Many who voted against the H.A.P. have disappeared, and I reckon there will be more than a few as passengers on this damn train.' He sighed, 'We were lucky: would have voted against them myself, but we were staying at her sister's on the west coast so didn't get round to voting.'

'So how come you are working for them now, Mr Thompson?'

He spat over the side. 'I ain't working for them as such, Mr Shaddick. I'm a train driver. Driven trains for nigh on forty years now. I drive the train and they provide the cargo. Don't like it, ain't happy 'bout it, but I got Mrs Thompson to feed and she's a big girl, if you catch my drift.'

I laughed and clapped him on the shoulder, 'I understand, Thompson.'

He shook his head again. 'You sure do divide opinion, Mr Shaddick. Tho' those in your favour seem to be getting less and quieter. Man can't voice his thoughts like before this war started. Say, I am pleased to meet you. You just keep on raising hell, boy, tho' I would consider it a favour if you didn't kill any more engine drivers.' He paused and laughed, 'You ain't gonna kill me, are you, Mr Shaddick, sir?'

I liked this man, I liked him a lot, and I was wracking my brain to find a way to let him live. Maybe throw him off the train before we reached the place where we were going to unload the prisoners or something. At the forefront of my mind was the fact that he would not escape interrogation, and thus I could not let him learn anything that could be used against us. I smiled, shook my head and passed him my hip flask. 'I'm not going to kill you Mr Thompson.'

I hate having to tell lies, but at the end of our journey together, and with much regret, I had to lose the kind support of Mrs Thompson and make her a widow; although I did give Mr Thompson, train driver, deceased, a fine send-off in a modern rendition of the ancient pagan burial, sending his train, with him slumped at the controls, at high speed south down a northbound track, where it crashed head on into a troop transport heading for the front.

There are many occasions where I have wished I could just rewind time and undo something I have just said or done. My main regret is obvious. In my top fifty was declining to go to see a movie with Abby Downs when I was fifteen. She took my friend Mike and made a man of him in the park later. But handing likeable Mr Thompson my hip flask is in my all-time top five as he took a swig and sealed his fate.

'That's a good drop, Mr Shaddick, a fine drop indeed. That's a drop of Si Kennet's best or I'm a stoker.'

I'm not heartless; I did let him finish the flask.

The train rattled on, and the men at the points turned us in the right direction. I consulted my map and my watch, did a few swift mental calculations and asked Thompson to slow us down. I wanted the partisan's friend, night, to have arrived before we stopped and unloaded. After some initial screams of terror, the voices from the box cars had stilled somewhat, and when Ferret, pulled up out of the car he had been put in, came to take over from me for a short while, I ventured across the tops of the cars, ripping off the hatches and explaining what was happening. This was far more difficult than I could ever have imagined it would be, as hysterical and panicked prisoners take a while to respond to rational discussion.

Eventually, I calmed them down, thanked them for their patience and managed to convince them that soon they would be freed and cared for by members of the resistance. It was a good moment for me, watching hope finally blossom in the eyes and demeanour of that close-packed group of humanity. Husbands hugged wives and adults clung to children. There were tears and shouts of gratitude. I smiled and asked them to remain calm and assured them that soon they would be free.

I had Thompson slow the train as we entered the wood, and roll to a stop. I had my men open the doors, help the prisoners down and lead them in groups to the edge of the thick woodland, where the waiting members of the resistance led them to the temporary camp. Once the train was empty, I remained on board with Thompson. I got him to slow down at a final set of points where I jumped off and ran ahead to change them to swap tracks. Once the train had passed I pushed them back again and sprinted to catch back up, fairly amazed that the trusting driver hadn't taken the opportunity to speed up and escape. I hauled myself back onto the train and returned the smile Thompson gave me.

'What happens next, Mr Shaddick? You know this is the northbound line?'

I nodded, 'Yes, thank you, Mr Thompson. I am aware of that. What happens now is that you push the lever that takes us to full speed and before the train gets too fast, we jump off.'

He grimaced, 'Not a great thing to be doing at my time of life, but never mind. On the plus side, if I don't break all my bones, Mrs Thompson might be impressed enough to shut up for a short while.' He pushed the lever forward and the train slowly began to accelerate.

As you know, Mr Thomson never made it off the train and his death hurt me far worse than the jump and ungainly roll which, for the record, seriously winded me and badly skinned my elbows and knees. Once the hideous struggle to breathe had passed and the sting from my skinned extremities had faded to a raw throb, I stood and saluted the departed train, wishing things could have been different and wondering at myself and my behaviour. Could a man really commit cold-blooded murder for a good cause? At what point does slaughter for the greater good become the greater evil?

So, in a dark and brooding frame of mind, I turned and began limping towards the camp. I exchanged words with the guard at the perimeter and made my way to the heavily camouflaged shelter set up as the HQ. Lewis, one of the previously released prisoners, was in charge, mainly as he would have more empathy towards those newly rescued. It also meant that those we had rescued today would see that there was a future to be had joining with us, which would give them hope. Moreover, it showed that I had faith in the new men and didn't just use the originals to perform the important tasks.

I checked everything was going smoothly. Lewis assured me that it was, so I took a walk around the camp, introducing myself to tired, beaten-looking souls who ate old bread with relish and cupped mugs of hot tea as if they held the Holy Grail itself. The thanks I received were quiet and effusive and as people began to realise who the man was walking amongst them, hands began to reach out and touch me. The murmur of gratitude was unending, as was the close-packed knot of people who wished to kiss my hand or my cheek. Children were lifted up to see me in the gloom and I began to feel sick. It was too much to be treated like a messiah simply because I had taken them away from the camps, too much to be treated like a hero after the acts I had committed to ensure their current safety. In my present melancholic state, with the pain from my skinned knees and the ache caused by the patch of guilt that was Mr Thompson, I found that I could not deal with their estimable regard. I shook a few hands and wished some well, told them it was nothing and retired back to the HQ shelter to get some solitude, some silence and some sleep.

I left early the next morning to attack as many targets as I could to keep attention away from this small area of woodland. Before I left, I told Lewis that once all the released prisoners had been shipped north, he was to soak the area with fuel and blow the track, making sure that the fire spread into the woodland to make the destruction seem like collateral damage. I left the camp and its refugees in the hands of him and his capable team and travelled further south to make my presence felt.

After a week of planting mines, blowing

bridges and destroying rail lines with various members of the cells, I took myself north again to return to the caverns. It was strange to hear the laughter of children echoing in the great gloomy chamber; it was a bittersweet reminder of why I was fighting. Venice greeted me with open arms, after disentangling herself from one or two of her persistent young admirers. I complimented her on a job well done. She just shrugged and gave me a kiss.

'You have done a good thing here, Fish. I am just glad you wanted me to help.'

I decided not to tell her about Thompson; there was no need to tarnish the victory for her.

The next couple of hours were spent trying to get reports from my various captains. Status reports from Harry and Jimmy, reports on current supplies and equipment from Oz, and reports on training and intelligence from Godfrey and Alex. All this I tried to do amongst a constant cacophony of thanks, and a seemingly endless number of handshakes from those we had rescued from the train.

It seems that Venice had been right: some of the women were just as eager to fight as she had suggested, and I had no hesitation in asking the training team to teach them the skills they would need. Some of the newcomers, both male and female, however, were too physically exhausted to undergo training and so they were assigned to Oz to help him with small jobs, but more importantly to look after the children and see that they played where it was safe and stayed within the confines of the cavern.

I got a meal from the kitchen, where I was served by one of the new women who gave me a smile and, with a wink, put an extra helping on my plate. I smiled back and went to find somewhere quiet where I could think unhindered for a while. I went and sat down by the lake in the rosy glow of the lights and mechanically spooned food into my mouth as I planned how to feed another five hundred mouths and also what use I could put them to. I finished eating and lay back, my hands behind my head, staring up into the blackness of the cavern roof. My thoughts were interrupted by Ven who sat down beside me. 'What you thinking, Fish?'

'Oh, you know, stuff.'

She nodded. She understood well the thoughts I had running through my mind. She leant over, kissed my forehead and looked deeply into my eyes. She held my gaze for a long time, stroked my head and jumped to her feet. 'You will think of something, Fish. You always do.'

Fairly sure that was a compliment, I grinned up at her, ‘I will try not to let you down, Ven. I have a few ideas, but nothing solid. I will talk to Jimmy later; he might be able to help me with something.’

‘Well, if there is anything I can do, Fish?’

‘Ven, you are always at the top of my list. If I need a beautiful, deadly woman for anything I will let you know.’

She smiled down at me and wandered off towards the communal area.

I got to my feet a short time later and went looking for Godfrey. He was showing a group of newcomers how to strip, clean and reassemble a rifle. He acknowledged my presence with a nod of his head and finished his demonstration before coming to talk to me.

‘Can I help, commander?’

I frowned for a second before I realised what he was doing. Hierarchy and discipline would be essential tools in our growing army. I turned towards the new recruits. ‘Do you mind if I borrow the captain for a moment?’ It was quite comical to watch them scramble to their feet and try to salute. I returned one of my own, told them that I hoped they were settling in well and to keep up the good work, before leading Godfrey off to the side.

'What's up, Danny?'

'I have been thinking, Godfrey. I think we need to make contact with the Coalition, see if we could help each other a little. If we could get some codes, Alex could keep them informed of troop movements and force build-up, that sort of thing. We could hit targets they see as a priority and maybe get some supplies and technical help by sea or something.'

Godfrey smiled and gave me his trademark approving pat on the shoulder. 'You amaze me, Danny. No training at all and you think more like an officer every day.' He laughed when I pulled a face and he continued, 'I had the same thought myself, but I have yet to come up with a workable idea for crossing the front lines, making it into friendly territory and presenting myself to the Coalition forces. It seems too dangerous and too far at present. I was hoping the tide might turn and when the frontline gets closer, try it then.'

'I don't think we can leave it that long, Godfrey. I have a sort of plan but to be honest, whilst it might be safer than sneaking across the lines, it is terrifying. Each time I try to think about it my mind runs away from the idea. I will try and get used to it and talk it over with you once I have forced it into some sort of shape. I have a more pressing matter for the present though, one I need to speak to Jimmy about. We need funds desperately: money to run the groups, money to settle people into the towns and villages and money to buy as many supplies as we dare.'

He nodded, his face grave, 'Good of you to think about the big picture, Danny. If we can send family groups out with new papers and the money to buy a house, with the story that they are relocating for whatever reason, that would be a great help. Let me know if you need any help planning.' He nodded, and for the benefit of the group behind him who were beginning to argue about what bit went where, he saluted and rejoined his recruits.

I found Jimmy sitting on a rock outcrop waving his flask expansively and counterpointing his dramatic gestures with a glowing cigarette in the other, telling stories to a group that included not just new recruits but some of the first wave of volunteers too. I realised with some sort of horror that the stories were about me. I listened from the darkness only long enough to be moderately embarrassed by his over exaggeration, before moving into the light, clapping my hands and telling people story time was over as I had things to discuss with the captain.

Jimmy took this as one last excuse to validate

his stories with his audience. 'See, the commander never stops. Always got some plan on his mind.' He raised his flask in the air, 'Death to the H.A.P.' There was some small cheering and a scatter of applause. I looked at them sternly and shook my head, before intercepting Jimmy's flask and taking a swig.

'Jimmy, if you wanted to get your hands on a lot of money, how would you go about it?'

He shrugged, 'We could rob a bank.'

'Exactly.'

His jaw dropped and he stared at me open-mouthed before throwing back his head and laughing. His laugh became a cough and he wiped his mouth and reached out to reclaim his flask. 'Always wanted to rob a bank.' He chuckled again, 'So what's the plan?'

I gestured vaguely at the large number of people in the cavern. 'Ask around. I know there are some in here with convictions, so see if you can find any with previous that will be useful. I want me, you and three others. Bring them to me when you have found them.'

I left him laughing quietly and shaking his head. I patted the lump under my shirt and went to find a private corner for some quiet contemplation and a chance to assuage the demons in my head.

HEIST

I sat with Jimmy discussing my plans a couple of days later. He assured me that he had found the right men for the job: a locksmith and two ex-convicts who had spent time in New Fold prison for breaking and entering. One of them told me that he claimed to be an expert at bypassing alarm systems. I had to be honest though, his claimed expertise when weighed against a five-year conviction did make me dubious of his boasts. However, when I quizzed them about the nature of the job, they seemed to know what they were talking about, particularly the locksmith, and as freed prisoners and newly committed members of the resistance I felt that I could trust them. They were also all I had to work with. I decided not to call them by their given names in the event that this episode could ever be used against them, particularly the locksmith, who claimed that he had never broken the law in his life. So for sake of the record, I named them Abel,

Bart and Chris.

We sat on the mountain top in the warm autumn sun, enjoying the fresh air, peace and solitude away from the busy cavern. Jimmy had his back against a tree, slowly shredding a leaf between his fingers. ‘So, Danny, how are we going to do this?’

‘I think we will try the main bank in Millfield. You know, the big mill town on the south central plain.’

‘I know it.’ He paused, ‘Ain’t there an army base nearby?’

I nodded, ‘Yup, that’s one of the reasons I want to hit that one. See if we can time it right to make off with the wages for the troops.’

He laughed, ‘Why not just intercept the truck carrying the money?’

‘I thought about that, but this way we will have more time to get away, and there will be other valuables in the vault. I’m hoping for some gems and precious metals as well.’

‘Fair enough, boss. How we goin’ to get in? Blow the safe, grab and run?’

‘Nah, I don’t want this job to be associated with our activity. We have few enough supporters on this side of the mountains, without further damaging our reputation by becoming labelled as opportunistic brigands. This has to seem like a common or garden bank job. If we could make it look like an inside job, then so much to the better.'

He snorted, 'Good luck with that! So, when are we going?'

'Well, we have ten days until the end of the month. I will travel down with Ven and have a look around, go into the bank and see what the security is like. You and the other three come down in seven days and we will take it from there.'

'Okay, boss. Sounds like a plan. Is there any kit you need me to bring down?'

I laughed, 'Jimmy, I have no idea what is needed to break into a vault. You had better ask your trio of experts; they should know what to bring. All I ask is that you keep it subtle: no striped jerseys, comedy masks or large crowbars.'

He threw a handful of shredded leaf at me. 'Gotcha. See you in a few days.'

I hadn't really planned on taking Venice with me, but the temptation of a week with only her company was too much. Anyway, I was sure that she could use some time out in civilisation, and I for one would be glad of the company.

So, travelling as husband and wife, with nice new papers that showed our commitment to the party and my occupation as a textiles manager, we decided to travel south by train. We organised a pick-up by our friendly taxi driver a few miles from the base, and were driven to Mallowdale where we caught the first-class train to Junction. The ride was quiet and uneventful, the food excellent and the company sparse. We changed at Junction and caught the train for Millfield. Our papers proved more than adequate for the task, and soon we were walking the busy streets of the large mill town.

I strolled arm in arm with the beautiful, well-dressed Venice. My eyes darted everywhere, taking in the movement of troops marching up the main street and the large warehouses full of cloth. Venice caught my attention by discreetly digging her thumb nail into my arm. 'For the love of the Saints, Fish, stop looking for targets and just enjoy the walk, will you?'

I grinned at her. I had been doing exactly that. 'Sorry, Ven.' I stopped trying to see everything and relaxed and began to enjoy the walk.

The bank was situated two-thirds of the way down the main street, sandwiched between a restaurant and a barber's shop. Almost directly across from it was a small hotel. I nodded towards it, 'How about there?'

'It looks nice, Fish. Good spot. I just hope the rooms are clean.'

We entered the foyer of the hotel, a place called The Loom. I can recommend it if you ever travel to Millfield: clean and friendly with impeccable service. It is, however, a little on the expensive side, but this was not something I was concerned with at that time as I hoped to have sufficient funds on hand to pay for our stay within the next few days.

We showed our cards and signed the hotel register, whereupon a bellboy led us up the broad wooden staircase to our room on the second floor overlooking the street. I gave him a tip, then changed my shirt as Venice showered. I tried hard to ignore her contented sighs as she relished the hot water and the perfumed soap. Then, because I loved her, I took her shopping.

A couple of times over the next week, we ate in the restaurant next to the bank, where I pretended to get lost looking for the men's room and ended up managing to get quite a good look at the backyard of the establishment.

I had an expensive haircut and a shave at the

barber's, where I exchanged idle chat with the man holding a razor to my throat. We wandered around the park and through the back streets, trying to glean as much information about our target as we could.

We entered the bank, and after a short conversation with a bespectacled officious little man at the front desk, we were granted a meeting with the bank manager. He was sitting behind a large desk, but he rose and shook our hands as we entered. He gestured to a pair of chairs and bid that we be seated.

'So, my clerk informs me that you wish to open a business account with us. Would you care to inform me as to the nature of the business?'

I nodded respectfully, 'Indeed, sir. I am in the textiles business, hence my relocation to this area. I intend to open a cloth warehouse specialising in the buying and selling of fabrics. I am particularly interested in procuring government contracts; you know, the supplying of cloth to the military outfitters and suchlike.'

He looked down at me from beneath his large eyebrows. 'Young man, it would take considerable resources to gain a foothold in that area.'

I adjusted my tone to combat his rather

patronising attitude, and I also dropped the sir. 'I have considerable resources. My parents left me a very tidy sum, and when I married Maria here I gained the backing of her family, a family who it may be conservatively suggested have vast resources at their disposal. Although we could both live comfortably on the monies we currently have, I for one have no desire to sit idle. I wish both to make my own way in this world and to aid our gallant armed forces in some manner. With this venture, I hope to be able to combine the two endeavours.' I leant forwards conspiratorially in my seat, 'It is my intention to buy my own warehouse outright as a first step. I trust your establishment would be able to store the large amount of funds I would deposit towards such an end?'

My act as the rich young man with money to burn and a powerful family behind him had the manager hooked. 'Of course, sir.'

I allowed myself a small smile at the reversal of respect, ingratiating as it was.

'My vault has the latest time lock mechanism on the door and there is a security presence on the premises at all times.'

I stood and looked down at his desk. 'Well, thank you for your time, Mr Hewitt. I look forward to doing business with you, and I shall return when my funds arrive.'

I nodded at him and turned to Venice, 'Come, my dear. We have property to inspect.'

So, with Venice on my arm looking every bit the pampered product of privilege, nose in the air I stalked out of the bank. We actually made it halfway up the street before we burst out laughing. I steered her into a nearby bar and we toasted each other's performance.

Jimmy arrived at the end of the week and met up with the other members of the team in the bar closest to the station after they had travelled down independently. I left Ven in the hotel room and went to meet with them. They were sitting around a table playing cards. I went to the bar and ordered a drink, and Jimmy leant against the bar next to me and ordered another. I engaged in some small talk with him before he invited me to join the game.

I introduced myself to the group and sat down to play, using the cover of the game to hide our previous acquaintance and to mask our conversation. I told them what I had learnt as I dealt out a fresh hand.

'There is a small yard at the back of the bank with a door with a security lock on it. Employees take their breaks there, have a coffee and a smoke. The restaurant is usually very busy, and it uses the cellar as a store. The barber's shop next door…' I looked at my cards, 'Raise you one. The barber's shop next door really only uses the ground floor. I didn't get to the cellar but it is still there; the upper floor is mainly used to store junk. I'll stick, thank you. The front door of the bank has heavy bars on it, while the vault door has a time lock and you have to get through a cage door before you can get to the vault. There is also a security guard on duty at all times.'

Abel grinned, 'The pot is mine, I believe.' He raked the tiny pile of copper coins towards himself and talked quietly, speaking around the black cigar in his mouth as I dealt another hand. 'The security guard actually makes things easier: no internal alarms, at least in the main room.' He paused a moment as we all inspected our cards. 'So, four ways in: through the roof, across from one of the cellars, or using either of the two doors.'

Chris laid down his stake, 'Two, please. There will be alarms on the door, and the cellar is a difficult option and would take too long and make too much noise. I reckon in through the back is the best bet. Last job I did, there was a small kitchen area at the back. If the guard is like most others, he won't have alarmed that if he uses it at all. Reckon there might be an alarm on the back door as well but two nails and a piece of wire will get us past that if I'm any judge.'

Abel threw his hand in, 'I have a trick for getting past those security locks. I will need to use a light for a short while tho.'

I nodded and raised my stake, 'Bart? You think you can get through the locks?'

Bart spent a moment sorting his hand, 'I can get through anything given time. The metal cage door will only take a minute, the time lock will take a few hours. I have all the kit I need: diamond bits, acid, picks and stethoscope. If we can keep it quiet and have enough time, we will get in.'

'Good enough. I will raise and see you.'

We spent the next three hours playing cards. I asked Jimmy to meet me in the park at lunchtime the next day and told the others that I would look forward to seeing them again at 10pm in two days' time.

Venice and I went for a stroll in the park after an early lunch the next day. We sat on a bench and enjoyed the scenery, before Jimmy, wearing a ubiquitous pair of overalls, came and sat on the same bench, where he pretended to read the paper. I spoke to him without turning my head.

'Jimmy, I need you to find some transport. Have a look around some of these warehouses; they all have trucks. See if you can find a loading bay with poor security. Your job will be to steal a truck – a canvas-sided one would be best, so that we can get in through the side of it without being seen. Use it to block the front door of the bank from view, and in five seconds we should be on our way. Park in front of the bank at half past three. We should be done well before that, but if we are not I will circle a light in the window. Give it half an hour and try again, only park at the back the second time.'

'Okay, boss. Got it.'

We left him to his paper and resumed our walk. Venice was to be my alibi. I wanted her to go down to the front desk in the middle of the night and request some indigestion medication for her husband, who was having trouble with his stomach. She would be able to check that no unusual activity was taking place and also explain my absence at breakfast if I was delayed in returning for whatever reason.

I made a point of retiring to bed early the next night, leaving Venice to entertain herself at the hotel bar and demurely decline the advances of a number of fellow guests who had been taken with her beauty and no doubt wished to entertain her for the evening with her husband so conveniently indisposed. At half past nine I changed into my dark slim-fitting clothing. I finished my outfit with a light overcoat and a hat that shadowed my features. Loathe as I was to do so, I left Harvey in my suitcase, but not before I had kissed his furry head and whispered my oft-repeated mantra, 'I'm on my way, little brother.'

I opened the window and climbed down the fire escape. I lowered myself by my arms and jumped the last fifteen feet. I hid a rope and hook behind some rubbish for my return and sidled into the street. As you may imagine in a busy mill town with a local base, it was extremely busy at this time of night, so I headed towards the park. When I was fairly sure that I was unobserved by anyone in an official capacity, I walked confidently down the narrow road that serviced the backyards of the establishments on the main road. Once on the roadway, I took off my coat and hat, rolled them up and stuffed them in a bin.

As I reached the backyard of the bank, the gate opened a fraction and a hand waved me in. Abel, Bart and Chris were already there, waiting in the shadows cast by the wall. I looked at my watch, pulled up my mask and gave them the signal to begin our robbery. I watched Chris slowly examine the door, the door frame and the wall around the door. He pulled on a pair of rubber gloves and slowly, using a rubber hammer, knocked two nails into a part of the frame I could not distinguish from the rest. Once the nails were in place, he carefully wrapped a wire around them, joining them together, and stood back. He gestured at Abel, who pulled out a torch. Shielding himself and his torch from view like an early photographer, he quickly inspected the key pad on the lock by the door handle. After a long minute or so he switched off the torch, stood up and punched four numbers on the pad. Moving with care he leant down and whispered in my ear, 'Open, boss.'

Although I realised the need for quiet, I couldn't help but ask, 'How did you do that?'

He was probably smiling under his mask, it is hard to say, but in his place I think I would have been. 'Look for the four dirty numbers, press the dirtiest first and the cleanest last, then like magic we are in.'

I patted him on the shoulder, readied my pistol and gestured at Bart to open the door. I signalled to leave it ten seconds before they followed and crept inside the bank.

There was, as predicted, a small kitchen area on the other side of the door, with the door to the main room of the bank directly opposite. I had a slight quandary as I waited for the others to join me: do I wait for the guard to come and get some refreshment before subduing him, or try and get him in the main room before he can raise the alarm? Time was of the essence and so I thought direct action was preferable, despite the increased risks. I had noted from my visit to the bank that the security desk faced the main door, so with luck on my side I would be able to overwhelm the guard before he could activate any alarm.

With the others silent behind me, I eased open the door and crept into the bank. My worries proved to be unfounded: the overweight middle-aged guard was asleep at his desk, chin resting on his chest, his hands clasped together on his rounded stomach. I reversed the grip on my pistol and with four quick steps, crossed the space between us and brought the pistol butt down hard at the base off his skull. He slumped to one side, and checking that he was still breathing, Chris and I tied him up, bound and gagged him and left him sitting in his chair. I pulled the chair backwards into empty space so no amount of thrashing against his bonds could trigger the alarm button under the desk.

I gestured to Bart. He unrolled a set of tools and began to work on the lock of the cage. It took him only moments to get past the lock, open the gate and head down the stairs to begin examining the lock on the vault door. He studied it for a few minutes and came over to talk to me. 'Best guess, boss, just over four hours to get in.'

I looked at my watch, 'Works for me, Bart. Let's get on with it.'

He set to, assisted by Chris as Abel and I wandered around the bank. I spent a while looking through the files of some of the bank's customers, more out of interest than anything else. They did give me some idea as to which customers might have the most in their safety deposit boxes. I discovered one belonging to a major general, who it appeared had some financial problems with over-investment in property. I decided on a whim to leave his safety deposit box untouched. A little obvious misdirection to be sure, but I will try anything to sow the seed of suspicion amongst the enemy.

I assigned Abel to watch the front of the building and went to make us all a cup of tea, making sure when I had finished to leave evidence of only one intruder. Then with nothing more to do,

I sat and waited, and then I sat and waited some more, fretting at the time and chewing at my nails.

Periodically I went and checked on the progress the other two were making. Each time I got a reassuring nod from Bart and I returned to my chair.

I was sitting staring into space, my mind on other things, when Bart called out softly, ‘We are in.’ Anxious and excited, I went to join them at the vault. There was a large stack of notes, which I ordered to be bagged up and made ready for transport.

‘Don’t take more than you can carry in one trip, lads. Get high-value notes and some good stuff out of the safety deposit boxes.’ I gestured to Bart, ‘We take what we can carry, then it’s out of the door and into the truck and away. Don’t get greedy; greed will get us killed. I don’t mind you putting some in your pockets, but again don’t get greedy. Having big rolls of cash stuffed into your pockets will be a bit of a give-away when you are trying to escape.’

I put a roll of notes in my own pocket and pointed out to Bart the boxes which were most likely to have the good stuff in. I watched him pop them open with quick manipulation of his picks. He was good at his job and we soon had a nice collection of precious metals and cut stones that I wrapped and put into a bag. I entrusted him with these items and began carrying sacks of money to the door ready for our pick-up.

We could manage two bags in each hand, and as Jimmy drew up right on time I slid the bolts on the door, picked up my loot and followed the others to the side of the truck. I heaved my load in behind them, shut the bank door and gave the thumbs-up to Jimmy. He drove off, nice and steadily so as not to arouse too much attention. Smiling with satisfaction at a job well done, I hurried across the road, retrieved my rope and was soon back in my room, climbing into the warm bed where I was elbowed away by Venice for being too cold.

I awoke early and stood by the window, waiting for a convenient outbound truck to pass beneath me, whereupon I threw my clothing and tools from the night before into the back of it. Satisfied that I had disposed of any evidence linking me with the bank robbery, a crime which for the time remained undiscovered, I went for a shower and prepared for breakfast.

We were sitting at our table eating a rather pleasant relaxed meal when the door opened and a group of civilian police accompanied by soldiers entered the hotel. They crossed immediately to the reception desk and demanded to see the register.

In due course we were all interviewed and our rooms searched. The night receptionist confirmed our story of my early retirement in the evening and of Venice's request for some stomach medicine for her distressed husband. No evidence was found, and the one witness statement of a truck stopping briefly outside the bank did lead to the report of a truck being stolen from a warehouse the same night. The truck was found abandoned some fifteen miles outside the town, and although a number of suspects were brought in for questioning, none of those involved were ever caught.

We stayed in the hotel for a couple more days, enjoying the comforts and fine foods before heading back via train and taxi to return to the caverns.

Abel disappeared with his share of the loot. I was furious with his breach of trust, and I asked Jimmy to select a couple of men and go to find him. Just over a week later, Jimmy returned. I did not ask him specifics, nor did I ask where Abel had fled to, but Jimmy did hand over the majority of the cash and valuables. Along with a box containing Abel's head. I had warned them all that greed would get them killed.

Contact

We now had recruits, papers and funds, but the issue of establishing contact with the Coalition was becoming increasingly pressing. As I mentioned to Godfrey before, I had formulated and discarded a number of plans to get across the front line and make contact with those I hoped would become our allies. The one plan I had in my mind that would not go away scared me in the extreme, and to think about it for too long made me nervous, although this fact in itself somehow only served to reassure me that it was the most workable plan. But, oh gods, did it fill me with dread.

The time, however, could not be put off much longer. Winter would soon be upon us, and if I could organise a supply line with the Coalition for a number of the things we needed such as medicines, winter clothing and weapons, our lives would become an awful lot easier. I also hoped to establish contact soon so that our forces could do what we could to blunt the impact of any spring offensive.

I gathered my friends and advisers about me one evening in the cavern and told them my plan. I expected Ven to be the most vociferous in her objections, given her past, but she just smiled and shook her head in amusement. Oz regarded me tight-lipped, Harry looked astonished, Godfrey nodded wisely and Jimmy fell off his rock laughing.

My basic plan was this: somehow hide aboard an aeroplane and force it to land on the Coalition side of the lines. I would get to speak directly to the Coalition, and they would capture a weapon that could prove vital to their war effort.

There were to my knowledge three main forward air bases serving the front line, situated on the south side of the Jeral Mountains, a base each to the east, west and centre. They provided machines for various duties along the front, which by this time was some eighty miles north of the mountains and creeping steadily further north despite some strong defence from the Coalition.

The central base, some fifteen miles east of Westridge, was chosen as my target, due mainly to its proximity and my excellent local knowledge. I spent three days and nights lying on frozen ground staring at the base through field glasses, observing the comings and goings of men and vehicles. I watched a number of aeroplanes lumber along a flat stretch of ground and climb unsteadily into the air. Each and every time I watched one of these flimsy-looking machines claw its way into the sky, I winced and cold sweat prickled along the length of my spine. But this was nothing compared to the stomach-lurching fear that gripped me when I saw one of the bloody things land. They would bounce and skid and turn when their wheels touched the ground; I even witnessed one flip over during a particularly bad landing. So in truth, although I spent those three days and nights lying in the freezing temperatures of late autumn watching the air base, I spent most of my time trying to work out alternative ways of getting across the front lines. I failed. There were none that I could see, or at least none with better chances of success. So, Mrs Shaddick's eldest boy was going to fly.

I discussed my findings back at the cavern with Godfrey and Alex. There were two men in most of the aeroplanes and it was Alex who surmised that one of them was probably a navigator and gunner whilst the other piloted the craft. That was the key, I suppose, that made the whole mad plan workable. I had intended to hide aboard and force the pilot to land at a place of my choosing, but it occurred to me that whilst I could never pretend to fly a plane, I could at least pretend to be a navigator.

I discussed the issues with Godfrey and Alex for a number of hours, trying to look at the problem from as many angles as possible, before I hit upon the solution. ‘Alex? Thorncross, the village next to the air base, do we have a safe house there?’

He nodded in the dim light of the cavern, ‘Yes, it’s the pub called The Goat, run by Peter Sherran, a sympathiser of ours.’

‘That works even better.’ I paused for a moment, thinking. ‘Can you get a man over there and see if Peter can put up two visitors for a couple of weeks: his niece from Junction and her friend? They are just visiting for a while; it seems they both have a thing for airmen. Tell him they can both help out in the bar and will be no trouble.’

Alex smiled at me and shook his head. ‘I can never fathom how your mind works, Danny. You pick a straight path and then follow the most winding route to get there. I will go myself tomorrow. Do these two lucky girls know they have volunteered yet?’

I grinned at him, ‘They will soon, Al.’

‘Who have you chosen, Danny?’

‘Why, only the two prettiest: Ven and Hannah!’

‘Does Jimmy know that you intend to use

Hannah on this mission? He has got a bit fond of her and her little boy.'

'Don't worry, Al, I will ask him; in fact, that's my next job. Come and find me when you get back tomorrow and let me know any other details we need to iron out.'

He saluted in the gloom and walked off.

I collected a cup of tea from one of the girls in the kitchen area, and once again was left feeling embarrassed and a little ashamed at the attention I received from the people working in the canteen. I mumbled my thanks and left in search of Jimmy. He was down at the generator, showing a couple of teenage boys how to maintain and operate his device, pointing out grease points and tension brackets with his wrench.

'Captain, a moment please.'

He smiled at me, 'Commander, what can I do for you?'

I beckoned him with a nod of my head in the direction of the shore line. We walked into the quieter and darker part of the cavern, up towards the washing area, sidestepping some children trying to spear fish from the black water.

'Jimmy, I want to send Hannah on an

information-gathering mission.'

He looked at me for a moment, and pointed at me with his wrench, his voice strangely tight when he spoke. 'Don't you dare put her in any danger, Danny. Don't you dare use her up.'

I looked back at him for a long moment, and to be honest I felt my anger grow. 'I ask out of courtesy, Jimmy. I know she will say yes if I ask; I know she feels she has a debt to me. I don't feel she has, but that is not the point. The point is, I am asking as a friend. She will be going with Ven to work in a pub for a couple of weeks, to try and wring some information from some pilots. It is a crucial assignment, Jim, one that no number of men could ever achieve.' I paused. 'Anyway,' I stabbed him in the shoulder with my finger, 'now you know how I feel each and every time Venice goes out on an assignment or a mission.'

His shoulders slumped and he nodded. 'Aye, fair enough, Danny.' He held out his hand for me to shake, 'Thanks for asking, boss.'

I pulled him into a brief hug, 'I will make sure she is looked after, Jimmy. It's nice to see you happy sober as well as half cut. Bring her over to my desk in a short while. I have to go and speak to Ven.'

He grinned and nodded at me, 'Okay, boss.'

I made my way over to the planning area, collecting Venice from the small group of women sitting around her. She was teaching something about sight compensation, not sure what it was but it certainly went over my head. I sat down with her at my desk and talked about her progress with her sniper group. I gestured towards William hovering in the shadows a short distance away, 'Have you allocated guards to the rest of the girls?'

She smiled that radiant smile of hers, 'One or two, Fish. I'm sure the rest will be selected before we need to undertake any action.' She paused and looked at me, her head tilted gently to the side. 'You need to rest more, Fish; you're looking tired.'

I shrugged, a common action for me at that time it seemed. 'One of these days, Ven, I promise I will relax. Until then, it seems there is always something to do.'

She reached across the table and squeezed my hand. We sat there like that, just looking at each other, until Hannah arrived. Pretty Hannah, with her honey blonde hair and deep brown eyes that always seemed to see everything and understand even more.

The father of her little boy had been killed

during their captivity. She had survived all the horrible things she had been forced to endure, and now it seemed as if she had been with us from the start. Jimmy in particular had been drawn to her and, from what I could tell, the feeling had been entirely mutual, and each had found something within the other that complemented and completed them. She smiled at me as she sat down and gave Ven a sisterly kiss on the cheek. I smiled back at them and began to discuss my latest plan.

The plan essentially consisted of waiting for the go-ahead from Alex, and then the two of them were to go and stay at The Goat for a couple of weeks, fraternise with the airmen drinking in the bar and get as much information from them as possible, such as the terminology they used, ranks, routines and flights. 'You know the sort of thing: anything that could help me pass as a navigator for a day or two. You know the score: flirt, promise and tease them until they tell you anything. Are you both okay with this?'

They both nodded.

'Excellent and thank you. When Alex gets back tomorrow, go and see him. Get any additional information you need and then go to see Godfrey to work out your back story and get the proper paperwork organised.' I stood and kissed Venice,

'Now I have to go and see Oz. You two go and pack.'

Alex returned the next day. It seemed that Peter was more than willing to play host to two beautiful women for a week or two. Alex also told me that new replacements came through the village before heading on to the base, and often stayed over at the pub if they arrived early. This information was crucial, and I thanked Alex for his efforts as the subconscious part of my brain that seemed to do all the work started planning my maiden flight. I went to see the girls off and walked them down to the pick-up point. I held Ven close and we shared a long kiss. I smiled my thanks at Hannah before waving them off and trudging back to the cavern entrance.

My next couple of weeks were spent with Oz and Godfrey, organising our winter routine. Many patrols and our lookout on the top of the mountain would have to be curtailed, as evidence of our passing would be far too difficult to erase. To this end, I gave Jimmy and Ferret permission to attack a supply train and make off with as many goods as possible. I could only hope that it would be a short winter – three hundred people take a lot of feeding and keeping busy. I also assumed that the ski lodge would be occupied again, although whether by civilians or the military I couldn't venture a guess.

After a fortnight of organising the winter protocols and worrying over Venice and Hannah, not to mention my forthcoming flight, I wrapped myself up warm in the morning before dawn, picked up both my military and civilian sets of false papers and set off to Thorncross.

It was a fairly long, brisk walk to the pub at Thorncross, but I enjoyed being outside and I was looking forward to seeing Venice again. I had to hide off the road twice to avoid troop trucks, but in the crisp cold air I could hear them coming from miles away. It was late afternoon when I arrived at my destination. The obligatory guards on the road into the village scarcely glanced at my papers, which stated that I was an engineer, and they waved me through. I asked them where there might be a pub or inn I could stay at for a few days and they obligingly waved me towards the centre of the town. I thanked them and continued on my way, making sure to seem as though I was a first-time visitor to the place.

There was no small blue toy in the upstairs window of the pub, and so I assumed that there might be members of the H.A.P. inside. Not really expecting otherwise, I opened the door and walked inside. I was greeted by a wash of heat and noise.

There was a large fire burning in the fireplace, and tables crowded with members of the military, eating and drinking and seemingly having a 'who can be the loudest' competition.

Sitting on the lap of an airman, one arm around his neck, the other holding a drink, was Venice. I swallowed the bitter taste in my mouth and the urge to start killing people and walked to the bar. I know that she saw me, but her performance was flawless and she gave no indication at all that she had seen me enter.

Hannah was standing behind the bar, and she greeted me as she would any other stranger.

'Hello, sir. What can I get you?'

'Beer, something to eat and a room, please.'

'I can do you the beer, and it's stew with bread on the menu, but I'm afraid we are booked up with off- duty airmen at the moment, sir, so we have no rooms free.'

I swore in a manner that might have been expected from a disappointed customer. 'Food and beer it will have to be, then.' I paid the bill and took a sip of my beer.

'If you find yourself a seat, sir, I will bring your food over.' I nodded my thanks and went to sit at an empty table at the far end of the main room, away from the fireside where Ven was flirting with two men in uniform.

I was halfway down my beer, letting my eyes wander over some of the old pictures on the walls and trying to quell my jealousy, when Hannah arrived with my food. I have to say that I was very impressed with her professionalism; there was not even the slightest hint of familiarity in her behaviour that might have indicated we already knew each other. She placed my food on the table, laid out my cutlery and handed me a folded piece of paper. 'Your receipt, sir.'

I nodded my thanks and slid the paper into my pocket. The food was good, and I was hungry from my walk. I finished my beer, caught Hannah's eye and waved my empty glass at her. She brought me another and I took out some tobacco to roll a cigarette to have with my drink. I used the small piece of paper she had given me instead of a cigarette paper in order to read the message she had written before setting it on fire. It read: go around the back and I will let you in when I see you leave.

I made my way to the bar and ordered another beer. I paid and asked Peter, the landlord, if he knew of any other places I might find some accommodation that evening. He directed me to a small guest house on the far side of the village that might have a free room. I thanked him and left.

I shut the door of the pub behind me, and waiting a moment to ensure that I remained unobserved, I walked quickly around the building, through the small gate at the rear and stood waiting at the back door. I was there less than a minute before the door opened. I slid inside.

'Second door on the left at the top of the stairs. Wait there.'

I nodded, went up the stairs as quietly as I could manage, and hurried through the second door on the left.

It was clearly the room the girls were sharing. I cleared a space on the bed to sit down, took off my shoes, placed Harvey on the pillow and lay down to wait. After a long walk and a few beers the inevitable happened and I drifted off into a gentle sleep in the sweet-smelling room.

I was woken a few hours later by warm lips on mine as Venice kissed me. My eyes opened and my gaze locked with hers. The kiss became longer and more passionate until she slapped me on the shoulder and pulled away.

'Missed you, Fish.'

'Missed you too, Ven.'

The door opened and Hannah entered wearing nothing but a towel after having clearly just showered. I grinned, 'Must be my lucky night.'

Venice tapped me on the nose, 'In your dreams, Fish.'

I love Venice, I truly do, but making me turn and face the wall as Hannah put on her nightdress was cruel. Also cruel and very distracting was the briefing they both gave me later – two beautiful women sitting side by side on the bed, wearing nightdresses as they told me of the information they had gathered, each comparing and contrasting various facts. They worked brilliantly as a team and complemented each other superbly, yet my mind kept wandering and I had to ask them to repeat a salient fact on more than one occasion.

The information they had gathered between them was astounding. It seems I was not the only man to find it impossible to try and impress a pretty girl. They had a long list of terms and slang the airmen used, as well as having gained rudimentary knowledge of how to plot a flight path and navigate from a keen airman, who seemed among the many who had volunteered information for a winning smile and a little attention. Also of great importance was the information that in the next week or so new replacements from around the country were coming to the airbase. I ended the briefing with raised hands, telling my lovely spies that that was enough information for now, and that I needed to sleep on everything I had learnt. I had to share one of the single beds with Ven. It was tight and we were close but I, for one, would ever be the last to complain about that.

The next week was one spent mostly in boredom. I passed the time learning the terminology used by the air force navigators as well as trying to gain enough proficiency with a protractor and set of compasses to plot a course on a map so that I didn't look like a complete novice if anyone saw me using these tools. As for the rest of the time, I remained hidden in the room. My meals were brought up either by the landlord or one of the girls. The only highlight of my time spent in that small room was the warm nights I spent entwined with Venice in the small bed.

The girls continued to work in the pub and to flirt outrageously with several of the airmen with whom they had become firm favourites. I waited with growing impatience for the replacements to arrive and for the rest of my plan to take shape.

I hated the wait. I was terrified at the thought of

flying, and the waiting and the silence of that small room played on my fears. I was desperate to be actually doing something, and by the time the replacement airmen arrived I was wired tight with nerves and frustration. Peter was under orders to give free drinks to the new airmen. They were to show their papers to prove that they were pilots or navigators in order to receive their free drinks, thus giving the girls the opportunity to select the appropriate victim. Since the new men were arriving from different parts of the country, I expected them to come in singularly or in small groups. My orders to the girls were that as soon as a navigator about my size entered alone, he was to be lured up to the girls' room before he could mingle with and introduce himself to the other aircrew. Once he arrived in the room I would swap places with him and head over to the airbase in the morning.

For two hours I waited for the girls to select the most likely victim. Two long hours in a delicately feminine room with my tie taut between my hands, which were clenching and unclenching as I waited for something to happen. Eventually, when I had almost convinced myself that tonight would pass without event, I heard Venice speaking on the stairs.

'No not that one, the second door on the left. Go in and make yourself comfortable, I just need to go to the ladies room.'

I moved quickly to the wall where I would be hidden when the door opened, and waited. The airman entered and I saw him look around the room. I pushed the door shut with my heel and slipped my tie over his head and around his neck, kicking the back of his knees to force him to the floor, where I slowly choked the life out of him. I was indifferent to his struggles and his choking gasps as his feet kicked quietly on the floor and his fingers clawed ineffectually at the back of my hands. His struggles slowed and then stopped, and I hung on for a minute or so more just to make sure that no more breath remained in his body. Venice entered quietly and together we stripped him of his clothing and dressed him in a set of mine. I put my papers in his pocket and changed into his uniform. I cautioned Ven to wait for an hour before she went downstairs, and to claim that the man was resting to get his strength back if anyone asked where he was. In the meantime, I filled in my papers with the name of the airman and made sure that his movement papers were in order and that he was in fact due to report to the air base in the morning.

I gave Venice a quick kiss before she went downstairs, and shut the door behind her again. I opened the window and manhandled the body out of the window so that it dropped quietly into the backyard. I then crept down the stairs, shouldered the body and, keeping to the shadows, made my way to the outskirts of the village, where I brutally obscured the facial features with a handy rock before partially hiding the body from casual observation with some branches and a bit of dirt. I sneaked back to the pub, loitering in the shadows until the place closed, then I crept back upstairs to the room. I washed, joined Venice in the small bed and had a restless night's sleep waiting for the morning.

Shortly after the sun rose, I picked up the kit bag, placed Harvey inside and prepared myself for the next chapter in my foolish venture. I thanked Hannah for her help and said a very obvious goodbye to Venice at the front door of the pub. The hug she gave me was fierce and the kiss passionate.

'Take care flying, Fish.'

I held her at arm's length, and smiled warmly at her, trying to conceal my fear. 'I will, Ven, I promise. I'm not sure how long it will be until I see you again, but I will return, you can count on it.' I kissed her again, 'Remember, when it snows, no one goes outside unless absolutely necessary.' I paused and looked around, 'Well, I suppose I had better get going. Love you, Ven.'

She smiled in reply and I swung the kit bag over my shoulder, waved a cheery goodbye and marched towards the air base.

My papers passed scrutiny, and I was shown to a barracks block. All the men in there were navigators. I gathered from the conversations that the navigator was also responsible for dropping any bombs that the aircraft carried, as well as using a mounted machine gun to strafe enemy troops. None of this worried me; once I was in the air my subterfuge no longer mattered.

The new men were paired up, pilots with navigators and navigators with pilots. I was introduced to my pilot, a man called Theodore. We shook hands and ironically he invited me to go for a drink at the local pub. It was a strange evening. I spoke to Ven as her conquest from the night before and was sharply rebuffed when I asked for a repeat, which made the men I was drinking with laugh. At some point towards the end of the night I proposed a toast to the glorious forces of the H.A.P., and arm in arm with Theodore we staggered back to the barracks where I learnt to sing some rude military songs.

I attended a familiarisation briefing to be shown a map of the surrounding area, the mountains and the region around the front line. This was followed by a briefing on the weather patterns in this part of the world, before I was informed that I would be undertaking a reconnaissance flight with my pilot at six in the morning.

I hardly need to mention how little sleep I got that night. But at five I was in the mess eating my breakfast, with Harvey tucked into my flight jacket. I attended another briefing about the weather and cloud cover, before donning my flying helmet and scarf and walking towards the aircraft as fear-induced sweat began to prickle my brow.

My time spent observing the airbase proved to be useful as I had watched men clamber in and out of these craft, so although I had never actually done it before I knew where to place my feet. I also knew enough to get into the rear seat; if I had not, the mistake would clearly have given the game away.

I plugged in my radio set to communicate with the pilot as I tried desperately to familiarise myself with the cockpit. I had no idea what most of the buttons, switches and levers did, so I opted to leave them alone for the moment. The only switches that really caught my eye were the three polished metal ones in front of me that were labelled bomb release. At the enquiry from the pilot, I answered in the affirmative, and leant forward and tapped him twice on the shoulder, as I had seen men do as I watched through my binoculars. The plane roared as the engine started and all was obscured in a pall of black smoke for a moment, as the plane turned and began to pick up speed.

I patted Harvey for luck and closed my eyes. I never even noticed when we left the ground, and I almost lost my breakfast when I opened my eyes and realised that we were some one hundred feet up in the air. I heard Theodore's voice in my headset, 'Don't worry about navigating to the front, I know the way. You can navigate on the way back. Just sit back and enjoy the ride.' I smiled to myself despite my bone-deep fear. Navigating back was not going to be an issue.

'Roger,' I replied, remembering after a pause to answer him, 'Be obliged if you could point out some landmarks.'

To his credit, he did so as we climbed higher and higher until the top peaks of the Jerals were below us. I spotted the peak where we had our lookout and had to restrain the urge to wave. I found with some surprise that I was actually quite enjoying myself and began to try to work out the best way of forcing the pilot to land on the Coalition side of the front line, while at the same time avoiding thinking about the landing.

We flew over the mountains and dropped lower

as the ground levelled out. I began to see formations of troops, columns of trucks and units of armoured vehicles, and decided to jot down on my note pad numbers and positions of enemy forces as we passed.

After nearly an hour of flight, the pilot pointed out that we were close to the front line. I peered at the grand horizon and saw that about five miles in front of us were flashes of explosions and the climbing black smoke from burning vehicles. The ground below us was churned to mud and pocked with dug-in fighting positions and shell craters.

I realised suddenly how I could make the pilot land on the far side of the front line and began to smile to myself. We were flying along the main supply road to the front, a road dug and maintained by units of troops with picks and shovels as they made the road passable for trucks and tanks. I knelt in the firing position behind the machine gun and flipped the switch to talk to the pilot. ‘Can you hear me, Theo?’

‘I can but you are supposed to use my call sign, idiot.’ He sounded annoyed.

‘Fuck your call sign, pilot. I want you to find a clear area well behind the Coalition lines and land there.’

'Are you mad? What on earth makes you think I am going to do that?'

He couldn't see my grin as I answered him with a simple 'This.' I reached out and flipped the bomb release switches one after the other as we passed over a line of tanks, which erupted into blooms of flame in our wake. I then opened up with the machine gun, spraying fire into lines of troops on either side of the road, mowing them down like falling wheat as they were slow to react to the attack from one of their own aircraft. I paused in my firing as the pilot tried to veer away from the road.

'Firing squad or prison of war camp, Theo. Your choice.'

'Are you fucking mad, you traitor?' He screamed, 'What the hell are you doing?'

'I'm a Coalition soldier – death or prison, your call.'

'What if I decide to take my chances with a court martial, tell them it was entirely your fault?'

'Well, you can take your chances with the friends of the men I just killed, or I can kill you before you land, otherwise. And anyway, I will just lie and make sure you are executed. Now land this bloody machine on Coalition territory or die.'

He saw sense quite quickly after that and flew over the lines for an hour at quite a high altitude to prevent us being shot down, before spotting a long green lawn in front of a large stately house, whereupon he did a remarkably neat landing that impressed even me.

The look he gave me as we clambered out of the plane was not a pleasant one, and if I hadn't relieved him of his pistol I have no doubt that he would have used it on me. Khaki-clad soldiers were running across the lawn to us at this point, and I walked towards them with a big smile on my face, waving. As the first of them reached me, I did not expect to be greeted with a rifle butt across the face and I collapsed senseless to the ground.

I regained my faculties in a small grey cell, stripped to my underwear and covered with a thin blanket. The entire left side of my face was swollen and sore. Moving my jaw made popping noises and caused pain to shoot up the side of my face. I had been left with water in an enamel bowl. I sipped some to relieve my thirst, although it took me several attempts to find a method whereby I could drink, and not drool it back into the bowl. I then soaked a corner of my blanket and used it to clean and cool the damaged side of my face. After a few minutes, despite a rather shocking headache, I was able to regain my feet and start pounding on the cell door.

A hatch in the door opened and a pair of eyes regarded me for a moment, before a bolt was noisily slid back and the door flung open. Two guards with pistols in hand stood before me. Even if escape had been on my agenda, I would not have fancied my chances against these two. 'Turn around, present your hands.'

I did as ordered and felt the cool metal of handcuffs encircle my wrists. I was led down a corridor lit by flickering lights, up a set of stairs and into another room. Here I was persuaded to sit in a chair that faced a similar one across a desk. My left hand was freed and my right attached to the arm of the chair. One of the guards left whilst the other stood behind and slightly to my right. The door opened and a bespectacled young officer entered, followed by a large soldier carrying several of the items I had had about my person when I landed. I have to admit I could not contain my forward lurch as he placed Harvey on the table in front of me, just out of my reach. The officer noticed, raised his eyebrow a little, but said nothing.

He sat down and organised his papers before him. 'Would you like a cup of tea?' Aware that this was some sort of highly unnecessary softening-up process, I grinned as well as my damaged face would allow and nodded. The large soldier stuck his head out of the room and less than a minute later a paper cup containing tea was placed before me.

I took a sip. 'How long was I out?'

He answered my question with another: 'Name?'

Refusing to play his silly game, and wanting to volunteer information instead of conceal it, I started talking, almost too fast for him to make notes.

'Daniel Shaddick, commander of the partisan unit working south of the Jeral Mountains. I'm here to make contact with your high command. I wish to coordinate our efforts with yours. I also need a couple of experts and some communications gear. I captured that aircraft to get here, and as I am a nice person you may have it as a gift.' I sat back and drank my tea, amused by the startled look on his face.

He took a moment to regain his composure, 'Your identification would suggest otherwise.'

I shrugged with one arm, 'It's fake.'

He held up my note pad, 'What are these numbers, positions and directions?'

'Those are another present for you. They are the

troop, truck and armour concentrations I saw as we were flying here.'

'We?'

'Me and the pilot I forced to land at gunpoint.'

He held up Harvey, 'This?'

'That belongs to my little brother. I have to get it back to him.'

He placed Harvey down again, and nodded. He beckoned to the large soldier behind him, who leant down to receive a whispered command in his ear. He left the room.

I sat back drinking my tea, and was just swirling the last few dregs around the bottom of the cup when the door opened again. The large soldier entered bearing another chair. He placed it down and stood back to let another officer enter. This one was clearly of high rank. He radiated calm assurance and was definitely used to being obeyed. He sat down and read through the notes the other officer had made. The first thing he did was to hand my notebook to the large soldier, with orders to take it to Intelligence for assessment and to pass it on to artillery as soon as any of it was verified. That done, he turned to me and introduced himself as Colonel Patterson.

'Well, young man, this is quite a strange tale you tell. I must admit I will feel somewhat happier about the veracity of your claims if and when Intelligence can verify the targets you have located for us. Your manner of entrance was unorthodox to say the least, yet you have to know that at the moment I don't accept your story and you are going to have to do a lot more talking for me to start believing you. Now, you should be aware that we do have some sources within the H.A.P. and we are aware of some significant partisan activity on the other side of the mountains, so what you tell me will be cross- referenced with what we already know. So start talking.'

So I talked. I told him everything about our efforts, about the raids we had conducted, the prisoners rescued and most of all I told him the story about my brother. He listened carefully as the junior officer wrote it all down, and paused my monologue just once to ask me a couple of questions when I mentioned Godfrey.

They took me back to my cell when I had finished talking. There was a hot meal and a large mug of tea waiting for me, along with a khaki uniform. I sat on the bunk wrapped in my blanket and ate before I dressed. After I put on the uniform, I lay back on the bunk and waited. After a couple of hours the door to my cell opened again. I stood and into the room strode Colonel Patterson. He held out his hand to me and I took it, and nearly had my arm dislocated by the hearty handshake I received.

'I must say, Daniel, your story pushes the bounds of credulity at times. However, I do believe that I have the pleasure of meeting the thus far unknown man responsible for all the havoc that is being wreaked upon our mutual enemies on the south side of the mountains. Come. Follow me.'

He took me up several flights of stairs until we entered a comfortable study somewhere within the grand building. At his insistence I settled into a sumptuous leather chair in the book-lined room. He pressed a large glass of brandy into my hand and offered me a cigar; naturally I took one. I lit it, took a sip of the remarkably fine brandy, and decided to venture a question of my own.

'Colonel, what happened to the pilot I forced to bring me here?'

He waved dismissively with his cigar, 'Already off to a camp, young man. I must say, his absolute loathing of you is one of the factors that made us take your story seriously. I doubt even the greatest of men ever to grace the theatre could fake that amount of hatred.' He smiled, 'We have been hoping to make contact with your group for some time now. We did entertain the idea of sending a couple of long-range insertion groups to that effect; however, we had no idea where to find you. So, Mr Shaddick, what is it you require from the conventional army?'

I saluted him with my glass, 'Well, sir, firstly I intended to establish contact so that we could liaise with the view of making a coordinated effort. We also need a couple of experts with communication equipment and a secure means of communication in order to do that, and some small pieces of specialist equipment such as fuses and timers. Ammunition and food are always a problem too, as we have to take both off the H.A.P., but obviously the act of taking them creates something of a diminishing return.'

He nodded, reached out and picked up a telephone. He spoke rapidly into it for a moment and settled back. 'The Intelligence section are working on solving those issues now. So, do you have any other observations from the field that we would find useful?'

I thought for a few minutes, sipping my brandy and letting the smoke from my cigar curl down my nose. I was about to answer in the negative when something occurred to me. 'Have you encountered the clone troops?'

He nodded slowly, 'Yes, we have. Something of a menace really. Totally committed soldiers who carry out orders with no heed to the preservation of their own lives. Fanatical fighters who come at us in waves and have to be shot in droves to blunt the attack.'

'We captured one early on at the start of the war. Still got him, in fact.'

'Really?' He raised his eyebrows, 'I imagine you have to keep him under constant guard. However have you managed to contain a remorseless fanatical soldier like that?'

'One of my men worked out how to break his conditioning. He now fetches and carries for our intelligence section.'

He took a pull at his cigar, 'We have had a number of experts working in that particular field with several captured subjects. Thus far nothing they have tried has met with any long-term success. In fact, each of the subjects had to be terminated after a while, due to their entirely intractable nature. I would consider it another remarkable gift, along with the aeroplane and the work you have been doing, if you could enlighten me as to how you perform this scientific feat.'

I grinned at him and held up my glass. ‘Not science, alcohol. Get them legless for a couple of days, and you can ask them anything after that.’

‘Really? That simple? Astounding.’

‘Oh, and if you shoot their officers and NCOs they stop attacking and go into a sort of pre-programmed defensive mode.’ He spluttered brandy back into his glass. ‘Really?’

‘Yes, sir. We operate with a sniper-heavy platoon structure. Their job is mostly to kill officers.’

‘That, young man, is vital information. I expect you to give the Intelligence section a full briefing to that effect and answer any questions they have this evening. Understood?’

‘Yes, Colonel. Tell me, do you know Godfrey?’

He smiled, ‘I certainly do. I was his company commander for a few years. Brilliant soldier, and to be honest, another fact that, to me, made your story plausible. What role is he operating in, if you have taken the title of commander?’

‘Godfrey is currently head of our small intelligence unit, and occasional adviser if he thinks I am making a wrong decision. In fact, it will be him and Alex, his second, who will be doing most of the liaison work with you.’

He seemed very content with this arrangement and we spent the rest of the afternoon discussing military matters until it was time for me to attend the debriefing about the clone troops. Once I had finished I was shown to a room, where I slept until I was woken by a young soldier claiming to be my aide for the duration of my stay.

The next couple of days were spent at the headquarters building, meeting various officers and being introduced to the two signal officers and the demolition expert who would be coming back with me. Strangely, none of them seemed too upset at their new posting, which I took to be a positive sign.

I attended a briefing on submarines, and it was then that I began to realise how we would be reinserted back behind enemy lines. It made sense, and if man could fly up in the air, then moving underwater should be really quite safe.

On the last morning of my stay at the HQ, Colonel Patterson had one last surprise for me. He told me to head to his office, where there was someone he felt I should talk to. I opened the door and stepped inside. There was a woman standing at the window, the sunlight casting her in sharp shadowy relief. However, there was no mistaking that silhouette. I staggered and caught the table with my hand. 'Sis?'

Neither of us had ever been prone to displays of emotion, particularly with each other, yet she crossed the floor in a few quick strides and threw her arms about me. I did the same, buried my face in her shoulder and tried not to let my emotions get the better of me. She held me at arm's length after a moment, to get a clearer look at me through the veil of her tears. 'Oh my, Danny, you have changed. I hear you are in command of the resistance fighters?'

I nodded.

'Not so long ago you were a useless layabout, and look at you now.'

I shrugged and failed to meet her eyes. 'Sometimes things happen.'

'Danny, where is Mathew? Is he safe?'

I looked at the floor again, shook my head and mumbled, 'He got taken in a round-up.'

She gasped and covered her mouth with her hand, anger flaring in her eyes and accusation in her voice. 'And where were you when he was taken?'

I could have told her the full story, I could have been honest, but the thought of condemnation and hostility from my sister was too much, and so, true to my character, I took refuge in a lie. I mean, why tell a painful and humiliating truth, when after I had rescued him, my previous conduct would recede from prominence, superseded by a happy resolution?

'I left him playing at a friend's house while I took a walking group into the hills. By the time I got back, the town had fallen to the H.A.P. and everyone had been rounded up and moved.' I watched her eyes and saw that she had swallowed the lie. 'I know where he is though, and to be honest the partisan group started as my effort to get him back.'

She looked at me for a long moment, studying my face. She knew me, you see, but the endless games of poker in my earlier life kept my face straight, and she saw no hint of deception in my features. 'You just make sure you get him back, Danny. You hear me? Bring him home safe and well.'

'I will sis, I will.'

For the rest of the short time we had together, she told me that her children were well, her husband was an officer in an armoured battalion and our parents were safe and well, if not a little frantic as they had been unable to return from abroad due to travel restrictions. I enjoyed hearing this cheering news of my family and I enjoyed seeing my sister, but in the end guilt drove me to shorten our reunion and go in search of my transport to the coast. I hugged her warmly, kissed her cheek and fled the simple warmth and honesty in her eyes.

Accompanied by the three specialists I had asked for, I was driven to a naval base in the back of a rattling truck. Military police checked our papers and we were waved through. We had a quick meal in the mess, were introduced to the captain of the submarine and taken aboard. We were shown a bunk room and politely asked to keep out of the way until the boat was underway.

'The captain will send for you when we are at sea,' we were informed by one of the naval ratings. The sub had much the same level of lighting as the cavern and I felt quite at home. Indeed, at home enough for me to swing my feet up on the bunk with Harvey under my jacket, and haunted as ever by the mute anguish in a little boy's eyes, I fell asleep.

Later I was taken for a brief tour of the boat. As well as being dimly lit, it was cramped and hot, with condensation dripping down the walls. It was, despite the number of men aboard and the constant activity of their various duties, strangely quiet. This, it appeared, was normal practice and I actually found it relaxing after the frenetic events of the previous few days. I was on board for two days on my journey beneath the waves, and it was while sitting with the captain in his cramped quarters sharing a small glass of rum that I heard the first confident statement about the outcome of the war. I had ventured to ask the captain the question I could not bring myself to ask the colonel – I had asked how the war was going.

Captain Bryce had shrugged. 'Well,' he answered, 'they have the aircraft, and the terrifyingly effective clone troops. They also for the most part have better tanks and armour. But the one thing they don't have is the sea. We in the north have a much larger navy; in fact, most of the pre-war fleet under Admiral Fowler-Heath sided with the Coalition. The H.A.P. have a few ships, and no doubt they will try and build or buy more, but all the submarine pens are in the north, and as far as our intelligence can ascertain, they have no subs. Just so long as our ground forces can keep them at bay, we can sink their ships and supply convoys, we can starve them of fuel and food. Mark my words, Commander Shaddick, this war will be won at sea.'

The boat halted at periscope depth in a bay just to the south of the Jeral Mountains. After studying the shore for a long time, and waiting for the darkest part of night, Captain Bryce ordered the sub to surface. We clambered up the conning tower onto the deck. A rubber dinghy was lowered into the sea, and the three specialists and I, now armed with sub-machine guns and grenades, shook hands with the captain and climbed aboard. Two of the submariners silently manned the oars and took us to shore. We whispered our thanks and swiftly, but as cautiously as possible, wormed our way through various beach defences and scurried into the dunes, where we waited and listened before crossing the coast road and disappearing into the trees.

This was my territory now, and completely at ease I led the specialists to the base, sleeping in the brightest part of the day and moving at night. On the fourth night I led them to the waterfall entrance, where Ferret was on guard with two of the younger men. He grinned when I replied 'Shut your face' to his demand for the password.

'Good to see you, boss. The others will be pleased you are back. How was your flight?'

'Tell you about it later. Let's get these new men in and dry.'

He nodded and led the way up the cleft in the back wall, where he picked up a lamp and escorted us to the main cavern.

After descending the rope ladder from the ledge, I moved through the cavern, nodding my reply to those who expressed their relief at my return. I made my way over to the planning area and introduced the astounded specialists to Godfrey and Alex. Even as I made the introductions and asked Godfrey to give them the tour and get them settled in, my eyes were searching the cavern for a certain graceful shadow. In the gloom, I saw her walking towards me from the darkness near the lake. I went to meet her. My feet picked up speed almost of their own volition and I could see her do the same. It was more of a collision than an embrace, and we wrapped arms around each other and held on tight. I buried my face in the raven cascade of her hair, breathed in her scent and held her, just held her. My body shook with relief and words became redundant as I held her to me. As we clung to each other the gentle clamour of the cavern faded away. In an island of solitude amongst the glow of fairy lights and the slow drip of growing stalactites, she said all I needed to know in the desperate grip of her arms around my waist as I answered in kind.

Later, I got very drunk and told them all the (slightly embellished) tale of my maiden flight.

Day After Day

The war continued, and the blue bear flag that was designed by the children in the cavern was left flying over scenes of carnage up and down the country, as we spent the next two years hitting targets of opportunity, as well as coordinating our efforts with the Coalition. For instance, the Coalition navy began shelling the coastal supply road, and the H.A.P.-built gun batteries at key locations to try and deter the attacks. It was our task to destroy a specific battery at a certain time to allow another navy bombardment. We usually did this with mortar fire on the back of the gun position, followed by an attack in strength from the trees. We would subdue the garrison, force them into their defensive bunkers and trenches, spike the guns and disappear back into the trees.

When the supply convoys began using inland routes to avoid the danger of the coast road, we mined the route using munitions delivered by submarine. Any convoy that hit the mines was sprayed with machine-gun fire before we slipped away, leaving burning vehicles and the screaming wounded behind us. This caused the H.A.P. to use more and more men in an effort to thwart our attacks. Special mine-detecting units became a favourite target for us and our pre-planned escape routes were always booby trapped to slow down our pursuers as we vanished back to the towns, villages and caves that we had come from.

The H.A.P. eventually got wise to our combined land and sea attacks on installations near the coast, and they began to attach groups of civilian prisoners to each installation. They were used to perform tasks such as the digging of largely redundant and obsolete earthworks or the repainting of the facility. Tasks that in reality served no useful function other than that of creating a human shield of innocents that proved very effective in preventing our attacks.

Over the course of the war I did many terrible things. I blew up trains carrying men and supplies to the front. I destroyed bridges, always waiting for an enemy vehicle to cross before I pressed the switch. I collapsed cliffs to sweep trucks full of men off the road and into the deep yawning gorge beneath them. I blew up factories and depots and stores of equipment vital to their war effort. These things I did from a remote place within, distanced from the death I wrought but no less responsible for all that. But the thing I was infamous for, the thing that motivated my fellow partisans and gave them cause to follow me, was the more immediate carnage I caused.

I threw satchel charges through the windows of crowded cafés filled with off-duty troops. I booked into hotels with Venice and left behind some of our luggage when we signed out in the morning. We would be well away as the bombs exploded. I cut the pallid and grimy throats of regular and clone troops, sawing through them with knives both blunt and sharp. I buried my hatchet in the grey-clad torsos of my enemies. I shattered the skulls of newly commissioned clone troops on the crumbling corners of crowded tenement buildings, my thumbs buried in the grey eyes of fully grown men who had only experienced a few short months of existence. I echoed their agonised screams with my own howls of rage, trying in vain to expunge the ever-present judgemental blue eyes that regarded my every move. But most of all, each and every time, I led from the front.

Every attack where my men had to do battle with the enemy, whether we attacked a patrol, or were killing the survivors from a derailed train, I led from the front. I was always the first to engage;

I would run screaming towards the enemy to get as close as possible as fast as possible. I would get in among the H.A.P. troops, blasting away with my shotgun until it was empty, then with my hatchet and pistol I would carve my way through them, running on fear and adrenaline, trying to wash away the image of mute anguish in a little boy's eyes in a crimson tide of cleansing blood.

Yes, I was reckless, but not as reckless as some might imagine, for behind me somewhere was my own beautiful guardian angel. I laboured at the bloody grinding edge of battle, sheltered by the skills of Venice. With William as her bodyguard and spotter, they identified the greatest threats to my person, threats such as other sharpshooters, soldiers moving to outflank me, grenade throwers or effective machine gun crews, and with her beautiful enigmatic quirk of a smile she shot them from afar. Positions I attacked would sometimes contain more dead than live soldiers. My trust in her was absolute, and after every fight I would thank her with a small bow and a longer kiss. At night, after I had cleaned myself of battlefield filth, she would bandage my hurts and knead away the knots in my aching body. She made me complete, she soothed my soul and her presence gave me permission to forgive myself.

The war continued in much this way for two

years: ambush, hit and run, mine laying, booby traps; indeed, the whole range of partisan tactics. Yes, we lost some people; it didn't always go all our way. I lost some very brave men and women, people who gave everything for something they believed in, people prepared to offer their own lives in the hope that their loved ones might be saved. Although I never intended to, and certainly the old me would not have cared, I felt each and every loss. None of us were ever captured, however. We could not afford to let any of us be taken by the enemy. The standard order was to take your own life before you fell into the hands of the H.A.P. This may seem a particularly savage doctrine, but I make no apology for it. If you were aware that your own capture would in all likelihood lead to the capture, torture and probable death of you partner and children in the cavern, what would you choose? Sometimes, if one of our soldiers was left in a situation where capture was unavoidable, for instance clubbed unconscious fighting like a devil surrounded by enemy troops, Venice knew what to do.

To those of my men or women who were wounded too badly to move, I gave my own personal benediction. I would clasp their hand, hold their eyes with my own, thank them for their strength, their valour and their loyalty, and slide my knife into their heart. Of the dozen or so for whom I had to perform this task, none were forgotten. I carry their names with me.

I am not a religious man, but I do often wish for an afterlife so I could meet up once again with these brave souls to kneel before them and ask for their forgiveness. Strangely, I do not feel that a single one would deny me that. They were good people.

All the names of the fallen were carved on a flat section of the cavern wall. There were too many names, but as much as I cared for my men, I would still sacrifice them all to free my little brother. I could only hope that the capricious bitch Fate would never make real my darkest fear, where circumstances would dictate that I had to choose between Venice and Mathew.

FEARMONES AND ENDZYMES

Two years into the war, the H.A.P. changed tactics and weaponry. They started using some sort of gas and chemical bombs, which were quickly dubbed Fearmones and Endzymes. The Fearmones were gas bombs that caused fear and panic, whilst the Endzymes contained a liquid that, once it had made contact with the skin, would begin to very slowly dissolve or digest the affected area. This process was, by all accounts other than mine, mostly painless except for a maddening itch. Quick work with a knife on the affected area would leave a messy scar but save a life. That is, unless the coverage was too great and then, well, benediction would be needed.

The first time we encountered these weapons was when we attacked an iron works at Bishops Heath in the south of the country. I came to two conclusions after the fight: firstly, that it had been something of a trap, and secondly, for some unknown reason, the Fearmones and Endzymes did not seem to affect me like they did everyone else.

I had assembled what for us was an unusually large group: some sixty men and women who were gathered with the intent of destroying the smelting works and roller mills in an attempt to disrupt steel production and hinder the H.A.P. war effort. Our intelligence informed us that there was a garrison of forty men guarding the factory. However, it seemed that our run of recent success had made us careless, as, in fact, there were more like two hundred. No doubt previous attacks carried out on other facilities had warned the enemy that this factory was likely to be on our target list, and they had quietly reinforced the garrison without our knowledge. It appeared that they had also decided to use this opportunity to test some of their new weapons.

As we waited out the coming of dawn in the trees, using a red flashlight for illumination, I drew a map on the ground, showing our attack route and our avenues of escape. I showed the sniper team where I wanted them situated, and pointed out to the three machine gun crews where I wanted them to site their weapons. The teams moved out an hour before dawn. I placed Harvey in a tree to watch, and as the sun rose I could see the four hundred metres of open ground we would have to cross and the two machine gun nests of the perimeter guard on our side of the complex. At the given time, the sniper team began to shoot at the soldiers manning the machine guns. Those who were not killed kept their heads down long enough for me to get close enough to lob a couple of grenades and neutralise their positions. Feeling confident, the heavily armed main assault team, with me in the lead, began to move out over the open ground, using whatever cover was available as we advanced on the factory. We had barely advanced over a quarter of the distance when I heard the sound of mortar rounds approaching. I shouted out a warning and we all dived to the ground and pressed our faces into the dirt, hoping that we would at least not be hit.

The salvo of mortar rounds went off with a strange pop, not at all like the hollow bang we were used to from conventional rounds. It was then that I noticed there was a faint green haze in the air. I stood up to scream a warning, to tell my men that we were under gas attack, and sucked in a deep lungful of the strange vapour.

All my fellows in the attack group were lying on the ground. Some were crawling back the way they had come, all were weeping and sobbing, and some were trying to dig themselves into the ground and cover themselves with dirt and rocks. I began to get irritated.

I glanced over at the factory and was horrified to see a large unit of H.A.P. troopers form up, all wearing gas masks, seemingly just waiting for the order to attack. My machine guns were silent. I began to get angry and ran to where the nearest machine gun was sited to find the two-man crew cowering in fear. As I reached them, I heard another salvo of mortar rounds impact on the ground amongst my oddly stricken men. Completely ignoring the other mortar shells for the moment, I saw that the enemy troops had begun to move forwards. I lost my temper.

How can I describe my rage? Volcanic? Apocalyptic? Incandescent? In truth, I only remember fragments. I raged and screamed, swore and gibbered. I beat the machine gun crews until the fear of me overwhelmed the psychological demons that held them in thrall. One of the survivors of the attack later told me that I reminded him of the legends about the barbarian warriors of old, who would enter a state of frenzy when battle was joined. Quite literally I went berserk.

I managed, with the butt of my shotgun and with dire howled threats, to convince the machine gun crews that they should begin firing into the mass of enemy troops. Luckily the sniper teams had been out of the effective blast area of the mortar bombs and were able to stay effective, although they proved to be hampered by a shortage of ammunition as the standard twenty-five rounds each had brought with them did not last very long. It is obvious with hindsight that one of the key objectives for the H.A.P. that day was to capture as many survivors as possible. Thus their return of fire was light and somewhat ineffective, more in the way of covering fire as each unit took turns to advance onto the open ground. Possessed as I was by my burning rage, I ran back to my attack group, who were still for the most part lying crippled by terror on the floor. I noticed in an abstract way that some were dead, their corpses looking like they had been hit by acid, while others clutched limbs and body parts that had raw wounds upon them.

I set about them with much the same techniques I had used on the machine gun crews. I, to my eternal shame, in the full view of my men, shot a couple that were too badly wounded to move and raged incoherently at the rest of them. Slowly, far too slowly, they began to regain their feet and composure; whether this was due to my unremembered efforts or to the effect of the chemical wearing off with time I am not sure. All I can remember is that the H.A.P. soldiers had increased their pace, presumably keen to get to us before we escaped. I could not allow that to happen. I screamed with hate and attacked the main force of the enemy. As I have said, I don't remember much more than lurid psychedelic flashbacks, but I remember everyone else seemed to be moving slowly, like they were wading through thick mud. I could hear individual bullets whipping past me in both directions as I seemed to float across the intervening gap and slam like wrath incarnate into their ranks. I fought with a holy fury, a pure burning violence. They were too slow and I was too fast, too angry and too deadly. I laughed and howled and in my madness I killed. I managed to kill a lot of men that day. I have no idea how many, but my rage drove me on to accomplish feats that I would have sworn were impossible. In all reality I fought for only a few short minutes but it seemed like hours as I ducked and cut and kicked and killed. Slowly and horribly this frenzy abated. I began to feel pain again and fatigue announced its arrival in the trembling of my limbs. My anger dissipated and reason began to return. With a desperate backward glance I saw that most of my men had stumbled to safety, so with one last surge of rage I cut myself clear of the enemy surrounding me and fled as fast as I could manage towards the cover of the trees.

Venice saved my life that day. I would have stood no chance: one lone man running on shaking legs from over a hundred enemy soldiers. She had moved to oversee the machine gun crews and was directing their fire and using the last few rounds she had saved to see me safely away. I ran past the machine gun positions, my breath laboured, my limbs dead to sensation and my head rolling as I struggled to keep moving, demanding more from a body that had nothing, absolutely nothing left to give. I must somehow have sensed my arrival into an area of relative safety, and utterly exhausted, like a puppet with severed strings, my legs gave way and I collapsed boneless into the dirt and passed out.

I found out later that Ven regrouped the survivors and wreaked havoc upon the H.A.P. troops who had advanced too far out in the open. The facility was destroyed but I played no part in that. Apparently I had a broken bayonet blade through my forearm when they found time to attend to me. I have the scar but I still don't recall the wounding.

It took me three days to recover from that gas attack. I could not really walk when I came to, and had to be helped into hiding. When I had recovered, I sent a report to the Coalition about the new weapons. I could only hope that our experience would help save some lives.

We did not encounter the new weapons very often, probably only half a dozen times over the next couple of years, but we learnt from our mistakes. Each time we took on a H.A.P. facility or attacked an entrenched enemy we always took gas masks with us, masks we had procured from our dead enemies. Of course I never bothered with one, preferring to ride the wave of violence to its brutal and exhausting conclusion, adding, I confess, to the legend.

We fought on for another two years after the Bishops Heath incident. The H.A.P. adjusted their tactics and we in turn adjusted ours. It was a knife-edge game, one in which we, the partizans, were marginally better players. We fought against clone units, and units we dubbed Naturals or Nats, hitting hard, causing the maximum damage and retreating before the enemy could get organised. One of my favourite tactics was to take a village or small town, clear it of enemy troops and loot whatever equipment they had. We would then run up the blue bear flag and disappear, leaving behind the bewildered civilian population and a pile of enemy dead.

The Coalition were pushed slowly further and further back into the north, fighting for every bit of ground, moving the whole civilian population northwards as they fought a slow retreat behind them. They left nothing for the H.A.P., pulling down buildings and destroying crops and supplies as they were forced yet another step northward. However, they began to consolidate their strength in the far north, so when the H.A.P. supply lines became hopelessly stretched and often infrequent at the end of the third year of war, with well-supplied and well-trained fresh troops they went on the offensive and the tide of war changed.

During the second and third year of the war, the H.A.P. had many men stationed in the south actively looking for us. However, as the ebb and flow of war began to turn in our favour, those men were sent back to the front, allowing us much more freedom of movement across the country. Instead, they began to rely solely on static garrisons at key points and a large well-equipped escort for any vital convoys moving by road or rail. There were still roving patrols, but these were too small and too infrequent to prove bothersome, and to be honest, very few we encountered made it back to their bases. We also liberated prison camps when we found them and had the opportunity to do so, and it was these people who made up the backbone of our partisan group. They were much more reliable than the free population for a number of reasons, but chiefly because we offered them and their families freedom and sanctuary from a regime that had taken everything from them and given them nothing but fear.

We did recruit a few from the general population, but we always had to be very wary. Much of the population in the south seemed to believe in the righteousness of the H.A.P. cause and many branded us traitors and bandits. I could only presume that these people had not seen the suffering of the prison camps, or the remains left by liquidation squads. However, there was, quite literally, a price on our heads. The reward for information leading to my capture was in reality astounding, but I gave all the new volunteers to Jimmy who, it seemed, could sniff out those with ill intent or deception on their minds in a matter of a few short hours. I have no idea how he managed this, but I assume the technique involved liberal use of his flask. Needless to say, none of those he rooted out were ever heard from again.

We fought for four years and for each of those years I aged five. Although still in my twenties, I looked like a man twice that age. My hair was going grey, and my body carried the scars of combat and the lines of worry that tension and loss had cut deep into the weathered skin around my eyes. Crawling through swamps, hiding in ice-filled ditches, or baking on white rock outcrops in the heat of summer had brought aches to my joints, and my body cracked and snapped when I rose from whichever floor I had made my bed on the previous night.

I hoped that soon it was all going to be worth it; all that killing and all that pain, the loss and the suffering inflicted in pursuit of my agenda. For finally, at long last, we were winning and the end was in sight.

If we were careful, we could move almost unhindered across the countryside, so the previous weeks had been spent preparing for my attack on Peremoss Point. All available men and women had been moved into the surrounding area. I met with an exhausted Oz, who assured me that he could equip and procure the necessary weapons and ammunition. With Godfrey and Alex back at the main base in the cavern, I gathered my commanders and sub-commanders in an old sawmill north of the targets and outlined my plan.

'There are two towns we have to take before we can attack the camp at Peremoss. Broughton and Alberts Crossing.' I pointed them out on the map. 'They both have garrisons that need to be eliminated before we can converge on Peremoss. We need to attack them both at once in order to prevent one from supporting the other, so to that end, Jimmy, I want you to lead the attack on Broughton whilst I lead the attack on Alberts Crossing. Harry, I want you to provide a screening force to the west. Make sure you intercept any relief force that might come to reinforce either of the targets.' Harry nodded his great wise head slowly. 'Consider it done, Danny.'

I smiled at him, 'Thanks, Harry.'

I turned to the sub-commanders, 'Gentlemen, if you could brief your section leaders, please. See to your units, check ammunition, water, first aid kits and make sure they have their gas masks. I want the first units moving into position for five in the morning, the attack to start at half past. Everybody clear on that?' There were various nods and murmurs of a positive nature then they filed out, leaving me with Jimmy, Harry, Oz, Ferret and, of course, Venice.

I looked up at them and smiled, 'Well, my friends, I can finally tell you that this war, and our part in it, is coming to an end. What I am about to tell you is for your ears only and not for other ranks, okay? To the south, below the horizon, is a Coalition invasion fleet. Once we have taken the Peremoss facility and liberated the work camp, and our flag flies from the tower, send the signal 'Dry Feet' to Alex, who will relay it on to Coalition high command.

We just have to defend the promontory until the fourth army arrives and then,' I grinned at them all, 'we can go on holiday.'

The joy was evident on the faces of my closest companions, and a beaming Jimmy passed his flask around. I hugged them all and thanked them for everything they had done. I took the opportunity to kiss Venice long and slow. 'Soon, Ven. Soon.'

She smiled in reply, 'Can't wait, Fish.'

Still grinning happily, I reminded them that there was fighting yet to be done but that the end was in sight. 'Jimmy, once you have taken your target, leave a capable officer in charge of the defence and meet me at Alberts Crossing with the body of your men. Harry, stay on post for twenty-four hours. Whether you clash with reinforcements or not, apart from a few scouts, rendezvous with me at Alberts Crossing for further orders. Good luck, gentlemen and lady, and I will see you all tomorrow night.'

Finally convinced that everything was coming together nicely, I left the shed to go and spend some time with the men who would be risking their lives in the morning. You know? Really I should have bloody known better.

The twin attacks were a great success. Resistance

was slight at Broughton: Jimmy had it very easy as he was fighting a clone garrison that appeared to have been commissioned without receiving full training and he pretty much overran the whole town in an hour. My fight was much harder: seasoned, well-dug-in troops that we had to clear street by street, room by room. None fled and none surrendered, and it took us all day, even supported by the arrival of Jimmy and his men, to finally clear the town and raise the banner over the town hall.

Something strange happened during the fight. One of the enemy soldiers had got behind me, and if it hadn't been for Ferret firing over my shoulder, I would have been killed. It disturbed me: my beautiful guardian had never once in four years let me down. I hoped that it had been something simple like a misfire, but worry nagged at me like a headache and I sent one of the men to check on the sniper team. His face upon his return told me all I needed to know. Half my world crashed down and I felt a great hole tear into my soul.

End Game

She was on a makeshift bed in a captured warehouse in Alberts Crossing, the small town we had just taken. Outside the small office where she rested, one of our team of medics told me in hushed tones that an Endzyme shell had exploded next to her as she picked off targets during the attack. William, it seems, had thrown himself on top of her, using his body to shield her from the blast, ever faithful to the task I had given him.

His brave sacrifice had only been partially successful and a fine spray of Endzyme tar had caught her down one side of her body. She had not been digested swiftly by the horror weapon, but whilst lacking the potency to kill her, the Endzyme was still effective enough to be slowly devouring her tissue.

I took a deep breath and tried to remain calm and civil to the dog-tired man who had done his best to save the wounded after fights up and down the country, and who had obviously drawn the short straw when it came to giving me the prognosis.

'So, what's the verdict, doc?' That my voice remained calm surprised even me. Inside I was panicking, fear running up and down my spine and nervous sweat breaking out over my body.

'No more than five days, Commander Shaddick. I can't stop the spread, it is across one side of her face and down one side of her body.' He gestured helplessly, 'If it was a limb, I could amputate and save her life. I'm sorry, commander, there is just nothing I can do to save her. It is a mild dose of contamination and thus quite slow, so five days until it reaches any vital organ. If it is any consolation, it is almost completely painless.'

It was and it wasn't. One drop of consolation makes scant difference in an ocean of turmoil, but I nodded and thanked him, opened the door and went in.

The room was illuminated gently in the light of a flickering candle. She was lying on the bed, a sheet pulled up over her body and her face turned away from me so that all that I saw was the flawless beauty I was accustomed to. I pulled up a stool and sat next to the bed. 'Hey, Ven.'

In answer, her good arm came from beneath the

sheet and reached towards me. I gave her hand a squeeze, brought it to my lips and kissed the smooth, warm skin. I kissed her long, elegant fingers and held her hand to my forehead as silent tears dripped off my chin.

She spoke, her head still turned from me, her voice quiet and small against the weight of the understanding of her own disfigurement and doom. ‘Tell me your favourite memories of me, Fish’

I was silent for a moment. I kissed her hand again to gain time to recover my voice and try to sound like my normal self. ‘Well, there was the time I saw you naked at Oldbridge.’

She made a derisive sound. ‘Seriously, Fish, please.’

I sat in silence for a while, ‘That time I saw you dance.’

‘I remember the dance. Tell me what you saw, Fish.’

I took a swig from my flask and winced at the rough hooch Jimmy had filled it with. I offered it to Ven, who declined with the smallest movement of her head. I closed my eyes and began to speak. ‘We were in Three Sisters, that garrison town in the southwest. Our papers said that we were husband

and wife, both committed party members, and that I was a civilian weapons system specialist, due to work as an instructor at the training base there. We booked in at the Pavilion Hotel, a hotel and bar that was used as a billet by ranking officers and civilian specialists. It also had a café attached that was open to non-commissioned officers for breakfast and lunch. Anyway, we booked in. Our suitcases, as was often the case, contained much more than clothes. We put them in our rooms and changed for dinner. You wore that black and white dress, high in the front, low in the back and split up one leg all the way to mid-thigh.

'That dress clung to your figure and caressed every graceful curve. It revealed everything yet showed nothing and made me glad to be alive. You, as ever, were beautiful, and as we descended the stairs you drew the eye of every officer in there and the jealousy of their wives. The meal was excellent, your conversation was dry, witty and intelligent and we smiled and laughed through the whole of the meal. After the meal we went to the bar.

'We had some drinks and talked a little to some of the officers in there, but the place was quiet and dull, just alcohol and polite, boring conversation. I remember that there was a jukebox playing quietly, just old-fashioned tunes, probably intended to provoke or entice those officer types to drag their stiff- necked wives around the dance floor, but nobody had taken the bait. You talked to the bar manager. I have no idea what you said, but you got some change off him, kicked off your shoes and walked over to the jukebox. I could see you thinking, one finger tapping your chin as you flicked through the selection of music. I saw you find one you liked, put the money in and signal to the bar manager, who obviously turned the volume up for you.

'The tune was not one I had heard before. The intro was delicate and melancholic, and after a few bars you moved into the centre of the dance floor and began to dance. Ven, it was the most delicate, graceful and sexy thing I have ever seen. You moved completely in time with the music, you somehow danced the words. I can't explain what I saw, but it was beautiful, Ven, really beautiful. It was the human form of reciting poetry, it was movement describing emotion. Everyone turned to watch and everyone watched in silence, stunned as they were. The song finished and you just walked back, put your shoes on and came over to me. You deserved the round of applause and the odd whistle you got, and those officers trying to buy you drinks.

'That's the night I asked you once again to marry me.' I shook my head at the memory. 'You said sex yes, marriage no; there would be time for that after the killing was done and we had rescued Mathew. Obviously I was frustrated but I understood. I didn't really mind. I was in love.

'Next morning we had breakfast, joined by a number of your new friends. We finished eating and asked the barman to keep an eye on our bags as we were going for a stroll along the high street to see something of the town we had moved to. As you know, we were already well away when the hotel full of officers having breakfast blew up, but I will never ever forget the night I saw you dance, Ven.'

Venice was quiet but her hand squeezed mine tightly and I could see tears on her cheek. That night must have made some impact upon me, as I could still remember the words to the chorus of that song:

'And how bitter flows this shallow stream

Over broken rock of heart and dream

Where I tripped and fell on roots that rose

In the place where perfect blossom grows.'

I leant across and blew out the candle. I had no need to be taunted by a flickering metaphor for hope.

I sat with her all night. She slept occasionally

but did not speak again until the morning. The doctor put his head into the room to check that we were okay and disappeared again. When the door closed behind him, she at last turned to me. I refused to flinch at the sight of the damage to her face as the Endzymes slowly digested her skin. I met her eyes with mine and forced a small smile.

'Send Harry in, Fish. I need to speak with him.'

I found Harry at the far end of the warehouse, surrounded by his staff and squad leaders as he organised the defences around the town.

'Captain, can I have a minute, please?'

He turned towards me, his face suddenly grave. 'Commander, what can I do for you?'

I led him to a quiet part of the large room. 'Ven wants to speak to you, Harry.'

'How is she, Danny?'

I shrugged helplessly, and my voice caught in my throat. 'Dying by increments and inches, Harry.'

The big man caught me in a hug and I fought hard not to break down.

'Gods, I'm sorry, Dan. What does she want with me? Do you know?'

I shook my head. 'How are the defences? Any

problems?'

'Not as yet. The perimeter is good; we have fought off a couple of probing attacks, but I don't think they have the troops to retake the town. Most of the troops are Tubes anyway, easy to predict, easy to defeat.'

'So you can spare some time for Ven?'

'Of course I can. You know me and Sara think of her as a daughter. Just let me hand over command of the defence and then she has got me for as long as she wants.'

He bellowed at the group of men clustered around his desk, 'Lieutenant Barrett, a moment, please.'

A young officer ran over to join us. His sympathetic look told me that the news had travelled. He saluted.

'Lieutenant, you are as of this moment in command of the defence, until such a time as I tell you otherwise. I have something else to see to. I forbid you to let any of the enemy through our perimeter, and do not, for the love of the Saints, make any decisions that you will have to explain to the commander here.'

Barrett turned to me and saluted. I returned the

salute and gave him my best death's head grin, the one I knew the troops talked about and were somewhat terrified of, never being sure what it signified for them. 'Lieutenant.'

'Commander.' He scurried off to the command desk and began issuing orders to the assembled squad leaders.

'Thanks, Harry.'

He smiled and gripped my hand briefly before heading off towards the room where Venice lay dying.

I spent some time getting reports off several of my men concerning losses, captured supplies and other issues. I made sure that patrols had been sent out into the surrounding area and that observers had been placed at the head of that bloody bridge at Peremoss. Jimmy, it seems, had as usual organised the patrols, and I issued orders that when Captain Parker returned he was to see me immediately. I detailed a couple of sergeants to process the volunteers we were getting from the townsfolk, then I drank a mug of tea and ate something before rolling up my greatcoat as a pillow and lying down on a bench.

Unlike many occasions when I went to sleep, I did not speak to Harvey this time, merely patted the place where I kept him in my coat and fell into a troubled sleep.

It was mid-afternoon when I awoke to find Jimmy sitting at the end of the bench. Despite everything, I smiled when I saw him. He still looked like a pirate: unbuttoned greatcoat, bearded, dirty, scarred and covered in weapons and ammunition. For once Jimmy was not smiling. He passed me a lit cigarette and raised his eyebrow, conveying without words his question.

'Not too bad, Jim,' I managed. 'Ven is fucked though, mate. Five days the medic reckons.' Some men, and Jimmy was one of them, know when words were useless, so we sat there in silence, passing his flask between us until it was empty. After the last drop, he sighed, ground out his cigarette with his boot and reached inside his coat. He pulled out a rolled map, which he spread out on the bench between us, and began pointing out pockets of resistance and places where his patrols had skirmished with the H.A.P.

'Most of the troops, Nats and Tubes, have fled across the bridge and are adding to the numbers on the Point. There are odd groups that have decided to defend a good position, normally a hill or farmhouse. I have men watching them so they are no threat at the moment. We can take them out one at a time or just ignore them for now.'

I thought for a moment. 'Send the new recruits under a couple of seasoned troopers, and just keep sporadic rifle and mortar fire on them. Keep them pinned in place, and if they want to surrender let them. When the Coalition are south of the mountains it shouldn't be too long before we can hand prisoners over. It makes these new recruits feel useful too. We haven't got time to train them properly, but keep the best half for our attack on Peremoss. They can soak up some of the bullets and save some useful men.'

Jimmy shook his head. 'You are still a hard man, boss. I could sometimes believe that most of what they say in those stories about you is true.'

I threw my empty tin mug at him. 'Jimmy, you little fuck. It's you made most of those bloody stories up!'

He was still laughing when Harry came over to join us.

He pulled up a chair and sat his massive frame down. He nodded to Jimmy and regarded me with sad eyes.

'She knows she is dying, Danny.' He sighed

and ran his hand through his hair. 'I don't quite know how to say this, but she wants her part in the attack on the camp.'

Perplexed, I nodded and gestured for him to continue.

'She knows that the second line of defence on the wall around the camp and factory complex is the strongest. There is lots of open ground to cross, against a strong wall with many emplacements and a heavy iron gate that they only open to let trains in. Danny, she has a plan for getting through the gate.' I cadged another smoke off Jimmy, 'Go on.'

'She wants me to rig up a truck so that it will run on the tracks. She wants me to fill it full of explosives and then she is going to drive it into the gates and open up a hole big enough to let our army walk in.'

I sat smoking in stunned silence, horrified and proud, until the glowing ember at the tip of the cigarette burnt my fingers. I cursed and threw it away.

'Can it be done?'

'There are one or two engineering issues to work out, but in theory, yes.'

'Harry, you have three days; get it done. Jimmy, we have two days to take the outer wall. I want as many patrols on foot and in transport as you dare. I want as much information on those defences as possible: numbers, guns and static defence points. I want them on a map. Send some men in on a dummy attack to expose emplacements we can't see. Prep the men for a night attack, the briefing to be held after supper in two days' time. Okay?'

Both men nodded, rose and went about their orders.

For the next day and a half I split my time between sitting with Venice and poring over maps and issuing orders. I went out on two patrols to examine the defences at the far side of the bridge myself, looking for a weak spot and formulating an attack plan. The time I had with Ven was spent trying to ignore the encroaching necrosis that was slowly devouring her, exchanging small talk and trying to make her smile. Not once did I mention her plan and not once did she try to explain. There was no need: I understood completely and she knew that I understood. More need not be said.

Preparations made, at 21:00 hours I briefed the men: two hundred of our bravest and best of the five hundred that had taken the town with me. Two hundred men and women in various pieces of uniform, faces blackened and weapons ready. Fifty volunteers led by Lieutenant Barrett would attack across the bridge at 01:00 hours, pushing a bogey fitted with a shield along the rails in front of them. They were to make a lot of noise and put down heavy fire at the gates. Before that the rest of us would float down the estuary in two waves to the old jetty at the abandoned whaling station behind the first line of defence. The first wave of twenty men led by me would float down to the old whaling station, creep ashore and despatch the sentries at midnight, to be joined by the rest led by Jimmy at 00:30. We would then move into position behind the defences, and when the group on the bridge attacked we would fall on the back of the enemy and roll up the wall, clearing out bunkers and trenches as we went. I detailed a squad to take the gate and let the first fifty in. I checked my watch against those of the other leaders, and sent the men to their ready positions.

I went to see Venice, kissed her on the cheek and told her I would see her tomorrow. I checked over my kit, hatchet, knife, grenades and shotgun, blackened my own face and went to join the insertion group. I patted Harvey for luck, and this time stared back into the brief vision of mute anguish in a little boy's eyes. 'I'm close now, little brother. I will be there soon,' I whispered. The vision faded and I slid into the cold, dark water.

Astoundingly the plan worked well. We slithered ashore at the old jetty, and lay still for a few minutes watching the sentries' routine before I gave some furious hand signals detailing men to different tasks. I then drew my blackened hatchet out of my boot and launched myself at the back of the passing sentry. They were mostly Tubes, and fell easily, unable to adapt and improvise without leadership. The Nats were all asleep in their quarters in the old office and my men tore through them like a whirlwind. All forty men on this post were put to the knife and not a shot was fired. We helped the other group ashore, dried ourselves off as best we could, cleaned our weapons and headed northwards to the first wall.

Barrett started his attack right on time. I waited a few moments for the defenders to turn their full attention towards the attackers on the bridge, and at my signal we fell on them from behind. It was a night of blood and fury, of explosions and gunfire. None of the heavy guns faced backwards and we rolled up the defenders from one end of the wall to the other. Every gun emplacement and fortification was cleared with grenades and satchel charges. Shocked H.A.P. troopers were mown down before they realised what was happening. The gates were opened and Barrett led his men to link up with ours. With fire and screaming, knives, bullets and bombs we hacked, killed or chased the defenders on the wall. Some fled across the killing ground towards the other wall, some dived into the sea at the other side of the Point to escape, but by dawn the wall was ours. I was blood soaked and battered, hoarse from shouting orders, and screaming wordlessly at the foe. I surveyed our surviving fighters from where I stood atop the smoking remnants of a bunker by the gate, and watched one of the corporals as he ran up the blue bear banner on the remaining flag pole.

When the flag reached the top of the pole I turned, and feeling nothing like triumphant but knowing what was expected, I raised my gun into the air and shrieked my triumph at the sky. My voice was joined by those of the others as they too gave voice to their feelings of relief and triumph and the joy of survival. I held my hand to my heart and then reached out to them as I saluted them for their endeavours.

After a brief moment to eat, drink and regain composure, I gave orders for the surviving guns to be turned towards the next wall a little over a mile away. These guns were to be used to suppress the fire from the wall to prevent the defenders getting off an oblique shot at the truck Venice would be driving. I ordered all fighters and vehicles to be brought forward over the bridge, and to prepare for an assault on the next wall. All, that is, apart from a small screening force and those engaged in containing the odd pockets of resistance that still held out. I sent word to Harry that the wall was ours, and set medics to tend our wounded. I leant my back against the wall of a trench, the sun warming my face, and I rested for a while before moving amongst the troops, thanking them for their attendance and commitment and asking that they give me one last effort to take that factory and tower, in order to help me release those poor souls, many of whom were kith and kin to my brave volunteers. Job done, I shared a bottle of wine that Jimmy had scrounged from one of the officers' quarters, before finding a surviving bunk, kissing Harvey on the head and falling asleep, with orders to only wake me if there was an attack or when Harry arrived with Venice. Venice: my Guinevere, my Isolde, my dream, my desire and the selfless key to finding my brother.

It was just after dawn on day four when a young soldier woke me with a nervous knock and a cup of tea to tell me that there was a strange vehicle approaching over the bridge. I picked up my weapons and followed him outside. It seemed that Harry and his team had worked wonders: a converted truck, its rims riding the rails, rolled slowly over the bridge, pushed by another wagon behind it. The front of the truck had been turned into a reinforced beak that tapered to a sharp point. I waited in silence for the strange convoy to come past me. I could not see into the cab of the first truck, obscured as it was by all the armour plating, but there was no mistaking the figure of Harry driving the one behind pushing the rolling bomb, and presumably Venice, before it.

He applied his brakes and rolled to a stop when he saw me, and clambered down from the cab. He looked harried and upset and there was a distinct catch in his voice. ‘Hey, Danny.’

I smiled, ‘Hey, Harry.’ I pointed at the front truck, ‘Talk me through it.’

‘Armoured beak on the front, angled to deflect fire. It will stand up to small arms and missiles, explosions should just roll over it. The point is the trigger; a hard impact on that will set off the charges in the rest of the beak. The theory is that the point will punch a hole through the gate and then the charge will go off. The charge is mostly shaped so that it will destroy the wall on either side, as well as the gate, to make as big a hole as possible.’

I nodded, ‘What’s with the other truck?’

His voice trembled again and he took a moment to conquer his emotion. ‘Ven can’t drive any more, Dan; she has to keep her good foot on the clutch.

We can put the truck in third gear for her, then this truck will push her up to a speed where she can dump the clutch without stalling. When I sound the horn, she knows to take her foot off the clutch and press the accelerator.' He went quiet, 'The rest is self-explanatory.' He paused for a moment and looked at me, anguish evident in his eyes. 'I don't want to sound that horn, Danny. I don't want to have to send her off.'

I reached up and brought his great head down on my shoulder. I held him tight and spoke quietly into his ear. 'You have to, Harry, for me and for her. This is her wish, this is what she wants to do. When she sets off, you can stop and turn away; I won't think any less of you, Harry. You have done an amazing job for her but you don't have to watch the end.' I patted his head and released him. 'That's my job. When the attack starts, Harry, I want you to head back to Alberts Crossing and take command of the defensive screen for me. When you hear that we have taken the complex, I want you to move all supplies and personnel onto the Point and turn it into a base. There will be released prisoners to look after and if our force is concentrated here we can defend against greater numbers. I don't expect much in the way of attack now though. The H.A.P. is on the back foot, and I don't suppose it will be more than a couple of days at the most until you see the first of the Coalition troops landing here.'

I realised I was keeping myself talking to put off going over to Venice. I drew myself to a halt. 'Anyway, you know all that. Thanks for this, Harry.'

I walked towards the cab of the modified truck, filled with dread and a kind of fatalism. The engine was running and I opened the door and climbed the steps. She looked as beautiful as ever, her long dark hair framing her perfect skin. On this side anyway. I could only guess what horrors the Endzyme was working on the other side of her face. She wore a loose pair of overalls but I could tell that her arm and leg on the far side were withered to invalidity.

'Hey, Ven.'

She turned slightly and I caught a glimpse of the side of her head where the Endzyme was eating its slow horrible way into her skull.

'Hey, Fish.' Her voice was quiet, but I knew her well enough to hear the fatalism and lack of regret in her tone. I lit a cigarette and put it between her lips, perfect on one side, marred on the other. She blew out smoke, and half grinned at me. 'Great, just what I always wanted: to die a fucking cliché.'

I smiled, tears in my eyes, amazed as always by this wonderful woman. I struggled for words and forced them past the lump in my throat, my head bowed to touch the side of hers. 'I love you, Ven.' She reached up and caressed my face with her hand. 'I know you do, Fish.'

'Ven,' I paused, fighting emotion and regret. So much to say and no idea how to say it. 'I just wish we had met in different times.'

She smiled a quiet sad smile, slowly shook her head and sighed. 'Oh, Fish. In different times I doubt we would have ever met. This was our time and well ...' she gestured helplessly with her good arm, 'this is where it has to end.'

Sometimes there are no words, and I couldn't for the life of me deny the truth of that.

'You ready?'

She nodded once.

I leant over to put the truck in gear and kissed the side of her face. 'Goodbye, beautiful.' I stepped down and as I swung the heavy door shut heard her call out, 'I love you, Danny.'

That was the first and only time she called me by my name.

Shaking with unexpressed grief, I nodded through the window of Harry's truck. The big man sat gripping the wheel, tears rolling unhindered down his great friendly face. He gave no indication that he had seen me, but he revved his truck, selected a gear and began to push her forwards, slowly picking up speed.

I stood and watched the whole mind-numbing event as the truck rattled and clanked, gaining speed. The horn sounded in harsh atonal requiem, and her truck roared and belched smoke and noise like a mythical creature of old, charging at the fortress gate, defiant, angry and determined. The larger captured weapons opened up against the defenders in a firework blaze to mark her passing. In the bedlam of ballistic fury I watched the armoured truck shrugging off small arms fire in flame and spark and clamour as it hurtled along the tracks towards its destination and detonation.

So what do you do in circumstances like this? When all you want to do is howl and claw at your own face to try ineffectively to externalise the internal? Well, in my limited experience I can only suggest that you bite down hard on the pain. You bite down. So. Fucking. Hard. You bite down hard on the pain and you chew it. You chew until you get used to the taste, and then instead of screaming, you smile. You smile, and as the anguish leaches from between your teeth, and your soul cries in desperate grief, you raise your hand and you wave goodbye.

Farewell to your beloved as she – the better part of you, the only person ever to fill your heart with joy – and all your half-formed dreams of a half-formed future are incinerated in a bright flash and a sonorous boom. Then, as the warm wind from the blast washes over you, you inhale deeply, trying in vain to capture one last gift of her scent on the breeze and you hold that breath for as long as you can, denying yourself tears or release, refusing to admit the death of half your hopes. Then you order the attack.

I flagged down a passing Jeep, and standing behind the machine gun mounted on the roll cage, I urged the driver to make haste towards the smouldering hole, the section of wall Venice took with her when she departed this life. Some vehicles raced up and down the length of the wall, the men within firing at anything that moved on the top of the barrier. Other vehicles like mine made with all haste towards the entrance into the final part of the compound. We bounced over the rubble and wreckage left by the explosion. Bullets ricocheted off the metalwork of the Jeep but I ignored them, focusing on the twelve low huts of the prison camp. I dismounted when we reached the tall barbed wire fence, and as other vehicles and men moved past us to attack the factory, I frantically shouted at the prisoners crowding the fence to move back. I gave orders for two of the Jeeps to back up to the wire, attached grappling hooks to the fence, hitched them to the back of the Jeeps and urged the men to drive. An entire section of fence ripped out of the ground and was dragged away. I signaled and two trucks laden with rifles arrived. The men on board began handing them out to the emaciated, wretched but angry prisoners, who poured forth from the hole we had made to eagerly claim their weapons and join in the attack.

The looming tower at the end of the promontory we ignored for now. It stood behind its own wall, and when this area was pacified, I would then consider how best to deal with it.

Once the flow of vengeful prisoners had ebbed, as all those fit enough or willing enough had gone to slake their own thirst for vengeance, quivering with anticipation I stepped into the confines of the prison camp. I checked Harvey was safe under my jacket and began wandering from hut to hut, calling out for Mathew. The foetid air inside the first hut made me gag and my cry brought no answer. I wandered amongst those too old, young or weak, calling for my brother.

'Mathew! Has anybody seen Mathew? Young boy, about so big, blond hair. Mathew. Does anybody know Mathew?' From hut to hut I went, anticipation speeding my feet, 'Mathew. Are you there, Mathew?'

I became frantic as hut after hut yielded no reply. My shouts got louder, and after the last hut failed to deliver me my brother, I began sobbing as I ran from wretched group to wretched group of prisoners. 'MATHEW! HAS ANYBODY SEEN MY BROTHER, MATHEW?' At least twice I ran around the camp shouting, gunfire and explosions cracking and banging as my men cleared the wall. I knew I should have been leading them, but I had more pressing concerns and Jimmy knew what to do. I fell to my knees in despair, my face in my hands, and I beseeched the fates. 'No, please, he must be here somewhere. He must, please.' I don't know how long I had been kneeling on the floor whispering into my hands before I heard the voice.

'Daniel? Daniel Shaddick?' I looked up at an old emaciated woman, in her prisoner overalls. Her hair hung in clumps from her mostly bald head. She had been plump at one time, but now loose, flaccid skin sagged from her jaw and gathered in folds around her neck. Most of her teeth were missing, but there was something in her voice that I recognised. I got to my feet and wiped the self-pity off my face, cleaning the sweat of panic with the dirty sleeve of my jacket.

She spoke again. ‘Is that you, Daniel?’

Her voice made me feel as if I was being scolded and then I remembered the comb.

‘Mrs Bancroft, is that you?’

She nodded. ‘We heard stories from new prisoners that there was a man called Shaddick breaking into camps and setting people free. I would never in all my born days have thought that it was you. Not the Daniel Shaddick I knew; still, you did say you would get help. Who would have thought it was you?’

I swallowed my irritation and impatience and led her to a wooden bench outside one of the huts. ‘Mrs Bancroft, where is Mathew? Where is my brother?’

Her eyes drifted past me, and for a moment it seemed like she would not answer.

‘I looked after him like you wanted me to. Such a sweet boy. Not a harmful hair on his little head, bless him. Such a sweet boy. Everyone loved him; we all looked after him.’

‘Mrs Bancroft, where is he?’

She looked past me again. 'They took him a couple of years ago, Daniel. We tried to keep him with us, but they just beat us and took him.'

'Took him where, Mrs Bancroft?' She looked past me again, her eyes staring at something beyond me. I turned to look, to see what she could see. She was looking at the tower.

'The tower,' she whispered. 'They took him to the tower.'

I sighed a long and desperate sigh. This was not good news and not the end of my quest, but at least I still had some hope of finding him. I stood to leave and she gripped my arm with surprising strength.

'They never come back from the tower. They take all the little ones but they never come back.'

I had to believe that my little brother was safe and well, tower or no tower. So I smiled and thanked her, and assured her that from now on she would be safe and well fed. I left her staring at the forbidding walls of the tower and went to wrap up the attack. There was some wreckage of men and machines at the base of the tower, which I found odd as there didn't appear to be any defenders on the tower wall. All the burnt-out vehicles and the bodies seemed to be inside a red exclusion zone marked on the floor of the concrete apron in front of the wall. Not sure what it signified but reaching the conclusion that it was a dangerous place, I gave orders to avoid the ground in front of the tower wall and placed guards to prevent anyone straying there accidentally.

All resistance had been crushed, and some of the former prisoners were still exacting their revenge on the bodies of fallen H.A.P. soldiers. I left them to it and called my commanders to me. I gave orders to interview some of the prisoners to see if any of them knew about the tower. It was my hunch that some would have been inside to carry out cleaning duties or something. I also asked that they should be brought to me if they knew anything useful. In the meantime, I ventured close to the steel wall that bisected the end of Peremoss Point, separating the tower from the rest of the compound. There was one small portal set in the wall and when I listened closely I could hear the static buzz of electricity. Mindful of the exclusion zone around the base of the wall that extended out for about ten metres, I didn't get too close, but picked up a fist-sized piece of rubble and hurled it at the wall. There was a hum of electric motors, and a low metal blister on top of the wall moved, obviously tracking the flight of the rock. A couple of metres before it hit the wall, there was smoke and light from the turret and the sound of a short burst of gun fire. The rock was pulverised in mid-flight. I found it impressive, terribly and efficiently impressive. I admit to being a little scared and I stepped back further away from the wall.

One of my NCOs brought onc of the released prisoners to me. He bore his new rifle like a protective charm and had clearly been involved in the fighting. I asked the NCO to scrounge up some food and a couple of cups of tea and spent an informative hour or so, sitting in the back of a truck, learning all I could about the tower. It was, it seemed, entirely staffed and run by a team of scientists and technicians, and apart from the occasional small detail of prisoners who were led into the building to clean and take away waste, no one else was allowed in. The prisoners who were on the detail were issued with a disc on a chain that they were ordered to wear over their overalls. It protected them from the automatic defence system, a system that would destroy anyone and anything moving within its range should they not have one of the discs in view.

I sat and thought about this for a while, whilst the prisoner filled his face with food. I ignored his satisfied sighs as I tried to find a solution to my new problem. Obviously I could bring up heavy weapons and blast the wall to twisted wreckage and then make a hole as big as I needed in the side of the tower. Had my brother not been in there, I would probably have levelled the whole lot from a distance, scientists be damned. I needed to get beyond the wall and procure one of the discs for myself. Almost facetiously I asked, 'Do the scientists ever venture outside?'

The man looked up from his plateful of food, and chewed hastily to empty his mouth. 'Sure they do. There is a table and a couple of benches on top of the cliff overlooking the sea. I have emptied the bins there. Some of them eat their lunch or take smoking breaks there; it's not allowed inside, you see.'

I smiled at him, patted him on the shoulder and jumped from the back of the truck. I had my way in. I knew I could climb that cliff, high as it was. If I climbed up and roped myself in a harness just below the top, I could wait until I heard someone above me and then with a bit of luck I could subdue them and take their disc before an alarm was raised. It was just a matter of timing and an uncomfortable wait of unknown duration tied to a cliff face sixty feet above the sea, but in reality no more difficult than some of the other things I had done. I just needed to get to the base of the cliff.

I suddenly remembered something, and knew just how I was going to get there. I drew a rough map on a piece of paper and stuck my head back into the rear of the truck to ask the prisoner to mark where on the cliff edge the benches and table were. Satisfied, I put the map in my pocket, squinted at the late afternoon sun and began issuing orders.

I asked Harry to occupy the defences on both walls and also to dig further defences between the walls to cover any retreat, something the H.A.P. had neglected to do. I also warned him to put a heavy dedicated garrison at the old whaling station to prevent the enemy doing exactly what we had done to them. It was also the place where the Coalition fleet would be landing and I didn't want any complications at this stage of the game. I asked Oz to collect up all the weapons, pile up the bodies and organize burial in the grounds of the prison camp. Ferret I tasked with keeping order, particularly amongst the newly released prisoners; and Jimmy, well I ordered him to find me something to drink, something strong to wash the bitter taste from my mouth, enough to drown the grief that was threatening to overwhelm me.

I requisitioned a well-appointed building that had clearly been the commanding officer's quarters within the compound. I stretched out my dirty feet on the clean bed, and Jimmy sprawled in a chair. We drank, I talked and Jimmy listened, then when I had run out of words we drank some more. I paced and raged, I drank, I broke things and I wrote a letter to Godfrey but it felt so sparse and inadequate. Jimmy listened and drank. When I had exhausted all the emotions and expressions I could manage I fell into a fitful sleep.

I was woken just before dawn by a soldier bringing me a mug of tea. I groaned, and after I had vomited in the waste bin by the side of the bed, I found the bathroom and soaked my head in a sink full of cold water. I straightened my mismatched uniform, downed my tea, and with water still dripping down my face I went out to confront the new day. I was still burdened by my grief, but I was at least positive that today would see me reunited with Mathew and I could at last gain my freedom from the vision that haunted my dreams. The mute anguish in a little boy's eyes.

Oz, my efficient little quartermaster, brought me some breakfast, and as I battled with a mouthful of eggs and bacon, I asked him to find me three men with boat handling experience. The men dutifully arrived, and I was surprised that one of the volunteers was Oz himself.

'I am a dab hand with boats, Commander. I used to sail up and down the river all the time before the war.'

'You sure you want to come, Oz?'

He came over to me and spoke quietly in my ear, 'All this time we have been working together, I have never been involved in any action. Now, I was happy with the work you gave me, in fact I really enjoyed the responsibility, but it would be nice to be involved in one of your actions before the war ends.'

What could I say? I shook him warmly by the hand and told him to go and find us a Jeep.

I threw some rope and what climbing kit I could improvise, along with my weapons, into the back of the Jeep, and with the sun breaking over the eastern horizon, I ordered the men aboard and began driving northwards along the river bank, looking for the hidden overhang and Godfrey's small sailing boat beneath it. She was where we had left her so long ago. I screwed my eyes tight against my emotions and took a deep breath as we removed the branches she had been concealed with. I had to oust a few nesting birds and there were a couple of mouse-bitten holes in the canvas of her sail, but otherwise she was in good shape. We pushed her into the water, and with Oz at the tiller we rowed towards the mouth of the estuary and the base of the cliffs.

As we passed the old whaling station, my men

stationed there waved and cheered and I stood unsteadily in the rocking boat and saluted them. I held my salute until we had passed from sight as a measure of my respect, then returned to my place in the bow, looking for a point at the base of the cliffs where the swell would allow us to approach without being dashed against the rocks. The tide was retreating which made my climb longer but increased our chances of actually getting me ashore. I pointed to a spot below the tower promontory, and Oz skillfully steered the little craft up against the base of the cliff. I timed my jump with the rise and fall of the waves and leapt upon a sizeable rock a few feet clear of the water. I made sure of my footing among the slippery green seaweed and gestured to the men in the boat to throw me my equipment. Once I had my climbing gear and my weapons I called to Oz.

'Can you stay around until you see me go over the top? I don't know how long it will take, but don't put yourselves at risk. Stand off if you need to.' Oz, battling with the tiller, briefly waved his reply and I turned and began studying the climb ahead of me, putting all thought of the boat out of my head. I checked the rough sketch in my pocket showing where the table and benches sat and realised that I would have to angle my climb to get to where I needed to be. Selecting my first handhold, my eyes looking for the next anchor point, I began to climb. It was hard, slow work. The rock was weathered with many handholds but it was also soft, quite rotten in places, and I had to test it and carefully place my weight as I climbed. But apart from being attacked by the odd seagull defending its nest and the occasional slip on soft rock, the climb went well: sixty feet and forty-five minutes of limb-trembling effort until I reached the top. I did not dare show my head over the top of the cliff, fully aware of the automated defence systems that protected the tower; so, I rigged myself a harness in a way that allowed me to hang scant inches below the top, listening and waiting. My plan involved somehow luring someone over to the edge of the cliff, where I could ambush them and steal their safety disc.

Working on a hunch, I tested my theory that small slow-moving items might not trigger an attack. With sweat beading on my brow, I very slowly, and when I say slowly I mean millimetres at a time, raised a small chunk of rock above my head and placed it on the ground at the edge of the cliff. There was no bang, no impact and the rock, and more importantly my hand, remained intact. Somewhat pleased with myself and more than a little relieved, I unbuttoned my jacket and took out my lure, more commonly known as Harvey, beloved toy of Mathew, symbol of the resistance and now the innocent little bear who would bait my trap. Reminding myself not to rush, I eased him up over the edge and sat him watching the tower.

Then I waited, and I waited, the rope cutting into my skin, the weight of my equipment hanging heavy off my shoulders and my limbs slowly stiffening. I eased my arms and legs as much as I could to keep them from cramping and ensuring continued blood flow so that they wouldn't fail me the instant I needed them. I took a sip from my water bottle and glanced at my watch. One and a half hours I had been hanging from a rope at the top of the cliff. I steeled myself, flexed my limbs and continued to wait.

Eventually I heard a door shutting. I grinned to myself, rolled my head on my neck, and slid my hatchet into my hand. I was confident that I could defeat anything up to six of these scientists, but as luck would have it there was only one. I heard a match strike and a moment later I smelt tobacco. A lit match sailed past my head and arced to the waters below. I heard the man exclaim, 'How the hell did that get there?' I coiled tense and waited as footfalls approached, hoping beyond hope and trusting that my devilish luck would hold out, and that his body would shield mine from the weapons.

When I judged he was within reach, I launched the top half of my body over the edge and buried the back spike of my hatchet in his foot. His mouth opened to scream, and reacting like any normal person would do, he bent over to grasp his wounded foot and remove the weapon that pinned it there. It is a mistake that few people who have fought for their lives ever make more than once: deal with the threat first and then see to your injury. Those not tempered in the hellish crucible of war are unaware of this rule, and so, as he bent double in shocked reaction, I reached up and slid the chain from over his neck. He stood in horrified reaction, a look of terror in his eyes; then his head exploded and his body collapsed to the floor. I looped the chain over my own head, and making sure that the all-important disc didn't drop below the level of the ground, I pulled myself up, turned to wave at the men in the boat and strode to the door. There was some sort of advanced lock on the door that could be opened by a light that scanned the hand of the person wanting to get in. Apparently my hand wasn't good enough, but I knew where there was another I could borrow and I just happened to have a hatchet.

The door swung open and I entered the pristine white corridors of the tower. The door closed behind me and I stood still for a moment to let my eyes adjust to the bright ceiling lights that reflected off the white walls and floor. Everything was either white and clean or of polished steel; the only other colour seemed to be the red writing on notices on the walls, notices no doubt that were expected to be obeyed. Steel doors with small windows set at head height lined the sides of the corridor: a corridor which led to a central room that had three other corridors and a stairwell leading off it. I peered in through the window of the door nearest to me. It was empty so I slipped in. It was obviously a lab of some description; I recognised some of the equipment on the tables from my own disinterested attendance at chemistry lessons at school.

There was a white coat on a hook on the wall. I put it on. Granted it was never going to disguise my sweat-stained dishevelled appearance, nor was it going to hide my dirty combat clothes and the larger- than-average number of weapons festooned over my body, but it might cause a moment's hesitation, and that moment could be the difference between life and death. Finding nothing else useful in the room, I left and began to walk cautiously down the corridor towards the main room. I glanced into other rooms as I passed. There were men in white coats working in most of them, and I hoped that break time was over and they had returned to work. I also hoped that they were all pre-occupied with their tasks as it would certainly make finding Mathew easier. I did wonder at the confidence these people had in their defences and security, however. If I was in a tower surrounded by an enemy, I am not so certain that I would have blithely continued with whatever task I had in hand. I could only assume that they had great faith in their weapons or expected a relief force to arrive in the near future.

Well, their wonderful technological defences had been breached by a rope, a teddy bear and a hatchet. I was going to find Mathew and any other children that had been taken, lead them to safety and then level the place with all the heavy weapons at my disposal.

In the main room at the base of the tower was a floor plan. The tower had seven storeys and I spent a few minutes looking at the plan, trying to work out where they might be holding Mathew. The top floor was smaller than the others and consisted of only three rooms instead of the dozen or so on the other floors. These three rooms were labelled Extraction, Processing, and the Control Room. I made a note of the position of the control room, sure that it was knowledge that would be useful. All floors could be accessed by taking the stairs or by using the service elevator. As I examined the tower map, I found that the most likely place to find Mathew was on the fourth floor, in a room labelled 'Subject Dormitory.'

I have to admit I didn't much like the sound of the word 'subject'. It was my guess that they were probably using sample cells from the children to grow the clone soldiers or something. I have to confess that science was never a strong point of mine, but that seemed to me to be a reasonable guess.

I reasoned that using the lift would be more likely to lead to my discovery, and so I took to the stairwell and began to climb. I moved slowly, listening for the sound of anyone approaching, my back against the wall and my hands upon my weapons. Moving from one floor to the next as I crossed the intersection of the corridors, ducking past windows and hoping that doors would remain closed was the cause of a few nervous moments, yet the stairs remained empty, and with a growing confidence I made my way up to the fourth floor. I stood for a moment before pushing open the double doors that led onto the floor. I remembered that the Dormitory was on the southeast side of the floor, so ducking below the windows of occupied rooms and trying to stop my boots squeaking on the polished floor, I came to the door that I thought was the right one. With my hand on my pistol, I took a deep breath, opened the door and swiftly stepped inside. I banged my shin on a broom and cursed under my breath. I had stepped into a cleaning stores closet. Smiling and shaking my head at my own stupidity, I prepared to step back out into the corridor and try the next door, a door which I was now certain would be the right one.

However, just before I exited the closet, I heard voices and froze with my hand on the door. These were the first people I had encountered within the confines of the tower and they were walking towards me. Judging by the voices, there were three of them. I waited, hardly daring to breathe. I let them walk past and counted to ten before I stepped back out into the corridor. I emerged from the store room in time to see the swinging doors to the stairwell flap closed behind them. I heard one of the men say 'Right, Doctor Blair, we have our duties to attend to in the extraction room; we shall meet up with you later for lunch.'

They exchanged their goodbyes. One man stepped into the lift whilst the other two took the stairs and went up. I mentally slapped myself. I had been so concerned with rescuing Mathew that I had completely overlooked the significance of the rooms at the top of the tower. The extraction room was next to the control room. If I got to the control room, I could switch off the defences, open the doors and let Jimmy come storming in whilst I kept the H.A.P. away from the dormitory. So, with one of my fairly common last-minute changes of plan, I cast one regretful backward glance at the door to the dormitory and slowly and carefully followed the two scientists up the stairs.

I caught bits of the conversation they were having as they casually strolled up the stairs. It seemed that they believed that their defences would hold, and even that they could stop shells from heavy weapons with a little adjustment. Fate, it seemed, had smiled again. Once more, mostly on a whim, I had made the right decision. They also talked about something they called milking the cow, probably something about funding for their work I imagined.

I followed them without incident all the way up to the top floor of the tower. Here both the stairs and the service elevator terminated at a single landing with a corridor that bisected the top of the tower, past the extraction room on the left and the processing room on the right, ending at the control room at the south side.

I gave the men I was following a minute or so to get into the room before I crept up to the door and peered in through the window. The room was well lit, with natural light from the windows that ran down each side of the room, as well as artificial light from a number of powerful electric lamps. These lamps were concentrated in the very middle of the room where something was occurring. The two men had donned surgical garb, and as one appeared to be administering electric shocks to some sort of bloated thing on a medical bench, half covered with a green surgical gown, the other seemed to be carefully tending to some strange tubework. I couldn't properly see the animal they appeared to be torturing. I thought it might be a pig, judging from the high-pitched squealing noises I could hear.

Content for the moment that they were busy, I took a look into the processing room, and found that it was empty. I turned my attention to the control room. 'Nearly there,' I told myself. 'Nearly there.' There was one solitary guard in the control room, dozing in his chair with his back to me. He didn't even manage to register my presence before he died. I pushed him and his chair to one side and studied the switches and dials on the control panel. It was quite complicated and I laid my shotgun down on the top of the unit and stood rubbing my temples as I tried to make sense of the controls. All I could hear was the damn noise of the tortured animal in the other room and I couldn't concentrate, couldn't make sense of what I was seeing. I decided I needed to put an end to the high-pitched squeals, just long enough to study the board in peace.

Whatever it was they were up to in that room, I am not a fan of torture and I don't appreciate those who seem to delight in it. So, my ire aroused, I walked back down the hall, stepped into the room and shut the door behind me. The first man saw me as I walked in. The look of anger on his face was comical, but it didn't last long as my hatchet turned gracefully over and over in the air and buried itself in his head. As he fell, my knife did something similar to the man with his back to me. As he dropped to the ground, his hand clawing at his back, I got a better look at the thing on the gurney. It was swollen and misshapen, thin tubes stuck into it in various places, particularly the large and deformed head. Its skin was stretched in some places, wrinkled and sagging in others, and mottled a nasty pallid pink and red. I realised with some anger that the mutated deformed thing lying there had arms and legs. I thought it might be some sort of chimp until the head turned towards me and it opened its eyes. Mute anguish in a little boy's eyes.

Everything went far away, blurred and spinning. Hot piss ran down my leg as my bladder voided, and I began to hear a distant screaming and felt a thudding in my head. The scream seemed to last forever and the thudding got more intense, the pain eventually overwhelming the static white noise of horror in my head. I realised that it was I who was doing the screaming, and the thudding was me bashing my own head on the floor again and again and again. I fell over onto my side, blood dripping down my face, unable to think, unable to function, catatonic in my horror and my guilt.

Some minutes later I heard a thin voice: Mathew was speaking. He was still alive, he was still my brother and I owed him so much. With an effort of will I got to my knees and shuffled over to where he was lying. I stayed on my knees and took his withered soft pink hand in mine and held it to my cheek. 'Hello, Mathew,' I managed.

His voice when he replied was thin and weak, his vocal cords strained from years of screaming. 'I knew you would come, Danny. You said you would.'

Tears ran down my face. I reached into my jacket and brought out the little blue bear, my confessor, whom I had carried for years, and cherished through fight and flight just for this one moment. I tucked Harvey under Mathew's arm.

'I brought him back for you, kiddo.'

His mouth turned up in what I hoped was a smile and his withered arm flexed around the bear. 'Harvey, my best friend Harvey. Harvey guarantee.'

I smiled at him through my tears, 'That's right, Matty. Harvey the guarantee. I had to bring him back to you, didn't I?'

His head moved a fraction, 'Yes, you did. You promised.'

I knew now why the Fearmones and Endzymes had not affected me the same way as everyone else. I don't know how they worked and what they were, but they were recognised by my body, and as a result the effect was entirely different since they came from my own brother. I struggled to my feet and kissed him on his bulbous forehead.

'Will you be all right for a minute, Mathew? I have something I need to do.'

'Harvey will look after me. You will come back though, won't you, Danny?'

I smiled down at him and flinched at the hope in his eyes. 'Of course. I promise I won't be very long, not like last time.'

He did his tiny nod and his attempt at a smile and I winked at him and walked back to the control room.

The view was magnificent, but I ignored it as I tried to make sense of the panel. I ran my hand over various controls thinking, or at least trying to order my chaotic thoughts. When I finally found the switch I wanted, I pressed it and a flashing dial assured me that the facility would be locked down in three minutes' time and counting.

I returned to the extraction room and went over to the trolley the two scientists had been using. I stared at it for a long while, my knuckles white as I gripped the edge, still deep in thought. In front of me in various slender glass vessels were the grotesque fluids they had been draining out of my brother. I could make a half-decent guess at which fluid came from which part of his body if I matched the colours with the residues in the thin tubes that still hung from him.

I was finished thinking, and as the timer counted down, and the light changed from the brightness that had illuminated evil science to the half-light of an emergency situation, and as the outer doors locked shut, I found a pipette and put two drops of the fluid from my brother's brain upon my tongue.

I entered that room at the top of the tower a vengeful warrior on a quest for the holy grail of my redemption. I left a bestial savage.

I have made many promises; and most I have broken, but this promise I keep. I have turned truth to lies and lies to truth, but this truth is a diamond truth and you can hold it close to your heart and believe in it utterly. Not one of the scientists or technicians in that tower died an easy death. Not one failed to scream his last minutes in unbearable pain and abject misery. I stalked the halls and the rooms of the tower, painting those pristine walls and floors with the dark blood of men who would torture children in the name of science. I do not know if the pure fluid was different in some way to that I had encountered before: I was just as fast and just as angry, but this time I knew what I was doing with an unexpected clarity, and my memory of the events remained unaffected.

I hunted in rooms, under beds and in cupboards until I had found them all. Strangely, the Subject Dormitory was empty. It seems that Mathew had been the only successful subject. Not one of those twisted bastards escaped my search until at last, beginning to tire and drenched in blood, I walked my way back up to the top of the stairs where I curled up alongside my little brother, and holding him close, I slept.

I awoke the next morning to bright sunshine coming in through the windows. Some of the black blood covering my body cracked and flaked off as I moved. Mathew was already awake, his arms wrapped tight around Harvey. I arose carefully so as not to disturb the wires and tubes that kept his little chest rising and falling. I had no idea what to do now. I had to go outside to stop the guns being turned on the tower and I had to get some medical help for Mathew, to see if we could move him and possibly reverse some of the damage that had been done. I picked up my shotgun from where I had left it on the control panel, and not sure what to do next I walked over to stand next to my brother.

He smiled his small smile at me, 'Hello, Danny.'

'Hi, kiddo.'

'I want to go outside, Danny, I like it outside. I want to go and play again.'

I gestured at the tubes and wires. 'Will you be okay?'

'You came back for me. Everything is going to be okay now.'

'I don't know if I can take you outside, Matty. I don't know what will happen if I take you off these machines.'

He stroked Harvey's head and a tear rolled down his cheek, 'Please, Danny, just take me outside.'

What else could I do? I switched off the tower defences, unlocked all the doors, detached the wires from him and cut short some of the tubes that went into his body. I picked him up in my arms and walked from the tower and out of the door in the wall.

Jimmy was the first to see me. He was standing with Oz organising the placement of a couple of large guns. His cheery smile and wave faltered as he saw my burden. A hush fell over the assembled men and women as I walked towards them, my brother cradled in my arms. Hannah, bless her, was the first to react. With a compassion in her eyes so deep it made me weep to see, she took Mathew's hand. 'Hello. You must be Mathew.'

He smiled his strange smile, 'I am. And this is my brother, Danny.'

'I know he is, little one. We are some of his friends.'

Mathew looked around from his place in my arms, 'What are you all doing here?'

'We came to help your brother find you.' He nodded slowly, 'Good, that is what friends should do.' He held up his teddy bear, 'This is Harvey,' he said, 'Danny brought him back to me.' He looked up at me and smiled. I smiled back, and as the sunlight bathed his face and the fresh sea breeze ruffled the remaining wisps of his hair, I watched the light fade from his eyes as his tortured body relaxed and he died holding his little bear, a quiet smile on his face.

I fell to my knees and surrendered to my grief: great gasping sobs of my own anguish as I cried for everything I had lost. I cried for all the dead; I cried at last for Venice, the only woman I had ever loved; I cried for Mathew and his lost future; and I cried for myself. So much emotion, so many tears, surrounded by my friends and companions, who, each in silent empathy, approached in turn and laid their hand upon my head. Eventually I ran out of tears and knelt purely in grief, rocking the body of my brother.

It was gentle, loyal Harry who helped me to my feet. I refused to relinquish the body in my arms and with an enormous effort of will I collected myself enough to issue orders. 'Oz, send the call sign. Harry, take command of the defence. Ferret, run up the flag. Jimmy, find a shovel and bring it to me. Everyone else I thank you for your help.'

I buried Mathew with Harvey tucked under his arm on a clear spot at the edge of the promontory overlooking the estuary. I did all the work myself, although Jimmy kept offering to help. When I had covered the small body, I shared a flask with Jimmy, tipping a libation on the fresh grave. We stood in silence. Consumed by grief I could not talk, and Jimmy, as always, knew when not to. When we had finished the brandy in his flask I hugged him hard and sent him on his way. 'Take care of yourself, Jimmy.'

He cracked a grin, 'Count on it, boss.' Then he turned and walked away.

I sit on the earthen mound that hides my shame and my failure as I finish writing this, the journal I began at Oldbridge. The smoke from the invasion fleet is on the horizon and it seems the war will soon be won. I am going to go for a walk, back to the Peremoss Bridge where it all began. There is a circle that needs completing. All my dreams are dust and the world is ashes in my mouth. I won all my fights but my only battle is lost.

AFTERMATH

Archaeological work by the Archaeology Department at the University continues and as of this moment, no remains or evidence of Daniel Shaddick have been found. Aside from his papers, scant archaeological evidence and apocryphal tales, no one is sure what happened to him at the eve of the end of the war. That I suppose is the subject of another paper.

In the meantime, I have taken the liberty of publishing extracts from these memoirs in one of the national daily papers. There has been some interest and yet still some controversy remains as to whether Shaddick was a hero or villain. I suppose he remains a little of both. However, I was moved by his tale and decided to use the money I was paid by the newspaper to commission a modest statue which, after a minor planning battle, I obtained permission to erect at the site of the old H.A.P. facility at Peremoss, close to where I believe Shaddick buried his brother.

The statue is of a man holding the hand of a small child, who in turn holds a teddy bear. The inscription caused much discussion within the department, and as we wish to evoke no bad feelings or memories, it reads simply 'Because some things are worth fighting for.'

The unveiling of the statue was discreetly advertised with a plea that no anti-Shaddick elements attend. Around sixty people did take the trouble to turn up, and one old man in particular caught my eye. He looked to be in his eighties and was in the company of a woman around ten years his junior and two large men in their late forties. I saw him reach up to the statue and touch the foot of the representation of Shaddick. I saw that his arm, where it showed from under the sleeve of his shirt, was covered in faded tattoos. I thought I knew who this was, and so I discreetly enquired of him, 'Forgive me sir, but would you be a retired ornithologist?'

He turned his gaze on me, his eyes sharp and intelligent, and waved the two men back when they moved towards me. 'It's okay, boys. I don't think this one means any harm.'

He regarded me for a long moment. 'I thought there was more written than you published. I take it you are responsible for this?' He pointed at the statue.

I nodded.

'Well, thank you. It's about bloody time.'

I plucked up courage to ask him another question, 'Jimmy, what was Shaddick like?'

He turned to the two men, 'Danny, Harry, go and look after your mother. I want a quiet word with this lady here.' He walked me to the edge of the cliff in the remains of the tower.

'He was the best man I ever knew: my dearest friend, funny, brilliant and totally focused. I miss him. It has been fifty years and I never met anyone I liked more.' He was silent for a moment, staring out over the sea. 'I knew immediately he told me to take care of myself that he was going to disappear, and who was I to stop him? He had lost everything he fought for. I reckon no one could cope with that much loss and guilt; it would have been purely selfish to try and stop him. I can only hope that he lived. There have been rumours from around the world of a man who has appeared in a number of nasty little wars to help those fighting oppression. I hope it was him … I have to believe it was.'

I could see that Jimmy was getting upset and so I thanked him and prepared to walk back to my car.

I had only gone a few paces when he spoke again.

'The night before he entered the tower, he said something to me that I have never been able to forget. He said that someone once said that it is better to have loved and lost than never to have loved at all. Danny said that was absolute bullshit and the man had clearly never really loved and he had clearly never lost.'

I too had heard the rumours of an ageing freedom fighter and I have to confess that my interest is not purely one of history. Mother always spoke fondly of her brother. I hope you found peace, Uncle Daniel.

Maria Phibbs, PhD 2216 AL.

About the Author

Dave Shaw is a farmer and archaeologist from Cheshire in the UK who passes the time in his tractor by creating stories.

As well as writing, his hobbies include medieval combat and archery.

He has appeared on TV with some of his archaeological work and is currently working on a fantasy trilogy.

Look out for the first book in the Life of Denial series, Hagan's Tale.

Lightning Source UK Ltd.
Milton Keynes UK
UKHW041100180522
403116UK00008B/365

9 781739 675608